COUNT BOHEMOND

COUNT BOHEMOND

ALFRED DUGGAN

with a preface by
EVELYN WAUGH

Pantheon Books
A DIVISION OF RANDOM HOUSE
New York

Preface

————————————————★————————————————

Alfred Duggan's death on 4th April 1964 brought to an abrupt end a literary career of peculiar interest.

The present, posthumous work is the last of a series of fifteen historical novels which began in 1950 with *Knight with Armour*. It was finished shortly before his death. Other projects were in his mind. He had planned, but not committed to writing a novel about Tancred in which the later stages of Count Bohemond would have been recounted. Besides these fictions he wrote three biographies, and seven historical studies for young readers, one of which, *Growing up with the Norman Conquest*, is due to appear in 1965. It is the opus of a full life-time accomplished in fourteen years, which has attracted the most dissimilar devotees and is likely to retain and multiply them.

The author shunned personal advertisement and the public performances of the literary world, so that to most of his readers he was a somewhat remote figure. A biographical note may be helpful.

Alfred's life was the exact antithesis of the familiar contemporary failure who starts as writer, loses his powers in middle-age and falls into impotent debauchery.

He was born in 1903. His father, who died when Alfred was a small boy, was a rich Argentine of Irish descent. His mother was the beautiful daughter of an American diplomatist. His mother brought him and his younger brother and sister to England for their education and in 1917 married Lord Curzon, then a member of the Inner War Cabinet and at the height of his powers. Alfred's boyhood and youth were thus spent in the heart of the dominant English class in his step-father's four great houses, with his own ample fortune to spend on pleasure and travel. Neither at Eton nor at Balliol did he show great application for work and he went down from Oxford prematurely. While there he kept a string of hunters for his use in winter and a night chauffeur to carry him to London night-clubs on summer evenings. None of his friends of forty years ago could have forecast the literary achievement of his later years. Lord Curzon was one of the very few who discerned his intellectual quality.

At the age of twenty he professed Marxism and atheism but a few years later he returned to the Church of his childhood and remained a devout Conservative Catholic for the last thirty-five years of his life. His travels took him far but his main interest was the remains of the Crusader occupation of the Levant and of the Eastern Mediterranean. He visited and studied many castles which were then unknown except to a few adventurous experts. His first novel, and this, his last, deal with the Crusades, the period with which he was most familiar and sympathetic. As his fortune dwindled and finally disappeared he read more and more, exercising a remarkable memory for historical detail. He read without ambitions to professional scholarship for sheer zeal for the subject.

He became a keen patriot and in 1939, though beyond the normal age of recruitment, not only enlisted as a private soldier but contrived to join a 'free company' (the forerunners of the Commandos), volunteers for hazardous service then being raised in a somewhat haphazard manner. In one of these bodies he was involved in the rear-guard of the retreat in Norway in conditions of great hardship which impaired his health and doubtless hastened his death. Invalided from the army he fulfilled his wish to serve his country by working for the rest of the war at the bench in an aeroplane factory.

In 1953 he married and in 1956 settled at Ross-on-Wye, devoting himself assiduously to his newly found skill in writing. The complete happiness of his domestic life sustained him in his work and he seldom left home in his last years.

This is all the biographical detail that the reader will need. Alfred's writing is strictly impersonal and offers little scope for the critics who seek to relate the novelist's invention to his personal experience. He spoke of his work with a modest detachment which concealed the dedication of an artist. When asked why he always concerned himself with obscure periods and places rather than with those more likely to excite popular curiosity, he would reply, with less than candour, that the scantiness of sources made research less laborious. In fact he was drawn to the dark ages by a real sense of kinship with them. Though in his working years entirely happy in his private life, he surveyed contemporary history with nothing but calm despair. He understood the Roman Empire and feudal Europe as he did not understand the world of the United Nations.

His literary style remained constant. It is as crisp and clear in this posthumous novel as in his first. Most writers come to maturity after experiments they regret. There is no groping in Alfred's work. At the age of forty-seven he published his first book. It was lucid and masterly, absolutely free of affectation or ostentation. He always in life, even in his years of dissipation, maintained a certain *gravitas* and formality. That is apparent in his prose but the severe good taste is lightened by dry humour, and a genial tolerance of the defects of human nature. His religious faith is latent in all he wrote. Never a propagandist or an apologist, he accepted the Church as the only proper milieu of man and man as being naturally prone to fall below Christian principle. Perhaps one of his finest passages is the ironical conclusion of *Conscience of the King* in which Cerdic, the remote ancestor of our royal house, reflects that he has survived the barbarian invaders, made his peace with them, defected from the Church, become a ruler among people of gross habits. He has seen a civilization dissolve but all is as well as could be hoped. And then the doubt: 'Suppose all that nonsense' (Christianity) 'that my brother used to preach is really true after all?'

Conscience of the King is my own favourite of Alfred's books. It is to that I should direct an inquirer who wanted a quick look at the quintessential Duggan. But each has his own favourite. The reader is never tricked. The books, for those who love them, are habit forming. *Count Bohemond* will not disappoint. It is highly appropriate that this, his last work, should end with the triumph of Christian arms against the infidel.

EVELYN WAUGH

7

CHAPTER I

The Name

———————————★———————————

The ancient brick building still kept out the weather, though it
had been scarred by fire. It was the only weathertight building in
the valley. For this was the year 1058, twelve years after the sons
of Tancred of Hauteville had come from Normandy on pilgrimage
to St. Michael at Monte Gargano. They had stayed on to conquer
Apulia. After twelve years of war and truce and treachery and
war again they were still busy at their conquest.

The long and spacious hall was roofed by three domes in line.
That was why it still had a roof; there were no rafters to collapse
when attackers set a torch to it. Once it had been the hunting lodge
of a great Greek noble, in the good old days when all Italy south
of Rome was the Theme of Langobardia, governed firmly from
Constantinople. This evening torchlight streamed from its un-
barred glassless windows, while a band of wandering foragers
feasted in it.

A few yards outside the main door rain hissed down on a trench
still lined with glowing charcoal, where the cattle for the feast
had been roasted. In the lee of a clump of trees horses and mules
stood tethered under crude lean-tos woven from branches. Only a
few grooms watched them. Most of the servants sheltered from
the rain inside the hall, and the draggled women of the camp with
them.

Although it rained the evening was warm, and there was no fire
within the hall. Most of the company squatted on the floor while
they ate off their laps; but at the far end an inventive steward had
dismembered a great plank door to make a proper trestle table. At
this improvised high table the leaders of the band sat on decent

9

heaps of turf or stone as though they were at home in a peaceful castle; there was even a long linen cloth to cover the rough planking of the table.

In the centre of the table, facing down the hall, sat the chief, Robert of Hauteville. But nowadays everyone called him Guiscard, the Weasel, even to his face; for his simple sense of humour delighted in nicknames. He was a big man, tall and broad, with a tangle of yellow hair falling to his shoulders and a silky golden beard fanned over his chest. With all that hair he looked older than he was, and his movements were ponderous; but his great frame was solid bone and muscle, not fat, and he held himself with dignified assurance.

On his right sat his wife, the lady Alberada, a very young matron with the blue eyes, fair hair, and scarlet peeling complexion of a northerner who lives under the southern sun. Both were dressed in rough travelling tunics of grey wool, stained by mud and rain; though the lord wore a great gold chain round his neck and the lady several bracelets and rings; because in troublous times sensible people keep their jewellery handy. In a corner lay a heap of mail and cloaks, but the lord's great sword was propped against his seat.

Also at the high table were four captains of horse, two Norman and two Lombard. They were decent men, though not exactly gentry; they wore the greasy leather jerkins that went under their mail. Beside each sat his female companion, wife or concubine or casual whore. The lady Alberada took her company as she found it. At one end of the table, feeling rather out of place, was a blowsy Italian peasant-woman, trying to hold on her lap a vigorous and nearly naked four-year-old boy.

Everybody in the hall had eaten as much as he or she could hold, and drunk all the wine that had been distributed. But it was too early for sleep, and at the high table the cups were still full; besides, the *jongleur* had not finished his performance.

He was not a true *jongleur*, whatever the lord Robert might call him by courtesy. He was a tall skinny Italian peasant, dressed in ragged patchwork, and the song he squeaked in a jerky rhythm was in the local Apulian dialect of Romance. He knew none of the noble stories about Charlemagne and Roland, for normally he entertained his fellow-peasants at fairs and weddings. He had called in at this lighted building hoping to find a band of local brigands, and because his empty stomach could not bear to pass the wonderful smell of roasting meat. He had feared a whipping; for his simple bawdy anecdotes would not appeal to Norman warriors. But he knew by heart one genuinely funny mock-epic, and it had saved the situation.

Now he had reached the climax, telling how this huge but slow-witted giant polished off his supper of a cow and a few sheep, with a netful of cabbage and some sacks of meal for garnish. After four barrels of wine he felt drowsy. Jack, who had been hiding in the brim of his hat, thought it safe to come out. Jack unfastened the giant's shoulder-brooch and found he could just wield it, though it was as long as himself; he plunged it into the ear of giant Bohemond, and so slew him. Jack's subsequent dealings with the forty-seven village maidens whom the giant had laid by as winter stores depended for their point more on gesture than on speech; but they amused the whole company and in particular the lord Robert, who liked his jokes simple. As the mountebank sat down there was a murmur of applause.

"Jolly good, jolly good," said the lord Robert with a chuckle. "Two silver pieces, even three, Alberada, don't you think? See that he gets a hunk of cold beef and a small skin of wine to help him on his way tomorrow. That bit about the hard luck of maiden number forty-five was really very funny indeed, and I've had a good lesson in Italian at the same time. But Giant Bohemond's dinner is the part I remember best."

There was a crash of earthenware from the end of the table, a roar of triumph and exclamations of dismay. Snatching at his sword the lord Robert looked up to meet the fierce gaze of his only son. The child had escaped from his nurse and climbed on the table, where he was now trying out his new teeth with concentrated energy on a cold and greasy rib of beef.

"Mark, get down at once!" called the lady Alberada. "Drat the child. It's not enough for him to tear out my inside when he's born. Now he must make a disturbance the first time I am warm and comfortable after a week of riding in the rain. Maria, take him outside, spank him, and roll him up in his blankets."

"Let him be," said Robert with another chuckle. "He's enjoying himself like a true campaigner. You're always nagging him about his birth, as though it were his fault that he was too big for you. I say he's an example to us all; never grumbles at hardship and makes the best of times of plenty. God's teeth, he looks just like the giant Bohemond at his dinner. That's it, the giant Bohemond. Butler, another mug of wine all round, so that the company may drink to the health of the new Bohemond."

The huge boy, still chubby with babyhood, did indeed look like a young giant, his dimpled legs sticking out from his brief shirt and the bone gripped in his mouth. Robert Guiscard enjoyed giving nicknames.

Everyone drank to the young giant Bohemond, and that started the party again. The wineskins went round until late in the evening. Young Mark-Bohemond knew he had done something clever, since all the common soldiers and their women were so pleased with him. But soon he fell asleep on his nurse's lap. He woke up again as the table was taken down and the leaders of the band prepared for sleep at their end of the hall.

By the time Maria had removed his single garment, doused his greasy face in cold water, and wrapped him in a thick blanket, he was wide awake and staring solemnly round him. He had a new name, which made this an evening to be specially remembered. But there was more to come, for instead of being carried off to sleep with Maria by the door he was dumped on the floor between the fur rugs which covered his parents at night.

"You're awake, Mark, aren't you?" asked his mother, squatting on her rug barefoot but otherwise fully dressed, for she did not often take off her clothes on campaign. "That's good. I can tell you the news tonight, and it won't come as a surprise in the morning."

"He's not Mark any more," said his father, standing over him naked and hairy. "From now on he is Bohemond, and I shan't call him anything else. But tell him the news by all means, so long as you tell it fairly."

"You and your nicknames," mother muttered with a sigh. "Very well, Bohemond then. Of course I shall tell you fairly, because father and I have not quarrelled. It's just that I am going away

12

tomorrow morning, and from now on you won't see much of me. But there's no quarrel, remember."

She stared defiantly at her son, challenging him to believe what she said.

"Of course there's no quarrel," father said quickly. "We are not parting because we don't like being together, but because the Pope says we must. It seems we ought never to have got married in the first place. We are related in the something-or-other degree, which means that we are descended from the same ancestor if you go back far enough. So your mother must go away, and I must marry someone else. I suppose she also will marry someone else. Of course you stay with me, little Bohemond, since you are my only son and my heir. But you will see your mother from time to time, whenever she can manage to visit us."

"It's the best way of parting," his mother chimed in. "The marriage is dissolved because we can trace a relationship. Annulment for consanguinity, they call it. But while the marriage lasted it was genuine, even though now it's over. I was a respectable wife, and your father was a respectable husband. You are legitimate, with no hint of bastardy. No slur on anyone's character, and yet we are free to make a fresh start. In fact we *must* make a fresh start, we should be doing wrong if we stayed together. Annulment for consanguinity is a pillar of Christian matrimony. It ought to be used even more widely than it is. "

Little Bohemond withdrew his attention. Mother was using long words he could not understand, speaking past him to score off father. She did that quite often, whenever she was in a bad temper; because a four-year-old cannot be insulted by his own mother, and anyone who happens to overhear ought not to take offence. He could see that she was getting at father; though how he saw it he could not have explained.

"Good night, mother dear," he said with a winning smile. "See you some day. Good night, father dear. See you in the morning."

After that neat summing-up of the situation he smiled with even greater charm at both his parents, snuggled into his blanket, and rolled over.

"Good night, little Mark." "Good night, little Bohemond," he heard them answer, with the hint of a sigh of dismay. It was comforting to know that he had scored off them both, though he was still not sure how he had done it.

He was too excited to sleep. He lay still, thinking hard. He did not really mind parting from mother. She was never unkind but she had some grievance against him—something about his size, something he did not understand. He knew that by now he ought to have brothers and sisters, he could tell that by observation of the women who lived with the common soldiers. Apparently it was his fault, not his mother's, that he was an only child. In some way he had injured her, not by his own wickedness but just by being himself. In her heart she would never forgive him.

On the other hand mother might be more important than father, and he ought to have chosen her side. For of course he knew that they had quarrelled, and were parting because they did not want to go on living together. Most of the common soldiers came from Buonalbergo, and had served mother's family before they took oath to father. But that meant only that there had been a time when Alberada of Buonalbergo had been grander than Robert of Hauteville, which was certainly true. For father used to boast that when he first arrived in Italy he was so poor he had to fight for wages, like any common trooper. But now father had become the famous Guiscard, able to hire as many soldiers as he needed; while mother was only the youthful aunt of the lord Drogo of Buonalbergo. In other words, mother's greatness lay in the past, while father grew greater every day. A prudent child would stay with the mighty Guiscard.

On the whole he preferred father, as a person. Father was brave and gay and cunning and successful. He was also a bit of a fool at times, but then you can't have everything. Father talked too long and too loudly, laughed too often and was too easily amused. All this playing with the sound of words was rather silly; especially when everyone spoke several languages at once, north French and south French and the many dialects of Italy, so that you could always find a word that sounded funny.

Little Bohemond himself knew exactly the quality which gave him pleasure, though he could not give it a name. When he saw a smith hit a piece of iron two or three times and produce a perfect horse-shoe, or a muleteer fasten a bulky load with one strong and complicated knot, or a cook start a blazing fire from one spark of his flint-and-steel, he would crow and dance with delight. What he admired was in fact efficiency, the exact fitting of means to ends with nothing wasted. Father possessed that quality, even though he was sometimes facetious when he was enjoying himself. There was a lot to be said for father.

By the time Bohemond was eighteen he was the son and heir of the famous Robert Guiscard, Duke of Apulia and friend of the Pope; and also the eldest of a large family. As soon as Alberada had been peaceably disposed of Robert had married the lady Sigelgaita of Salerno, a princess of a noble Lombard house. She was tall and fair and stately, and better adapted to cope with the sunshine of Italy than any immigrant from Normandy. Every year she presented her husband with another bouncing child.

Bohemond had grown until he towered above even his mighty father. He was so much taller than his companions that he had got into the habit of stooping from the shoulders, to talk to them more easily. He had inherited the blue eyes and fair hair of a Norman, but in the quality of his skin he was luckier than his parents. While their cheeks were always scarlet and peeling Bohemond's pink-and-white complexion was merely tinged with a golden glow. He looked as handsome as the statue of St. Michael in a church. He kept himself always very clean, and had a barber shave him every day when he was not fighting; if he was too busy for a shave he would rub his jaw with pumice stone, so that you could hardly make out what would have been the colour of his beard if he had allowed it to grow. His hair also was clipped as short as a priest's, so that it never became tangled and sweaty under the hauberk.

In private life he was almost as blameless as the real St. Michael in Heaven. He had learned to read and write in Latin; Italian was his native tongue, but he could speak north French and south French and understand Greek. Every day he practised with his weapons, and he never ate or drank more than was good for him. He seemed to take no interest in women; but his father was relieved to note that he was not interested in boys either. Such a mighty horseman and jouster must be adequately virile, but apparently the temptations of the flesh did not bother him. His greatest pleasure was to see difficult things well done, or to do them himself.

Guiscard doted on his magnificent heir, and his stepmother admired him. But his half-brothers and half-sisters disliked him, for he did not conceal his contempt for them.

Soon after his eighteenth birthday Bohemond went with his father on yet another pilgrimage to the shrine of St. Michael on Monte Gargano, the goal that had brought the first Normans to Apulia. After they had prayed at the shrine, and given a suitable offering, father and son stood on the open summit of the mountain.

"Splendid place, this," muttered Guiscard. "I like it better every time I come. You know, my boy, quite apart from the famous and authentic visit of St. Michael, this mountain has a claim to be the very high place from which the Devil showed Our Lord all the kingdoms of the world. They say that about a lot of other mountains, too. But here, if you look with the eye of faith, you can see Rome over there, or at least a hint of the hills round it; and over there the high peaks of Romania, the other half of the famous ancient Empire. Rome the Great and East Rome, or bits of them. That's a fair sample of all the kingdoms of the world."

Bohemond squinted into the shadows of the sunset eastward. "I don't know that I can see solid land, but from the way the clouds gather I know there is land below them. Pretty high mountains, they must be. So that's Romania. The part they call Hellas, I suppose?"

"Hellas or Macedonia or perhaps Sclavonia. The boundaries are a bit tangled and I'm not sure which we are looking at. But they all obey the Emperor in Constantinople, and so does the wide country of Thrace to the east of them. Constantinople is the richest and most populous city in the world, as any of the Greeks round here will tell you. Then beyond an arm of the sea, the Straits of St. George, you come to the parts of Romania that lie in Asia. That's supposed to be richer and more extensive than Romania in Europe. And so it goes on, for hundreds of miles. It all belongs to the Emperor, just as much as my horse belongs to me. He can make what laws he likes, levy what taxes he likes, set his subjects to planting mulberries for silkworms or to carting stones to improve his roads. They have no rights, he can do what he likes with them. In all Romania there is only one free man, the Emperor. The rest are either paid soldiers who carry out his commands or wretched serfs who obey them. Only the paid soldiers carry arms and no one holds land freely by military service."

"That's not exactly news, Father," said Bohemond with a shrug of boredom. "Everyone round here has heard of the tyranny in Romania. That's why even our local Greeks were quite glad when the Emperor withdrew his Catapan from Bari."

"Everyone knows that, as you say. Here's another bit of news that isn't so widely known. Last year the Emperor fought a great battle against the infidel, far off to the eastward. All his soldiers were killed or taken, and he was made prisoner. At present Romania has no Emperor, and when there is one he will have no army."

"What's that?" Every muscle tensed in Bohemond's huge body. "That wide land, that rich land, with no army to defend it? There, only just across the water?" His lips closed in a thin line as he peered steadily eastward.

"A Norman landed at Brindisi a few days ago, and I had a talk with him. His right hand had been smashed and he was going home to live with his cousins in Normandy. He came from Romania, and he told me all about it.

"Do you remember a knight from Bailleul who used to serve your uncle Roger?" Guiscard continued. "I suppose not. He left Italy when you were too young to take an interest in such things. He was a true Norman, and a good knight. I forget his name. We all called him Roussel because of his red hair. I gave him the nickname, and it stuck. Well, the Emperor hired him and all his band to fight for wages in Romania. This crippled sergeant had been one of his men. He didn't see the battle. All the Normans were somewhere else, besieging an infidel castle. I expect that's why the Emperor was beaten, fighting a great battle without his best troops. But this man was in the retreat afterwards, after this battle at a place called Manzikert, and he said the disaster was more complete than anyone can imagine. The people who beat them are a new breed of infidel, Turks like you get on the lower Danube. The army of Romania has been utterly destroyed. Think of it. Thirty thousand paid troopers and as many followers of the border chiefs, sixty thousand warriors and every man of them mounted. The greatest army the world has ever seen. At the end of the day they were all dead or taken or scattered in flight. They can never be replaced, either. Because the Turks have overrun the eastern Themes, where the soldiers were recruited. There's money in Constantinople, and they will be able to hire mercenaries. But never again will there be an army of native Romanians."

"Why are we waiting?" asked Bohemond simply.

"All in good time," Guiscard answered with a smile. "How big is Normandy, and how many Normans live in it? We have conquered Apulia and Calabria, and we are beginning to nibble at Sicily. It's not six years since Duke William conquered England. We are spread rather thin on the ground. The great Empire of Romania will take a lot of conquering."

"That's true. But we ought to begin now, before they can hire another army. Why don't we invade that bit opposite, Hellas or whatever they call it; and go on from there as we recruit more Normans to our banner?"

"There just aren't any more Normans, that's one good reason. Anyone who wants to leave home can get land in England, where our Duke has been crowned and anointed and the people recognize him as the lawful King. That's easier than conquering a fief in Italy or Romania. We can't recruit more true Normans. We must make do with the knights we have now, or Lombard knights who are nearly as good, or the odds and ends of common troopers from all over the world who have come to Italy to fight for wages. Besides, conquest isn't the only way to get a footing in Romania."

"It's the only way for Normans to get in. The Greeks don't like us because we are faithful servants of the Pope."

"So we are, and I should like to stay that way. But if the Greeks offer me a fortune on condition I serve their Patriarch I might be open to conviction. Theology is a subject beyond the understanding of a simple knight. God won't damn a layman for serving the wrong spiritual superior. But Normans can do more than fight. Look here, young Bohemond, you must get this into your head. Normans can govern—we are the best governors in the world. The revenues of Apulia and Calabria are greater than before we came, though then they were ruled by clever Greeks and during the conquest nearly every valley was plundered. Greeks are bright, but they're all crooked. As for Lombards, they are lazy as well as crooked. Half the villages didn't pay tribute because no one came round to collect it. Others bribed the collector with a little something for his own purse, much less than the due payment. Now everything runs as smoothly as a water-mill. No use trying to bribe a Norman collector, because he won't take less than the full tribute even if he keeps it all for himself. A man who has to look after his irrigation-ditches jolly well must repair them once a year. A man who ought to collect toll from every traveller can't let his friends pass free. In my fiefs only I plunder caravans of merchants; there are no other brigands. The peasants pay us rather a lot, but they don't pay anything to anyone else. We can govern a country so that it prospers. Now don't you suppose that whoever is the next Emperor of Romania would like to hire Normans to help him run his Empire? Things will be rather disturbed after a few civil wars."

"You think a new Emperor might hire us to work for him?" asked Bohemond. "Would it be worth while to go there just for wages?"

"We should want wages, of course, and good wages. Those Greeks pay for everything in money. But I was thinking more in terms of a Greek marriage for one of the girls, and so working our way into the Greek nobility. They choose their Emperor from the great noble houses, and some of them were founded in the first place by foreigners."

"A good plan, if you can find a Greek willing to marry one of us. But why not? To them Normans are foreign barbarians, no better and no worse than any other Frank. I suppose they don't distinguish between Hautevilles and fitzRollos."

"Nor does anyone else, my boy. We have come up in the world. My father, your grandfather, was a simple country knight, but the Pope has recognized us as rulers of Apulia, on a par with the Dukes of Aquitaine and the Counts of Provence. The Hautevilles are grand enough to marry anyone."

"Then I shall wait until I can get the King of France's daughter. For the present I don't want a home, anywhere. While you lead our band I want to be ready to go anywhere and do anything as your second in command."

"Very properly expressed, my boy. There isn't a princess in the world who won't be eager to jump into your bed as soon as she sees you, or a prince who wouldn't be honoured to have you as son-in-law. I'm your father, and proud of you; but any stranger would say the same. But we mustn't tie you down before we know how high the Hautevilles can climb. If you married a Greek, or even a German, we couldn't get the match annulled for consanguinity. It's lucky your mother was a Norman."

Abruptly Guiscard fell silent, blushing. He was inclined to allow his tongue to run ahead of his discretion but it never ran very far ahead. It was not frightfully important, he consoled himself. Long ago Bohemond must have guessed that his mother had been discarded, with no hard feelings on either side, because she was not quite grand enough for the most eminent of the Hautevilles. Dear Alberada, she made no fuss when the time came to part, and in the beginning the two hundred horse she brought as dowry had been the foundation of his fortune. Now she was happily married to a decent Norman or her own rank in society, Roger of Pomaria, and when she met her first husband at social gatherings there was no embarrassment on either side. But she had never produced another child. The huge though perfect body of Mark-Bohemond had been too much for her.

Young Bohemond continued to live at home and help his father, the pattern of a good young knight. He was too proud to be led astray by low companions, too prudent to gamble heavily, too dignified to be amused by debauchery. His life was as regular and blameless as any monk's. Even his father, who kept a close eye on him, suspected that at the age of twenty-one he might be still a virgin. Yet he was the fiercest jouster and the bravest horseman among all the daring Normans of Apulia.

His half-brothers were perhaps the only men who knew him and did not like him. Sigelgaita, their mother, was exceptionally courageous, but her children were, after all, only half Norman. The Lombards had been tough and savage barbarians when first they crossed the Alps, but some centuries in pleasant Italy had softened them. Of course any Lombard could chase any native Italian; but any Norman expected to chase any Lombard. Lombards lord were cruel and merciless, like any lord of any race who wished to hold an Italian fief; but they were more inclined to rely on poison or the dagger than their Norman competitors. In Bohemond's eyes Lombards ranked below Normans, and Sigelgaita's sons ranked low among Lombards. They knew it, and resented it.

Otherwise all the descendants of Tancred of Hauteville, that almost mythical ancestor who had lived and died on his muddy Norman fields, felt respect for one another, if not affection. Among themselves they fought incessantly, for each one of them was trying to make himself supreme over the whole family; but when danger threatened from outside they closed their ranks. As a united clan they were invincible.

CHAPTER II

First Trip to Romania

————————————————★————————————————

When Bohemond was twenty-four, and the best knight in Italy below Rome, his father gave him an independent command. The Hautevilles were trying to cope with a rebellion of their Norman followers, who felt that they were getting less than their due of the fruits of conquest. The Hautevilles were not entirely successful, though by tricky juggling with Lombard and native Italian warriors, and by buying off separately the less greedy of the rebels, they managed to fix up a compromise peace. So Bohemond's quite honourable but unfortunate defeat at Troja did not make him stand out as less successful than his uncles. He had charged in front, and done great execution with his own hands. More could not be expected from a youth in his first command.

During the Christmas feast of 1080 his father talked with him privately in the solar.

"As soon as Apulia is genuinely at peace I shall be ready for Romania," he said, holding his hands towards the brazier. He sat in his luxurious chair, which had sidepieces rising up to support the elbows. It was the only chair of its kind in those parts, the work of a cunning Greek joiner; more like the throne of an Emperor than the seat of a mere Duke. "We've got an excuse to intervene, and with any luck a party among the Greeks will support us. That's much easier than naked conquest."

"Apulia will never be genuinely at peace, in your lifetime or mine," Bohemond answered him. "If we keep the Normans happy the Lombards rebel, and if we satisfy all the gentry then the Greek burgesses feel wronged. But now there may be peace for a year or so. What's our pretext for invading Romania? I thought we had some kind of marriage treaty with the imperial house?"

"We did, my boy. That's the pretext," said Guiscard with a chuckle. With increasing age his conversation had become very obvious; though in the actual operations of politics he was as devious as ever.

"Do you remember your baby sister Helen?" he went on. "You never took much notice of her. But perhaps you haven't forgotten that I fixed up a splendid marriage for her. She was betrothed to a boy of her own age, Constantine the son and heir of the Emperor Michael of Romania. We sent her to Constantinople as soon as she was old enough to leave her mother, so that they could bring her up as a proper Greek princess."

"And the Greeks have cried off? That gives us an excuse to fight them, but I don't see why it gives us Greek allies. Surely there isn't a party among the Greeks who pine for an alliance with the Hautevilles above all other things?"

"You think too meanly of the Hautevilles. Nowadays we matter. In this particular case, as it happens, you are right. No Greek cares about Hautevilles. But a considerable faction among them are loyal to the noble house of Ducas. The Emperor Michael is a Ducas, and his father was Emperor before him. That's as near a legitimate dynasty as you get among those faithless Greeks. Now a fellow called Nicephorus something, a name I don't know, has overthrown the Emperor Michael and cast him into prison. Young Constantine is also in prison, and our little Helen has been shut up in a nunnery. Doesn't your blood boil? It ought to. So we invade. But there must be a lot of important Greek officials who owe everything to Emperor Michael, and they will be on our side if we proclaim that we will restore him. It seems to me a very good opening."

"How can we restore the Emperor Michael?" cried Bohemond, who could never keep track of Greek dynasties and did not share his father's interest in them. "His gaolers will cut his throat before we can rescue him. Why didn't they kill him when they turned him off his throne? It seems slack of them."

"They never kill dethroned Emperors if they can avoid it. That's prudence as much as mercy. The next Emperor hopes that his enemies also will be merciful. In this case they can't kill the ex-

23

Emperor Michael even if they want to. By a remarkable stroke of luck he escaped from his dungeon and has now made his way to Italy."

Guiscard twitched his eyebrows fiercely and stared straight at his son, as though to compel belief.

"Did he now?" said Bohemond with a smile. "Very lucky for him, wasn't it? Of course if you back this chap he can't be an impostor. You must have seen him in all his glory while you were arranging the marriage treaty."

"You know as well as I do that I've never been to Constantinople. The betrothal was arranged through envoys. But it's not for me, or for you, to decide whether Michael is genuine. The Pope has recognized him. He will come with us on our invasion of Romania, with the special blessing of the Holy Father. When he has regained his throne he will restore the Greek church to its rightful subjection to the See of Rome."

"If that's his programme even the partisans of Ducas won't help us. If there's one thing the Greeks won't stand it's subjection to the Pope. He may be the best Emperor they ever had, but if he's a papalist they won't follow him. Seriously, since it isn't your responsibility, do you think this man is the Emperor Michael? The Pope can't go wrong in a matter of faith or morals, but he might be mistaken on a question of identity."

"How the devil should I know? He's a Greek. My clerks tell me he has the manner of a Greek nobleman, which isn't as easily copied as all that. Every Italian recognizes his claim, while in Romania they laugh at him. I suppose it's just possible the real Michael escaped, though his guards must have been remarkably careless or disloyal. Anyway, what does it matter? He can't harm us and he may help. I shall take him along, to make speeches to the locals after we land."

"Will he be allowed to give orders to the troops?"

"Of course not, though that doesn't prove anything. Suppose he were the real Emperor, with a birth-mark of an imperial diadem on each cheek of his arse, I still wouldn't allow him to command Norman knights. No Greek is worthy to command a Norman. But there is one thing you must remember. The reigning Emperor, this Nicephorus, hasn't any troops at all."

"There are garrisons in those seaports to the east of us."

"Oh, garrisons, infantry garrisons. They recruit them from the local farmers. The people they used for real fighting were regular horse, heavy cavalry covered in mail. The Turks killed them all at Manzikert and they can't collect any more."

"Nicephorus must have some soldiers, or he couldn't win even a civil war."

"He has mercenaries—Patzinaks, Magyars, Turks, Germans, even a few Franks. They don't trust one another, and their employer doesn't trust them. We don't want to rouse all the Greeks against us, so we shall go gently to begin with. Capture a few walled towns and see how they like Norman rule. If it works out we might advance slowly to Constantinople, and take over the half of Romania that lies in Europe. The Turks already have the other half, the Asiatic provinces, what they call Anatolia."

"The Emperor, now, this Nicephorus? I suppose he is a famous general?" inquired Bohemond.

"A famous general, of course. That's why the Greeks followed him against their true lord, and his. A trained general, like all these Greeks who read books to learn how to fight. But he was trained to command regular Greek cavalry, very fine men except that they don't want to be killed. He'll take it for granted that his men can live on the country without causing a famine, that they will be there whenever he wants them, that they will camp where he says. On the field he will expect them to wheel left or right at a single blast from the trumpet, and to stand fast until he commands them to charge. You can't do that kind of thing with strange mercenaries. He won't know how to control them. Now this is how we begin. . . ."

They discussed men and supplies. The opening of the campaign would be the trickiest part. Norman rule in Apulia was precarious, and if they were checked at the outset they would face rebellion at home. They must begin with an easy but striking success, and Guiscard himself wished to remain in Italy until he could reinforce a victorious army. Therefore Bohemond would lead the invasion. He must snap up some poorly defended port, say Valona, before he settled down to besiege a great fortress, Durazzo or Corfu. His father would join him once a base had been secured.

Transporting an army by sea was known to be dangerous and difficult. But of recent years, since Duke William had taken his knights and all their horses to England, people were no longer frightened of it. Bohemond pointed out that he knew nothing of fighting at sea, and his father admitted he was in the same position.

"But it can't be difficult," he said cheerfully. "Look at the sailors you meet in Bari. They voyage to Romania and come back alive. You have to fight dismounted; but then you dismount to defend a wall. Think of your ship as a castle to be held, and trust your shipmaster to move it to the right place. Anyway, I don't think the Greeks have a navy in the Adriatic."

In May 1081 Bohemond, commander of the Apulian forces in Romania, welcomed his father to the siege of Corfu. Everything had gone well. The little ports of Valona and Butrinto had surrendered after a trifling resistance. The local peasants were resigned to feeding the invaders. The troops were lodged in a well-built camp before the walls of Corfu town.

His father had brought enough men, he saw with satisfaction. The whole channel between Corfu and the mainland was alive with clumsy round cargo ships, and with the slim speedy dromonds which protected them. This was an army, prepared for conquest; not a fly-by-night band of raiders.

He stood on the shore to welcome his father. There were a good many passengers in the boat. He could make out his stepmother in the place of honour at the stern, with his father on one side of her and on the other a Greek nobleman who must be this alleged Emperor Michael. If the claimant to the Purple ranked third among the leaders he would not try to displace Bohemond from his command, which was all to the good.

You had to put up with Sigelgaita on campaign. She had influence among the Lombards, so in Italy she was useful; perhaps father thought he would find more Lombards here in Romania, though he ought to know better. Danger never frightened Sigelgaita, and she endured hardship without complaint. The trouble was that in a crisis her noble blood rose to the occasion; you never knew when she might flourish a sword and incite the last

26

reserve to charge, just when it was important that they should remain in reserve. Perhaps one day she might be used as a banner, something the men would follow when common sense told them to run away. But father would never let her be sacrificed, even in a worthy cause. He admired her, and indeed she was admirable. What a pity that he also doted on the wretched half-Lombard brats she had given him. Luckily those children seemed to have been left at home.

Bohemond bent his knee to greet his father and stepmother, and after a moment's hesitation kneeled again to the dubious Emperor Michael. The pavilions were ready, and a hot meal steaming on the fire. It was all passing off very well.

The Greek was handsome, and wore very fine armour. His manner was oddly deferential in an Emperor, and he quickly motioned Bohemond to rise. It seemed that he did not speak Italian, though obviously he understood it; his eyes darted among the chattering Hautevilles.

"Hello, Mother. Where's Roger?" asked Bohemond. "Surely he is old enough to lend a hand in the conquest of Romania?"

"Roger the Purse has stayed behind to govern Apulia," said his father. "He is of full age, and the documents he seals must be valid. I don't know whether he will make a good governor, but at least he will keep track of the money in my treasury."

"It was your father's idea," Sigelgaita said quickly. "I wanted him to come with the army. But of course a young man who knows Lombard ways will be popular with the Lombard barons."

Bohemond gave a perfunctory smile in acknowledgement of his father's joke. Roger the Purse had become an established nickname, because the boy was always fiddling with the coins in his wallet. Bohemond knew this for the nervous trick of a lad who felt he did not quite achieve the ferocious standards of other Hautevilles. But Guiscard chose to regard it as a sign of avarice, and dragged in the nickname every time he mentioned his second son.

It was rather more serious that young Roger had been left behind to govern Apulia. It was true that he knew the country well, and was related through his mother to most of the leading barons; but Bohemond was the eldest son. Still, what could young Roger do, if Guiscard suddenly fell down dead and it came to civil war? Hold Apulia against Bohemond, the best knight in Italy and the favourite of the troops? The idea was absurd.

"Don't apologize, Mother," he said soothingly. "I am sure Roger will govern Apulia as well as he would fight Greeks."

Let her think that one out.

"The Emperor wishes to know what you think of the prospects of the siege?" said a young Greek clerk. Bohemond did not believe him. The Emperor Michael, if he was the Emperor Michael, did not seem interested in the military activity which surrounded him. But this was a question he could answer as an expert, and he gave it careful consideration.

"It's a very strong place," he said, regarding the walls with his head on one side. "If they really try to hold it we won't get in for a year or two. But they don't fight so desperately as all that. My guess is that the garrison don't care very much whether their town is ruled by Greeks or Normans, and that the governor has despaired of relief. He's probably a noble from the city, with a wife and family in Constantinople where the Emperor can be revenged on them. He must put up a show, to prove his loyalty, but at bottom he is resigned to defeat. In a month or six weeks, I should say, they will open their gates if we promise not to plunder."

All listened in silence. Bohemond's opinion on the prospects of a siege were treated with respect.

"The true Emperor is here," observed the Greek, "though in the city the tyrant Nicephorus ravages unchecked. So that from fear the commander of Corfu must pretend to serve him loyally."

There was no need for a reply to this necessary formality.

As soon as Guiscard was alone with his son he reverted to the resistance of Corfu. "We haven't all the time in the world, you know. Next week I shall try an assault. In Constantinople there has been a change of command. Nicephorus is out, replaced by a young fellow called Alexius Comnenus. A fine soldier, so they tell me. He will come here to meet us in the field. They don't know that in Corfu, and I haven't told our Michael though I expect he knows. In the other fortresses they will hear of it, and they will hold out in hopes of this army of relief. The Emperor intends to lead it in person. It puts a new complexion on the war."

"Comnenus—yes, that's a famous house. Alexius—I've never heard of him. You say he is a young man?"

"And therefore more dangerous than an elderly general who was trained in an army which no longer exists. He didn't come to the fore until after Manzikert had been lost. He can manage mercenaries, and odds and ends of troops picked up from here and there. He makes do with them. He fights by ambuscade and sudden surprise. They say he is willing to risk his own neck. Understands Frankish warfare. Brave. Devout after their Greek fashion. Descended from previous Emperors. The Greeks will follow him with devotion. It makes it much more difficult."

"But in Corfu they don't know that—yet," said Bohemond. "We must hurry. That assault of yours goes in tomorrow, not at the end of the week."

On the last day of May Corfu yielded on terms, after an honourable but not desperate defence.

It took the Apulians a fortnight to move camp from the island of Corfu to the mainland before Durazzo, their next objective. Durazzo was ready for them.

The new Emperor had acted swiftly. There was no time to bring troops from Constantinople, and anyway there were no troops in the city. But he had sent a famous general, George Palaeologus, to take command of Durazzo; and his envoys were riding through Christendom, laden with bags of gold, to gather mercenaries. Alexius was said to be immensely popular with the Greeks, who had quite forgotten the dim glories of the House of Ducas; so that there was no point in keeping the Emperor Michael in the Apulian camp. He did not care for military life, which seemed odd in such a distinguished general. He went back to Rome, where the Pope liked him. Guiscard did not feel himself weakened by his departure.

There could be no short cuts to the capture of Durazzo, strongly walled and strongly garrisoned. A bowshot from the defences the Apulians set up a line of hurdles covered with canvas. Behind these hurdles cross-bowmen waited with their weapons wound and loaded, ready to shoot any defender who showed himself. Farther back were catapults to hurl stones at the walls; but it would be a very long time before they made an impression on the ancient masonry.

The defenders were more worried by cross-bows than by catapults. The cross-bow was a new weapon, hitherto unknown in Romania. The instrument was made of so many little pieces of horn and wood and gut that it was hard to maintain in working order, especially in bad weather; men trained to its use were high-class mercenaries, who demanded good wages. But it was most effective, shooting straight with a low trajectory and carrying farther than an ordinary bow. Guiscard did not grudge the money needed to hire good cross-bows.

For two months no progress was made. But any serious siege would last much longer than two months, and the Apulians were not disappointed. Few Greeks dared to show themselves on the wall, and if ever the catapults made a breach it would be hard to repair under a rain of well-directed arrows.

Then ships sailed down from the north, neither Greek nor Italian in rig but a mixture of the two; since they were crammed with men and high out of the water they must have come for war rather than for trade. They made for the harbour of Durazzo; but when the Apulian fleet barred the way they altered course and came to anchor in a shallow bay a mile up the coast. A rowing-boat put out, flying a great banner; it made for the headquarters of the Apulians by the entrance to the harbour.

"You're an Italian, Sigelgaita. Do you know these people? They can't be Sclavonians; they look too civilized for that. I don't think they are the German Emperor's men. Those usually display some kind of eagle, and this boat wears a flag with a great lion on it. But it's only one boat, so it comes in peace." Guiscard was puzzled.

"They come prepared for war, but they aren't quite certain which side to fight on," Bohemond put in. "Pirates probably, who want to watch the fighting before they help plunder the losers. We can't allow that. I'll deal with them."

The man who stepped out of the boat, waving a leafy branch, called in good Latin; he must be a Frank, since no Greek ever knew that language. Bohemond took off his sword and went forward to speak to him.

"We are the navy of St. Mark, from Venice which lies in the sea. We have come to free the town of Durazzo, as our Emperor has commanded us. But we are Italians and we don't wish to fight other Italians. Send one of your leaders to talk with our admiral and we may be able to come to some arrangement. Meanwhile will you agree that there shall be no fighting between us today or to-morrow?"

Bohemond climbed into the boat. At parleys he often re-presented his father, who was too quick-tempered to be good at negotiation face to face; though at long range he could deceive an enemy as well as any man. Some hours later he returned in the same boat, and walked stiffly to headquarters.

"I took the responsibility of refusing their terms," he said wearily. "I knew they would not be good enough for you, so the war begins at sunrise the day after tomorrow. They don't offer enough. It's like this. The new Emperor of the Greeks, Alexius, has hired them to fight for him. That's fair, for in a sense they are his subjects. They don't pay him tribute, or obey his laws. But they pray for him in their churches and claim his protection against the German Emperor. Well, they took his money and set out to drive us away. Now they see our strength. So they will split the money with us if we go away quietly. But we shall get more from the sack of Durazzo. Besides, it doesn't do for us to get the reputation of being easy to buy off. We are conquerors, not pirates."

"Normans—northmen. How long since your ancestors were pirates?" asked Sigelgaita. "But in this case you did right. We don't know how much Alexius gave the Venetians, and we certainly can't trust them to give us a fair half of it."

"H'm, it means fighting at sea, which I have never done before," muttered Guiscard. "But you are right, Bohemond. We can't back down so late in the day, though if they had offered the money before we left Italy I might have been tempted. We'll go on board our ships tonight, and practise what we must do when the battle comes. Then we sail against the Venetians, ready to fight as soon as they start."

That evening most of the warriors in the Apulian army were embarked on the ships; which then proceeded, slowly and clumsily, to the mouth of the bay which sheltered the Venetians. Guiscard,

Sigelgaita and Bohemond were on the same vessel, the largest and stoutest of their carracks. It was a three-masted sailing ship with very thick sides, almost as broad as it was long and very awkward to move. But its castles were the tallest in the fleet, so that it was the obvious citadel to hold the chief commanders. Guiscard took over the forecastle, with Bohemond on the aftercastle and Sigelgaita roaming at large in the waist. The master explained that the stern was the post of honour and the usual station of the admiral; but Guiscard replied that he was in the habit of leading his men from in front.

All night they tossed at anchor in extreme discomfort. A ship anchored short in a seaway pitches abominably. By the morning no Apulian felt very warlike. About midday, with the wind fresh and gusty from the east, the Venetians hoisted anchor and bore down towards Durazzo.

"That's cheating," shouted Guiscard in anger. "We gave them a truce when they asked for it. Until sunset we are at peace. By to-morrow we would have got over our seasickness, that's why I got the men on board yesterday. Why did they ask for a truce and then break it? The dirty dogs. We shall keep them out of Durazzo. Display the banners and sound the trumpets."

"They needed that truce to raise their fighting-tops," grunted the shipmaster. "They have cross-bows in those platforms high on their masts, and heavy stones to drop on our decks. They couldn't sail the open sea with all that clutter aloft. Dirty work, as you say, my lord, but effective."

"Where are our fighting-tops? Why haven't we got them?" Bohemond demanded.

"We also are ready to voyage in the open sea. Nobody told me we were to fight this afternoon. We've been caught napping," was the angry answer.

"Never mind, we have swords. We don't need more to deal with Italian burgesses," said Sigelgaita gaily. In addition she carried a cross-bow, which she could wind as well as any man.

The Venetians came on steadily, their carracks under sail, their dromonds rowed slowly not to get out of line.

From the start the fight went badly for the Apulians. Venetian ships were bigger and faster, and their crews very much more

32

expert. They could sail with the wind abeam and shift from place to place in the line, while Apulians could only keep station while they remained still. Three Venetian dromonds singled out Guiscard's carrack. Each hit it a mighty whack with its bronze-shod prow and passed on to make way for a tall carrack, which grappled.

In the rolling swell the two great ships bumped together. As the fighting-top of the Venetian loomed over the Apulian deck a great lump of iron hurtled down. It landed amidships, where there was no upper deck above the hull; the jagged metal smashed the bottom timbers and continued into the sea. Of the leaders only Bohemond saw this, as he took cover behind a tall mantlet from the cross-bows. His father and his stepmother were scrambling over the bulwarks at the head of a boarding party.

Of course Normans and Apulians fought better when it was a question of fighting hand-to-hand. When the flagship seemed likely to founder Bohemond joined the rest of the family. After a short struggle the Venetians gave way, but there was no opportunity to take prisoners or massacre unresisting fugitives. At the right moment a Venetian dromond came up on the other rail, and the beaten defenders jumped neatly to safety. Unhandy Norman knights and scared Apulian fishermen managed to beach the captured ship.

By sunset the Venetians had pierced the Apulian line and most of their ships were within the harbour of Durazzo. But the Apulians, beaten by superior technical skill, were not disheartened. Their battered ships still watched the harbour mouth, and the Venetians would face another stiff fight if they tried to come out again.

Wrapped in warm cloaks the wet and weary Hautevilles huddled round a fire outside the headquarters pavilion.

"Never again will I fight on the sea," said Guiscard. "You can't stand up, and any miserable rascal can kill you at any time just by dropping a heavy stone. Those Venetians gave value for the money Alexius paid them. I wonder what they charge for the hire of their fleet?"

"More than we can afford," Bohemond answered him. "Anyway, mercenaries who are willing to change sides are not worth hiring. I still don't know who won. They sank some of our ships

33

but we sank some of theirs. They got into Durazzo but they can't get out again."

"On balance they won," Guiscard grumbled. "They will take over the defence of Durazzo, and if they fight as they fought today the place won't fall for a long time. They broke a truce to do it, though. We must remind all Italy of that. Those confounded fighting-tops. Now Alexius has plenty of time to reach here with his army of relief."

"All the better. We must fight him one day, and now we shall fight him far from his own city. It was a nasty business, but now it's over. We are not really any worse off."

"It was the greatest fun," put in Sigelgaita. "I'm pretty sure I killed a Venetian with my cross-bow, and that time when I fell in the water was warm and I hadn't forgotten how to swim. I like fighting at sea, with your bed and your dinner handy and none of that bumping about on a hard saddle."

For another two months the siege of Durazzo continued.

"Of course Alexius leads a great army, as big as ours. I know that. What kind of army? Who are his troops? I suppose this wretched yokel can't tell us anything so useful as that." Bohemond fingered his dagger, as though tempted to murder the peasant then and there.

"Patience," his father said soothingly. "This fellow is a peasant, but he says he was a trooper in a Greek band until he deserted after Manzikert. He knows what an army ought to look like, and he has seen this one. We shall keep him in chains for a bit, in case he's a liar. But if what he says turns out to be true I shall make him a rich man for life."

The shaggy countryman twisted his sheepskin cap, but he went on talking to the interpreter. He could not understand Italian, but he guessed that these two foreign lords were deciding whether to kill him or reward him.

When the interpreter had finished Guiscard summed up. "Two or three bands of regular Greek horse, successors I suppose of the bands that missed Manzikert. Household cavalry. They will be gallant young nobles, eager to show off before the Emperor. A great many Patzinaks, light horse who skirmish with bows. A few

34

German knights, but he may not trust them to fight other Franks. No one there who can face a Norman charge. I just can't guess whether his foot will be any use. The Varangians, the axe-bearers —they have a great reputation."

"Palace guards," Bohemond answered scornfully. "Lackeys who stand in ante-rooms. Gentlemen of good birth, naturally, because they wander through his public apartments. But they fight on foot, which proves they are only for show. I don't care how strong their armour is, how sharp they keep their axes. If they can't charge on horseback they are obsolete in modern warfare."

"It proves that Alexius is hard up for soldiers. Those palace guards don't normally leave the city. All the same, they are famous. I wish I could imagine how brave infantry fight. After all, there used to be brave infantry. Our forefathers fought on foot, when as heathen they pillaged all Christendom. So did those ancient Romans who left such remarkable buildings all over Italy. Quite part from these Varangians, how do we deal with mounted archers?" Guiscard was obstinately determined to take Alexius seriously.

"We shall find out when the time comes. What's the use, anyway? Our men know how to charge with the lance, and it's too late to teach them any other way of fighting. I shall charge those Patzinaks and start them running away. If they run fast enough they won't stop to shoot arrows."

Of course Bohemond was right, Guiscard reflected. There was only one way in which Normans could fight, and when they met the Emperor Alexius they must try it. If it turned out to be not good enough, well, they were near their ships. That gave him an idea.

Next day the Apulian army was drawn up on the shore, to witness the burning of their transports. All the baggage was stacked in camp, and the sailors were transferred to fill gaps in the crews of the warships. Guiscard did not deliver a formal speech, though of course all later chroniclers of the campaign supplied him with one. He spoke casually to his leading knights. "Alexius is over there. We can't get away from him. We must beat him, or lie here until the Resurrection. Remind your men of that before the battle."

35

On 17th October 1081 the Apulian army was drawn up for battle. Guiscard had attempted nothing fancy. His men were in their conventional formation: three squadrons of horse in the front line; cross-bows immediately behind, as close as they could get; in the rear a crowd of grooms and servants and sailors, who looked to the casual eye like a reserve and might help to defend the palisaded camp if the worst came to the worst.

Bohemond commanded on the left flank. Guiscard himself led both right wing and centre. Sigelgaita had insisted on riding beside her husband, in mail and fully armed.

They waited, for there was nothing more to be done until the enemy should appear. But it seemed that Alexius did not know the etiquette that governed the fighting of a decisive battle. The Greek army did not appear.

Presently a few Patzinaks trotted out from the wood half a mile in front. They had learned by experience in the first brushes of the campaign that a cross-bow carried farther and hit harder than a short horseman's bow, and they kept out of range. Dutifully they spread out and found the Apulian flanks. The Greeks would have a clear picture of the numbers and position of the invading army.

Bohemond was fretting with impatience. He knew that he ought to do something, not sit still until the enemy were ready to attack; but he could not think of anything to do. It would be rash to charge blindly into that thick wood against unknown numbers. All the veterans advised waiting to receive the first attack, so that you could see the hostile force you were up against.

Ah, here was something, a little knot of enemy horse. But when they were clear of the wood he knew them for Alexius and his personal staff. He could see the purple housing on the Emperor's horse, and on the spare horse led beside him. It would be stupid to charge the enemy commander. That was just what they wanted him to do. There would be an ambush concealed in the wood.

His squadron could deliver only one real charge, though that one would be very deadly. After he got them galloping the well-armed knights would stretch out to the front while the common troopers lay back. The knights would go on charging after the trumpet signalled the recall; for no knight would draw rein until he saw another knight had pulled up. The common troopers would stop dead at the first toot. If he ever did get his men halted they would assume that the battle was over, and leave their ranks to plunder. He must not start them until the right moment.

From the rear came sounds of alarm. Looking over his shoulder Bohemond saw that a party of horse had sallied out from the main gate of Durazzo. He sent a few troopers to protect the Apulian camp, but did nothing otherwise to impede the sortie. From the banner in their midst they seemed to be led by the eminent George Palaeologus; probably all the Greek cavaliers in the garrison had come out to help their Emperor. As they rode round the left flank of the Apulian host and disappeared into the forest Bohemond saw it as one up to the besiegers. Their best course, their obvious course, would have been to wait until the crisis of the battle and then attack the Apulian rear. The strange tactics of Alexius, who hung about behind the trees instead of advancing, had puzzled his own side as much as it puzzled his adversaries. Now what might have been a dangerous diversion had become a trifling reinforcement.

At last the Greeks were on the move. A column of horse emerged from the wood, opposite his father. At first they advanced rather slowly; then, just when they were near enough to begin the charge, they halted and dismounted. The Apulians stared in amazement. What incredible behaviour, to ride to the battle and then fight on foot!

"Those must be the Varangians," said an elderly knight who rode behind him. "I was with Duke William in that English battle, though afterwards there was so much law and order in England that I came on to Apulia. Harold's men rode to the battle and then dismounted. They need both hands to swing their great axes, so they can't control a horse or carry a shield."

As the Varangians marched steadily nearer, Bohemond saw that they wore long mail shirts under gilded helms. Short swords hung from their belts, but each man's main weapon was the axe he carried resting on his shoulder. They marched in a broad column, very close together; evidently they thought it nothing extra-ordinary that infantry should attack horse.

But they were going to attack Guiscard's wing, and Bohemond must hold himself ready to meet the rest of the Greek army. As yet there was no sign of them. Even the Emperor and his staff had vanished into the trees.

At the last minute, of course, Guiscard led his men in a charge. Horsemen should never stand halted to receive attack. There was still no sign of the rest of the Greeks. Something must have gone wrong; either the Varangians had advanced too soon or the right wing had not been ready when expected.

It was astonishing. The Varangians were winning. Horse were giving ground before foot. Bohemond tried to make out what was happening. Horses, it seemed, would not gallop into men who stood firm; normal foot were always turning to break at the moment of impact. He could see his father prancing cautiously just out of reach of the axes. Some common troopers were pulling their mounts right round and getting ready to ride off the field. This was absurd. Why didn't the cross-bows shoot? . . . Then he saw that they dared not shoot, while Guiscard and his knights were so close to the enemy. The Varangians advanced steadily. Soon they would break through the right wing.

He would have to wheel his own men in a right-handed charge, though it would break the line and uncover the camp. Why didn't the rest of the Greeks come up and keep him busy? There must be a trap somewhere, though he could not see how it would work. He would have to charge. He could not sit still while his father and the right wing were defeated before his eyes.

Then he saw Sigelgaita. Her fair hair, escaping from its coif, streamed down her back; the wide skirt which should have hidden her legs was hitched above her knees; she had dropped her reins to wave a sword in one hand and a banner in the other; her spurs were plunged into the bloody sides of her maddened horse; the polished rings of her mail gleamed in the sun. The middle-aged mother of so many bouncing children might have been a Battle-Maiden out of the old heathen songs.

Luckily her horse would not carry her into the ranks of the close-set Varangians. But no knight could shrink from the onset when a lady set such an example, and the common troopers took heart when they saw the knights charge again. Sigelgaita had restored a dangerous situation. Guiscard had got his men in hand. The Varangian attack was held.

38

At that moment masses of Patzinaks issued from the wood, directly before the Apulian left wing. This must be the main attack, which should have been synchronized with the advance of the Varangians. Yes, the Emperor was leading them. Bohemond settled his long shield before his chin so that his body was covered from neck to left ankle. He trotted forward. His men followed in good order.

Patzinaks would not meet the Norman charge, though that was what the Emperor had intended. Alexius waved his sword, his great banner of the Labarum snapped in the wind, trumpeters on either side of him blew the battle-call. But the Patzinaks wheeled their horses with their knees as they shot arrows at the charging Apulians. Those men were already beaten, Bohemond knew it; as many other foreigners had been beaten when first they encountered the knightly charge. Must he gallop into the wood, following a beaten foe until his men were scattered on blown horses? Or could he do something more useful while his men were still behind him and obedient to his commands? With knee and rein he forced his horse to the right, waving his lance to direct his men.

Of course more than half of them galloped straight on. When a charge of that kind had started some riders were too busy keeping in the saddle to notice anything else. But some followed him towards the flank of the Varangian column.

His horse stopped so abruptly that he nearly went over its head. It just would not gallop into that line of immovable men. He poked with his lance, until a great axe cut off its point. It seemed that a knight could do very little harm to Varangians who stood firm.

But while the knights were so close the Varangians could not move. They were beginning to retire towards the rest of the Greek army; but with Guiscard pressing on their front and his son on their flank they must halt to dress their line. Bohemond called to a knight beside him.

"Bring up the cross-bows. Tell their captain that both Hautevilles and most of their knights are here to protect him, and that the battle is going well. Here, take this ring to prove you come from me. I know cross-bows hate to move after close fighting has started, but it's really quite safe for them. Tell them that these people are the imperial bodyguard, all hung with gold chains and gold collars. Any cross-bow who shoots a Varangian may keep the plunder from the corpse."

Presently the cross-bows arrived, looking round them timidly for fear Greek horse might charge. But they were encouraged when they saw knights ready to protect them, and they settled down to their shooting.

It was a grim, relentless slaughter. Whenever the Varangians tried to move the knights charged; while they stood in rank the cross-bows shot at an easy mark. The column of steel-clad foot grew smaller, but it did not waver. Towards the end the remnant of them sought shelter in a chapel close by. Stone walls kept out the arrows but the tiled roof was supported on wooden rafters; when those had been set alight the defenders must come out. By sunset the last Varangian was dead. There were no prisoners, either wounded or whole.

Before the massacre was quite finished the rest of the Apulian horse dropped in, on their way back to camp where supper should be cooking by now. Their charge through the wood had been wholly successful. They had ridden into a Patzinak ambush, of course; every Greek commander hid Patzinaks in ambush. But unless their first flight of arrows brought victory those lightly armed skirmishers always fled from charging Franks.

On the far side of the wood they had come on the Emperor Alexius trying to rally his men. But they were too shaken to face another attack. Soon Alexius had retired eastward along the great road, with no escort save his regular Greek horse; while his mercenaries streamed north to get over the Danube and away from this war. It had been a most famous victory and they had pillaged the imperial camp before any baggage could be removed.

The dead Varangians were piled thickly, tall long-haired men with bloody wounds in front. Their naked bodies glimmered white in the dusk. Their mail and their clothes had been stripped from them before they were cold, sometimes before they had ceased to bleed. That was one reason why there were no wounded prisoners. Cross-bows, already dismounted, are quicker at this sort of work than troopers or knights. In a day or two those naked bodies would look very nasty. They must be burned, or shovelled under-ground, as soon as possible.

Bohemond felt vaguely sorry for all those noble stark corpses. A pity they had to be killed; if they had asked for quarter he would have granted it. But there had been nothing else to be done with them. They would not run away, they would not yield, they just went on swinging their great axes until the arrows struck them down. Obstinate men, and after all it was what they were paid for. He would have a Mass said for their souls, here in this roofless chapel. Bohemond contributed generously to the support of religion, and already a great number of Masses had been offered for the repose of the souls of his enemies.

His father and stepmother sought him out where he mused among the corpses. They were in high spirits, and he remembered to congratulate Sigelgaita on her gallantry. "I enjoyed myself," she answered. "It was fun. I wish I could do it more often, but all those confounded babies kept me at home."

"You won the battle for us, my dear," said her proud husband. "I shall make sure the *jongleurs* get the story right, so that every-one knows it. But now that the battle is won, what shall we do next? There is no army to oppose us, no army to defend Romania. We can chase Alexius all the way to the city, and plunder his dominions in Europe. There's a lot of good plunder to the south and east."

"We must stay here and make sure of Durazzo," Bohemond answered at once. "We can hold that place once it's ours, but if we ride on to plunder Thrace they will chase us back again after a year or two. Even this battle has weakened Durazzo. Palaeologus and the Greek nobles of the garrison rode out to link up with the Emperor, and they never had a chance to get back again. There can be no one but Venetians inside it."

"Those Greeks did muddle their battle, didn't they?" Guiscard chuckled. "Their timing went wrong on every move. It's the mis-take they all make, even Alexius who is better than most of them. They can't really remember, when the crunch comes, that their troops are barbarian mercenaries. They imagine they have only to issue an order and it will be obeyed. They always move too fast or too slow. But that infantry bodyguard was a nasty surprise, eh? There was a time when I thought they had us beat. Clever of you to change direction after you had started your charge."

"I remembered something I had heard about the battle in England," Bohemond explained. "Mailed foot can't move if you threaten to charge them, and then archers can shoot them down. Luckily our cross-bows were brave enough to come close. But what a muddle it was, even on our side. Half my knights galloped off where they were no use at all, and the cross-bows on your flank never shot an arrow from first to last. I wish I could lead an army where every man did what he was told. Only ten years ago there was an army like that, here in Romania. It's maddening to think it was destroyed before I could see it. How on earth did the Turks beat it?"

"That was treachery, my boy, or so they say. If the second in command wants to overthrow his Emperor more than he wants to beat the foe the best army in the world will get beaten. But you've got to admire one thing in those Greeks, they never give in. Young Alexius has no native army at all, but with one thing and another he manages to keep his end up."

"He keeps his end up with money. When that is spent he will be finished," said Bohemond with relish. "He can't go on for ever, hiring Venetians and Patzinaks."

"I enjoyed fighting his bodyguard," Sigelgaita murmured dreamily. "What a pity he lives so far off."

"The city is far away, but one day I shall go there," said Bohemond with sudden decision. "I want to get into Anatolia, where they used to recruit those wonderful soldiers. The same kind of men must be living there now, if only we could drive back the Turks. Think what an army it would be, Greeks led by Normans. The man who had an army like that could be greater than Charlemagne."

"It's too difficult," said Guiscard, shaking his head mournfully. "No Frank can cope with those artful Greeks. You remember that fellow Roussel I told you about? He did well for a time until he was poisoned by a Greek, more or less by accident in the course of some Greek feud. Come to think of it, Alexius was mixed up in that, before he was Emperor. For a Greek, he knows rather a lot about Franks."

"No need to make plans now," said Bohemond. "We must stay here until Durazzo falls, and that may be a long way ahead."

In February 1082 the defenders of Durazzo yielded on terms, after an honourable resistance of more than eight months. They were permitted to withdraw to Venice with their ships, baggage and arms, and the town was not sacked. Even after this long battering the walls were little damaged, and the Venetians claimed that hunger had compelled them to surrender. But a few timely bags of Apulian silver had helped them to make up their minds. The Venetians were honest mercenaries, who gave good value for money. They had earned their pay from Alexius, and if they took a little present from his enemies as well that was only common prudence. The Apulians loaded their baggage on mules and rode off down the great road to drive Alexius from his base at Salonica.

It was a pleasant march. They saw no Greek troops though local bandits could be dangerous. Romania was an empty land of tall mountains separated by wide valleys. Walled towns were rare, though where they existed their walls were strong. But their governors, used to constant revolution, were usually willing to admit the Apulians provided they levied an orderly ransom instead of promiscuous plunder. By May they had reached Castoria and there was still no Greek army in the field.

In Castoria a messenger reached them from Italy with important news. Guiscard summoned Bohemond and Sigelgaita to talk it over in private.

"Alexius deserves his wealth," he said with a rueful grimace. "He knows how to use it. There are half a dozen rebellions in Apulia. The rebels hire all the soldiers they need, I suppose with Greek silver. I hate to leave here while things are going so well, but I ought to get back. There's another reason too, a secret one. The Pope wants me. The German Emperor is making trouble again. We must help the Pope when he calls on us, remember that, Bohemond. The Pope's friendship is the only thing that keeps us even moderately respectable. Without it we would be nothing but land-pirates. So I must go, and of course my dear wife will come with me. But perhaps we need not wind up this lucrative foray. Bohemond, could you stay here with most of the troops, and keep the pot boiling until I return?"

CHAPTER III

Bohemond Against Alexius

————————————————★————————————————

Bohemond was then in his twenty-eighth year; so naturally as soon as he was on his own he changed the plan of campaign his father had laid down for his guidance. Instead of marching down the great road that led to Salonica and then to the city, the road by which Alexius expected him, he turned south to conquer a Greek province. Romania was a good land to rule. The Greeks were accustomed to paying heavy taxes, in cash, to some arbitrary tyrant who had been appointed in the city, and who gave the provincials nothing in return for their tribute. They were quite glad to pay money to a Norman instead, who hanged thieves and chased away Sclavonian brigands. Bohemond thought it more prudent to take some of the empire, and keep it, rather than ride on with the bare chance of sacking the great city if all went well.

While he was blockading Janina he got word that Alexius had broken camp. Greek peasants willingly brought information, once it was known that he paid well for it. To them any marching soldier was an enemy; their only hope of surviving military requisition was to gather silver coins and bury them.

It seemed that Alexius brought no great force with him. The mercenary army scattered last autumn outside Durazzo had been replaced only by a few bands of Patzinaks. Patzinaks were cheap, and there were always plenty of them seeking wages; but they would not fight hand-to-hand, because that was not their custom at home.

Alexius, therefore, would not force a battle. But he would not have left his secure base at Salonica unless he intended to break the blockade of Janina. He must be going to try one of those cunning Greek dodges.

But a secret weapon is little use if it must be handled by untrustworthy mercenaries. A patrol of Patzinaks came into the Apulian camp with information for sale, and after a little trouble in finding a competent interpreter Bohemond was forewarned.

On an open grassy plain south of the town Alexius led a full-scale attack, though his men followed him without enthusiasm. When he had probed the Apulian line of battle and discovered its flanks he launched a sudden charge of scythed chariots.

Chariots had gone out with the Trojan War, as a cultivated clerk remarked to Bohemond. Even so they might have worked if the Apulians had not been expecting them. Each was drawn by four horses abreast, the scythes were sharp, and to make them more frightening each had inside it a flaming brazier. Perhaps the horses of the Apulian knights would have bolted rather than face them. As it was, cross-bows shot them down.

Alexius withdrew, with few casualties but great loss to his reputation. Soon afterwards Janina surrendered on the usual terms. Bohemond was elated. He was doing better than his father. This campaign seemed very easy. He led his army southward and laid siege to Arta.

Alexius still kept the field, though he dared not launch another attack. He was a gallant warrior, who did not seem to know when he was beaten. But what could he do? His army was just not fit to meet the Apulians in the open field.

He could do quite a lot, Bohemond discovered. His presence was a tiresome handicap. Knowing that their emperor was in the neighbourhood the garrison of Arta fought with great devotion, confident that he would find some way to rescue them. He would have to be driven right away.

The Apulians found him holding a strong position on a ridge, his whole front entrenched. He seemed anxious to stay and fight it out, so Bohemond gave orders for an attack next morning. Then, luckily, as he tossed on his bed during the night before the battle, he smelt a rat.

Why did the emperor stand his ground, at the head of such a puny and discredited army? Because he wanted to be attacked

45

where he stood. A wise man never does what his enemy wants of him.

By dawn he was inspecting the field. There would be an ambush farther back, of course, because Alexius was fond of ambushes; though so far they had done him no good. As well as the morning mist allowed he searched the ground in front of the enemy for pits and mantraps. The turf had not been disturbed, and it was fair going for heavy horses. But the whole shape of the enemy line, the way the archers were drawn up on the flanks with the few mailed horse and the best of the Patzinaks massed in the centre, showed that the Greeks expected him to charge in the usual Frankish manner: with his knights in the centre and his cross-bows on the wings. Very well, he would do just the opposite.

It took a lot of explaining, and some pushing and shoving; for no one else in his army could understand what he wanted to do. But in the end he was ready to advance with his foot massed in the centre and his horse divided into two wings.

After the Greeks had fled he discovered that the ground in the centre of their position, where they had expected the Frankish charge, had been sown with caltrops. If he had done the usual thing the Greek archers would have shot down all his horses.

Alexius had lost his second army within two years. With only a small escort he fled right back to the city; Salonica was already too near the Apulian advance.

But when Arta surrendered the season was very late; instead of returning north to the great road Bohemond led his army eastwards to the town of Trikala, where they found warm winter quarters.

Soon after Christmas came cheerful news from Guiscard. In Italy all was going well. His father added, as something to bear in mind during this joyful season, that in all Christendom there were only two emperors: during the Christmas of 1082 Robert Guiscard, son of a simple knight from Hauteville, had been chasing the German Emperor Henry; and Bohemond, son of Robert, had been chasing the Greek Emperor Alexius. That would be something for their descendants to remember.

As soon as the grass began to grow Bohemond moved east to

besiege Larissa. That was the last barrier before the coast of the Aegean; as soon as he had conquered it, and collected a fleet, the way would be clear to Constantinople.

But during the winter that undaunted Alexius had hired yet a third army. Word came that he was marching westward, ready to fight before Larissa fell.

"He's a good man, almost as brave as a Norman," Bohemond remarked to his captains. "It seems a shame to beat him again and again, and kill more of his mercenaries. Yet what else can we do when he won't give in? I wish he had the sense to do a deal with us. I wonder what he would say if I suggested that he keep the city, and Thrace, and what the Turks have left of Anatolia; and let us have Salonica and everything to the west of it? That's all I want, at least for the moment. I don't think my father, or any other Norman for that matter, could govern Constantinople."

"Alexius is willing to part with some of his land," said John of Brienne, a well-born Frenchman who was second in command. "I had a letter from him today, or the spy said it came from him. He offers me Arta and a good fief round about if I will desert you to join him. I can't think of a polite answer, and I don't want to insult a brave man. So I shan't answer at all."

"It does sound a dirty business," said Bohemond in answer to the look of disgust on Brienne's face. "But these Greeks have different standards. They buy traitors. It doesn't follow that they themselves can be bought. How much did they offer you, Aulps?"

"I haven't heard from them. Is that because they think I am not worth buying? That's another kind of insult. Should I be annoyed by it?"

Peter of Aulps led the cross-bows, though in rank he was a knight. He was a simple and greedy mercenary, though a competent commander.

Bohemond kept his eyes on the ground. Spies had warned him that Alexius might be trying to buy Brienne; but they said there had been two messages, the other for Aulps. If Aulps chose not to report it he might have been tempted. He was a man who yielded easily to temptation. Well, the best way to guard against desertion was to win the next battle. Aulps would never desert to the losing

47

side, and if he did his men would not follow him. But it must all be kept in mind.

Towards the end of April Alexius again challenged battle. It was all as it had been before. Bohemond led the Apulian horse against a cloud of Patzinaks, while on the wings his cross-bows skirmished with the Greek foot. This time Alexius was not in the front line. As the knights chased the timid Patzinaks they encountered him some way back. He charged from the flank with a body of light horse, in one of his usual ambushes. The Apulians thought little of it. Alexius placed his ambushes cleverly, but what was the good of that when the men he led would not charge home?

This time, however, they did charge home, against the un-shielded right side of the Franks. They were a new breed of mer-cenary, heathen Turks from the far east. Although they rode light ponies and wore armour of leather instead of iron, they carried sharp slashing sabres and were willing to use them. Their charge halted the Franks, and then the Patzinaks turned about and began shooting in earnest. After a good many horses and some men had been disabled Bohemond decided to retire. Meanwhile Russian axemen had charged the Apulian cross-bows and got rather the better of the encounter.

A straggling disorganized fight, covering a great deal of ground, continued until nightfall. Bohemond could never see in one glance all that was going on, though Peter of Aulps did not seem to be pulling his weight. There was never any danger of a rout; but each Apulian detachment in turn found it necessary to fall back to keep in touch with their comrades. For once the complicated Greek system of tactics seemed to work out better than the simple Frankish charge.

When darkness fell the Apulians were still in one body and willing to go on fighting. But they had been pushed well north of Larissa, so that the siege was raised. Worst of all, a band of Turkish horse overran their camp, and they had lost the plunder of two successful campaigns. Most of their Italian servants got away while the enemy was pillaging, but of course all their Greek foragers and concubines and grooms stayed behind to join the winning side.

Luckily the night was warm and dry as Bohemond led his defeated and hungry army northward in the general direction of Durazzo.

In Trikala they found food, but they burned the place from sheer spite as they retired from it. After that the retreat continued in growing misery. In a strange land they must go back by the roads they knew, though during the advance their foragers had taken all the available food and now they had no native foragers. Turks and Patzinaks followed close behind. The paychest had been lost in the captured camp, and unpaid cross-bows grumbled. After a few days Aulps deserted, though most of his men remained faithful for fear that the Greeks would murder them. Bohemond discovered that war on the losing side could be a very unpleasant experience. He did his best to encourage the troops. Brienne remained loyal, which helped; but Alexius published the letters in which he had offered him great rewards, so that many common soldiers suspected that he was about to betray them. Some troopers went over to the Greeks, who paid punctually; many others just went home to get away from such an unlucky war.

By the time they reached the Adriatic the Apulian army was very much smaller. Alexius was too cautious to follow, but they found an enemy waiting for them. The energetic Venetians had come back again to lay siege to Durazzo. Bohemond found safe and warm winter quarters in Valona. But in the spring of 1084 he despaired and sailed home to Apulia.

By autumn of the same year the Hautevilles were back again. It was their settled policy, on which their prestige rested, never to give in. Robert Guiscard had made his name by his four-year siege of Bari, and he would batter at the ports of Illyria until they were firmly his. To show that he was in earnest he brought with him most of his family: not only Bohemond and Sigelgaita, but three of Sigelgaita's sons, Roger and Robert and Guy. After a great buffeting by autumn gales they reached, in December, the island of Corfu where the Venetians were besieging the port.

It seemed an unlucky enterprise, haunted wherever they went by the memory of earlier failure. Bohemond, though still nominally second in command, found himself shut out from the family councils. Sigelgaita treated him as a mere hired expert, and Guiscard

49

was more and more influenced by his gallant wife. The younger boys, with more of the Lombard in them than of the rapacious Norman Hauteville, seemed to forget that he also was a member of the family.

But Guiscard was still all Norman and all Hauteville. During December, when all prudent warriors lie up in warm winter quarters, he prepared to drive the blockading fleet from the harbour of Corfu.

There was a long day of fighting among the cold wet squalls of the harbour. At sunset the Apulians sailed back to their beach on the other side of the island, while the victorious Venetians mocked them. In the council that night Guiscard explained his plans.

"All our big ships are damaged, so we must waste tomorrow in repairing them. A pity, though it will pay in the long run. So the next attack on the harbour must be postponed until the day after tomorrow."

"My squadron will be ready," said Bohemond curtly. Once he would have helped his father to make these plans; now he learned of them at the same time as baby Guy, aged sixteen.

"Isn't that a bit strenuous?" piped up the squeaky voice of Roger the Purse. "This is the middle of winter. My ships can't be repaired in a single day."

"I pay sailors to fight, not to loiter in winter quarters," Guiscard boomed firmly. "We are Hautevilles. When we are beaten we fight again, and again until we win. Before Bari, I remember—but you don't want to hear that again." At mention of the famous leaguer of Bari an expression of glazed boredom had settled on the faces of all his family.

Two days later there was another sea-fight, in even worse weather. Once again the Apulians were beaten.

"One day for repairs, I suppose?" said Bohemond at the usual evening council. "It's lucky this island has plenty of timber."

"One day," his father assented. "Get this into your heads, all of you. We fight three days a week until all our ships are sunk, or until the Venetians leave Corfu, whichever comes earlier."

Sigelgaita's three sons grimaced with disgust.

Next day, while their carpenters were busy, they saw Venetian ships sail north, and hoped this was the beginning of a retreat. But their own shipmasters explained that it was nothing so gratifying. On the contrary, it showed that the Venetians were resigned to fighting all winter. These were their light fast scouting ships, dromonds and such, which were usually laid up for the winter in the dockyard at Venice. The big sailing battleships remained in Corfu harbour.

"So they fight with big ships only, while we have every kind. That ought to give us an advantage. I shall attack with all we've got. Think out a plan, someone: fireships, ramming with galleys. Third time lucky, or so they say." Guiscard was in good spirits.

The third time was indeed lucky. When night fell five Venetian battleships had been taken and two sunk with all hands. At last the siege of Corfu was lifted.

By Christmas, when even the most predatory Hauteville thought it too late for campaigning, Guiscard had his army in winter quarters on the mainland.

It was quite a good camp, on the shore facing the Corfu Channel; but there was something wrong with the water supply. The Sickness of the Host struck suddenly.

Whenever an army sat down for some time in one place the Sickness of the Host made its appearance. Men suffered from pains in the stomach, with diarrhoea and vomiting; it was especially disabling that the victim could not ride. Some died within a few hours, of violent cramps in the stomach; others faded slowly away, apparently because they could not keep down enough food to sustain life; a few recovered, though it took them a long time to get back their strength. Nobody knew what caused the Sickness of the Host; though it was usually more deadly when troops, short of food, were eating anything they could find. It was just one of the unavoidable difficulties of warfare. Commanders seldom allowed it to interfere with their plans.

During this winter the sickness in the Apulian army was very bad indeed. Luckily there was nothing urgent to be done before spring, so they could just stay where they were. They buried the dead and nursed the invalids. The Greeks did not bother them.

One evening Bohemond felt pain in his stomach, and knew the disease had attacked him. At once he sent for his confessor, so that all could be put in order while his mind was still clear. But when it came to the point he had very little to confess.

He had never been very strongly tempted by sins of the flesh. He admired pretty girls, as he admired everything beautiful; but his enormous and handsome body was in fact undersexed. At thirty he was unmarried. He had never been in love, he kept no concubines.

He was intensely avaricious, of course; but no more than was natural in a Hauteville. He had always paid his due tithes. He gave adequately to the support of religious foundations. In battle he had killed many men, but he took no pleasure in cruelty and never tortured captives for his own amusement. On the whole he kept his sworn promises, as much as could be expected from a man in his position. In the struggle against the German Emperor he had been wholeheartedly on the side of his overlord the Pope.

The confessor asked some probing questions, and was agreeably surprised by the answers. On his deathbed even a great lord tells the whole truth. Bohemond was absolved, and told he had little to fear in the next world. The pain in his stomach was still very great, but he felt encouraged.

Then his father arrived, bringing a Greek physician who had a great reputation in Durazzo. Guiscard flapped about foolishly, repeating unanswerable questions and demanding that the physician do something at once, bleed the patient or cup him or scarify him. The Greek said only that Bohemond must expect to feel worse before he felt better, but that there was a fair chance of recovery. He must be kept warm, and washed whenever he dirtied himself. If the next foraging party should bring in a cow they might see if he could swallow a little warm milk.

The thought of swallowing anything seemed so intolerable that Bohemond fainted, and presently fell into a high fever. For many days he was delirious. But the Sickness of the Host was not invariably fatal. In the end he awoke, in his right mind.

He was so weak, from continued weakness and starvation, that he could not lift his head. His valets nursed him lovingly, for it irked him to have women by his bed. The Greek physician pronounced that one day he would come back to his full strength, but that it would be a very slow business; he must rest for all the coming summer. In fact, since he could play no part in the campaign he would be wise to return to Italy. At Salerno was the best medical school in the world, and nearby were hot springs which would help his recovery. Bohemond sailed as soon as he was strong enough.

On a scorching July afternoon Bohemond lay on a pile of cushions under a trellised vine. He gazed down from the hillside on the pleasant bustling town of Bari. The sun glowed in the sky. Even in the shade of the arbour he could feel his body taking in new strength from its dry heat. Italy was the best land in the world, especially now that it was ruled by Normans. In the cold damp north he would have recovered more slowly, if at all. There was only one thing to be said for ancestral Normandy; there, so he had been told, Normans ruled without a rival. Here the Pope was inclined to claim the rights of his tenuous suzerainty, and the German Emperor was always trying to displace the Pope. The ideal land would have a hot climate, like this; an industrious and obedient population, like this; and no famous potentates to covet it. Perhaps there was such a land somewhere, beyond Romania for example; one day when he felt more energetic he would get on a good horse and find out.

Two sergeants of his bodyguard were bringing a messenger, a common trooper covered in dust and sweat. He was sorry to be interrupted in his reverie, but of course they had done right. If a man had ridden hard to bring news he must be heard at once; if the news turned out to be unimportant he might be flogged for his foolishness, but he must never be delayed. This man, a cheeky Italian, had evidently thought out his approach.

"Important news, my lord, secret news, bad news, news that affects you closely. In all Bari no one else knows it. What reward will you give for my secret news?"

"How important? Worth a piece of gold?"

"Twenty, my lord. If you don't think so when you have heard it your guards may flog me."

"That's fair enough. Twenty pieces of gold to a flogging, after I have heard what you have to say. Go on."

"My lord, your noble father the Duke of Apulia is dead in

53

Corfu, dead of the Sickness of the Host while his army waited to sail against Cephalonia."

"God rest his soul. But he was an old man and his time had come. Such news is not worth twenty gold pieces."

"His army was left leaderless. They would not follow Roger the Purse, though the lady Sigelgaita proposed him as their next commander. All the Normans and the Lombards and the Italians are packing their baggage to sail back to Italy. They will bring with them the body of the mighty Duke Robert."

"Come, that is more important. So the men wouldn't follow Roger? I can't say I blame them. Not a competent commander, though he tries hard enough. Alexius will be encouraged. You can have your twenty gold pieces."

"Thank you, generous lord. Then the worst news will be given free, as it should be. When the lady Sigelgaita asked that her son Roger should command the army she added that by the will of the mighty Guiscard he was to be the next Duke of Apulia. The soldiers agreed. They have recognized him as Duke, though they did not trust him to lead them against Alexius. The new Duke of Apulia, at the head of his great army, will now be setting out for Bari. That's bad news, and it's important news, and it concerns you, my lord."

"God's teeth but it concerns me. Hey, guard. Fetch my steward, and tell him to bring my purse. Unlike my brother Roger I don't know how much I have in it, but you may keep the lot, my man. That's in addition to the pay you will draw in the new army I shall be raising. Duke Roger of Apulia indeed! We'll see about that. Where do I come in, Bohemond fitzRobert, Guiscard's eldest son? Those soldiers who are running away from Corfu would have been safer if they had stayed in Romania. Hey, you, the other guard. Go and fetch the constable and the commander of my mercenaries."

Hautevilles stood together against the outside world, but if there were no external menace they could fight one another like tom-cats from the same litter. For the next four years war raged through Apulia, Calabria and Sicily.

Bohemond recognized accomplished facts. Guiscard had not in-

herited Apulia, he had conquered it with his own sword; therefore
he might bequeath it wherever he would, disregarding his legitimate heir. That was in accordance with the new feudal code, already thought of as immemorial custom. Just so had the great
Duke William left his ancestral duchy of Normandy to his eldest
son Robert, but his conquered Kingdom of England to his second
son William, the heir of his choice. Roger the Purse was undoubted
Duke of Apulia, by the nomination of his father; even though
that nomination had been procured by the undue influence of
Sigelgaita, bullying a dying man in his last hours on earth.

But, though Roger must remain Duke, Bohemond might hold
land as a vassal of his younger half-brother. By the time peace was
made, in the summer of 1098, Bohemond was recognized as lord
of Taranto and Bari, and of many other fiefs in Apulia and Calabria. He was so rich and powerful and famous that most people
called him the Count of Taranto. He preferred to use a simpler
and prouder title: on legal documents his seal called him merely
Bohemond son of Duke Robert.

The town of Bari was *en fête*. Following the old Greek custom
the burgesses, mostly Greek in language and manners, had hung
gay woven cloths from their upper windows. The cobbles outside
the cathedral had been covered with flowers laid in a neat pattern.
It had been arranged that a fountain, a marble lion's head set in
the wall of the Exchange, should spout a jet of wine; though as yet
it had not begun to flow, and the cistern at the back was guarded
by two sergeants with drawn swords. Burgesses in their best
clothes, many of them wearing tunics of bright Greek silk, crowded
the pavements, while their wives leaned from the decorated
windows above. As the great doors of the cathedral were flung
open the high nasal sound of a Greek processional hymn swelled
louder above the shuffling of many feet. First emerged the choir,
and a number of clean little children scattering rose petals; then
came most of the clergy of Apulia and Calabria, walking two by
two; then the canons of the cathedral, with their bishop behind;
last of all, which is the place of honour at a religious function, the
Pope, God's Vicar on earth, walked beside Count Bohemond, his
host, ally and protector.

The new Pope Urban could carry off these stiff ceremonial occasions with genial ease. He was middle-aged and vigorous, so that he walked with dignity. By birth he was a north Frenchman of knightly stock, which meant that he shared the origin and ancestral background of the Hautevilles. It was only a year since he had been chosen to fill the See of Peter, so that he still took unfeigned pleasure in the deference accorded to him.

The two great men walked right across the square, so that the crowd could see them and cheer. But the Pope's white mule and Bohemond's most showy warhorse were waiting at the head of the street to carry them up the hill to the castle. A King or an Emperor might walk beside the Pope to lead his mule; Urban understood that a Count of obscure family must be a more careful of his dignity in public. He had ordained, through his Master of Ceremonies, that Bohemond should ride at his right hand whenever he himself was mounted.

As they clattered gently up the street he made polite conversation.

"This is a handsome town, and obviously you keep good peace in it. I like those eastern carpets, and the silk tunics of the burgesses. I am glad they have chosen such a holy patron. Now his body is lodged splendidly, and I pray that it may remain in your new shrine until the Resurrection. Better not inquire whether all the people of Myra were willing to part with St. Nicholas; but I gather your merchants bought the relics from someone, they did not steal them or take them by force. Myra now lies open to the ravages of infidel Turks, and St. Nicholas will be safer in Christian Italy. He was a very holy Bishop, though some of the stories about him may have been garbled in the telling. The fame of Bari will increase, though we must do something to appease the injured feelings of his Greek flock. I should like to talk to you about that, after dinner."

"If you say so, Holy Father. I get on well enough with these Italian Greeks. In Romania they don't like me. But then why should they?"

Bohemond himself hated nobody, but the behaviour of the Greeks of Romania irritated his tidy mind. They would be much better off under the rule of competent Normans, and their struggles

---

against the Hautevilles seemed to him more obstinate than courageous.

Pope Urban did not dine with his host, for reasons of etiquette. Wherever he might be Christ's Vicar must take the head of the table, yet the lord of Bari would not wish to sit second in his own hall. When dinner was over Bohemond was invited to walk with Urban in the walled garden.

The pope at once began to talk business. "You may think I give myself too many airs, but in my position I have to insist on the full ceremonial. Just as you, my dear son, cannot demean yourself by leading my mule. A King may do that, but not a Hauteville. In all Christendom I am obeyed as Pope only in Norman Italy; even my bishopric of Rome is held by the Emperor for his absurd antipope. I must not give scandal by appearing as the tame bishop of the Hautevilles."

"Of course, Holy Father. I am proud to be the most obedient of your subjects."

"Soon I shall have more subjects, in France and Spain and England. It's only the Emperor and his people who are obstinate against me. One of the reasons why I came here was to tell you that. You have been faithful to the rightful Pope; soon I shall be the recognized Pope. That ought to comfort you. The other thing I want to say is this: Couldn't you patch up a peace with Alexius of Romania? In himself he is a good man, a brave warrior and a wise ruler. He has a very keen nose for approaching failure, like all Greeks. He sees that the German Emperor must be beaten in the end. I have heard through third parties that the Emperor Henry will get no more golden bezants from Constantinople. Alexius dare not offer me full submission, because his own clergy would not stand for it. But his Patriarch will make some sort of promise of obedience, a first step to reunion. All that stands in the way is his fear of the Normans of Italy. It isn't a matter of faith or morals, so I can't command you. But I beseech you."

"Why pick on me, Holy Father? I am only a mesne vassal. My uncle Roger is head of the House of Hauteville, and my young half-brother Roger the Purse is Duke of Apulia and Calabria."

"That's lawyers' language. I am talking about real things. Where the famous Bohemond leads all the other Normans of Italy will follow. Alexius doesn't fear either Roger, he fears *you*. You are Bohemond the giant, the hero of those nursery tales. Set his fears at rest."

"Yes, I am Bohemond the giant, the mightiest of the mighty Hautevilles. And I don't own a foot of land anywhere, except as the vassal of my younger brother. My stepmother cheated me out of my inheritance. I want land of my own, land somewhere oversea. I can get it only by attacking Romania."

"Oh no. You could get it by defending Romania. Alexius must fight constantly against infidel Turks on his eastern frontier. Why not help him to win land from the Turks? There will be enough for both of you. The people of that land are Greeks, like the people of Bari whom you govern so well. They are used to paying taxes in money. Their ruler will be richer than any ruler of the Franks."

Bohemond hesitated. But Pope Urban was famous for his wisdom, and the thrill of a complete reversal of policy appealed to his adventurous spirit.

"Very well, Holy Father. I will make peace with Alexius and thus unite Christendom," he said after a pause. "But I won't help Alexius, at any rate not just yet. Let him fight his own infidels. Perhaps one day, who knows, I shall win a great realm in the east."

"Thank you, my son," said Pope Urban, and for about the tenth time that day gave him the special papal blessing.

CHAPTER IV

To the City

— ★ —

The walls of Durazzo, so often breached and so often repaired, gleamed parti-coloured in the sun. On the highest tower a look-out shouted a familiar call.

In the commandant's office three or four officers hurried to take their usual places round the council table. "Well, gentlemen," said John Comnenus when they were seated, "this is it. 'Warships approaching' the sentry called. These must be the Normans of Apulia, the most dangerous of the Frankish fleets."

"The garrison is under arms, Highness," said the castellan. "Shall I close the gates and raise the drawbridge?"

"Not yet. But have men standing by the windlass. You might also pull back the ropes of the catapults, and load stones in them. It's just possible that these people may accept our condition. If they come in peace we must carry out the orders of the Emperor my uncle. After all, the brother of the famous King of the Franks gave no trouble when it came to the point."

"He's a fool, Highness," said another councillor, "and he did not see what was happening to him until it was too late. This Bohemond knows us."

An officer at the lower end of the table began to splutter excitedly to an interpreter, who then spoke deferentially to the Prince.

"My lord Peter of Aulps understands the tongue of civilization, but he distrusts his skill in speaking it. Therefore he speaks through my mouth. He says that if these Franks are led by Bohemond of Taranto then he, my lord Peter of Aulps, must get out of Durazzo at once. Our Emperor pays him to fight Franks, and he earns his pay. But not for all the gold in the world will he meet Count Bohemond."

"That sounds very extreme," Comnenus said pleasantly. "Is this barbarian so very disgusting?"

After another splutter from Peter the interpreter resumed.

"Bohemond is the biggest man in the world, and the strongest. My lord Peter came to Romania in his following, before he entered the service of the Emperor. He fears that giant Bohemond may tear him in pieces with his bare hands."

"Turning your coat brings these difficulties," Comnenus replied. "Don't translate that bit. Tell the lord Peter that within an hour a guard of Patzinaks will escort him to the city. He is not to go anywhere else, and he is not to take any of his mercenaries with him. In the city the Emperor will find him suitable employment. Good-bye, my lord Peter. This interpreter will stay. I want to talk with him."

When Peter had scurried out Comnenus turned genially to the interpreter. "I am sure you translated faithfully all that was told you in Frankish. Do you know whether any of it is true?"

"Oh yes, Highness, all of it. I am a Greek of Bari, and I lived in the west until I came here with the Frankish invaders. Count Bohemond is indeed the mightiest warrior among the Franks, and the biggest man I have ever seen. My lord Peter deserted him treacherously while on campaign in these parts. He is wise to fear his vengeance."

"His size doesn't frighten me," said Comnenus. "My uncle has many foes, nearly all of them bigger than he, for he is a small man. But he continues to hold his throne by the sword. This Bohemond may come in peace after all. He has said so, and I suppose even a Frank speaks the truth sometimes. For the time being we follow our instructions: Resist if he attacks, otherwise speed him on his journey. I suppose free food and free wine is the biggest inducement you can offer to these pirates. They will march to the nearest supplies. Yes, my man, you have more to say?"

"Highness, there is something you ought to know about Count Bohemond, something well known in Italy but perhaps not in Romania. He is a mighty warrior and a powerful ruler, but as the Franks reckon birth he is of lower rank than the leaders who have come before. His grandfather was little more than a free peasant. His father came to Italy with nothing but horse and arms. Bohemond is his eldest son, but he was passed over as heir in favour of the children of a second marriage. In my hearing my lord Peter has described him as an upstart."

"Thanks, that is worth knowing. You will be rewarded. Now go off to your Peter, and remember everything he says. But he won't let you hear much. He must know as well as I do that you are a spy."

"We have learned something valuable, gentlemen," he continued when the interpreter was out of the room. "We must flatter this Bohemond, and treat him in every way as the equal of the other Frankish lords. Then the others will dislike him. We don't want a united front of all the barbarians against civilization. The more they quarrel among themselves the better. It really is true, absurd as it must seem to us, that some barbarians consider themselves better born than others."

Count Bohemond stood on the ship's afterdeck with his young nephew Tancred. Bohemond was now forty-two years of age, but from a distance the pair might have been brothers. Both were immensely tall, with broad shoulders, narrow hips, slim waists; both moved easily in their heavy mailshirts; both carried long double-edged swords. Bohemond's clean-shaven face, brown from exposure so that his grey eyes gleamed with unexpected emphasis, peered from a mail hauberk which covered neck and ears. Tancred let his hauberk hang on his shoulders like a hood, to leave his long black hair undisturbed; and his soft black young man's beard fuzzed over the front of his mail. Long hair and long beard were the fashion among the young knights of Italy, though the elder generation thought the fashion unmilitary.

Bohemond gazed ahead. "That's Durazzo. Since I saw it last they have repaired the walls, and the Greek banners give it an ugly look. Gates closed, of course. I have opened them; but not this time if I can avoid it. I have explained to the shipmaster. We make for that shelving beach to the south. We get the troops ashore as quick as we can, and then march inland. I know the country, and our route is clear in my head. Not the route the Greeks advise, of course, because we must show them from the start that we don't take orders from their Emperor. I don't suppose they will attack us before we attack them, though we shall observe all military precautions. It doesn't look as though you will see your first fight today."

"That beach on the right? A good place. Cross-bows on the ridge inland can cover the disembarkation of the stores."

"It's on the right, as we look at it. But on campaign you should always say north or south. There are men in this army who would look for a beach to the right of this town if they were coming from the east, just because they heard you call it that. I hope you don't mind me putting you right. Is it true that you have never yet drawn your sword in anger?"

"Quite true, and I am not at all ashamed of it. I am old enough to think for myself. It seems to me the plain teaching of the Gospel that one Christian should never kill another Christian. There are a lot of Christians who never fight, monks and hermits and such. I wanted to see if a Count could live without fighting. I wonder what would have happened if the Pope had not started this pilgrimage?"

"You would have had to become a monk or a hermit, as many other Counts have done before you. It's the only honourable way to dodge fighting, and not a mode of life that appeals to me. The abbots of Italy should be grateful that this pilgrimage came in time. By blood you are half a Hauteville, and our House doesn't take kindly to canonical obedience. In your opinion is it all right to kill infidels?"

"Of course, especially when the Pope advises it. And it is equally right to kill false Christians who hinder the Holy War. If we have to charge those Greeks my horse's head will be level with yours. Oh, it's a wonderful idea. At Clermont, I'm told, men saw the Holy Ghost in the form of a dove hovering over the head of the Pope as he spoke. My brother is as keen as I am, in fact keener. He joined the first band of French pilgrims. By now he must be near Constantinople. I'll see him again when we all march in one body to free Jerusalem."

"To free Jerusalem, or to free the Christians of the east from infidel rule? I know we are to do both, but I wonder which should

62

come first? Have you heard from your brother since he set out? Rumours are floating about that Count Hugh, brother of the King of France, is in some sort of trouble. But we can cross that bridge when we come to it. Our immediate job is to get the men and horses ashore, before those Greeks in Durazzo come out to interfere. I shall feel a lot happier when our knights are mounted."

"They intended to dodge us, and by God they have pulled it off," said John Comnenus at the next council in Durazzo. "My uncle sent me to keep an eye on these mad Frankish pilgrims, and I shall feel pretty silly when I report that a large army has slipped through our fingers. It was Bohemond of course. Luckily my uncle knows him. I gather that a few years ago they chased one another all over these mountains, taking it in turns to win a battle. Well, his men haven't plundered, and he seems to be trying to keep the peace. I shan't bar his way. In fact I shall have depots of provisions waiting for him. That was the second half of the imperial orders: If the Franks come in peace get them to the city as quickly as possible. Don't let them linger on the road."

"Certainly don't bar their way, Highness," said the Greek officer in command of the Patzinaks. "In confidence, I don't think we could do it with the troops we have available. I suggest that my mounted archers follow behind them—far enough behind to avoid an accidental collision. One danger is not covered by the imperial orders. Those barbarian cross-bows defend a wall very stubbornly, and I am told the Franks know something of fortification. Suppose they think it prudent to safeguard their line of retreat? We might suddenly find all Macedonia dotted with Frankish castles, while the main body marches peaceably towards the city. If I come behind them I can mop up any Frankish loiterers without bringing on a pitched battle."

"A sensible proposal. March behind them as you suggest. But keep at least ten miles behind their rearguard, and think twice before you attack. Don't go too far east. These are not the last barbarian pilgrims. Another army of savages is struggling through Dalmatia, having a bad time from the Sclavonian mountaineers. I expect they will be glad to reach the safety of Durazzo, but I must have troops in hand when they arrive. Oh dear, there's no end to them. It seems that every warrior from the barbarous west is coming to live at free quarters on the bread and wine of Romania."

The Greek officers looked at one another nervously. They had been trained in the tradition of a strong regular army, but ever since the disaster at Manzikert more than twenty-five years ago there had never been enough troops to go round.

Castoria in upland Macedonia was unwalled, though populous and well provisioned. There the Normans of Italy celebrated their first Christmas on pilgrimage, the Christmas of 1096. The mountains that ringed them were higher than any they had seen in Italy; but at least they were accustomed to the idea of mountains, and did not feel so lost in exile as pilgrims from the northern plains.

The army kept good discipline, all the more readily because the local inhabitants had fled. The Castorians remembered that Bohemond himself had plundered their fields little more than ten years ago, and naturally they could not believe that this second time he came in peace. With some reluctance he had plundered the valley a second time, so that his men should not go hungry at Christmas. But he saw to it that only food and drink and baggage animals were taken, and that none of the peasants were killed. Their absence from the camp was in itself a good thing; camp followers, especially female camp followers, are the root of all indiscipline. So far there were few concubines with the army; pilgrims in a Holy War could not bring them from Apulia, and so long as the natives were hostile they could not pick them up on the march. Bohemond announced that any man found guilty of rape would be hanged, and was rather taken aback when his nephew questioned his right to give such orders.

"My dear uncle, is this your army? Or are we a band of pilgrims travelling together for safety? If these knights are your vassals, even so no vassal can be compelled to follow his lord on pilgrimage. What about the foot? Do you pay them? If so, what are the terms of their engagement? To come down to personalities, I have never in my life sworn to obey anyone. I never shall. I made up my mind about that on my sixteenth birthday, three years ago. Would you like me to leave this camp, where it seems that you rule?"

"If I called on my knights they would obey me, and I could hang you within the hour. Get that straight in your mind, nephew. It won't happen, of course, because you are my sister's son. But I have the power to command it. I hope you will stay with this army, but if you prefer to travel independently you may go in peace. By what right this is my army, how far these knights will follow me, how long my power over them will endure, are questions still unsettled. Come for a walk, where no one can overhear, and we can go into the matter."

"Why not ride? The fields are muddy."

"Another campaigning lesson. Never ride when you can walk. I have three good destriers, and I suppose you have more than one. But between Durazzo and Jerusalem you won't find another decent warhorse, trained to charge straight. No warrior of the eastern world wants his horse to charge straight. They like to hover out of reach of their foes while they shoot their arrows. Among all the soldiers of the Emperor I met only one body of men who were eager to fight hand-to-hand; and they fought on foot. They turned our charge, so we had to shoot them down. We killed them to the last man, but I believe the Emperor has hired more. So if you run into a company of foot bearing great axes, treat them with respect. Now walk with me."

They walked among the muddy pastures of the valley, where now no oxen were to be seen.

"I wish the Pope had explained more clearly what he wants us to do," Bohemond began. "By the way, do you realize that no one knows exactly what he said at Clermont? No record was taken at the time and he himself can't remember all of it. Never before has there been anything like this pilgrimage. As you pointed out, in law there is no reason why any of these men should obey me. But that goes for all the other armies too. The Duke of Normandy is the head of the whole Norman race; but that gives him no right to rule Normans in Romania, or in Italy for that matter. I hear that my silly brother Roger the Purse has been making all sorts of extravagant offers of fealty. But I for one won't acknowledge the Duke as my lord when he catches up with us—if ever he does. And what is supposed to happen when all the pilgrims are assembled in one body?"

"I suppose we choose a leader, and obey him for the duration of the pilgrimage. It seems to me quite easy," answered Tancred at once.

"Yes, yes, quite easy if we are all of one mind. But that is impossible unless God grants us a miracle. Who chooses the leader? All the pilgrims? If that groom over there disagrees with my choice does his voice weigh as heavily as mine? I shall have a voice, or I shall go straight back to Italy. Will you have a voice, though you are not twenty years of age? Will each army have one voice, so that your brother is counted as a follower of Count Hugh and you are counted as my man, which you are not? Do the knights choose, without consulting the foot? Is every rascal who owns a horse to be reckoned a knight? I don't see how we are ever to join in one army."

"God wills it. This pilgrimage will drive the infidels from the Holy Sepulchre. Perhaps the Pope has named a commander for the united army."

"Perhaps he thinks he has. That's no good since he hasn't made it clear to all of us. Do you know Pope Urban?"

"He has given me his special blessing. But I was twelve years old at the time. I can't say we had much intimate conversation."

"I used to see quite a lot of him. At one time we Hautevilles were the only secular rulers who acknowledged him. He is a holy man. Perhaps you couldn't say that of every Pope. He is also a Frenchman of noble birth, who understands French knights. In fact he can twist them round his little finger, or we wouldn't be keeping Christmas in this outlandish plain. But it seems to me that he feels more strongly than he thinks. The west ought to march to the rescue of the east. A noble sentiment, so he gets us all marching. But it isn't what they wanted, those easterners. I happen to know that the Greek Emperor began the whole business. He asked the Pope to send a few western knights to fight in the Greek army for the usual wages. Instead he gets this huge pilgrimage. I wonder how he will cope with us when we are all gathered in the city."

"Do the Emperor's wishes matter?" asked Tancred with a shrug. "So far he has given us food, and directions for the journey. But if we choose another road he can't stop us, any more than he can

66

stop us taking supplies by force. I hope he marches with us
against the Turks, because then his mounted bowmen can
skirmish with their mounted bowmen. We haven't any troops of
that kind. But if he prefers to stay at home we can manage without
him."

"My guess is that he won't want to help us. You don't realize
how deeply Franks are hated over here. I'm glad you saw that
point about the mounted bowmen. You will make a leader when
you have some experience. I bet no other knight has spotted it,
except my own followers who have fought Patzinaks and know
how awkward they are to deal with. But the wishes of Alexius *do*
matter. Get that into your head, young Tancred. He is brave and
intelligent, and he has brave and intelligent men to serve him. Also
he has nearly all the money in the world. If it comes to an open
breach between the Greeks and the pilgrims he can put us in a very
difficult position. I shall try to make friends with him. The trouble
is that these Greeks can never make friends with any foreigner.
They serve us if they must, and rule us if they can; but they will
never treat a barbarian as an equal."

"Perhaps we had better take over their empire. We could run it
better than they do." Tancred spoke idly, in a tone of casual
speculation.

"That's just what the Emperor fears," Bohemond answered
sharply. "It's crossed the mind of every one of us from time to
time, but you must never say it out loud while you are in Romania.
Put it right out of your thoughts. Now to govern a province of
Romania, as a faithful vassal of the Emperor of course, would be
quite another thing. That might be worth trying. One day there
will be a weak Emperor, and then your grandchildren would
prosper. But that's all in the future. For the present, Alexius is as
brave as a Frank and as cunning as a Greek, a dangerous combination."

Bohemond turned about.

"Is everything clear, young Tancred?" he asked sharply. "Until
we reach Constantinople I command this army—because my
sword is the heaviest in it if for no better reason. What's more, I
can get you there safely. Not everyone could do that. In the city
we meet the Emperor, and the other pilgrims. I don't know what

comes after that. If it's something absurdly dangerous I shall go straight home to Apulia. My vow will be unfulfilled, but I can get some bishop to absolve me. Even the Pope can't command a Christian to commit suicide. If you wish to leave my army you may go tomorrow. Once we are on the march again any disobedience of my orders will be punished."

"Until we reach the city I shall obey your orders, and if need be fight under your banner, uncle. After that, we leave the future to settle itself. Will that do?"

They turned amicably to the little cottage where they slept side by side on the mud floor.

In the New Year the army resumed its march, a little north of east until it reached the Via Egnatia, the paved road from Durazzo to Constantinople. It was easy to travel on the great road, and at every halt provisions awaited them. But they must submit to Greek guides and a Greek escort.

The guides were officials of high rank, polite and always willing to talk through their interpreters. By this time Bohemond had accepted as a fact of natural history that no Greek understood a word of any foreign tongue, and that all their interpreters were renegade foreigners. He himself was fairly fluent in the Greek of Bari, which was not quite the Greek of the city. Of course he could not read anything written in their strange alphabet, so Greeks of the upper class, all literate, took it for granted that he could not understand their language. He encouraged the mistake by always discussing official business through an interpreter. One never knew when that kind of thing might come in useful.

The pilgrims saw no Greek soldiers, except a few Patzinaks standing at forks in the road to indicate the right way. These heathen knew no Christian language, so it was impossible to question them. They would merely point and grin, unless some pilgrim was obstinate about taking the wrong road; then they would draw their bows and shout what was evidently a threat. Knights did not take kindly to being directed by traffic police, but Bohemond commanded them to do as they were told. He guessed that there must be other Greek soldiers within reach, or these savages would not be so bold. Then a few words overheard while they

68

passed through a village told him that a large body of Patzinaks followed behind.

Discipline was as good as could be expected, when the pilgrims were bored by their long slow journey. They had landed in October, and they were still in Macedonia by February. There was only one nasty outbreak, when the pilgrims discovered that the village through which they were passing was inhabited by heretics. Bohemond already knew this, though he wondered how the rank and file had managed to find out. Of course they sacked the place.

The Greek officials were annoyed, protesting that the heretics had been exiled to this spot by imperial command and were thus under the Emperor's protection. Bohemond wondered whether someone had deliberately tried to cause an incident. Why bring the pilgrims through a village of heretics, and then let knowledge of its leak out? But when all was over the officials accepted his apologies. Perhaps some other Greek had been trying to discredit them as inefficient. All Greeks were cunning and devious.

In the third week of February they reached the River Vardar, flowing through a green and pleasant valley. There was plenty to eat, and it seemed a good place in which to rest the horses and observe Ash Wednesday. But the guides explained to Bohemond that the pilgrims were not supposed to stay in one place for more than three nights; rather than quarrel with them he gave orders to resume the march.

The River Vardar was too wide to be bridged; but there was a good paved ford and a ferry for the baggage. As always, crossing was a slow business; as always, the non-combatants were slowest. Ferry-boats returning were nearly as full as those going east, as cooks and servants came back for something they had forgotten. Bohemond led his knights through the ford, and then rode on to get away from the noise and confusion.

After a short stage they halted, in the hope that the baggage and dinner would soon come up. Bohemond was sitting on the grass with his back against the peak of his war-saddle, when an excited Italian sergeant galloped up from the rear.

"To arms, my lord," he cried. "Heathen Patzinaks are killing our men on the far side of the river."

"Do they hold the ford?" asked Bohemond, as a groom placed

the war-saddle on the still-damp back of his horse. "They do? Then we need cross-bows to clear it. Hugo, get the cross-bows moving, all of them. Hurry them back. And you, dry that horse's back before you put the saddle on. Dry it with your breeches if you can't find a rubber. You'll give the beast a sore back, and there isn't another good horse for sale this side of Brindisi. Now, gentlemen, we are in no great hurry. We can't cross the river until the cross-bows have opened the ford for us. Where is lord Tancred?"

"I told him first, sir," said the messenger. "He has already gone back."

"Then there is absolutely no hurry for the rest of us. No one is to break down a good horse by galloping to this petty affair. When we do move off, trot or canter gently."

While Bohemond looked calm and almost bored his mind was racing. If once the pilgrims began fighting in earnest they would not stop until they had ravaged all Romania or been killed by the Greeks. This might be a treacherous assault planned by the Emperor; in that case they would all be dead in a few hours, for no Greek took chances. He must assume that it was an accidental collision, and damp it down by showing no interest; it had been a mistake to hurry those cross-bows. But he was always sensitive about his rear and they were the right men to drive Patzinaks from a ford. It was hard to turn in a moment from the alert commander into a bored nobleman, but he had managed it. A pity if young Tancred were killed by a Greek mercenary before he had met an infidel, but that strange young man must see his first action some day. He continued to lounge, apparently without a care in the world.

An hour later he was armed and mounted, on his way back to the river bank. Suddenly a squadron of knights galloped to meet him. Or were they knights? They rode destriers; but they were clad in tunics, without shields or mail. Young Tancred reined in before him.

"Don't gallop so fast. That horse has to carry you to Jerusalem. Where is your mail? What have you been doing?"

"Sorry, uncle. Sorry, my lord, I should say. I have just ridden in my first charge, and I am still excited. But my horse is sound, and we have taken some remounts." He pointed to a knot of bound Patzinaks who rode under escort behind him.

"Those ponies are no use to us, except perhaps to eat. You're dripping wet, and filthy. Whom did you charge, and why?"

"Those Patzinaks, of course. They had attacked some of our knights who were still on the far side of the river. They held the western end of the ford in force, so I turned south. As soon as I was out of their sight I swam my horse across the river. That was why I thought it prudent to take off my mail, but I left a groom to guard it. Some of your knights followed me. On the far bank we charged the Patzinaks, and cornered them against the river bank. We killed some, and a few got away. The rest surrendered, so I brought them to you for questioning. Have we anyone who speaks their language?"

"Of course not. But some of them may speak Greek, and here comes a Greek lord complete with interpreter. You left your mail, and I suppose you shield and lance, so that your horse could swim more easily? I'm glad you remembered to take your sword, or I might have supposed you were deserting to the enemy. But it has all turned out well. Thank you. Now we must try to find out what these savages were trying to do."

The interpreter questioned a Greek-speaking Patzinak; Bohemond, with an expressionless face, privately checked the translation and found it accurate. It seemed that these brutes were too stupid to do anything but obey orders. They had been told to keep the pilgrims on the move, and here were knights delaying at the river crossing. They had shouted to them to get on, and been surprised that their message was not understood. So they had loosed a few arrows. Where they came from that was rather a gesture of emphasis than a declaration of hostile intent. Then one thing had led to another, just because they were faithful mercenaries who obeyed orders.

"I believe what they say," Bohemond declared to the Greek interpreter, "though I know they haven't told everything. At some point it struck the brightest of them that they had cornered a handful of knights, and might win some of our precious western mail if they murdered the lot of them. Otherwise they wouldn't have held the ford. But I don't want to deprive your Emperor of

71

their services. Officially we shall call it an accidental clash, brought on because they obeyed orders too zealously. Try to keep them a bit further from my rear unless you want more trouble. From now on I shall order my cross-bows to shoot at any Patzinak who lingers within range. A cross-bow carries much farther than the short bows they use. Now they may go off and earn more pay. I suppose, Tancred, they lost their purses in the scuffle, and some of our men happened to pick them up? Then that's all, interpreter. Tell them to get moving."

As the relieved prisoners trotted off, free, Bohemond rode aside with his nephew. "That's another tip. Those mounted archers have no fixed home, so they carry all their wealth in their belts. Even the shabbiest corpse or prisoner is worth robbing, if you can spare the time. You did very well, and I'm proud of you. Next time you charge you should wear mail. It's safer. But you have an eye for country, and you make up your mind quickly. When we meet the Turks you shall have an independent command."

As Lent advanced the army settled into a routine. The great road led them east by easy stages. At every halt provisions awaited them. Armed Patzinaks barred every side road, so that no pilgrim might wander off by himself; but that was a sensible precaution which could not annoy a veteran. Some pilgrims complained, especially the clergy among them, that they were never permitted to enter a walled town. They might not pray even in the famous shrines of Salonica, endowed with plentiful relics of the Apostles, or indeed see any of the wonders of the civilized east. But the Greek guides answered that men who were marching to worship actually within Christ's Holy Sepulchre should not delay their journey to visit the tombs of mere saints. Bohemond was disappointed. He was quite sure that his own shrine of St. Nicholas at Bari was more beautiful and more holy than anything Romania had to offer; but he would have liked to examine some of those gates from the inside. Unfortunately a man of his great height and striking appearance could not get near the walls in disguise.

Unexpectedly, he had found a competent deputy and second in command, the young nephew whom he had barely known when they landed beside Durazzo. It was probable that Tancred would get himself killed in his first stiff fight, for the lad was utterly fearless. To take off your mail to get at the enemy quicker was a strange beginning to warfare. But Tancred saw in a flash what ought to be done, and was willing to take responsibility. While he lived he would be as useful as an extra sword-arm. His gallant rescue of the stragglers at the crossing of the Vardar had made him the hero of the army; even veterans would follow without grumbling a young knight of such prowess.

The Emperor sent an envoy of high rank to supervise the approach to the city, a pleasant young lord who was willing to be polite even to Franks. He was a distant kinsman of the imperial house, handicapped with the name of Alexius Comnenus; so he was always addressed by his title of Curopalates. He used his interpreter with such practised grace, and the interpreter was so quick and unassuming, that Bohemond could gossip with him by the hour and forget that his companion spoke no Frankish.

On 1st April 1097, the Wednesday in Holy Week, the army encamped outside the town of Rusa in Thrace. At last they were nearing the end of the march they had begun in October; Constantinople was not more than a hundred miles away. When Bohemond suggested that they might be permitted to halt for more than the agreed three days, to celebrate Easter in such a pleasant spot, the Curopalates readily agreed. As a return gesture of friendship Bohemond commanded that the survivors of the baggage animals they had taken from Castoria should be returned to their lawful owners.

They were now within range of the gossip of Constantinople, which the Curopalates was always willing to pass on. Bohemond took him aside for the usual walk in a meadow which was the only chance of private conversation in that crowded army. He inquired for news of the other pilgrims.

It was hard to remember that the interpreter walked with them. He spoke in the first person, and copied the tone of voice used by each speaker.

"Yours is not the last army to arrive, lord Bohemond. Count Isangeles is not far behind you. Have I got his name right?"

"Very nearly, Curopalates. His name is Raymond of St. Gilles, a very great lord. He is Count of Toulouse and Marquis of Provence."

"With him, but leading a separate army, marches the Count of Flanders. I know that is his correct title. His father once served the Emperor in arms, our good friend and still remembered in Romania."

"Is he the last?"

"There are no more Franks in Romania. But in Italy another army is getting ready to sail to Durazzo. Their leader styles himself the Count of the North, which sounds rather a magniloquent title."

"A mistranslation. He is Count of the men from the north, now dwelling in a Frankish province. My own grandfather came from those parts, so I know I am right. Duke of Normandy is a better version. Are you sure he has not yet landed in Romania?"

"He arranged to land just after Easter. I don't know what is happening in Durazzo today, and he may be there. But have you ever heard of an army that arrived before it was expected? Soldiers usually find it hard to be punctual."

The jest gave Bohemond an excuse to smile; at such good news he could not keep his face unmoved. Since he left Apulia he had been wondering how the Duke of Normandy would receive him. The lord of Bari and Taranto was a great Count and a famous warrior. But to Robert fitzRollo, Duke of all the Norman race, he would be merely the son of a country knight who had gone abroad and done well for himself in a foreign land. That his silly brother Roger the Purse had been so humble before the Duke would make things worse.

Now Duke Robert had delayed in Italy. He had a reputation for muddle and incompetence; probably his journey to Constantinople would be slow. Before the Normans of Normandy arrived Bohemond should have at least six weeks to get on terms with the other Counts. But Duke Robert might lift his eyebrows at the pretensions of an upstart Hauteville. There was no time to be wasted.

"What of the pilgrims ahead of me? Has the Emperor received them graciously?"

"Count Hugh, brother to the King of all the Franks, is now lodged in the Emperor's own palace. There has been a little trouble

74

with Count Godfrey, the one who led his army overland through Hungary. The Emperor offered to ship them into Asia, but they prefer to remain outside the city. There have been riots in the suburbs—perhaps a few swords drawn—nothing serious. They will all settle down when your supreme commander arrives, this Count Isangeles whom you call by another name."

"Count Raymond our supreme commander? Who says so? I don't for one, and there will be others who think as I do."

"Count Isangeles says so himself, in a message his envoy brought to the city. At least those aren't the actual words of the message, but it comes to the same thing. He said that your religious leader, a Bishop appointed by your Pope, marches under his command. Since a Bishop cannot bear arms I suppose the Count who rules him will command in the field."

"Oh dear, you've got it all wrong. The Emperor has Franks in his service. You ought to consult them. Our Bishops often bear arms. No Bishop obeys the Count who happens to defend his diocese. Count Raymond is rich and well born, but the other Counts won't defer to him. There is going to be a nasty muddle, and just outside the walls of the city. Look, I must stay here over Easter, to hear Mass after the Frankish fashion. Then I shall leave my followers under the command of my nephew Tancred, and ride on as fast as I can to clear up this mess. Riding post I can be in the city by Tuesday. I have seen your Emperor in the old days, even if it was only on the battlefield. He's a good soldier and a man who takes quick decisions. Give me a token to show to the postmasters, send a message ahead to say I am coming, and beg the Emperor to grant me a private audience. It really is important. I may have to reason with the other Counts, or there will be bloody war all round the city. But get this into your heads, all you servants of the Emperor. We have come on this pilgrimage because the Pope asked it of us, but neither the Pope nor his deputy will command us in battle. We shall choose our own leader."

Bohemond was surprised at his own vehemence, but his tongue could not keep up with his racing thoughts. There was deadly danger that the whole pilgrimage would dissolve into war between Franks and Greeks. The Franks could probably sack Constantinople, even if the Greeks wore them down in the end; though it would be tactless to say so at this moment. He was sure that Pope Urban had not appointed a commander. At Clermont he could have done so; but he would never do anything so rash at this late stage, especially without consulting all the leading Counts.

The Curopalates was persuaded. He would give orders to the postmasters. Bohemond could start on the afternoon of Easter Day and reach the city by midday on Tuesday. A courier would carry a message at once, begging that the Emperor would receive him as soon as he arrived. While he was away Tancred would be recognized as his deputy.

Bohemond found Tancred treating a sick horse. He poured out his news as quickly as he could.

"Is there any truth in the story?" asked his nephew. "Has this Count Raymond any sort of commission from the Pope? What kind of man is he, anyway?"

"At least ten years older than I am, very rich, a good organizer. He fought the Moors in Spain, though I don't know which side won. He holds Toulouse from the King of France and Provence from the German Emperor. In other words, a foot in each camp. Just the sort of man the Pope might appoint to lead us, in fact. But if Urban had appointed him he wouldn't tell the Greek Emperor first, before his own faithful pilgrims had heard of it."

"Then Raymond is lying. If he has allies both in the Empire and in France then he will also have enemies in both realms. That's the way the world goes. But you must get in your story first, or he may carry it off by sheer impudence. Shall I wait here with our knights and knock him off his horse before he reaches the city?"

"That's no good. He might win—his army is stronger than ours. Even if you won all the other Franks would turn against us, for breaking up this great pilgrimage before it gets properly started. That's the real trouble, you know. The pilgrimage has grown until it is out of hand. If we do unite into one army it will be the greatest the world has ever seen. But I doubt if all of us will ever follow one commander. . . . Thank God our Duke is a month behind us. When he catches up he will find me a great lord, too great to be dislodged."

"My father was a noble Lombard Marquis," said Tancred, "but for all that I'm proud that my mother was a Hauteville."

CHAPTER V

Alexius

———————————★———————————

The little party galloped down an empty road, which seemed ominous when they were so near the city. Bohemond rode in mail, because that was the easiest way to carry it; but a groom bore his lance and shield, so that he appeared peaceful. With him galloped his Greek guide and the interpreter. In the rear a few servants led packhorses, with clean linen and the silk tunic he would wear for his audience with the Emperor.

Bohemond had thought out the details of this journey. He was taking a chance. The Greeks might murder him, or throw him into a dungeon. But he must waste no time in contradicting this absurd rumour that Count Raymond had been appointed commander of the pilgrims. If he brought a small escort of faithful knights he would merely put more lives in danger; if he brought his whole army the Greeks might attack him. He must come alone.

As they climbed a gentle slope a party of Greek regular horse came out of a side road and took station as escort. "Partly to do you honour, my lord, and I regret to say partly for your safety," said the interpreter. "Lately the suburbs of the city have been disturbed, though the main camps of the pilgrims are beyond the harbour."

As they reached the summit of the ridge they saw half a mile ahead a mighty wall. The paved road continued straight before them to an imposing gate, but their escort turned left along a dusty track.

"The city, my lord," said the interpreter. "That's the Golden Gate. But your lodging is near the Emperor's palace, five miles away. It will be quicker to ride round outside the walls rather than force a way through the crowds in the streets."

That was more tactful than to say that he would not be given a chance to look at the great gate more closely. Bohemond increased his pace to get clear of the dustcloud raised by the escort; as he rode he stared at the wall.

There were at least two complete lines of defence, each set with towers; perhaps a breastwork in front of the moat might be reckoned a third outer line, though it was so grassgrown that it might be ruinous. In Bohemond's mind a set of facts fell into place without deliberate thought. Besieging catapults could not batter the base of the inner wall until they had completely demolished that in front; a storming party would meet arrows from at least four different levels, two battlemented walls, two lines of towers. The land walls of Constantinople were impregnable.

He gazed ahead for the corner where the walls should turn away to meet the harbour, but he could not see it. "How far does this wall continue?" he asked in a deliberately casual voice. "I suppose there are pastures and vineyards within. That is what I have seen in Old Rome."

"On the contrary, the city fills its wall completely, and it is growing. No houses may be built outside this wall, for reasons of defence. The new suburbs lie across the harbour, the Golden Horn. That is where the pilgrims are lodged, those who have not already crossed to Asia. Would you care to ride more slowly? It is less than five miles to your lodging, by the Blachernae Gate near the harbour and the palace."

"Five miles? The city extends so far? Most remarkable, most interesting."

Bohemond kept all interest out of his voice. He might have been remarking on an unusually large cabbage. He was trying to work out in his head how many inhabitants it would take to fill a built-up area five miles long by at least one wide, but the arithmetic was too much for him. He slowed to a gentle trot. His guide wished to impress him with the size of the city, and he was quite willing to look at it.

Five miles of wall more or less in a straight line, just for one side of the city. A wall of dressed masonry set with towers, as strong as the Aurelian wall of Rome; and another even bigger just behind it. What must it have cost to build it, even in the days of the mighty ancients? The Emperor was absolute master of all the Greeks who lived behind it, and of all their possessions. Pilgrims from the west must have felt stunned with awe when they saw it. But he, Bohemond, had chased this mighty Emperor from the battlefield, had killed to the last man his guard of gilded axe-bearing heroes. While he kept in mind the campaigns of his famous father he would not be awed by this Emperor of an innumerable multitude.

Presently they arrived at the head of the Golden Horn, and the small but luxurious villa where Bohemond was to lodge. There were mosaics on the floors, and a complicated steam bath; but such things were not unknown in Apulia. Servants were ready, with the usual interpreter. For some reason Bohemond felt a strange quirk of suspicion; he rejected the savoury dinner waiting ready for him, picked a live sheep from the flock at random, and dined on it as soon as it had been killed and roasted. He did not believe that Alexius would poison him. But he knew how bitterly all Franks were hated in Romania and he personally had killed a good many Greeks; what he feared was private enterprise among the servants.

It was sunset before he was ready for his private audience. He was dressed in red leather shoes, trousers of white linen cross-gartered with red leather straps, a white linen shirt and a tunic of red silk. He smoothed his jaw with pumice-stone and combed his short hair. He decided that he would wear nothing at all on his head, so that no chamberlain could command him to uncover in the presence of the Emperor. For the same reason he left his sword behind. Indoors the heavy weapon would be of little use, and it would be better manners to show that he trusted the Greeks utterly. Instead he wore a handsome girdle of red leather.

The Emperor had sent a riding mule with an upholstered saddle, so there was no danger of staining his white trousers. There was another mule for the interpreter. Half-a-dozen palace guards walked; tactfully, they were not Varangians.

Night was falling as he passed through the Blachernae Gate into the city. The gate itself was of the usual Roman style, a short tunnel of masonry with plenty of loopholes for arrows. The barrier at the inner end would yield easily to a battering-ram, except that the bearers of the ram would be shot at close range before they could get it there. In the gathering darkness he could just make out that only a single wall shut off the city from the harbour. The quay was so narrow that boarding bridges slung from the masts of ships might reach the battlements. A determined assault from the harbour might penetrate into the city. But a chain would bar the harbour mouth. The assailants would have to carry the defences on the far side of the Golden Horn before they could approach the quay.

He pulled himself together. He was not planning an attack on the Emperor in his own city. It was just that he could not see a strong place held by someone else without looking for the spot where he could break in.

The Palace of Blachernae was smaller than he had expected; but within it blazed like a jewel. The ante-room, faced with coloured marble, shone as bright as day. As he walked on the inlaid pavement double doors flew open before him; chamberlains, dressed like flowers in green tunics and wide headdresses of gaily coloured gauze, motioned him to enter.

He strode in alone, save for the unobtrusive interpreter who was so easily forgotten. At the far end of a long hall, among guards and councillors, the Emperor of New Rome sat on a throne of purple silk and chased bronze. Around him were tall feather fans and smoking censers, as when the Pope gave formal audience in the Palace of the Lateran. Bowing his head, Bohemond touched the floor with his right knee. It was the salute he had decided on before he set out. If any chamberlain tried to make him do more he would explain that it was the salute he gave to God before the high altar of a cathedral.

He had done the right thing. At his elbow the interpreter was speaking: "Rise, noble Count. The Emperor salutes you graciously. Now you are to follow him through that little door behind the Throne of the World. He will honour you by conferring with you in his private chamber." This was getting better and better.

There were only three of them in the little room, the Emperor Alexius, the inevitable interpreter, and Count Bohemond. He wished his grandfather could see him now; he had come a long way from Hauteville. The room was cool, though lamps burned everywhere; in the middle was a little marble table strewn with writing materials; and round it, glory of glories, three backless stools and a tall chair of state.

"Sit on my right, Count Bohemond." But the interpreter made no move to be seated. Bohemond perceived that he was now literally the Emperor's mouth. Trembling with delight, he sat on a stool and for the first time looked hard at his host.

Alexius was a little man, though neat and well made. His face was very dark, and his full beard quite black. He wore a long tunic of silk, embroidered with various religious and imperial symbols; on his head the imperial crown, a close-fitting jewelled cap from which hung a camail that seemed to be made entirely of pearls. He looked anxious and worried, as well he might; but not at all frightened.

"Well, Count, you are as big as they told me. I'm glad that outside Durazzo I did not stay to encounter your lance. You chased me then, there's no denying it; and though I pushed you back to Italy in the end I never made you flee from the field at full speed. I feel that after all those campaigns we are old acquaintances. Certainly you know more about the affairs of Romania than any of your fellow-pilgrims. So I want to talk things over with you. To begin with, what exactly are your aims? Suppose everything falls out as you wish it, what is the most you hope to accomplish?"

"I did not hear the Pope speak, your majesty. I can't answer for those who heard him. But none of the other great lords were at Clermont either. The object of this pilgrimage is to free Jerusalem from the infidel. To get there we must fight your enemies the Turks of Anatolia."

"And when Jerusalem is free, do you all go back home again?"

"Some will go home, some will stay to defend the Holy City. I don't know yet which I shall do."

"The last Christian ruler of Jerusalem was my predecessor, the Emperor Heraclius. Will you recognize my right as his heir?"

"Your majesty's predecessor the Emperor Constantine ruled Paris and all Gaul. Has Count Hugh, brother to the King of the Franks, recognized your right to his native land?"

"A sensible answer. At one time or another either Old Rome or New Rome ruled every corner of the known world. A claim that no one has enforced for centuries is no claim. For more than four hundred years we have prospered without Jerusalem, and we can manage without it in the future. We can't manage so well without Anatolia, which was lost very recently. I am not an old man, yet when I was born our Emperor ruled as far east as Armenia. What about this as a compromise? You pilgrims recognize our right to the frontier of thirty years ago, before the Turks beat us at Manzikert? In return we recognize your right to anything you may conquer beyond that frontier."

"Your majesty is righteous and fair-dealing. But I have an even better plan. At home we may be Normans or Flemings or Frenchmen, but we are here because we are Christians. Let a united Christian army march against the infidel. I for one shall recognize your leadership. I know by experience that you are a cunning warleader. There is also the point that you have plenty of money, while we are poor pilgrims. This is a chance that may never come again. The onset of our knights is irresistible; our cross-bows are more deadly than your archers. Frankly, the rest of our foot are poor material, our knights do not always obey orders, and we get muddled over questions of supply. You know the roads of Anatolia, there must be veterans among your soldiers who have been inside all the cities now held by the Turks, you have disciplined foot and skilled engineers. Let us fight under your command."

"That's a generous offer, Count Bohemond. Will the other Counts agree with you? I have heard that this Count Isangeles, who is nearly arrived, claims that the Pope has appointed him to be your supreme commander."

"What of it? No Frank will believe his claim. I rode here in haste to warn you against his pretensions. As for the other Counts, I can talk them round if you will let me offer them something. Let them have all the lands and castles they want, on condition they hold them from you and admit your supremacy. You will have to keep them obedient in the mean time, before they have conquered their fiefs. That's where your money comes in. Feed them and pay them generously, and they will follow you."

"A splendid chance, as you say. A campaign to free all Anatolia. It is also a heavy responsibility. It may take years, and I shall have to be absent from the city. I have to do other things than fight. In my spare time I must govern this Empire."

Bohemond jumped to seize this magnificent opening.

"Your majesty need not accompany the army throughout the campaign. Let me represent you. That's it. I remain with the army, and command it in your absence. Pay your subsidies through me, so that I can cut off supplies from the disobedient. I shall need to hold some rank in your service, some post that will impress your men as well as the Franks. How would this do? Your commander-in-chief is called the Grand Domestic, isn't he? Well, make me your Grand Domestic in Anatolia. I shall swear any oath of fealty you choose to draft, before any witnesses you name. We were made for one another, you and I. You are the most resourceful and steadfast commander alive, and I don't think there exists any-where in the world the man who can withstand my charge. With your brain and my sword we shall drive back those Turks to Scythia, and together restore all the glories of New Rome."

"Very probably we would," the Emperor agreed. "The question is: after the Empire had been restored to all its past glories, which of us would be ruling it? My dear Count, I suspect that you also have a brain, just as I also have a sword. Seriously, it is just half an hour since we met in peace for the first time. What would my councillors think if you came away from our first conference com-mander-in-chief of my army? Affairs move more slowly in this complicated eastern world. But it's a plan worth bearing in mind. I don't say No and I don't say Yes, so far. There remains, how-ever, the question of your oath of fealty. I suppose you are willing to swear obedience while you are within my dominions? The other Counts have already sworn so much. As witnesses, what do you say to Count Godfrey and his brother Count Baldwin? Both of them happen to be staying as my guests in this palace tonight, and they are anxious to meet you. Their armies, by the way, have al-ready been ferried over to Anatolia. Shall we move back to the throne-room? Then we can summon them from their chambers."

Bohemond's thoughts were racing. It seemed odd to do any-thing so formal as oath-swearing after sunset; but then these Greeks, with their bright lamps, notoriously turned night into day.

If these two great lords had already sworn fealty there could be no harm in doing the same. When they met him for the first time they would see him as the honoured guest and friend of the Emperor, which was all to the good. Now what did he know about those two leaders?

They were of high birth, descended in the female line from Charlemagne, like so many noble Franks. Godfrey had been a Duke in Lorraine; but by appointment from the German Emperor, not as a hereditary ruler. Baldwin was a landless younger son. Both must intend to remain in the Holy Land for the rest of their lives, since they had no estates waiting for them at home. Their eldest brother, Count Eustace of Boulogne, had come with them and indeed paid for the journey; but he was not so famous a warrior as either of his brothers, and while they were abroad was content to take third place.

Ushers brought in the two Counts. They were handsome warriors, younger than Bohemond, and of course not so tall; he had never seen a man taller than himself, and only his nephew Tancred equalled him in height. He was pleased to note that their clothes of ceremony were not so grand as his. They wore the usual white trousers and coloured leather shoes, but their tunics were of blue woollen cloth; very closely woven, very well dyed, but all the same nothing but wool. Of course silk was a great rarity in northern France where they came from. Only in one point of dress did they surpass him. Over their shoes they wore little spurs of gilded steel, to remind the world that normally they rode instead of walking. A very pretty little mark of distinction. Bohemond vowed to have such spurs made, though of genuine gold, as soon as he could order them from a craftsman of the city.

What really mattered was their greeting, when the interpreter introduced the noble Count Bohemond. They must have known that he was the grandson of a simple country knight, for in their world everyone knew the ancestry of everyone else. But he stood there, the tallest and most stately warrior they had ever seen, better dressed than they and evidently a favoured friend of the Emperor of the Greeks. The descendants of Charlemagne bowed to him as to an equal. He had got safely over a difficult hurdle.

The ceremony of fealty followed exactly the Frankish custom.

Bohemond bowed his right knee to the ground and placed his folded hands within the hands of the standing Alexius. In Italian he swore to be loyal to the Emperor so long as he was within the realm of Romania. Of course the interpreter who put it into Greek omitted the qualifying clause; Bohemond had expected as much, and did not greatly care. His fellow-Counts were witnesses to what he had said, not to what the interpreter repeated; what bound his conscience was the oath he had sworn in his own tongue, not the version of it altered to please the Emperor.

The other Counts approved; it seemed they had taken more or less the same oath. But Bohemond had no chance to talk things over with them. As soon as he had sworn a chamberlain indicated that the audience was at an end, and the foreigners were ushered to the door. As they turned at the entry for one last bow Alexius broke through all the rules of etiquette. "Come and see me to-morrow morning, Count Bohemond," he called. "Come an hour before midday. I shall be in my cabinet. The sentry will take you straight there. No need for further ceremony. Don't be late. I want to discuss this campaign with you."

Overwhelmed by this public mark of favour, Bohemond bowed again. Not until he was half-way back to his lodging did he realize that he had made public the fact that he understood Greek.

The Emperor's cabinet was a large room on the first floor of the palace, lit by tall windows. Chairs and stools stood round the walls in no particular order, and the centre was filled by a long table. When Bohemond entered Alexius was standing at this table, bent over a large sheet of paper. There was no one else in the room.

Bohemond halted in astonishment. He had not imagined that an Emperor could be alone. No Frankish Count, no baron of any standing, was ever alone. A few servants or guards or clerks were always loitering about, to run errands or fetch him anything he wanted. Perhaps this was just another queer Greek custom. Alexius seemed to take it for granted.

"Your Imperial Majesty," Bohemond began, taking pains with his pronunciation.

"In here we drop titles," the Emperor interrupted. "This is

where I work. You couldn't manage the correct titles, anyway. It takes my courtiers years to learn them. Just say what you mean, and don't bother about how you say it. I ought to have known that you understand Greek. You can't rule the Greeks of Apulia without picking up some of their language. Now come here and look at this map. Have you ever seen a map?"

"In Brindisi there is a map of the way to Rome, engraved on marble by the mighty men of old. I know what a map looks like. But this is the first I've seen that's new, and drawn on paper."

"It's new, as you say, but it represents an old state of affairs. This has been copied specially from an old map of Anatolia, as it was before the Turks ravaged it. It's twenty-five years since a Christian travelled some of those roads, those lines marked in red."

"I see. This is the coast, I suppose. I can't read the names, though I can read Latin. One of your clerks must explain them to me."

"I shall explain them. You and I will plan this campaign together. See, here near the edge is Manzikert, where the great battle was fought. Jerusalem is beyond this other edge, for it was not then part of the Empire. But here is the road leading to it. Those broad lines are mountains, and the crosses mark passes. Our frontier was pretty strong in those days, before the Turks broke in."

"Indeed it was, sir. This bit seems to stick out beyond the mountains. Was it an outlying fief, perhaps paying tribute but not directly under your rule?"   ·

"No, this was all in the Empire, as directly subject to the Emperor as the city itself. That bit was the Duchy of Antioch. Beyond the mountains, certainly; but a very strong town, quite easy to defend. It has a Patriarch of its own, who is just as much the successor of St. Peter as your Pope in Rome. Would you like to be the next Duke, when it is Christian again?"

Bohemond's eyes gleamed with simple avarice. "How big is the Duchy?"

"About fifteen days' march by eight broad, I suppose. It used to be very rich, though I don't know how much the Turks have left of it. Such a fortress needs a good commander, and you are the best soldier among the Franks. We should have to make various arrangements. In the old days the Duke always left a hostage at court, just to make sure he stayed loyal to the Emperor. Let me see, what family have you?"

"There are dozens of Hautevilles, if not scores by now. The trouble is that most of them are my foes. I am the only child of my mother, and my half-brother would not stand surety for me. My nephews on this pilgrimage are all good knights, too good to be wasted as hostages. I have no wife, and no children."

"That's an obstacle. Not married, at your age? Perhaps I can find you a bride. What would you say to the daughter of a Greek nobleman, with a good dowry of course?"

"I'm not the marrying kind, my lord. I'm just not interested in women. I am a pilgrim, with no ties anywhere. In my young days they were always pestering me to marry, and I swore a great oath that I wouldn't marry anyone except a daughter of the King of all the Franks. Of course the King of the Franks will not give his daughter to a Hauteville, so I shall never marry."

"I gather that plenty of ladies are interested in *you*. My own daughter saw you from a window last night, and wants to meet you. She can't believe that anyone so tall is really human. I should add that she is already married, and she hates Franks. So I can't offer you an imperial princess. If you don't want a noble Greek lady we must think again. But there will be a lot of fighting before the Christian army gets anywhere near Antioch. At present the King of the Turks holds his court in Nicaea, right on this side of the map. But just keep that Duchy of Antioch in mind, and serve me faithfully. If we get so far it will be yours."

Bohemond straightened his shoulders, took a deep breath, and asked an important question.

"My lord, in your heart of hearts do you really believe that we can liberate Jerusalem? Since the Turks have triumphed over your mighty army, why should the Franks drive them back?"

"I don't think you Franks stand a chance—by yourselves. I have seen your terrible charge, and run away from it myself. The Turks also will run away, but they will shoot behind them as they run. In the end they will shoot down all your horses. You know my Patzinaks? They can be a nuisance, can't they? Their trouble is that at bottom they are cowards, so you generally chased them right off the field. Turks fight just like Patzinaks, except that they are very brave. Brave horsemen, who carry sharp swords as well as bows. At the beginning they shoot from a distance, but when the right time comes they will charge home. How do you deal with them?"

"With your Patzinaks, of course, sir. The Patzinaks won't panic if they know they have Frankish knights behind them. They skirmish with the Turks, and draw them on until they are close enough for our charge to catch them. A genuine Greek type of battle, which all your officers will understand. But I see what you mean. We must act in concert with your army. That means we must carry out your orders. I shall, for one, and so will all the other Counts who have sworn fealty. Some pilgrims may make trouble. They aren't used to obeying orders even from their own natural lords."

"I am glad you see it so clearly, my friend. Do what you can to convince the other Counts. It's our only chance of success, and it's what your Pope had in mind when he got up to speak at Clermont. I had asked him to send me Frankish knights, to take my wages and serve in my army. But the plan was such a good one, such a holy one I may say, that the whole west volunteered. Even I can't pay, in gold or silver, all the pilgrims who are making their way to the city. But if all goes well I shall win plenty of land, to provide rich fiefs for my vassals. Then there's Jerusalem, and all Syria. I don't claim to rule beyond Antioch, you know.. Any Franks who care to defend the Holy Places on the border of the infidel may rule in complete independence. They will lead hard and dangerous lives."

"Antioch is enough for me. I am not worthy to rule Jerusalem, and as you say it will be very dangerous. When do we start?"

"As soon as you have all taken your oaths of fealty. This campaign begins to look promising. I was disappointed, I confess, when the first pilgrimage arrived, that rabble led by Peter the Hermit. Hardly any knights, and more women and priests than fighting men. They wouldn't heed my advice; they wanted to cross into Asia and begin to fight the infidel. Since I could not hold them I sent them on their way, and of course most of them were killed by the Turks. I saved as many as I could. Peter the Hermit is here in the city, and will tell you all about it. Now look at the map. Here's what we do."

They stood side by side, leaning over the table.

"The Turks have no ships, so we go by water as far as we can. The first lot, Peter's, landed at Civetot here, but you would do better to go to the head of the gulf, to Nicomedia. It's a strong fortress with a Greek garrison, so you can camp near it in safety. When you are all gathered into one army you march south to Nicaea, here. I shall send guides, and engineers, and of course plenty of provisions. But for the moment I can't leave the city. When Nicaea has fallen I shall meet the pilgrim army, and we can decide what to do next."

Bohemond nodded, absorbed in the map. He was beginning to get the hang of it; he must remember all he could, for he was unlikely to see it again. After a few civil nothings he took leave of the Emperor, who was evidently very busy.

All afternoon he sat in his lodging, thinking over the plans he had agreed with the Emperor. It was not going to be quite so straightforward as he had supposed. He had volunteered to serve Alexius, and the offer had been accepted. Now some instinct warned him to be wary. Alexius had planned a sensible and prudent opening to the campaign, and then at the last minute slipped in a hint that he might be unable to march with them. He had prophesied quite openly that Franks without Greeks could not beat Turks in the open field, and in the next breath assumed that they could liberate Nicaea. Did he suppose that by gracious compliments he could hoodwink Bohemond son of Duke Robert, the most wily of the wily Normans of Apulia?

No, that wasn't quite fair. Alexius had said that in open country Franks might not be able to catch Turks; but if the infidels stood to defend a walled town Frankish swords could reach them. It was not really a contradiction. In fact it was a compliment, for the Emperor judged Bohemond capable of working that out as soon as he heard the plan. Very well, they were to take Nicaea and then the Greek army would join them. There was justification for that. The siege might drag on a long time, while the Emperor sat at home and amassed money and provisions for the march. Nicaea, only a short distance from the sea, stood at the head of the great road to Syria. With that as their base they would all advance together, as fast as their horses could carry them. The Turks must assemble to bar the way. That would bring on just the kind of great battle the pilgrims wanted. After that had been won the road would lie open, the road which led to the Duchy of Antioch.

These Greeks were always reading and writing papers; that was how Romania was governed. Even the Emperor looked at papers on a fine hunting morning, and at night discussed important business by lamplight. No Frankish lord ever worked after dinner, unless immediate danger threatened. The Emperor was genuinely a very busy man, who could be excused from attending the boring routine of a siege. So far there was no ground for suspecting him to be a deceitful ally—except for that busy guardian angel in Bohemond's mind who warned him to be very careful.

He sent orders to Tancred, bidding him bring up the army as soon as convenient. Even though there was no danger that the Duke of Normandy would catch up with them it would be well to reach Nicomedia before Count Raymond of Toulouse.

Bohemond did not try to penetrate further into the city than the Palace of Blachernae just within the gate. Probably no guard would stop a great lord who had spoken familiarly with the Emperor; but it might happen, and it would be most humiliating. He managed to do a little shopping, since various merchants came to wait on him. He bought his golden spurs, and several silk tunics in different colours; also a light càmpaigning cloak alleged to be woven from the hair of camels. The Greek majordomo attached to his villa advised him what price to offer, and he did not think he had been cheated more than was proper to any visiting foreigner.

On the third evening he was commanded to supper in the palace. It was a formal banquet, and except for the honour of the invitation rather a bore. The food and wine were excellent, the dishes all of gold; but there were as many ladies present as men. He spoke little, for he was afraid of saying something uncouth in his poor Greek, picked up from grooms and common soldiers. Before the meal began he was formally presented to the Emperor's daughter, the Princess Anna; and he sat between two of her waiting ladies. But all the females were so amazed at his size that they did little but stare; he felt that he was on show as a dangerous animal, not welcome as an eminent pilgrim. He was expected to eat with a fork, which made matters worse; though once or twice he had seen forks used by wealthy Greek merchants in Bari. The Boulogne brothers were at the table, Count Godfrey and Count Baldwin, but he had no private conversation with them. Their interpreters were always beside them, and would presumably repeat to the Greeks anything he said in Frankish. He felt rather disgruntled when he came back to his villa outside the walls.

It was late at night, but he found waiting for him his nephews Richard of the Principate and Tancred. They were both in a towering rage. They shouted and boomed at him, though the heat of the banqueting hall had given him a headache.

"Uncle, what's this I hear?" Tancred began. "Have you already betrayed our sacred pilgrimage? Is it true that you have offered to become the paid servant of that miserable heretic, the King of the Greeks? Do you command your followers to swear allegiance to the tyrant? Richard and I will do nothing of the kind. Both of us are willing to prove on your body that what you did was wrong."

"Quiet, you silly boy," Bohemond answered with a groan. "It's been a hard day, and I want to go to bed. If you are trying to challenge me to a fight may I remind you that all private quarrels are suspended until the finish of the pilgrimage. Which of us is breaking the vow, you or me? To turn to something more important, what have you done with my army? I put you in command. Then I sent orders for you all to march here. If you have left our men leaderless in a foreign land you aren't fit to command a patrol of light horse. What are you doing here?"

Tancred was so full of righteous indignation that the counterattack silenced him for the moment. But he soon collected his thoughts.

"I have carried out your orders, in so far as any honourable knight can fulfil them. All your men are encamped within a mile of this house. They are safe and well lodged, and I saw their dinners cooking before I left them. But your orders for tomorrow are more than I can bear. All knights to assemble, on foot, to swear fealty to the Emperor when he visits them. After that he will graciously ship them to Anatolia, where they will fight for him. Richard and I came here as pilgrims, not to serve heretics for pay. We can reach the field of battle without help from any Emperor. We have got hold of a Greek ship's master, a smuggler by trade. He knows how to dodge the Emperor's guardships, and he will land us in Anatolia tonight, before sunrise."

"We came only to tell you where we are going, so that you should not look for us tomorrow when we are missing," broke in Richard, speaking more peaceably. "In these matters of fealty and oath-swearing every good knight must judge for himself. I guard my own honour, just as you guard yours. I suppose you had private reasons for what you have done. I do not condemn such a famous warrior. Surely we may part in peace? It's just that we don't want to swear fealty to this Greek."

"If you go in peace I shan't try to stop you. I must stay behind for a few days, to arrange with the Emperor about provisions. Whose bread have you been eating all this year, since we landed at Durazzo? Whose bread will you eat while we besiege the Turks in Nicaea? Don't you think we owe Alexius some return for his help?"

"On the whole I think we owe him nothing," said Tancred. He had recovered his temper and was willing to argue. "It is the duty of every Christian to a pilgrim help on his way. Alexius, who is very rich, can afford to feed an army of pilgrims. But I suppose, uncle, you have not heard of the latest crime committed by these Greeks? You tell him, Richard. If I begin to speak my tongue may run away with me."

"Well, my lord," began Richard, looking down at his shoes and choosing his words with care. "Yesterday morning Count Raymond and his south Frenchmen caught up with us. They are not in very good shape. It seems they had a hard time on the march. We knew that the Pope's legate in charge of the whole pilgrimage, the Bishop of Le Puy, was travelling with Count Raymond's army, so some of us rode over to ask for his blessing. We couldn't see him. He travels in a litter because he has been gravely wounded. Near Salonica a heathen Patzinak shot an arrow into him, and it is not certain that he will recover. When they heard of it your men grew very angry."

"That's not the half of it," Tancred was shouting again. "While Count Raymond's men rode through the mountains they were repeatedly attacked. The savages rolled down rocks on them as they struggled through the passes. But the Greek soldiers in Durazzo were afraid of them. They received them in peace, and gave them food. Then we get this attempted murder of a holy Bishop, appointed by the Pope to lead us. Count Raymond won't bring his army any closer to the city. He fears that if his men see the Emperor they will snatch him from his bodyguard and hang him from the nearest tree. If I saw them doing it I would join in. Can't you see, Uncle? The Greeks plan to murder our leaders. Then they think it will be easy to massacre the leaderless remainder. They are heretics. You can't really call them Christians. I suppose the Turks have bribed them."

"It looks bad, I know," answered Bohemond, "but I don't think it's a treacherous plot. Of course Count Raymond had a rough journey. He chose an absurd road, just because he would rather ride hundreds of miles through mountains than sail for a day on the open sea. The mountaineers who attacked him are not the Emperor's subjects, but his enemies. As to the misfortune that befell Bishop Adhemar it must have been a misunderstanding. A Bishop wouldn't halt just because a common trooper hailed him, but those Patzinaks shoot after the first challenge. A heathen wouldn't recognize a holy man. When he reaches the next world he will know better. Finally, Alexius is not trying to murder our leaders. On the contrary, he is always looking for some supreme commander of all the pilgrims so that he can negotiate with one man instead of a mob."

An encouraging thought struck him. He hastened to share it.

"This is indeed a sad misfortune, but it may turn out to the advantage of the Normans of Apulia. Don't you see, my nephews, that if the papal legate were here we should all be bound to obey him? Except perhaps when we were actually fighting. But he might, he just might, order us to obey Count Raymond; and it would be hard to defy him openly. Now Count Raymond will arrive without his tame legate, and if he tries to take command we can tell him to think again. All the Counts will be equal, and that will include the Counts from Italy. It's lucky that Godfrey and

Baldwin saw me as the honoured guest of the Emperor. That will help them to forget that my grandfather was a simple knight when their grandfather was Duke of all Lorraine. This campaign may go better if a Hauteville leads it. That may happen."

Tancred agreed in words, though he was still clearly very angry. The cousins still insisted on crossing by night to avoid taking the oath of fealty. But there was no open breach among the Hautevilles.

CHAPTER VI

The Pilgrims United

————————————————★————————————————

Nicomedia was a Christian town, held by a Greek garrison. But the Turks had overrun it in their first victorious rush after Manzikert, and a town took many generations to recover from such a barbarian visitation. It was a poor place, without shops, without craftsmen, without inns. Frankish lords preferred to lodge in their own pavilions outside the walls; the poorer pilgrims clustered round their leaders in makeshift shelters, where no Greek would ask them to pay rent.

Several armies were encamped side by side: the Lorrainers and Flemings and north French who had followed the three Boulogne brothers, the French knights who followed Count Hugh of Vermandois, another great host of Frenchmen with no particular leader, nearly half the Normans of Apulia who had crossed into Anatolia with Tancred while Bohemond still lingered in the city. Every day Greek ships brought provisions, the gift of the Emperor. But the supply was beginning to diminish; it was time to get on with the war.

Godfrey of Lorraine had invited his equals to a council. Sending out the invitations had been a tricky business. In Lorraine Godfrey had been a Duke, which in the German lands was a higher title than Count. But out here the Greeks, who used the same titles, held that Count was above Duke; and Godfrey had resigned his office when he set out on this pilgrimage. Anyway, a Count by descent ought to be grander than a Duke by imperial appointment. To avoid quarrels it was better to spread the net widely.

They sat on trusses of hay in the shade of a grove. Each had beside him a roll of spiced bread and a mug of nasty Greek resin-flavoured wine, but supplies were so short that even Duke Godfrey could not provide a feast for this business meeting. He sat in the middle of the semi-circle, his two brothers on his left and Count Hugh in the place of honour on his right. Other French Counts, some of rather doubtful eminence, extended the line on either hand. On the leftward extremity, the lowest places, sat the young Hautevilles, the brothers William and Tancred and their cousin Richard.

Duke Godfrey stood up to speak formally, above a hum of desultory chatter. "It's about time we began this war, after riding so far to find our enemies. The King of the Greeks threatens to cut off supplies altogether, unless we march south to lay siege to Nicaea. It seems a reasonable move in itself. I have no objection. Do you know, by the way, that these Greeks never bothered to make a road between Nicomedia and Nicaea, though for centuries they ruled in these parts? I have sent out pioneers to clear the way, and to put up markers for those who come after. Will you gentlemen bring your men to join me when I begin my march?"

Richard of the Principate jumped up. He was smaller than the other Hautevilles but still taller than most Frenchmen. "I should not interrupt such great lords, but we know the Greeks and you northerners do not. If you speak of the King of the Greeks we shall get no more Greek bread. They consider it an insult. Alexius styles himself Emperor; not Emperor of anywhere, just Emperor. Refer to him as the Emperor Alexius. You ought not to mind. Most of you have sworn fealty to him, though my cousin and I did not."

"I swore to serve him while I was within his dominions," Godfrey answered with a frown. "By all accounts your Count Bohemond went much further. He offered to serve him as a mercenary, for wages."

"Alexius is a very good chap," said Hugh of Vermandois. "He treated me with all the deference due to my birth, and the food in his palace is magnificent. By all means let's give him the title he likes. Here's to the Emperor Alexius." He sipped his wine, and quickly put it down with a grimace of disgust.

A suppressed chuckle ran down the line. Everyone present knew that Count Hugh had been lodged in the palace as a hostage for the good behaviour of the French; if he had tried to leave it he would have discovered that for himself. But so long as chamberlains bowed before him, and stewards served him with good meals, he had been content to remain where he was.

"Very well, that's decided," Godfrey summed up. "The Emperor Alexius and no lesser style. Anyway, he's the lord of most of us, so long as we are in his town of Nicomedia. To return to more important matters. Will you march when I do?"

"Of course," said the Count of Toul. "But there are other things to be settled. If Duke Godfrey has made this road he is entitled to be the first to use it. We follow after. But when we reach Nicaea we shall need a single commander. Duke Godfrey? The Pope's legate? The Emperor Alexius? I'm not in the running, I know, so I shall obey anyone the rest of you agree on. But we must have a single commander."

"I'm not in the running either," Godfrey said quickly. "I'm not grand enough, nor rich enough, and anyway I don't want it. Neither Alexius nor the legate will be with us at Nicaea. The legate has not yet recovered from his wound, and the Emperor says he will be busy at home. We must think of someone else."

"Why go to Nicaea at all?" asked Tancred. "Alexius desires it, which is a very good reason for going somewhere else. The legate can't be with us because Alexius ordered one of his archers to shoot him. At any rate that's why the rascal escaped punishment, he claimed that he was carrying out the express orders of his paymaster. I've seen a good road leading due east from here. That must be the general direction of Jerusalem. Let's march along it until the Turks come out to fight us. If any Greek heretics try to come with us let's treat them as they treated the Pope's legate. But they won't try, they are too afraid of the Turks."

"We would all enjoy doing that." Godfrey spoke with a confidential smile. "But for various reasons it would be imprudent. I believe Jerusalem lies south of due east, though I'm not sure. Without Greek guides we would never find it. Without Greek food we would soon be hungry. Anyway, I for one couldn't march with Count Tancred, since I have given my oath to the Emperor."

Hugh of Vermandois summed up. He was not a famous warrior

or a powerful ruler, and in addition he was not very bright. But he was so sure of the deference due to his birth that he was always willing to take the initiative.

"We'll go to Nicaea and besiege it. It's what the Emperor wants, it's the only way to make sure of supplies from the city, and from a military point of view it seems the right thing to do. As to choosing a leader, this isn't the time for it. Some of the most famous pilgrims have not yet reached the army. Count Raymond, Count Bohemond and the legate are still in Constantinople. The Duke of Normandy and the Count of Flanders are still marching through Thrace. Wait until all of them have joined us. For the present this council of leaders will be able to manage a simple siege."

Early in May Bohemond joined the besiegers of Nicaea, with those of his men who had not gone ahead under Tancred. His arrival was as impressive as he could wish. Beside him rode an eminent Greek soldier, Manual Butumites, who commanded a large corps of engineers. At the tail of the column, behind the ox-drawn siege-engines, came boats mounted on wheels, which were to blockade the lakeside wall of Nicaea. Every man in his army was well fed and carried an emergency-reserve of biscuit. Their horses were fat and newly shod. As soon as the boats had been launched at the western end of the Ascanian Lake, Greeks began to ferry supplies to the besiegers, who had been on short rations. It was a most convincing demonstration of the benefits of co-operation with the Emperor.

Hugh of Vermandois came out to greet Count Bohemond. Before a cheering crowd of pilgrims the royal Count reined in his warhorse and embraced Bohemond as an equal. Butumites made a gesture as though to dismount, but Hugh graciously signed to him to stay in the saddle. Then Bohemond presented him, without waiting for an interpreter. He had become quite fluent in Greek, which added to the amazement of the pilgrims from the north.

The council of equal commanders seemed to be running the siege without difficulty. Of course Bohemond, who had brought such valuable help, was given a place on this council. No one could sneer at the birth of a Hauteville immediately after the brother of the King of France had kissed him on both cheeks. Godfrey and his brother Baldwin welcomed him as an old friend, and his nephews were obviously willing to let bygones be bygones. It could not have passed off better if he had planned every move in advance. As a matter of fact, nearly every move had been planned in advance.

Manuel Butumites was also invited to attend that evening's council. But the other lords forgot to invite his interpreter and Bohemond forbore to remind them; so he could speak only through Bohemond. That also helped.

Butumites asked a good many questions. Like all other Greek soldiers, he wanted to know what the enemy intended to do; as opposed to the sensible Frankish custom of keeping your weapons handy and charging the enemy whenever he chose to appear. There were local peasants in camp, come to sell what the Turks had left them of last years' harvest; they seemed to know all the news of besieged Nicaea. The King of the Turks had ridden eastward to make war on the Armenians; the garrison had asked him to save them, and he was now hastening west at the head of a great army. All this Butumites related to the council, and then suggested that they should fortify their camp before the impending attack.

Bohemond translated what was said, and saw at once that his fellow-Counts did not like it. Godfrey spoke up at once.

"To fit out my men I sold all I possessed. Then for a whole winter I rode through strange lands. I wished to reach the infidels and charge them, not to hide behind a palisade for fear they should charge me. If this Greek won't face them let him go home to the city."

Bohemond did not translate that in so many words, though he also thought Butumites too cautious. "Look, my lord Manual," he said soothingly, "I know that you speak as a veteran. You fear that in open country these Turks will overcome us. They will shoot their arrows from a distance until they have killed our horses, and then finished us off with their swords. They can't do that here, before Nicaea. They want to break into the town, and we want to keep them out. They must ride to meet us, and we shall kill them all."

Butumites appeared to be persuaded, though Bohemond noticed afterwards that he never strayed far from his fastest horse. Before a battle these Greeks always thought more of flight than of victory.

A few days later Count Raymond led in his strong army. The legate came with him, fully recovered and riding a warhorse. Bishop Adhemar was the son of a French baron; he was fully armed, and as willing to fight as to pray. Like most Bishops he never expected a miracle, and disapproved of those enthusiastic pilgrims, chiefly drawn from the lower clergy, who counted on God to get them out of all difficulties. He took his place quite naturally on the council of leaders, but he did not expect to be asked to preside.

He was polite to Butumites, and to every other Greek he met; he never spoke of the wound he had received outside Salonica. But he did not conceal his dislike of the schism. Bohemond, who could suck in gossip as a fish sucks air from a stream, gathered that he had raised the question of submission to Rome with Alexius, and been disappointed with the answer.

Count Raymond was by nature a bore. Some years older than Bohemond, who was the oldest of the other leaders, he continually drew on relevant experiences from his own past. He was expert in feudal custom; but it was the custom of Provence, which differed from that of the Normans and north French. He sneered at those Franks who had sworn fealty to the Emperor, and explained that his own oath—not to harm him—was much superior. He took it for granted that he had known exactly what was in Pope Urban's mind when he spoke at Clermont, though it was the common opinion that the Pope had not known what he was going to say until he heard himself saying it. Finally, he never explained himself in one word if he could find ten to make his meaning clear.

But he was eager for the fray, as even Tancred admitted to his uncle. On the very evening of his arrival, while his men were pitching their tents, a small band of Turks tried to cut their way into Nicaea. Count Raymond charged bravely and drove them off. Later his engineers cut off the heads of the dead and threw them over the walls of Nicaea from catapults. That gave the besieged Turks something to think about.

The Count of Flanders was the next to arrive, with a good army. He had travelled through the winter with the Duke of Normandy, and he knew well all the great families of the Normans. But he also treated Count Bohemond as in every way his equal.

Within a few days Duke Robert would arrive, which would be the final test of Bohemond's position. But before that the pilgrims fought a considerable battle—and Bohemond was unable to take part in it. The King of the Turks led his men in a fierce attack on the besiegers. Count Raymond and the legate met them, and presently the Flemings charged them from a flank. All day the battle raged, at very close quarters. But the garrison of Nicaea could be seen massing just inside a gate, ready to charge out and join the other infidels. The Normans of Apulia, posted opposite this gate, dared not weaken their line.

It was astonishing, and rather frightening, that light horsemen without mail could encounter western knights and dispute the field for hours. These Turks were fantastically courageous. They were killed by the hundred, but they killed many pilgrims. Count Baldwin of Ghent, as well armed and well mounted as any other good knight, was unhorsed and done to death before he could get to his feet. In the end the King of the Turks and the remnant of his men fled to the eastward. The pilgrims might concentrate on their siege. They began to mine a tower.

At the beginning of June the Duke of Normandy and the Count of Blois at last rode into camp, with a great following. Duke Robert turned out to be a gallant and charming knight, so assured of his own social eminence that he was eager to be friends with everybody. By birth he was the head of the Norman race everywhere, but even in Normandy he could seldom enforce his will; he did not expect the Normans of Apulia to obey him.

He greeted all the Hautevilles in friendly fashion, and sat down beside Bohemond at the council of leaders. The trouble was, as Bohemond said to Tancred afterwards, that he never noticed where he sat or with whom he was discussing the campaign. "I feared he might not treat us as equals, and he does. But he is just as friendly with common troopers, so his friendship does not really enhance the eminence of the Hautevilles."

The Count of Blois kept greater state, but seemed bewildered by everything he saw. He made no particular suggestion about the conduct of the campaign, except that if they marched beyond ·

reach of convoys from the city they would all starve. He explained frankly that he had joined the pilgrimage only because his wife had commanded him to; he must stay with the army or be disgraced as a recreant, but the sooner they all went home the better he would be pleased. His wife, Duke Robert's sister, evidently ruled the County of Blois; perhaps it was as well that she did not rule Normandy also, or she would have tried to enforce her authority over the Normans of Apulia. Stephen of Blois was obsessed by the danger of starvation in this unknown land. He had with him an elaborate abacus, which he worked himself instead of leaving it to a clerk. His calculations had convinced him that the great host of pilgrims, who included thousands of non-combatant women and children and clergy, would need much more food every day than could be gathered by all the armed foragers they could put in the field.

The other Counts agreed to let that problem solve itself when it arose. Foragers could gather enough to feed the fighting men; the others must stay behind in some friendly town, or go home. The pilgrimage could not be planned entirely to fit in with the arrangements made by the Emperor for supplying them.

Meanwhile the siege-operations suffered a set-back. Count Raymond, after some blustering about his past experience, set to work all the pioneers in the united army to dig a mine under one tower of the defences. It was a good mine, as even Tancred admitted; soundly dug, with a minimum of casualties, to reach right under the foundations of the tower. Unfortunately Count Raymond made a mistake in his timing. As soon as the chamber had been filled with dry fuel it was duly set alight. But the fire took some time to catch hold, and the ancient foundations were stubborn. The pilgrims heard a great rumble as the tower came crashing down, but since it was the middle of a pitch-black night they could not assault immediately. By sunrise the Turks had built another wall behind the breach, and the proposed assault was cancelled. All the dangerous and exhausting work had gone for nothing.

In the whole pilgrim army only Butumites the Greek was cheerful. He explained to Bohemond, with whom he often supped at the end of the day, that he expected an early capitulation. "The garrison know that their King has deserted them. If the town falls by assault their lives are forfeit. They are sensible men. They will yield while their defences are intact and they have something to bargain with."

"I see. Have they already approached you?" This was how Greeks sometimes broke the news of important developments to mere Franks.

"Not officially. My agents in the blockade ships on the lake can sometimes communicate with the Greek townspeople. The Turks would yield tomorrow if the terms were good enough. I suppose your people agree that their lives should be spared?"

"I suppose so, if they yield a place while it is still defensible. That's a law of war in the west, though I don't know how far it applies to infidels. If we let them live we must allow them to come out with horse and arms or the common pilgrims will massacre them. They will probably try that anyway. The brothers of those pioneers who were shot as they dug the mine will feel themselves cheated. On the whole I am against a capitulation. We can take Nicaea. We would have taken it already if Count Raymond had been bright enough to tell the difference between night and day. Let's take it, and kill the whole garrison. We are in no hurry, and a brisk slaughter of the infidel will encourage the lesser pilgrims."

"Nicaea is a strong fortress. It used to be prosperous. The Emperor would like to get it back undamaged. Those are his commands, and while you are in his dominions you are sworn to obey them. I must insist that tomorrow my interpreter put the proposal to the full council."

"Of course, my dear general. We are faithful allies. But I am not the council, I cannot agree on their behalf. Now it's getting late, and I want a word with my nephew Tancred before I go to bed. Will you excuse me?"

At the council next morning Bohemond seconded the very prudent suggestion of their valued ally. Then Tancred jumped up to denounce in a fiery speech this underhand attempt to cheat the poorer pilgrims of their rightful plunder. Even his uncle announced himself persuaded, and it was agreed to order a general assault for the next day. Since there was no breach it would have to be an escalade, and a day was needed to make scaling-ladders.

But no Frank can cope with a Greek ally, as Bohemond complained bitterly afterwards. "If you treat him honestly he cheats you, and when you try to cheat him he does it better. Either way he makes you look silly."

On 19th June 1097 the pilgrims looked very silly. As they formed up at sunrise for the assault, in full armour and weighed down with scaling-ladders, they saw Greek banners on the walls of Nicaea. On the battlements were Patzinak archers with drawn bows, and the gates were closed. While the pilgrims hesitated Butumites explained, through his interpreter, to Duke Godfrey. He thought that would be less unpleasant than explaining directly to Count Bohemond.

"Last night the infidels in Nicaea made terms with the Emperor. They are now embarked on our boats on the lake. They will be taken to the city where we can discuss their ransoms. A condition of the surrender was that Nicaea should not be pillaged. It is now a walled town of our glorious Empire, and the rule applies that governed your march through Europe. Franks may not enter the fortifications. Exceptionally, as a reward for your gallant efforts, small parties of unarmed pilgrims may visit the town under escort. But the Emperor does not wish to deprive you of the spoil. The wealth of Nicaea will be taken, under armed guard, to the imperial camp at Pelecanum beyond Nicomedia. There the Emperor will divide it among his faithful Franks."

"We can still take Nicaea," Godfrey answered, "and if we did we would still be fighting the heathen. It's a pity that your great Christian Emperor won't hire Christian soldiers. But if the Turks and their treasure are already on your ships the capture of the town will gain us nothing. I shall advise my fellow-pilgrims to disperse. How soon can we call on the Emperor at Pelecanum?"

All the Frankish knights were angry and dismayed. Men of good birth had been killed during the savage fighting against the King of the Turks. The lesser pilgrims, equally angry at first, were mollified that same evening. Before withdrawing from Nicaea the Greek engineers distributed all their stores, a great mass of bread and salt pork and wine; there was a lavish feast for all comers. At that stage of the long march sensible camp followers valued a full stomach more than a wallet full of heavy plunder.

Bohemond persuaded the other Hautevilles to come with him to Pelecanum. Tancred was naturally reluctant. But it was now, for the crossing of the deserts of Anatolia, that they needed help from the Greeks; and unless Tnacred swore fealty they might not get it.

"I gather the Emperor really wants an oath from you," Bohemond explained. "You are not a man who swears lightly, but in this case I think you might. Consider the honour done to you. Until we reached Romania you had never drawn your sword; you have only charged once in your life, at the River Vardar. That one charge earned you such fame that the mighty Emperor does not think himself safe until you have sworn to serve him. By the way, I don't suppose the pact between Alexius and the pilgrimage will bind us for very much longer. If he does another deal with our enemies, behind our backs, we shall all defy him."

"It was a deal, it was with our enemies, it was concluded behind our backs," Tancred answered carefully. "But we can't say that Alexius is forsworn until we see what he offers us at Pelecanum. If his presents are worth as much as we should have got from the sack of Nicaea we have lost nothing. If he insists I shall take oath. When we meet the Turks in open country we shall need those mounted archers of his, heathen though they are."

The camp of the imperial army was very unlike the disorderly settlements of the pilgrims. A large square enclosure was marked out a by a palisaded earthen bank, pierced only by four genuine wooden gates which might be opened or shut. As the Counts rode through a gate a strong body of guards saluted them. Within, tents of a uniform pattern were arranged in straight rows, so that it was easy to move from place to place. A broad main street led to the imperial pavilion, made entirely of purple cloth; a few yards away stood the imperial chapel, a smaller purple tent; its walls were looped up to display a rich portable altar, on which candles burned. In the entry of his pavilion Alexius sat on a gilded throne, which itself stood on a thick carpet laid on the ground. He wore his robes of state and his imperial crown. Behind him stood a motionless line of guards and courtiers.

It was so obviously all laid on to impress the barbarian that Bohemond would not allow himself to be impressed. All this grandeur, all this ritual, had come down from the days when the Emperor was a mighty ruler; since the battle of Mankizert, twenty-five years ago, that was no longer true. Alexius was richer than any Frankish Count, probably richer than all of them put together. But they had come here, at the urging of the Pope, to protect him from his enemies; and therefore the army of the pilgrimage must be stronger.

After they had gazed at their leisure at all the splendour set before them the Emperor rose graciously from his throne to receive his guests with all honour. He spoke, of course, through an interpreter; but he must have recalled that Bohemond could understand Greek, for what he said was exactly what the interpreter put into French.

"My loyal followers, you have yielded to me the town of Nicaea in accordance with your promises. Now follow me into this tent and you will see that your loyalty has cost you nothing."

They began to crowd towards the tent, curiosity and greed overcoming their fragile Frankish dignity. Tancred alone stood firm, so immovable that his uncle had to walk round him. "Come on," muttered Bohemond. "If we don't hurry the others may get more than their share."

"Then you go on, and grab for all the Hautevilles. You are expert in that, my dear uncle. I have not been invited. The Emperor wants only his loyal followers."

"Don't be silly. You are missing great riches. Slip in with the crowd and help yourself."

But Alexius noticed everything. "Count Tancred, I believe?" said the interpreter. "You were so eager to reach the foe that you could not wait in the city to swear fealty to the Emperor. If you will do so now, before these other noble Franks as witnesses, you may take first pick of all the wealth stored in this tent."

Everyone stared at Tancred, who stood irresolute. "Come on, young man, swear and get it over," urged Godfrey. "It isn't pleasant, I know, but we have all done it. It's no worse than swearing fealty to your natural ruler at home."

"I have never sworn fealty to anyone," Tancred answered. "The Normans of Apulia have no natural ruler. We rule ourselves. If I defy this heretic here and now, who will stand by me? Why take a share of his wealth? With our swords we can have the whole of it."

"I for one won't stand by you," said Bohemond sharply. "Do you suppose we would have sworn fealty to the Emperor if we thought we were strong enough to overthrow him?"

"Besides," added Godfrey, "no one here can help you without being recreant. The rest of us are already the Emperor's men."

"Very well. I give in. The welfare of the whole pilgrimage must come before my private independence. Bear witness to what I do. Here, interpreter, ask the Emperor to take my hands in his. Tell me what I must say. "Tancred fell on one knee where he stood, so that Alexius had to step forward to grasp his hands.

"That's that," he said a moment later, ostentatiously dusting his fingers as he stood erect. "Now I choose my gift. Don't bother to show me the treasure inside. All the gold I want I can win from the Turks. Instead I choose this pavilion. Please tell your servants to strike it. The one I have now is too small."

There was a rapid interchange between the interpreter and the scowling Emperor. "You silly boy, you can't have the imperial state pavilion, thirty camel-loads of royal purple cloth. Because of your impudence the Emperor rejects your fealty. You are not important. It does not matter to the Emperor whether you are his friend or his enemy. Now leave the camp."

As Tancred strode towards his horse, waiting at the camp gate, he snarled over his shoulder: "You are all witnesses that Alexius does not hold my fealty, since he has broken his side of the bargain. But I think that one day it will matter to him that I am his foe."

It was embarrassing for all concerned. With scarlet cheeks the interpreter invited the Franks to enter the pavilion, and they hurried in with their eyes on their shoes. Bohemond stole one glance at the rigid back walking to the gate. It seemed likely that if Tancred lived long enough his prophecy would come true. It was comforting to remember that he was half a Hauteville.

All the same, the heap of gold, silver and jewels waiting for them within made up greater wealth than any of them had expected, greater than some of them thought existed anywhere in the world. Even Count Stephen of Blois, who had married the managing daughter of the mighty conqueror of England because of her splendid dowry, was quite dazzled by the Emperor's generosity. The quarrel beside the imperial throne had sobered the Franks. There was little jostling or grabbing as they watched its division. It was much more than they would have taken in the sack of any town, even such a great town as Nicaea.

Count Raymond felt a little anxious; but he got his share like everyone else, though the oath he had sworn to the Emperor was less binding. Count Stephen was ecstatic. Even Bohemond was satisfied. It did seem, after all, that the Emperor dealt generously with his Frankish servants.

When the money had been sealed into sacks and deposited with the waiting escort the Emperor once more seated himself on his throne and prepared to address the assembled Counts. He sat in full state, his sceptre in one hand and the orb of the world in the other, the imperial crown on his head. His interpreter declaimed formally, as though in a court of law.

"Gentlemen, the mighty Emperor and his invincible army cannot march with you to conquer the Turks. Troubles on the lower Danube require his presence in Europe. He will give you all the assistance in his power—ample provisions, expert guides, a general of high rank who will march with you and report direct to the throne. General Taticius is familiar with Turkish methods of warfare. In fact he is a Turk by race, though a Christian veteran of the imperial service. You will find his advice of great value. He now awaits you in your camp before Nicaea. The Emperor suggests that, after suitable refreshment, you should ride there and confer with him."

The Emperor did not wait for an answer. As the interpreter finished speaking he rose from his throne and vanished into the recesses of the great pavilion.

Servants led the Counts to another pavilion, where a long table bore a cold collation and many wine-jugs. They ate hastily, almost in silence; for there was a long ride before them and they did not care to speak among Greek spies. Within an hour they were mounting their horses at the gate of the camp.

CHAPTER VII

The Pilgrims Divided

———————————————★———————————————

The quickest way from Pelecanum to Nicaea was across the Gulf of Nicomedia. But no prudent Frank would carry gold by water if it was possible to ride. The Counts took the great paved road to Nicomedia twenty miles away; from there they would follow Godfrey's marked track to Nicaea.

First came the mules laden with treasure, escorted by a strong guard. The Counts rode behind, where they could see that all went well and charge quickly to the rescue if danger threatened. The width of the road made it convenient to ride three abreast; Bohemond noted with interest how these great men, his equals and rivals, spontaneously sorted themselves out.

Count Raymond rode in front, with a south French nobleman on either hand. Count Raymond often inserted himself in the front rank, because he had persuaded himself that it was the will of Pope Urban that he should lead the whole pilgrimage. He was a very great man at home, and the others were quite willing to grant him precedence; but it was unlikely that they would obey his orders in the field.

Behind Count Raymond the three Boulogne brothers rode abreast, Godfrey in the place of honour in the middle. It was curious how in that family Godfrey always took the lead, though the Count of Boulogne was the eldest. But then Count Eustace intended to return to his rich fief when the pilgrimage was over; whereas Godfrey and Baldwin were landless men who would remain in the east until they died. Besides, it had already become evident at the siege of Nicaea that Godfrey was an outstanding commander.

The Count of Vermandois came next, with a French courtier on either side. By right of birth he should have ridden first, and when Raymond had pushed himself in that position he had avoided the second place. But it was hard to know where to put this rather foolish Count. In Paris he was the King's brother and a very great man. Here in Anatolia he was only the leader of a small contingent. Besides, this was a pilgrimage and that eminent brother of his was under the ban of the Church—woman trouble, of course. Pope Urban tried to make great lords live as chastely as peasants, though in this degenerate age that was to ask too much. Bohemond was very lucky not to be bothered by these temptations, but he congratulated himself that it was partly due to his own virtue. These great lords ought to fight harder, and go hunting if they were so unfortunate as to be at peace with all their neighbours. At the end of the day they would be so tired that they would live faithfully with their own wives.

Robert of Normandy, Robert of Flanders, and Stephen of Blois rode side by side. There was nothing wrong with the Duke of Normandy, and not very much right either. It seemed odd to remember that all the Normans of Apulia had feared his arrival. He might be the head of the whole Norman race, but he did nothing to impose his authority. He was pleasant to everyone he met, even to his creditors who were numerous. He was a gallant knight and a skilful warrior. But he was so indifferent to danger that he would make a reckless leader ; he concentrated on the foe before his own lance and forgot the rest of the battlefield. The Normans of Apulia would never be so foolish as to follow him, and he never tried to persuade them that they ought to be his subjects. Count Stephen was another unmilitary ass, not even terrible in the charge like the Duke his brother-in-law. Count Robert was the best of that trio, and a single-minded pilgrim into the bargain. But though everyone admired him it was known that he would go back to Flanders as soon as he had done his duty. There was no danger that any Norman of Apulia would be tempted away from the Hautevilles to follow the banner of Flanders.

Best of all, every one of these lords accepted Bohemond son of Duke Robert as fully his equal. There need be no more worrying about the status of a Hauteville. The next thing to worry about was the desertion of the Greeks. On this pilgrimage there was always something to worry about. He would ask Taticius some pointed questions as soon as he met him.

Late on the following day they reached the camp before Nicaea. Immediately every leader set about distributing the Emperor's gifts among his faithful followers. There was no point in keeping a reserve of treasure. During the next stage of the march they would eat Greek supplies for as long as they lasted; and then forage in the lands of the infidel where bread was won by the sword, not exchanged for money. After the distribution there would of course be a great feast. Late on the following morning, when the headaches were beginning to wear off, the council of leaders would meet to consider their next move.

Bohemond did not wait to reward his followers in person. There were important inquiries to be made, and he was unique among the great lords in having a completely trustworthy deputy, his nephew Tancred. Tancred was waiting for him, still in a very bad temper. He cheered up when he saw the great pile of gold, for he regarded anything gained from the Greeks as stolen property at last returned to its rightful owners. In his opinion those cowardly heretics should long ago have made over all they possessed to their gallant defenders.

Tancred had gathered a titbit of news.

"Today some Christians rode into camp from the east. Armenians they call themselves, and they accuse the Greeks of heresy. So they must be decent Christians like ourselves. The man I spoke to said he was quite willing to submit to the Pope, though until he met us he had never heard of him. They look like warriors—light horse only, but tough. They speak a language of their own, which none of the local peasants understand."

"Then how did you speak with them?"

"Because this man had learned Arabic as a hostage among the infidels. That's the same tongue the infidels use in Sicily, where I learned it. These Armenians are subject to the Turks; that is, they pay tribute. Otherwise they manage their own affairs. The men who have come here would prefer Frankish lords, though they are also in rebellion against their Armenian ruler."

"They sound a rebellious lot. I have heard of Armenia, though I don't know whether Armenians are good warriors. Still, it's worth bearing in mind. Christians who don't like Greeks and are willing to join up with Franks. We might make something of it, if ever we get so far."

That was one of the questions he was going to put to Taticius.

The eminent Greek general did not keep much state. His tent was a humble affair with a single ridge, amid a group of tents of the standard Greek pattern which presumably housed his corps of guides. The doorkeeper was a mere servant, though he carried a short sword. He announced Bohemond.

Inside the tent Taticius squatted on a little square of carpet laid on the bare ground. One of those excellent Greek lamps stood beside him; he was studying a map unfolded on his knees. He sprang to his feet and came forward, bustling with hospitality.

"Ah, the famous Count Bohemond who speaks Greek. No need for an interpreter. I am honoured. Have a carpet? Oh no, you Franks like to sit on something high. What about that box? I'm afraid there's no chair. Will you take a cup of wine? Supper will be ready in an hour or so."

Taticius was a wiry little man, grey and bent with age. Baggy woollen breeches covered his legs to the knee; his shins and feet were bare but a fine silken tunic hid his torso. His hair was clipped short, as was his scanty beard. Obviously an active old boy, at present in casual undress. All this Bohemond took in at a glance. But even good manners could not stop him exclaiming at the other's face.

"Good God, what is that on your nose?"

"This *is* my nose, a very fine nose, made of pure gold. I wear it always, for I look very horrible without it. Our steel caps have no noseguard, such as you Franks so sensibly employ. An infidel sabre cut off the nose I was born with, so a goldsmith in the city made this substitute. It had to be gold, the surgeon told me; for any lesser metal would rust, and the rust might poison me. I think it looks very handsome, but people *do* stare when they see it for the first time. Will you warn the other Counts, so they are prepared for it? But you didn't come here, after a long ride, to discuss my appearance. Is there anything I can tell you? My orders are to give the pilgrims any assistance in my power."

"You are most gracious, general. Forgive the astonishment which overcame my courtesy. I must explain that I come of my own accord. I do not represent the council of leaders. But I should like to be able to say, at the council meeting tomorrow, how much military help you can give us, and what you can tell about Turkish methods of warfare."

"Military help? I suppose the honest answer is none at all." Taticius opened his mouth in a gap-toothed grin. "I command about a hundred men, experienced scouts who know the country to the eastward. They are mounted, and they carry bows as well as swords, just like Turks. We call them Turcopoles, 'Turk-fighters'. But their job is to tell you the way to Jerusalem, and what lies behind every ridge you pass on the road. I wouldn't trust them to stand firm in a line of battle. On the other hand I know all about Turkish warfare, for I was trained in it. Do you know that I am myself a Turk?"

Seeing Bohemond frown he explained further.

"No, I'm not a renegade. I didn't change my religion to escape from captivity. I was carried to baptism in my mother's arms. We Turks are divided into different hordes, and in the old days we worshipped nothing more impressive than a few magic rags stuck on a pole. When we rode west we wanted to be civilized, so we all joined a civilized faith. My father heard that the Seljouks had turned Moslem; since they were his most bitter enemies he commanded his horde to turn Christian. That was before I was born. Then the Seljouks proved too strong for us, so we all took refuge in the Empire. It's more than twenty years since I joined the imperial army, but I was already a trained Turkish warrior."

"Then you are indeed just the man to help me."

Bohemond liked this tough little savage; who so neatly gave the information, without appearing to boast, that his father had been a great chieftain of the Turks.

"To put it as frankly as possible," he went on, "do you think that the pilgrims stand any chance by themselves? Can we cross Anatolia without help from the Emperor's Turcopoles? Or ought we to stay here until the Emperor is at leisure to march with us?"

"You might have a long wait, though perhaps I shouldn't say so. Why not give up the whole enterprise and go back home? Those who have no homes can serve the Emperor for wages, as I do. On the other hand, it's not exactly suicide to go on. The Turks will hover out of reach and pester you with arrows; but that heavy mail of yours is proof against their arrows. Sooner or later they must go away, or charge. In the open country they will go away, but in the end you will reach some place they want to defend. Then they will charge, and at close quarters you may beat them. What I don't know is how steadily Franks stand up to skirmishing. Keep in line. Hide your horse behind the foot. Don't charge. Get your cross-bows to the front. That's a new weapon, which will puzzle the infidels. I can't say more."

"You have said enough. I see you are an honest man and a friend to the pilgrimage. Unfortunately what you advise is just what Franks won't do. My knights never keep in line, they charge without orders, and nothing would induce them to hide their horses on the battlefield. So I suppose we shall be beaten. Will you still come with us?"

"Those are the Emperor's orders. But I am not under the orders of any Frank, so I may choose my own post when the battle comes. It may be well to the rear, if things look unpromising. I have not been ordered to defend your banner with the last drop of my blood, and I shan't do it. I am well mounted, and so are my Turcopoles. If there are any survivors I shall be among them."

"You have made the position perfectly clear. When next you report to the Emperor please include my congratulations. He has arranged matters so that whatever happens he will win. By autumn he will once more rule Anatolia, or he will be rid of this intrusive Frankish army. You might add best wishes from my nephew Tancred as well. I am sure the dear boy would like me to send them. What an elegant little carpet you sit on. Is it one of those infidel praying-mats?"

They chatted together for another half-hour. Taticius allowed Bohemond to inspect his golden nose, and described vividly the fight in which he had lost its predecessor. He admired the strength of Bohemond's mail, but thought his great sword too heavy for close combat. They understood one another perfectly. Bohemond was sure that Taticius would give the pilgrimage all the help in his power. He was equally sure that the Emperor would not.

Next day's meeting of the council was stormy. Count Raymond took the chair, by the simple method of getting there first. So Duke Godfrey when he arrived went quietly to a place on the extreme right of the semi-circle. "Sorry if I'm late," he said in careful south French. "That legate of yours must be a good man, St. Gilles. I saw him begin his Mass only twenty minutes ago, so I thought there would be no hurry. He must read even faster than my own chaplain. I hope you ate a good breakfast."

Count Raymond, who had cut breakfast to be sure of being early, grinned an embarrassed smile. The smile changed to a frown when he saw the two giant Hautevilles, Bohemond and Tancred, moving into humble places on the extreme left, but with the Duke of Normandy between them. He rose to speak.

"Gentlemen, our work in Nicaea is finished, and the Emperor has rewarded us generously. It is time to move on, and again our next step has been made clear by the prudent foresight of the Emperor. I have been talking with the lord Taticius, who has been sent to advise us on our route. He has maps, you know, and I can read them. When most of you were too young to bear arms I was using a map to find my way through Moorish Spain. We can go due east, by the great road which leads ultimately to Armenia. It's the best road, and it runs through fertile country; but Armenia lies a long way north of Jerusalem. The shortest road to Jerusalem heads a little more to the south; but it runs through a desert, beside a great lake of foul salt water. Our guides say it is unsuitable for an army. A third road, even farther south, goes by Tarsus and Antioch to Jerusalem; a little bit out of our way, but the country is fertile and inhabited by Christian peasants. Of course these Christian peasants are now ruled by Turks, but our Greek guides can slip on ahead and warn them to collect provisions for us. So I have arranged that we march by this southern road, at sunrise tomorrow. Warn all your men, and see that they get their baggage packed today. It would be a good idea to try out the pack-saddles this afternoon, to avoid sore backs. Now are there any questions?"

"Not questions, exactly, but I propose to make a few observations." Bohemond slowly unfolded to his enormous height, his hands tucked in his swordbelt. "In the first place, all these roads diverge at what used to be the town of Dorylaeum until the Turks destroyed it. I also can read maps, Count Raymond. Dorylaeum lies several days' march to the eastward, so we need not choose our route until we get there. In the second place, Count Raymond seems in some unexplained way to have become your leader. He isn't mine. I have never taken oath to him. If the majority of this council of equal leaders decides to march tomorrow the Normans of Apulia will march with them. If not, not."

As he took his seat again Tancred reached an enormous hand across to pat him on the shoulder; but what really mattered was that Duke Robert, sitting between the two giants, smiled approval.

Half a dozen angry south Frenchmen were on their feet to shout at the Normans, who shouted back. Though Yes in south France was *Oc* and in the north French *Oui* there was no language barrier; for all were shouting No.

Duke Godfrey restored peace. He had no home, and might be described as an adventurer seeking a fief in the east, but he was a dedicated pilgrim whose only aim was to free Jerusalem, and everyone knew it. Besides, as he pointed out, there was very little in dispute. If they were to continue the war they must march to Dorylaeum. Only if they decided to wait for the Emperor could they stay outside Nicaea, and then if the Greeks chose to cut off supplies they would have to move somewhere. Sitting at the extreme edge of the council, he first announced that he would march with Count Raymond and then asked his neighbour. By the time the question reached Bohemond, on the farther edge, the council was nearly unanimous and he would be foolish to object. With few courtesies the meeting broke up and the leaders separated to arrange the march.

The Duke of Normandy still walked between the two Hautevilles. "Is it true that Alexius believes that we shall all be killed by the Turks?" he asked doubtfully. "How wicked, to send so many fellow-Christians to their doom. But everyone says now that he is a very wicked man. On the other hand, I remember that sometimes my father would repeat what someone else had said, and what he repeated sounded much worse than what the other fellow had intended. There was that tangled business about Count Harold and some oath. Nobody will ever know the rights of it. Of course you would never lie, Count Bohemond. But did the Emperor mean exactly what you have told us?"

"I think it is his genuine opinion," Bohemond answered gravely. "But his opinion may be mistaken. When he spoke he was trying to persuade the pilgrims to march under his command. Now he wants us to go off on our own. Perhaps that will make him change his mind."

"He has changed his mind about our value as allies, that's all," said Tancred savagely. "He knew that we could take Nicaea for him. Now he hopes that we shall starve in the wilderness. Can't you see, Duke Robert, that whatever happens he stands to gain? Already we have given him a strong town and a rich province. What have we got out of it? Enough biscuit and salt meat to keep us alive."

"And a good many sacks of gold," answered the Duke. "Though that didn't make me any richer, because it all went straight to my creditors. But he has done as much as you can expect from a Greek. Anyway, he would not be so base as to send his friend Taticius to certain disaster."

"No wonder his brother took England from him," Bohemond muttered to Tancred. "My lord, Greeks and especially Greek Emperors, have been known to sacrifice their friends in return for some great advantage. Taticius hopes to get home safely, by running away in good time. I've spoken to him, and he let me see as much. Alexius expects the Turks to win. Well, let's prove him wrong. Together we shall all set out on this great road to the eastward. But I won't take orders from Count Raymond. He may be the oldest leader in the pilgrimage, but I am a better knight and a better warleader."

The whole pilgrimage did not march out together, which emphasized once again Bohemond's efficiency. Before midday he issued orders that his men should march at sunrise, and it was so. The other leaders gave the same orders, and some of their armies took three days to get on the move. The Normans of Apulia felt smugly superior as they waited for their comrades. They were camped by a bridge over a small stream. On the far side of the stream could be seen Turkish scouts. The war had woken again. The final breach came at the council of leaders that evening. Duke Godfrey brought it on, lest worse befall. He explained that he had heard from Taticius that beyond the river were only a few rare springs, which filled slowly. They would find it difficult to water all their horses in one evening. Therefore the army should divide, the second division marching one day behind the first. Let Count Bohemond, who got his men on the move so quickly, lead the first division. Count Raymond would lead the second, and Duke Godfrey would march with him.

That worked out in practice as a division between Normans and the rest. Of course Count Hugh chose to march with the second party, since the Normans of Normandy were the most dangerous enemies of the King of France. Duke Robert, with the Count of Flanders and the Count of Blois who had accompanied him across Christendom, marched with the Normans of Apulia. Taticius and his little band must also march with the Normans, since as pathfinders they must go first. The many little independent contingents of Frenchmen were almost equally divided.

"We Hautevilles are still coming up in the world," said Richard of the Principate to Tancred. "Uncle Bohemond is not yet supreme commander of the pilgrimage; but Duke Godfrey's order of march has made him leader of about half of it."

"It's going to be frightfully hot in the middle of the day," Duke Robert grumbled. "Must we ride in full mail?"

"It would be prudent," answered Bohemond, "except perhaps for young Tancred, who likes to charge in his tunic. Yesterday evening those scouts seemed confident, as though there were a lot of other Turks behind them. If I were a mounted archer this is the sort of country I would choose to fight in. Open grass, where a horse can go anywhere; and yet so broken with hills that they can hide within half a mile of us. I smell danger—though before such experienced warriors it seems presumptuous to say so. The foot are already taking down our tents. Could we explain to them that it would be better to wait a bit? There's water here, and a good many thirsty miles before we find more. Can the Turks ride over grass without raising a betraying cloud of dust? May I ask Taticius what he thinks?"

When asked Taticius shrugged his shoulders. But Bohemond noted that he was riding his fastest horse, and carried a bag of money tied to his belt.

Pictures were forming in Bohemond's mind, pictures so vivid that it was hard to grasp that they were not memories of something that had already happened. He saw knights, charging across the boundless rolling plain until their sobbing horses came to a stand and Turks shot them down at leisure. He saw the wretched foot and non-combatants, separated from their natural protectors, scurrying in aimless panic as the Turks rode in to sabre them. That was what Alexius had prophesied. That was what would happen before sunset of this very day.

Just as clearly he saw the way out. Cross-bows shot harder and straighter than any horseman's arrows. But the man with a cross-bow must feel safe while he wound his cumbersome machine. The guy-ropes of a tent ought to halt any charging horse. Western mail, especially with a shield before it, was proof against Turkish arrows. If the knights would consent to fight on foot their vulnerable horses might be hidden.

If only he were in command of disciplined soldiers, as a Greek general in the old days commanded obedient troops. But these pilgrims were volunteers, not even vassals doing their feudal duty; and he was only one among a group of equal Counts who advised rather than commanded them.

Urgently he caught Duke Robert by the arm. "If the Turks attack today we shall be in for a stiff fight. But I know what we ought to do. It's not what we do usually. Follow my advice and your men will follow you. Let's try to get the whole army to act as one unit. Today I shall command, but that's only because I have already made up my mind. Next time it may be you, and I shall obey you. But there must be a supreme commander. Will you order your men to leave the tents standing as a barrier against Turkish horse?"

"If you say so, my dear fellow," the Duke answered easily. "Since you have views and I have none let's do as you say. I came here to fight the infidel and I don't much mind how I do it. When

I can get hold of a messenger I shall tell my boys to leave their tents standing."

The casual council of war was already breaking up. They had encamped for the night among the grassy hills just west of ruined Dorylaeum. It had been agreed, without any formal vote, that the whole army should move by the southern of the three roads which divided here. Since no one had suggested delay the poorer pilgrims were already loading the baggage and striking the pavilions of their lords. They had learned one fact from the local Greeks, and were proud of their knowledge: that it was wise to march at sunrise and rest during the great heat of the afternoon.

Robert of Flanders had overhead the conversation. His mind was quicker than the Duke's. "You want to use the tents as an obstacle against a Turkish charge? It's not our kind of fighting, and anyway you are too late. With a different kind of army it might be a good idea. But you know the old saying: 'Order, counter-order, disorder.' Look, there's my pavilion coming down. If some of us halt while others press on the pilgrimage will spread over miles of road. We must march all together. But I'll tell my men to keep well closed up, and if there's a battle I shall follow your advice. Perhaps the Turks won't attack until tomorrow, though I agree that their scouts ride as though there were an attack coming."

Within an hour the pilgrimage had stretched out into column of route. Ox-drawn waggons and pack-animals plodded along the narrow paved road, and with them the countless women and children of the poorer pilgrims. Spearmen and cross-bows guarded the long train of non-combatants, and all the knights rode in one body at the head.

The rear of the column was just leaving the old camp site when a great roaring came from the hills to the north. Taticius cantered up to Bohemond, which was quicker than explaining through his interpreter.

"Turkish kettledrums, the things my people use instead of trumpets to hearten them for battle. But never in my life have I heard so many, not even when the whole horde of the Seljouks drove my father within the Empire. See, those are their standards on the brow of the hill. Horse-tail after horse-tail. I could count them and guess at their numbers, but now there's no time. This is it! The greatest battle since Manzikert! By nightfall there will be heaps of dead men. Make sure there are plenty of infidels among them."

"Will you be leaving us?" inquired Bohemond.

"My Turcopoles are off, and I don't blame them. They say they will fetch help from the other column behind you. Of course no one will understand them, or believe them. You must send Frankish messengers at once—and get those tents pitched."

"But you will stay?"

"Blame my handsome nose. I can't mingle with the infidel like my followers. My head is famous in these parts, and the King of the Turks will pay generously for it. I stay. Now do get those tents pitched, and the horses under cover. If you can keep your men in line some of us may see another dawn."

Bohemond spoke briefly to the knights of Apulia. "Gentlemen, the enemy seems to be all round us. Hold hard until I tell you to move. I must get the tents pitched. Count Tancred will command you until I return."

The non-combatant pilgrims were excited, but not yet frightened; for the knights stood between them and the Turks. They were glad to here definite orders, and eager to carry them out. The servants hoisted tents and stretched a maze of guy-ropes along the ground. Some cross-bows took station among the tents, others moved up to join the knights. Women and clerks unloaded the waggons and drove beasts to shelter behind them. The more active women volunteered to carry water to the knights and their horses in the front line. Already the sun was hot, and by midday it would be much hotter.

All the non-combatants, without distinction of race, willingly obeyed Bohemond. His height made him unmistakable, everyone knew who he was, and no other great lord was issuing conflicting orders. He sent back a patrol of well-mounted troopers to beg urgent help from Count Raymond. The south French ought to be about a day's march to the west, but they might have caught up a bit; anyway knights could gallop twenty miles in a couple of hours if they left their foot behind. The Turks seemed to be attacking from the north, though their numbers overlapped both Christian flanks. Pools and marshy streams covered the south, the Christian rear. The western Turkish wing seemed puzzled by the tents and unwilling to close. If the troopers were lucky they might get away safely.

As Bohemond galloped back to his knights he saw in imagination thousands of little figures riding over the rolling grassland. The Turks would not charge, they would shoot. The cross-bows would damage them. Then he recalled that Turkish arrows would not fit into the western machines. The cross-bows would be helpless when their quivers were empty. He must go among them and make sure they aimed carefully. If he were alive tomorrow he would set the smiths to making waggon loads of spare bolts. He should have thought of it earlier.

A Turkish arrow could not kill a mailed knight. But it could kill his horse, unless he dismounted and stood before it. Would knights do that? Normans, perhaps; but the French volunteers would charge out against their tormentors. The line would waver. As men were killed the survivors would close up, round the banners of their lords. Once the line broke Turks would get in behind and hamstring the horses. A Frank might be a match for five Turks, but a score of them could get him down and cut his throat as he lay on the ground. With his left elbow Bohemond felt the hilt of his great sword. Turks would be dead before that hung as a trophy in some infidel tent.

By the time he reached his knights he was smiling cheerfully. A leader must always appear gay and confident. But he was also pleased at what he saw. For once, the Normans of Apulia were doing as they had been told.

His men stood motionless in a solid line. Some knights had dismounted, and every horse was shielded by a footman of some kind, cross-bow or spearman or dismounted knight. On the right of his line the Normans of Normandy stood in the same formation. On the extreme right Robert of Flanders, that intelligent captain, had curved back his right wing to face the outflanking Turks. The left wing was anchored to the camp, the rear was guarded by the stream. Now all they had to do was to stand firm until the Turks charged or until night fell, whichever should happen first.

Three hours later even the most conscientious leader could not smile to encourage his men. So far neither side had won or lost, but the pilgrims were suffering much more than the Turks. Perhaps the noise was as unpleasant as anything else. Every battlefield is noisy, but here the sounds were unfamiliar. The thudding of the kettledrums never ceased. The main Turkish line stood two hundred yards away, but bands of archers galloped by at very close range. They rode from east to west, so that they might shoot in comfort from the near side of their horses; and all the time they gabbled in high outlandish voices.

Sometimes a cross-bow brought down a Turk or a Turkish pony. The best shot of all hit an infidel in the thigh and killed pony and rider together. When Bohemond saw this he inquired for the man's name, and promised him a reward after victory was won. But the pilgrims had few bolts left, and the Turks rode so close that they were past in a flash.

Little groups of knights had disobeyed orders and tried to chase away their assailants. That always led to disaster. Ringed round by archers, their horses were shot down; the few knights who struggled back on foot had been horribly gashed in the face and legs by the razor-sharp Turkish sabres. Few got back. While they lay under their dead horses the Turks, quick to discover the weak points in unfamiliar armour, stabbed them in the throat or under the skirts of their mail. The sun was high, the dust-cloud thick, and Frankish mail felt desperately hot and heavy.

Three spearmen left their station in the front line and stumbled towards the camp. Bohemond, dismounted, strode after them. The man he caught by the shoulder went back to his duty, but the others got away. A dismounted knight looked longingly over his shoulder. In a slight lull in the din Bohemond bellowed: "Hold fast, gentlemen. Here's a new war-cry. Trust in God and end the day rich. Pass it down the line. It's true. When we have broken the Turkish charge we shall pillage their camp."

A woman splashed water over his head. He was surprised not to see a cloud of steam. As she recognised him she called: "My lord, send some knights to the camp. In a few minutes the Turks will break in, and all the children will be martyred." He knew her voice. She was not a common woman of the camp. She was a waiting lady who looked after the two small children of the lady Godvere, the Norman wife of Baldwin of Boulogne. A waiting lady would know something of warfare. Her warning must be taken seriously.

Here was a mounted Christian. He must be ordered to get off his horse like everyone else. Oh no, it was good old Taticius who did not take orders from any Frank. With his Turkish bow and an unlimited supply of enemy arrows he had been busy since the battle began; though he had to keep carefully behind the front line unless he wanted every archer on both sides to shoot at him.

"Taticius, see what's happening in the camp. I haven't time to go there on foot, and if I mount everyone who sees me will panic. Tell me if they need help there."

"Sorry, but I can't get near the camp. Turkish ponies are floundering among all the guy-ropes, and I don't want to be killed by a Christian cross-bow. That's what I came from the left flank to tell you. I can say it without spreading alarm, since you are the only Frank who understands Greek. In about half an hour the camp will be overrun. Perhaps that's the best way. In their hurry to get at your rear the Turks will kill the non-combatants. It's better that they should be killed while the knights are still fighting, better than leaving them alive for the slave-market. Whoa, pony. I've done enough riding for today."

Taticius rammed his bow into its case on the saddle. As he slipped off the pony's back he crossed himself in the Greek fashion, and then drew his sabre.

"So it's come to that?" Bohemond sighed. "I suppose it's my fault, though I still don't see what I should have done different. All the same, keep your pony. When the Turks get round behind us I shall tell my knights to mount. We like to end a battle on horseback, you know. It's considered a mark of good breeding. And we may corner a few infidels against the stream behind us. So far we have killed very few of them."

Taticius slipped as he grabbed at the dangling reins of his pony. He put one hand to the ground to save himself, and then stared at it intently. Then he bent his head right down beside the hand. As he stood erect he was smiling all over his face.

"A Frank wouldn't feel it, but I can. A throbbing. Big horses, ridden hard. I think this fight is just beginning."

"Count Raymond," whispered Bohemond with an answering grin. He beckoned to his trumpeter.

"Blow, 'Get mounted.' Blow it three times. Afterwards say a Paternoster to get your breath back. Then blow, 'Charge' until you burst. Here's a gold bezant. It's my last, but if I have timed this wrong money will soon be of no use to me."

As the first call rang out there was a bustle all down the line. Other trumpets took it up. As Bohemond swung himself into the saddle he kept his eyes on the skyline. Most knights would have considered rescue a happy ending, but he was gambling the lives of all the pilgrims on complete victory. If the Turks were driven off they would come back again tomorrow. They must be caught by a simultaneous charge of the whole army while they were still too close to disengage.

Here was the first sound of the "Charge". It was a long call, and Bohemond had seldom heard its last note; usually it was drowned by the thunder of galloping hoofs.

Over there, just behind the camp, were the long wriggling banners of Toulouse and Provence. As he pushed his horse through the front rank he saw far to the right the banners of Lorraine and Boulogne. Best of all, as he cleared his lance from the body of a Turkish archer, he saw the stiff gold and silver banner of the legate, right behind the infidel line. Adhemar, that warlike Bishop, had taken the enemy in the rear. Everything had worked out according to plan; according to God's plan, of course, for no sinful Frank could have brought off such a perfectly timed converging attack.

CHAPTER VIII

Which Road to Jerusalem?

─────────────────────★─────────────────────

The united army of the pilgrimage rested for two days beside Dorylaeum, to recover from the strain of the famous victory. It was decided to continue the march in one body for greater safety; though the division in the council of leaders was even greater than before, since there were now only two rivals for the supreme command. All the Normans and their companions in the first column swore that Bohemond was the most cunning warleader since Alexander; everyone who had galloped with the second column attributed the entire victory to the skill of Count Raymond.

A wonderful victory it had been. Many Turks got away, for the Frankish horses were already exhausted when the pursuit began; but the infidels were utterly demoralized. They did not attempt to defend their camp, though as homeless nomads they carried all their wealth in their tents. Local peasants reported gleefully that for many miles to the east the road was lined with Turkish ponies, ridden to death by their terrified masters. The spoil had been even richer than the gifts of the faithless Alexius.

But when the pilgrims marched out from Dorylaeum, on 3rd July 1097, they were beyond the edge of the known world. Taticius reported formally, through his interpreter, that he knew no more of the country ahead than any Frank.

"This map shows the road, and the towns, and the cisterns set up by past Emperors for their troops at the end of each day's march. But I'm told none of this remains. The road is broken up, the towns are deserted, the cisterns are dry. This country was always short of water, and in less than thirty years the Turks have made it into a desert. I advise you to strike south-east, marching fast and carrying as much water as you can. Beyond the desert you will find Christian Armenians. You already have Armenian exiles with you. They can tell you more than I can."

These Armenian exiles were a subject of great interest, though for lack of interpreters few pilgrims could speak with them. During the midday halt after they left Dorylaeum, Tancred discussed what he knew with his uncle.

"I am more alone than ever before," he began. "My brother William was killed, charging with Count Hugh and his Frenchmen. He should have stayed among the Normans, who care for their comrades. You and I fought for five hours, and never got a scratch. He charged for about ten minutes at the end of the day. A Turkish arrow opened a vein in his leg, and because no Frenchman stopped to help him he bled to death. It's the end he wanted when he left home, so I mustn't complain. His vow is fulfilled. I can kill enough infidels for two, to make up for his loss. It's because I want to go off on my own, killing infidels, that I came to see you. Can you spare me some knights if I leave the line of march?"

"My dear boy, a great many knights will follow the hero Tancred whatever I say. But you set a bad example. We shall never free Jerusalem unless we remain in one great army. What is this idea of yours, anyway?"

"I have been talking to that Armenian who speaks Arabic. Far off to the south-east, but more or less on the direct road to Antioch, lie some walled towns. One of them is Tarsus, where St. Paul was born. The burgesses in these towns are Christians, Greek or Armenian. Turks hold the castles, but there are not very many of them. If a Christian lord were to take one of these castles the Armenians would fight for him and the Greeks would pay him their taxes."

"But suppose the Christian lord had vowed to liberate Jerusalem? How could he fulfil his vow?"

"As far as I am concerned no date was set. I shall never go back to Apulia. As lord of Tarsus I could one day help to liberate Jerusalem."

"I see, but it's all in the future. Look here, young Tancred. At this moment the army of the pilgrimage is pretty well divided into two. All the Normans want to follow me, all the south French want to follow Raymond. That's much worse than it was before the battle, when we had at least a dozen rival leaders. Don't make any move on your own, I beg you. If you go there will be a real split. Is any other lord planning to take over these Armenian towns?"

"Yes. That's why I don't want to wait too long. These Armenian exiles are the guests of Count Baldwin, the youngest of the Boulogne brothers. How they talk to him I don't know. I suppose he has found one of them who speaks Greek, and of course he has Greek interpreters. I must move before Baldwin, though I'll wait as long as I can. Is it really true that the Pope started this pilgrimage without making any arrangement for the leadership? I'm quite sure Count Raymond was not appointed leader, whatever he says now. If there is no true leader, then I am not deserting my lord if I go off on my own."

"I have heard different rumours, but I agree with you that the Pope never appointed a leader. Like everyone else, he took it for granted that we had one. The Greek Emperor wanted help from the west. We came to help him. He ought to be leading us now. I still can't decide why he was afraid to take it on. He's no coward, as I know to my cost. If he thinks the campaign is hopeless why did he suggest it to the Pope in the first place? It doesn't make sense. Yet everything Alexius proposes makes sense, from his point of view."

"What about this? It isn't my idea, it came from my bright Armenian friend. Alexius wishes to restore the old boundaries of his Empire. He doesn't want Jerusalem. As things stands he never has any trouble from his Bishops. One of his titles is Isapostolos, equal to the Apostles. He appoints and dismisses his Patriarch. He makes new rules for his Church. The Patriarch of a Christian Jerusalem won't like that, and the Emperor won't be able to control two Patriarchs at once, three if you include Antioch. If he were under the ban of Jerusalem, as the King of France is under the ban of Rome, his crown would sit uneasily."

"I never thought of that. Of course your Armenian friend hates the Greeks even more than we do. Still, it explains things. Do you see what it means? Alexius doesn't stay at home because he thinks we can liberate Jerusalem on our own, or because he is neutral in the Holy War. He actively wishes us to fail, because we are a danger to him. To think that when we met I offered him my help! But Taticius isn't in this. He's an honest old veteran."

"Perhaps. He may be guiding us the wrong way on purpose. But you agree that we have no genuine leader, and that any pilgrim may take what measures seem best to him so long as he does not harm the common cause?" Tancred was persistent and single-minded.

"You owe no fealty to any man. But I am your mother's brother, and I suppose the most eminent of all the Hauteville knights. I ask you, out of family affection, not to leave us just yet. We very nearly lost that last battle and there are still a great many Turks in Anatolia. Let us all march in one body at least until we reach these Armenian towns."

"I'll promise that much, unless Count Baldwin leaves us first. I'll even promise to obey your commands in battle, though it is more than my duty. Would you like an oath?"

"Not from you. I heard you promise."

It was the right thing to say. Tancred went off in a glow of happiness.

The journey was even worse than Taticius had foretold. Throughout July and the beginning of August they struggled through a waterless and empty desert, in greater heat than any Frank had experienced. The map showed villages, ploughlands, cisterns; thirty years ago the Empire had drawn rich taxes and stout recruits from this province. Taticius explained that what Turks liked was an open grassy plain where their sheep might graze. That was what they had tried to produce here; but lack of springs and too much salt in the ground had instead produced a wilderness.

The pilgrims managed somehow. At dawn there was dew on the scrub; to chew a leafy bough would moisten the mouth, and they were all too thirsty to feel hungry. But horses died by the score.

The loss of a warhorse meant, at least for the time being, the loss of a knight. They had captured some Turkish ponies, and if ever they reached Syria horses would be plentiful; but native horses were smaller than those from the west, and they must be trained to charge straight. Every time Bohemond saw a dying beast on the ground he felt as though he were losing blood from his own body.

He plodded on foot at the head of the Apulians, leading his last remaining horse which bore his mail. In this heat no knight could march dismounted in his mail; some piled their mail on the baggage waggons, even throwing away good plunder to make room for it. That was better than nothing, since western mail could not be replaced in the east and there was plenty more plunder waiting for them in Jerusalem. But Bohemond considered it unmilitary. If an alarm came he did not wish to run to the baggage, or fight in his tunic.

Only Taticius and his pony did not feel the heat. About half of the Turcopoles had rejoined the pilgrimage after the great victory; the rest had either joined the Turks or been killed as they tried to do so. At present Turcopoles were valued scouts, all the more useful because they would certainly fall back on the Franks at the first sign of the foe. Little Golden Nose rode easily beside the plodding Bohemond.

"Can't you lighten that burden of mail?" he asked anxiously. "In an emergency like this my people would throw away their cuirasses. Anyone who keeps shield and sabre can rob an armed corpse after the next battle."

"That's no good to us," answered Bohemond. "Frankish mail is made in one piece, from head to shins. No knight would dare to charge without it, and if we can't charge we can't fight. I suppose the Emperor knew this desert would finish us even if we beat the infidels in the first battle. That's why he went home."

"Come, you mustn't say that to me," Taticius replied sharply. "Other pilgrims say it, but they can't say it in Greek so it doesn't bother me. I am the Emperor's faithful servant, and he would not send me to my death. No one in the city knew that this desert existed. Shall I show you the map once more?"

"What's the use? Here is the desert, and here we are in the middle of it. Can you make a guess about how much more of it we have to walk through?"

"Not a guess. I know. Look, here on the map is Iconium. Only a year ago that was an inhabited town, and there are streams and orchards in the suburbs. Even if the infidels have killed all the Christians they can't dry up the water. Make for it as fast as you can, and then you can rest the surviving horses. Besides, if you push on hard you may kill Count Raymond. I hear he is very ill."

"Another reason why I can't hurry. If he dies while I lead the army everybody will say I murdered him. At least he is dying decently, of fever and hardship. He didn't go off to fight bears when he ought to be fighting infidels."

"My dear Bohemond, you ought to serve the Emperor. You don't think like a Frank. Of course Duke Godfrey had to fight the bear when his men had found it for him. That's one of the things I like about Franks. Turks have the same point of view. In fact the two peoples are so alike that they must descend from a common stock. After all, if Duke Godfrey is gravely wounded the bear was not only killed but eaten. No dispute about which of them won the fight."

The pilgrimage struggled on. Bohemond noted that knights, who had eaten well all their lives, could stand starvation just a little better than the poor. Thousands died, but few of them were noted warriors. If he could find horses to mount his knights the army would be as strong as before Dorylaeum.

Just in time to avert complete disaster they reached the valley of Iconium. The town was almost empty; a few squatters reported that the Turks had driven off all the inhabitants they could catch just before the pilgrims arrived. But even Turks could not make a desert of the fruitful, well-watered valley. The pilgrims settled down for a long stay, to give the sick a chance to recover.

As Bohemond lay in green grass, in the shade of peach trees, he tried to make plans for the future. The desert lay behind them. Not far off to the south and east were settlements of warlike Armenians. They had passed a barrier which Alexius had considered impassable.

Their next stop must be Antioch, an indispensable base for the liberation of the Holy Land. There were several roads, though all were barred by high mountains. They might go where they wished. The Turks must be utterly cowed. Otherwise they would not have abandoned this precious valley, with a defensible walled town in its centre. No one could tell him very much about the Armenians, newcomers who had settled in these parts after the Turks had driven out the Greeks. What mattered most of all was whether the Armenians bred good horses, with which he could remount his knights.

The army would go wherever he decided. Fortune had placed him, for the moment, in supreme command. That would not last much longer. Duke Godfrey was recovering from the wounds received on that frivolous bear hunt. But though Godfrey might be a rival he was not an adversary. They could work together.

Count Raymond, if he lived, would be a greater obstacle. He opposed anything suggested by Bohemond, and most unfairly he had gained prestige by his part in winning the battle at Dory-laeum. All he had done was to gallop towards the enemy, which was the duty of any good knight; but Bohemond had persuaded his followers to dismount, and then induced them to stand firm under the Turkish arrows for the better part of a long hot day. Of course the Normans alone had won the· battle, and the south French had merely helped them to drive the defeated foe from the field. But public opinion makes these odd mistakes.

It would be best for all concerned if Count Raymond should now fulfil his vow to liberate Jerusalem or die in the attempt. He was a very sick man. He had been anointed, so he must be in danger of death; but these south Frenchmen were cautious, wishing to be prepared for all eventualities. It would be just like Count Raymond to get well after all.

Then little bow-legged Taticius bustled up with exciting news. "Another horde of Turks has come out to bar the way. They are not Seljouks, the people you beat at Dorylaeum. This is the Danishmend horde, and they have never met Franks before. They are gathering to the east of us, outside Heraclea. Here it is on the map. I know I'm right. My scouts have seen them."

"Eastward, and on the main road? That helps me to make up my mind. We march there as soon as we are fit to move. But why should they bar the way? Forgive me, but it doesn't seem to me the way Turks usually fight."

"It isn't. We like to attack from the flank or the rear. We don't usually hold a river crossing. My guess is that these people don't want to bring on a battle, they want to persuade you to take the southern road, through Cilicia. They aren't interested in what happens to the infidels of Syria. The Danishmends graze their sheep in what this map calls Cappadocia, all this mountainous region south of the Black Sea. They don't like strangers marching through it. They are a famous horde, you know, supposed to be even fiercer than the Seljouks. It might be a good thing to avoid them. You can get to Antioch just as well by the southern route."

"I expect we could, but we must think of the pilgrims who will come after us. No road may be barred to Frankish knights, and the sooner all the Turks know that the better for Christendom. I won't ravage their land, because that would mean marching north, away from Jerusalem. But if they come out and challenge us to fight we shall just knock them over in passing."

Taticius shrugged. "I suppose that is the right thing, if you enjoy fighting."

Within a few days Count Raymond took a turn for the better. Once his fever had broken recovery was certain, and to Bohemond's annoyance it was speedy. Duke Godfrey was also well enough to attend the council of leaders, so that once more the pilgrims were led by a wrangling triumvirate. Because Bohemond has said so often that the Emperor had deliberately sent them to their doom Count Raymond was now a stout supporter of the Greeks, making excuses for everything they had done. Duke Godfrey held the balance. He was landless, and by now penniless, but all the pilgrims respected his birth, his honesty and his courage. Luckily he in his turn respected the military skill of Bohemond, who could usually persuade the army to do as he advised; but Bohemond had to argue and persuade, he could not issue commands.

When the pilgrims were ready to move they found they had reached the end of the desert and could once more plan the day's march on the Greek map.

Before noon on a bright sunny day they sighted the Turkish horde. The weather was cooler, and the army reasonably fit. Godfrey, Raymond and Bohemond drew aside from the dust of the march to examine the enemy position.

"A Turkish army waiting to be attacked," murmured Godfrey.

"No attempt at surprise. We ought to be able to deal with them."

"Let's show that we can be as careful and thorough in our tactics as the Greeks," said Raymond. "Those Turks must have a ravine or some kind of obstacle in front of them. They want us to charge them, and therefore we won't. We'll send forward our foot. While cross-bows and Turks exchange arrows the knights make a wide sweep to the right, cross the ravine out of sight, and come in on the flank. We shall catch the lot of them."

"Unless they scatter our foot and plunder our baggage before the knights arrive," Bohemond answered. "I can't see a ravine. There may be no obstacle. We won't use elaborate tactics against these men, let's just scare them to death. I'll charge their centre as hard as I can. If that doesn't work it will be time to call up the cross-bows."

"I'm not really fit for a charge of that kind," Raymond objected. "My doctor says so, and I don't feel up to it. My way will be slower, but in the end we shall kill more infidels."

"Your way will kill more Turks, if they wait for us," said Godfrey. "But we haven't come here to kill Turks. There are too many of them, anyway. Life just isn't long enough. It's better to frighten them so badly that they don't interfere while we are liberating Jerusalem. I prefer Bohemond's plan. I'm not yet fit either. Raymond and I will ride gently in the rear rank, just to show that all the leaders are in agreement. Come on, Bohemond, show us how it should be done. Never before have I seen a charge from the outside, so to speak. I've always been in it, or riding to meet it."

"Taticius," Bohemond called in rapid, confident and ungrammatical Greek. "I want to knock over the king of those infidels. Can you spot him?"

"In the middle of their line. He has a banner beside his horse-tails, and the kettledrummers ride just behind him."

Bohemond and Tancred began to muster all the knights who still rode sound horses. They were pitifully few.

Even these horses were so weak that the squadron advanced at a gentle trot, until they were almost within arrow range. Now they could all see that the ground stretched level between them and the Turks; who were actually preparing to charge them, instead of drawing their bows. Bohemond called, "*Deus Vult*," the war-cry common to the whole pilgrimage.

For just a few seconds it seemed that there would be a splendid head-on collision, the kind of fight that every Frankish knight enjoyed. The Turks came on bravely, making a tremendous noise. They shouted and waved their sabres, their drums banged away, their ponies neighed, their holy men in the rear began a high quavering chant. Their king, gleaming in silk and furs, stood high in his short stirrups.

He saw galloping against him two huge men, Bohemond and Tancred. Their horses were twice as big as Turkish ponies; behind their long shields appeared only fierce eyes glaring beside the steel noseguard; two long lances pointed unwavering at his breast. The Danishmend jerked at his pony's bit; he turned it about while it stood on its hind legs. All his men followed as he galloped off to safety.

Bohemond nearly caught him, because his horse was already at full stretch as the Turk started. A gallant drummer saved his lord. His pony was knocked over with a great clangour of kettledrums, and the rider at once trampled to pulp under charging hoofs. But Bohemond's horse checked to jump the fallen pony. A moment later the Turks were drawing away from the weary horses of the pilgrims.

"I hope some of them have been genuinely scared to death," said Bohemond to Godfrey as the column re-formed. "Apart from that I don't think we hurt a dozen men."

"Does it matter? They have nothing that we wish to take from them. The Greek Emperor can attend to them, while he rescues their Christian subjects. Surely it's enough that Turks dare not face our charge. Perhaps they won't hold Antioch against us."

That evening the pilgrims rested comfortably in the battered but still inhabited town of Heraclea.

In the morning the leaders met in council, principally to decide on their route to Antioch. It was already September, four months since they had left Constantinople, a full year since the north Frenchmen had left home. It would take them at least another year to liberate Jerusalem and ride back. They were growing impatient.

Taticius appeared with his interpreter and his famous bundle of dog-eared maps. Not far to the south of Heraclea lay the rich and fruitful province of Cilicia, inhabited by warlike Armenian Christians. From Tarsus a well-known road led to Antioch. It was the obvious way to go, but Taticius advised against it.

The only way into Cilicia from the north was by the famous Cilician Gates, a narrow pass which had been deadly to many armies; the only way out, from Tarsus to Antioch, was by the almost equally narrow Syrian Gates. Whereas if they travelled northward for about a hundred miles they would join a good Greek road which led down, by an easy passage through the mountains, to reach Antioch from the north. That was the road used by Greek merchants in the old days, when Antioch was a Greek fortress.

As soon as the interpreter had finished Count Raymond jumped to his feet. "I agree with our guide. What's an extra hundred miles in a year-long journey? Besides, I've had enough of narrow passes. Before we reached Durazzo my men came through the mountains of Sclavonia, and the mountaineers did us great harm. When a savage stands on top of a cliff and rolls down great boulders a mailed knight cannot catch him. We have thousands of unarmed followers, women and children. Our stores and wealth are carried in ox-drawn waggons. We must take the easier road."

At once Tancred replied. "It's enough for me that the Greeks recommend the northern road. When have the Greeks done us anything but harm? I say we must go south. The way to Cilicia may be dangerous, but at present the infidels are too frightened to hold it against us. If I go with a few friends and occupy this pass, will the rest of you come after me? It will be safe, safe enough even for the mighty Count of Toulouse. The infidels may rally before we are ready to use the second pass, into Syria. Then we go by sea. Tarsus is a port, or was. If there are no ships there now we can wait while they build some."

"A voyage is a troublesome business," put in the Duke of Normandy, without bothering to rise. "Embarking the horses . . . not that we have many horses . . . let's go north. . . ." His voice trailed away.

"I'm for the long way round, if that's what Taticius recommends." Duke Godfrey was on his feet, to make sure everyone saw which side he supported. "We can't usefully discuss country none of us have seen. By hearsay the northern route sounds safest. What do you think, Count Bohemond?"

"I agree with Count Raymond." Bohemond also stood, to notice more easily the gasp of relief and amazement which greeted these simple words.

He could not say what had decided him. He trusted Taticius, but he distrusted Greeks in general; so that more or less cancelled out. He did not like the idea of a dangerous pass; he was sure the pilgrims would get through it to Jerusalem, but it would be troublesome for small parties going home after fulfilling their vows. At bottom he was trying an experiment: would Count Raymond be friendly when they were both on the same side, or was he such a determined rival that he would have second thoughts just to disagree with him?

"Count Robert of Flanders? Agreed? Count Hugh? Is anyone against? My lord legate?" Duke Godfrey collected the voices like a skilled chairman. Any decision was better than a long debate, in their total ignorance of local geography. It was notorious that the Bishop of Le Puy never intervened in a military discussion, and never gave an opinion unless he was asked.

"I have no objections, gentlemen. I do not presume to direct the movements of the army. Do both these routes lie within the limits of the Empire? Perhaps it is time to remind you of the oaths you swore in Constantinople. Soon we shall be liberating flourishing cities."

"No bother about that," said Raymond quickly. "Since both Heraclea and Antioch lie within the Empire, so must all the country in between."

"Then that's settled. Tomorrow we march north to what's this place, Mazacha. All fortresses we take must be held for the Greek Emperor. That's all, gentlemen. Issue orders accordingly." Godfrey hurried away before anyone else could begin a speech. Some of the lesser Counts snatched at any chance to address the assembled nobility of Christendom.

So that's what Raymond is after, Bohemond said to himself. He doesn't mind which way we go, he will even help Alexius to whom he would not give his oath when it was really needed for the welfare of the whole pilgrimage. He only wants to make sure that I don't get Antioch, though it was promised to me by Alexius himself. Only because I defeated the whole Danishmend horde with my single lance, when he said he was too sick to charge. There's jealousy for you.

He knew that he himself was being petty and jealous. Raymond had indeed been sick. About the Duchy of Antioch nothing had been finally settled, though the question had been discussed privately. The trouble was that he, Bohemond, who saw his way clearly through every difficulty, who could plan a campaign and picture a battle before it was fought, was beginning to be lost in a fog.

Some great lords were happy to live in a fog all their lives. Duke Robert of Normandy, for example. He spent any money he could lay his hands on, he hit any foe who came within reach, he gorged when food was plentiful and starved without complaint if there were none; he took what came and did not try to alter Fate. His brother had stolen a great Kingdom from under his nose, and Robert had not even noticed until it was too late.

But the Hautevilles, and Bohemond in particular, made long-term plans and stuck to them. Once he had planned to conquer the whole Greek Empire. With his father, who had risen from nothing to be the mighty lord of Apulia, he had attacked the Venetian navy thrice in one week because the Venetians had to be removed. When the situation had changed, not because of any weakness of will, he had planned a partnership with Alexius which would free all Christendom from the Turks. A Hauteville did not give up just because his goal seemed to be out of reach; he saw his aim clear and stuck to it, as Guiscard had stuck to his entrenchments during the famous siege of Bari.

Now he was puzzled. He did not know what to do next. Alexius expected the pilgrims to fail; it was likely that he hoped they would fail. But he had given them Taticius, an honest man who did his best to help. At Constantinople Count Raymond had so hated the Greeks that he would not swear to serve Alexius; now he was an advocate of imperial claims in Anatolia. It didn't make sense. He must wait for the situation to clear.

Bohemond supped, as usual, in his own pavilion. They would march at dawn tomorrow, but by this stage of the long journey the servants had learned to pack everything at the last minute. The pavilion, even the chests and stools in it, were exactly as they had been in Thrace last autumn.

For supper there was local wine, new bread, and some of the salt pork infidels never stole. Tonight he would sleep dry and fed; tomorrow he would ride through strange lands. Why worry over the future? Why not take everything as it comes, like those boobies Duke Robert and Count Hugh? So far they had fared as well as any far-seeing Hauteville. They were all embarked on an endless pilgrimage. Let them wander day after day as Taticius or that feckless council of leaders should advise, until it pleased God to send them a pillar of cloud to guide them to Jerusalem.

Then Tancred burst in, and brought his mind back to politics. The boy was very angry. He must be heard with patience.

"Uncle," he stormed, "have you been blinded by that Greek trickster? Will you really march north to gain more fortresses for Alexius, when you know that Jerusalem lies to the southward? Even if you are so foolish they can't deceive me. In the morning I take the road for Tarsus, with any knights who will follow me. If you come too, with all the Normans of Apulia, we shall conquer the whole land. Even on my own I shall win a good fief, and perhaps reach Antioch before you. I came to tell you in good time, so that you won't try to stop me at the last minute."

"You should have said all this to the council. Golden Nose, by the way, isn't a Greek. He is a Christian Turk, and an honest man. The Emperor may be a scoundrel, but he has honourable servants. I think we have chosen the best road, but I can't stop you going by another. I won't come with you, because I have already given my word to the council. How many knights will follow you?"

"About eighty, I expect, and several hundred foot."

"Then if you get through that narrow pass you will be strong enough to take over Cilicia. The Emperor may try to take it from you afterwards. Don't come to open war with him if you can avoid it. Otherwise I have nothing to say. I wish you luck. It's just that we see the campaign differently."

Tancred felt disappointed. He had come along in expectation of a heart-warming family quarrel, and Bohemond seemed barely interested. "What will happen to Cilicia if we don't liberate it?" he asked belligerently.

"It will fall into our hands as soon as we hold Antioch," Bohemond answered. "You haven't studied that map properly. Cilicia faces the sea. In the old days Tarsus was a great port. Our great weakness is that there are no Frankish ships in these parts. When Antioch is ours Italian ships will come. Then the Armenians of Cilicia, who hate the Greeks, will ask us to rule them."

"Unless the Emperor grabs it."

"Yes, that is a problem. In the end who will be stronger, the Emperor or the pilgrimage? The pilgrimage is a much bigger thing then I expected when I joined it, bigger than you expected. We'll liberate Jerusalem. Then what? How many will stay? You will, I will. Count Raymond will, confound him. Who else? I have a feeling, something I can't prove, that there won't be room for both pilgrims and Emperor. But we must wait and see. The Empire is much stronger than most of these Franks suppose. It would be good to see the Greeks properly obedient to the Pope, and one Frankish realm from Jerusalem to Constantinople."

"Emperor Bohemond, eh? Well, why not? Time will show. So I go south with your good will? I'm glad. See you in Antioch, or in Heaven."

Next morning Tancred slipped off as quietly as he could. But a knight of his stature could not avoid notice. His adventure immediately became the talk of the pilgrims; before evening Baldwin of Boulogne had led another band towards Cilicia. Although Baldwin was the youngest and least of the Boulogne brothers his following greatly outnumbered Tancred's small mesnie.

CHAPTER IX

Armenian Discords

—————————————★—————————————

Bohemond trudged cautiously along the narrow trail, thankful that his temperate Armenian horse never tried to push him in the back. At a convenient turn in the road he looked behind at the long column of dismounted knights who followed in single file, each leading his horse. On the edge of such a precipice it would be suicide to ride.

It was hard to believe that the whole army of the pilgrimage had travelled this rocky path; but a glance into the depths brought confirmation. Dotted throughout the gorge were the remains of pack-animals and a few men; where the trail first narrowed, at the beginning of the pass, they had seen many abandoned waggons.

If this was the safe and easy road, what had happened to Tancred and Baldwin who had chosen the dangerous one? Or was Taticius, after all, a traitor who deliberately led the pilgrims to destruction? Bohemond began to distrust his own judgement of character, until with relief he found a simple explanation. The Emperor and all his servants were absurdly afraid of the Turks, but they were used to mountains. On this road there would be no danger of attack, since the peaks on either side were impassable. Thirty years ago the path must have been much wider, if it had really been the main caravan route between Antioch and the city. This must be a bad patch. Once they began to go downhill travelling would be easier.

They were certainly on the right road; the wreckage of the main pilgrimage proved it. For his present troubles he must blame only his foolish pride. Taticius had warned him that mailed knights

could not catch fleeing Turks. But it had seemed a splendid opportunity to demoralize the Turks even further.

The Turks were already demoralized. As the pilgrims approached the mountains from the south-west they had heard that
the Armenians of Placentia were beset by an infidel horde. That
horde, the same Danishmends who had already fled before Bohemond, had once again disputed the advance of the army. Again
they fled in disgraceful panic after a short fight. The pilgrims
nearly trapped the besiegers against the walls of Placentia; the
Turks barely escaped, and the rescued Armenians offered fresh
horses to their saviours. Bohemond led the knights of Apulia in
hot pursuit.

From a narrow military point of view that was the right course.
Once an enemy is in full retreat you must push him as far as he will
go, without giving him a chance to reorganize. But the Danishmends
fled north, and the road to Jerusalem led south-east. It had been
agreed that the main body of pilgrims should cross the mountains
while no enemy opposed them, and that Bohemond should follow
after. It was evident that their journey had been unpleasant.

Of course Bohemond had not caught the Turks. When he found
a deserted bivouac with its cooking-fires cold, and on the same
evening one of his fresh Armenian horses died of exhaustion, he
had given up the pursuit. On the return journey they had gone
slower. From the condition of the dead animals he passed he
guessed that he must be at least a week behind the main army.
He hoped that the council of leaders had not done anything
foolish while he was not there to advise them.

By nightfall his men were over the crest and the path had
widened into a steep wooded glen. They could camp in one body.
After Bohemond had seen to his own horse he inspected the
others before they were hobbled and turned out to graze. No
knight would shirk the care of his own horse, but some had rubbed
them down very clumsily. It was one of the many tasks every
gentleman learned in his youth, and never expected to practise
again after he had grown to be a knight. In Europe they would
have mounted grooms with them, or catch local peasants and
make them work for their betters; this glen was uninhabited.
Some knights ate biscuit and cold bacon; others, including Bohe-

mond, must fast until they caught up with the army. His wallet was not empty, but it held barley for his horse.

They slept huddled close together on the bare ground, for it was very cold. They had no fire because they had no servants. A gentleman might tend a horse, he might not cut firewood. It was a gloomy camp.

But next day things went better. Before midday they reached an Armenian village where the peasants gave them goats and wine, though they explained, by gestures, that the main army had already taken all the bread, Before sunset they found baggage-mules waiting for them and tents spread, under the direction of the Count of Blois.

Count Stephen embraced Bohemond. He seemed genuinely glad to see him.

"Did you catch those Turks? No? I thought you wouldn't. But it did occur to me that you and your knights would be very hungry. This was the worst stage of the march for us, though now we have bread in plenty. I know what it is to travel just behind a hungry army; it's happened to me more than once. But I have never travelled without any servants at all. Surely even the Holy War does not demand such extreme hardship? I was working out the supplies we should need—I manage my own abacus, you know. Suddenly it came home to me that you must be without provisions. So I brought back these pack-mules. Take your time and rest your horses. The army is waiting for you."

Bohemond thanked Count Stephen with genuine gratitude; at the same time he reflected on the curious character of that noble pilgrim. Stephen should never have been a Count; they ought to have made him a Bishop. Of course he must know what it was like to travel behind an army; very likely he had been just too late for several bloody battles. All the same, he could think straight and he thought of the welfare of others. Bohemond would have thought of a party of his own vassals, travelling on weary horses through a ravaged land; he would not have turned back to bring food to fellow-pilgrims to whom he had no responsibility. Stephen was not an inspiring leader in the charge, but they ought not to waste his unusual capacities. Perhaps the council of leaders might appoint him to superintend the fair division of supplies among the whole army? The honour of such an appointment would keep him happy, and that would be another good thing.

After Bohemond had given due thanks, promising to pay for the rations from the next plunder he acquired, he asked for the latest news of the campaign. "Has my nephew Tancred rejoined the march? I suppose he is well? Did Baldwin of Boulogne come with him?"

"Count Tancred is flourishing. A splendid young hero, though of course his size helps him. It's easier to be brave when you are a head taller than all your foes. Oh dear, I shouldn't say that to *you*. Forgive me. He didn't actually come back with Baldwin. It seems they had some sort of quarrel, though I don't know the rights of it so don't ask me for details. Anyway, Tancred's back. Baldwin hurried back to say good-bye to his wife. She died of sickness, poor thing; a noble lady and a true martyr of the Holy War. So now Baldwin is a widower. He's gone off again, to the eastward. He has all these shady Armenian friends, and the gossip is that he will marry some Armenian princess for her dowry. There, I ought not to repeat such rumours. Baldwin is a very good knight, and he was in floods of tears as they buried the lady Godvere. Your nephew Tancred is a very good knight also. In fact every pilgrim is a good knight. The wicked knights stayed at home. I only wish good knights could agree better among themselves."

"So Tancred has been quarrelling? I'll straighten that out when I meet him. He's a strange, headstrong boy, very sure of himself. But he's a gallant leader and an ardent pilgrim. I can usually make him see sense. In the end he was willing to take oath to Alexius, and when that fell through he scored off the Emperor quite neatly. Now let's sit in the shade, and while we eat you can tell me everything that's happened."

Gnawing at the inevitable lump of salt pork Bohemond returned to his questioning. "What did they do with Placentia after I left you? I hope we have an open road behind us, if anything goes wrong."

"Oh yes, Count Raymond thought of that too. He reminded us of our treaty with the Emperor, and that it would be dangerous to offend him while we were so far from home. So we decided to keep the terms of our oath to the letter, even though Alexius has withdrawn from the Holy War. Placentia had been within the Empire until the Turks came; we are bound to give it back to the Greeks as we gave back Nicaea. We looked round for a Greek to give it to, but we couldn't find one. Count Raymond suggested that we give it to Taticius, that nice Christian Turk with the golden nose. He was very pleased at the offer; but he explained that the Emperor had commanded him to march with us to Jerusalem. He dared not stay behind, even to govern a rich town. He proposed a compromise. He knew of a Frankish knight who had long been a faithful servant of the Emperor. This Frank could talk to us, he knew the customs of the west, and he would hold the town as though he were a western vassal of the Empire. That was a clever idea, don't you think? So we left this Frank in charge and crossed the mountains. A terrible journey."

"Yes, but who was the Frank? A pilgrim?"

"No, not a pilgrim. He has been in the Emperor's service for many years. I don't know when he joined us. After Nicaea, I should think, because I usually remember faces and he was a stranger. Not a man of very noble birth, naturally. I suppose he would rank as a knight, the kind of knight who hires out his sword for wages. His name is Peter, but I can't remember the rest of it. At least, I do remember, but I must be remembering wrong. The lord Peter of the Alps? Would anyone call himself so? There is no fief 'of the Alps'. But some knights choose rather grand titles when they live among strangers."

"You've got it very nearly right, my dear Stephen," said Bohemond with a chuckle. "Peter of Aulps, not Peter of the Alps. I knew him in my youth. I heard he had taken service with the Emperor. I should like to meet him again, just to stick his head on a pole in memory of the old days."

"Dear me, is he an enemy of yours?"

"Not really an enemy. Merely a recreant who sold himself to the Greeks while he was fighting under my banner. He tried to betray me, but my other knights wouldn't follow him. That was years ago, when I was helping my father to invade Romania. I suppose he has been in Greek service ever since. Since the pilgrimage arrived he must have led a hunted life, dodging about near our army and yet keeping out of my sight. If it wasn't such a frightful pass over the mountains I should like to take my Apulians back to Placentia. But we must put the welfare of the pilgrimage before our own frivolous pleasures. Well, well, Peter of Aulps in charge of the only road back to safety. What a pretty little piece of Greek planning."

"I'm sure it's nothing more than a mischance. Old Golden Nose is an honest man."

"Golden Nose is honest, but his master isn't. Alexius fixed this. Probably he fixed it before we left Nicaea. Just an extra precaution. He doesn't want me near his city, so he makes an extra drawbridge out of Peter. But doesn't it look pretty? The pilgrims give back his fortress to Alexius, and in return Alexius installs a Frankish knight. A compromise that should please everyone. All done so neatly, while I am away chasing Turks. I wonder how they put it to Golden Nose? 'Put this Peter in command of a strong fortress, but it must be done while Count Bohemond is away.' An order that must have puzzled Taticius."

"Well, it's done now, and unless you go to war with the Greeks you can't undo it." Count Stephen was at once shocked and thrilled by this glimpse of Greek intrigue. "Pilgrims are forbidden to make war on fellow-Christians, and I suppose even Alexius is a Christian of sorts. Now Peter the recreant is anchored. He can't follow us to stab you in the back. Anyway, you may be imagining things. Alexius may have forgotten that Peter once betrayed you. Now when all your men have eaten I suggest you bed down early. From now on it's a good track. By tomorrow night you will be back with the army."

Bohemond found his pavilion standing as before. His servants had everything in order, and a hot bath waiting for him. There was bread for his knights and fodder for their horses. The pilgrims were encamped in a pleasant valley, amid a friendly population of warlike Armenians whom the Turks had never plundered; though even these warlike Armenians thought it prudent to pay tribute to the infidels of Syria. That was an added excitement. The pilgrimage had traversed Anatolia from end to end, and now was almost on the threshold of the Holy Land. Henceforth there would be hard fighting, but no more of those terrible marches among deserts and

146

mountains. The infantry twisted new bowstrings out of unfamiliar silk, the knights tried out their new Armenian horses. They were almost within sight of their goal.

After he was bathed and fed Bohemond asked to see Tancred. His nephew swept in with a vigour that made him almost feel tired again.

"If you see Count Baldwin, the brother of the Count of Boulogne, kill him at once. There is blood-feud between us. He has killed three hundred of my men."

"Of course I share my nephew's blood-feud. But are you sure of your facts? Three hundred men? With his own lance? He is a good knight, I know, but I never thought of him as that kind of paladin. Is he in camp? Why haven't you killed him already?"

"He didn't kill them with his own lance, the recreant. He betrayed them to the Turks. Of course he isn't here in camp. He fled eastward, to the castles of those Armenian scallywags who are his friends. In any case *I* can't kill him, even if we meet again. We have been formally reconciled; the Kiss of Peace, Communion, kneeling side by side, all the trimmings. That's although he was in the wrong from start to finish. But it's a complicated story."

"If it's complicated you must tell me all of it, slowly. Before you begin I'll make this clear. I gather you think yourself in the right, but even if you are in the wrong I stand by my sister's son. In any blood-feud Hautevilles stand together. Now begin, and slowly."

The boy collected his thoughts.

"Well, you remember that I set out for Tarsus. I had a hundred knights and two hundred cross-bows, enough to liberate the whole country. The pass is dangerous, as the Greeks said; but no one held it against us. Then at Tarsus we had a stroke of luck. The Turkish garrison, who had never met Franks, rode out to meet us in the open field. They charged instead of using their bows. We drove them back to Tarsus a good deal faster than they had come out. Then I remembered your advice about prudence and avoiding traps, so I halted the pursuit outside the gates of the town."

"That was sensible," Bohemond commented. "I hate fighting among houses unless my men are already dismounted and in good order."

"For three days we sat before Tarsus," Tancred continued. "The

147

gates were shut, but the walls were not properly manned. Some Greeks got out and told my interpreter that the Turks hadn't made up their minds what to do. They felt frightened, but they were safe inside the very strong castle. The Greeks wanted me to offer terms. The Turks would come out if they were guaranteed a safe retreat with horse and arms. I wouldn't promise that because in fact I couldn't guarantee it. Obviously the Greeks planned to murder them by shooting from the housetops while the Turks were entangled in the streets, and once fighting broke out my men would join in. I believe I did right. Some say there's no need to keep faith with infidels. That may be true as a general rule but a knight must always keep faith."

"Only clerks want infidels to be massacred, and even they want someone else to do the killing," answered Bohemond. "Even with infidels, stick to the rules of war. If the infidels break the rules you may treat them as they deserve. You did right."

"Well, on the evening of the third day Count Baldwin came up with a much bigger army than mine, five hundred knights and a lot of foot. He set up a separate camp, and we more or less ignored one another; though naturally the Turks supposed he had come to reinforce me. So in the middle of the night they rode out from the castle, right out of Tarsus and clear away. As soon as it was light the Greeks told me what had happened. I rode in with my men and raised my banner on the castle."

Tancred had been pacing the floor. Now with a smile of apology he dropped to a stool. He was coming to the crisis of the story, and he wished to give an impression of fair-minded calm.

"Count Baldwin called on me. He suggested that we should join forces to pillage Tarsus. I answered that I had not come on this pilgrimage to plunder Christians, and that the Greeks and Armenians of Tarsus were now under my protection. His rejoinder to that was that I could not protect them. He wanted the town, and his army was strong enough to drive me out. But if I would lead my men eastward without showing fight he would let me go in peace. I thought it over for a bit, and then I fled from Tarsus."

The young man looked appealingly at his uncle.

"There were other things I might have done. I might have hanged Count Baldwin from the battlements of the castle. But when I let him in to talk with me that implied a safe-conduct, don't you think? It would have seemed dishonourable. I couldn't hold the town. I hadn't enough men. I could have held the castle for as long as my provisions lasted. But they were Turkish provisions and I had not yet counted them. My men might have begun to starve that very evening. And I didn't want to be the first to draw sword on a fellow-pilgrim. Surely anything is better than war among the pilgrims? I fled."

"There again you did right; though if you had murdered Baldwin when he threatened you in your own castle I for one would have stood by you. So far Baldwin has behaved very badly but no Christian blood has been shed. What is this about the blood-feud?"

"It comes later. I wanted to explain what led up to it. I went off eastward. Cilicia is a rich province, full of Christians. Everywhere the Turks were getting out, fleeing north to join the Danishmends. The Greeks, of course, just wanted someone to protect them. They can't or won't fight, so they are bound to be ruled by foreigners. Every Armenian is willing to fight against the whole world; but that includes fighting against all the other Armenians, so their lords can't set up strong fiefs. I took two fine towns named Adana and Mamistra, and I thought I would soon be Count of Cilicia. But Baldwin came after me, still threatening force. It was then I heard from some Greeks what he had done to our comrades in Tarsus as soon as my back was turned."

Tancred stood up again. He was much too angry to sit still.

"Soon after I left Tarsus three hundred Apulians arrived there. Mostly foot and unarmed followers, with a sprinkling of troopers. They were tired of the long march. They had been told I was lord of Tarsus, and hoped to garrison the town for me. Baldwin would not allow them within the walls, so they camped in the open. A wandering band of Turks broke into their camp in the middle of the night. There were no survivors. Three hundred men—Apulians —men who had marched with us from Brindisi—men who looked to us for protection. They died because Baldwin would not let them sleep safe in Tarsus. That's blood-feud. To even the score we must kill three hundred of Baldwin's Frenchmen. It would be splendid if we could kill three hundred knights. A French knight for every Apulian groom. If we follow him now, with all our men, we may be able to do it."

"Yes, but there's more to come. You have been reconciled. I want to hear about that. First tell me, did his knights approve of what he had done?"

"Of course not. They are good knights. They talked of leaving his banner to seek some other lord."

"That's when you should have attacked him, when his own men were unwilling to fight. Instead you gave him the Kiss of Peace. How did that come about?"

"Because Baldwin has amazing luck. Suddenly he found more followers. They came literally out of the sea to help him. A fleet of north-French pirates put into the port of Tarsus. Just think of it. They had fought their way from the English Channel to the Levant. Somehow they got through the Straits of Gibraltar, between the Moors of Spain and the Moors of Africa. They were led by a man of Boulogne, a ruffian named Guynemer. He was delighted to take service under the brother of the Count who had chased him into exile with a price on his head. That made Baldwin too strong and we called off the attack. But I got into Mamistra before him and kept him outside the walls when he arrived. My cousin Richard tried a night attack on Baldwin's camp. But it's not a trick that comes off twice in the same campaign. He retreated when he found ten times his numbers waiting for him. I didn't want a battle in the open field, and by this time all the clergy with both armies were being a nuisance. So I went through this public reconciliation before the high altar of the main church in Mamistra."

"Then you ended the feud, my boy. I don't see why I should start another just to oblige you. I suppose you don't want to break your reconciliation and be recreant? When you give your oath you must keep it, even if you have given it to a man you dislike. Henceforth you and Baldwin must be at peace, though that doesn't mean you have to trust him. You say he has gone east, so you won't have to meet him in council. Forget the whole business. That is the only advice I can give you."

"Yes, he has gone off to look for a fief in the east. He has broken his vow to liberate Jerusalem. Baldwin is an oath-breaker, and recreant besides."

"But Tancred is not recreant. Keep that in mind. I'm sorry to hear pilgrims have fought fellow-pilgrims, though it was bound to come sooner or later. Perhaps things would have gone smoother if the Pope had chosen a leader for us. But we must face conditions as they are, and liberate Jerusalem in spite of them. Everything you have told me is important and interesting, but you rather slurred over the most important development of all. Ships from the English Channel cruising off Tarsus. The ports of Cilicia held by Franks or Armenians. They may be nasty Franks or nasty Armenians, but they are not Greeks; and the nastier they are the better will they get on with a gang of pirates from Boulogne. You see what that means? A new route to Italy. Alexius doesn't bar the way home any more."

It was late before Tancred went back to his own pavilion, but Bohemond had persuaded him against further revenge. That boy could always be guided by an appeal to honour. It was just that his honourable thirst for vengeance was stronger sometimes than his other honourable sentiments. After hearing the advice of an older and wiser man he would always do the right thing. But how that boy enjoyed his emotions, how he wallowed in the luxurious depths of his honour! He must be the centre of attention. Probably he had been just as happy exchanging the Kiss of Peace with Count Baldwin before a crowd of admiring spectators as he would have been, if things had turned out a little differently, kneeling on Baldwin's chest to hack off his head.

So Bohemond mused, sitting over a last cup of wine. The fleet from Boulogne, that was what really mattered. He closed his eyes, the better to contemplate the map now engraved on his mind. Antioch was not a port, but it stood near the mouth of a river. The lord of Antioch could not offer secure shelter to Christian ships.

Most sailors considered the Straits of Gibraltar an absolute bar to Christian traffic. Of course no Moors would want to attack a fleet of armed pilgrims—little profit in victory and plenty of hard knocks however the battle went. Ships from the north were better equipped for warfare, and their crews better armed, than the merchant fleets of the Mediterranean. Every Norman remembered that he was descended from Vikings.

All his life he had taken it for granted that the Greek navy ruled the Levant. Greek Fire was a secret weapon, deadly to all ships not equipped with it. Some Turks had taken to piracy but there was no organized Turkish fleet; there had never been a Turkish victory at sea to depress the morale of Greek sailors.

But all Italian sailors were not timid merchants. Amalfi and Bari, in his own Apulia, had a reputation for daring voyages and hard fighting. The Venetians had stood up to the Hautevilles. The Pisans were said to be as brave. A stiffening of North Sea pirates would make them more formidable still. They seldom visited Anatolia or Syria, because they did not trade with infidels. But a Christian Antioch, still more a Christian Jerusalem, would draw them. Sooner or later they would fight a stand-up battle with the Greek navy; and then the Greek navy, like all other Greek institutions, would be revealed as a sham living on its past repute. That was it. He would open a safe sea-route to Rome and all the lands of the Franks. Alexius could be ignored in his remote corner of Christendom. To reach Antioch Alexius must cross the desert and the mountains as the pilgrimage had done. If he ventured so far another Emperor would be proclaimed during his absence from the city. Never mind Cilicia, or the warlike and independent Armenians. Antioch was the key to future greatness. He, Bohemond, must rule it.

In the morning he attended another meeting of the council. It had become by now a smaller gathering. The lesser Counts, who used to come chiefly to assert their independence, now mostly adhered to some particular great man. The Normans of Apulia hung together, usually in alliance with the Normans of Normandy. In the same way Count Godfrey and Count Raymond each controlled a powerful and united army. If there should be a division of opinion no one would try to settle it by counting heads.

Nevertheless there were a few independents still who were worth conciliating: the Count of Vermandois, the Count of Flanders, or the numerous leaderless minor Counts from central France; and of course if any question of religious policy should come up, though that was unlikely, they must all defer to the commands of the legate.

As had now become the custom, Duke Godfrey took the chair.

As soon as the meeting opened Bohemond seized the opportunity to repay a debt and gain an uncommitted supporter. He proposed that all provisions offered by local Christians or brought in by foragers should be put into a common stock, to be administered by the Count of Blois.

No one else wanted the troublesome task, and Count Stephen was delighted. The proposal was carried by acclamation. It was probably a good thing in itself, Bohemond considered. Stephen liked doing sums, and with his abacus he would get the answers more nearly right than any other great nobleman. If the provisions were divided fairly everyone would gain; and if they were divided unfairly, Stephen, who had helped Bohemond when his knights were starving, was the right man to profit by it.

Bohemond had spoke at the beginning of the meeting to get everything settled before Count Raymond should arrive. Raymond was often late, unless he cut breakfast; and he always opposed any suggestion put forward by Bohemond.

They went on to discuss the buying of horses from the Armenians, and the best road down to the plain of Antioch; and still Raymond did not appear. When the meeting broke up Bohemond strolled over to inquire from Robert of Normandy.

"What's become of the hero of Dorylaeum, the gallant Count Raymond who rescued you and me from those ferocious Turks? Is he sick again? If he is, will you join me in a prayer that he may have a swift and painless journey to Heaven? I suppose that's too much to hope for. Where is he? He's not a man to go hunting when he might be making speeches."

"He's a pompous ass, isn't he?" the Duke answered cheerfully. "He really believes that he rescued us, and that we ought to be grateful. But he couldn't come to the council because he isn't in camp. Don't you know? Of course, it all happened while you were chasing those Turks. He galloped off to liberate Antioch with his single lance. Then he heard that the Turks might stay to meet him, so he very prudently halted half-way. As soon as we march again we shall join him."

"This is important news. I wish they would keep a record of what happens in council so, that I can read it up if I miss a meeting. I suppose they'll never do that. It's too professional and tidy for gallant carefree Counts. Come to my pavilion and tell me all about it."

"I'll tell you all about it, but in my own pavilion. My steward found a little cask of wine that needs drinking. Why not stay to dinner? I can offer you a veteran he-goat, who defended his life most valiantly. That's a better dinner than you will find anywhere else. The others are eating mule, which is even worse."

There was an air of cheerful squalor about the quarters of the Duke of Normandy. The servants were friendly and inefficient, the furnishings dirty and comfortable. Bohemond dined on excellent new bread flavoured with a scrap of old goat, served on a dish of massy silver. The Duke ate from a wooden platter; he explained that he had just sold his gold plate, the gift of Alexius. But Duke Robert was a judge of wine; the little cask held a rare vintage.

"About dear old Raymond," the Duke began. "It was soon after you left us to chase those Danishmend Turks. Do you realize that Armenian castles stretch all the way from the mountains nearly to Antioch? Well, at a place called Coxon, just on the far side of the mountains, we picked up an Armenian rumour that the Turks were fleeing from Antioch. We believed it. The Turks are so scared that they didn't hold Iconium. They might very well be too frightened to hold Antioch. It was important to put in a garrison before the Turks got back their courage. Raymond offered to send ahead a few hundred of his best-mounted knights, and follow more slowly with his main army. We were all glad to let him go, because we wanted to help our waggons over the pass. Raymond's men know all about mountaineering after their troubles in Sclavonia. But the rumour turned out to be false, as you must have guessed. The Turks are not fleeing from Antioch. On the contrary, they are gathering supplies and reinforcements in preparation for a long siege. Raymond's knights advanced until they bumped into the Turkish pickets. Then they halted in a comfortable Armenian castle. Raymond has joined them. In a few days we shall join him. Do you think we shall have any trouble in taking Antioch? Everyone says you are the great expert on Greek fortresses."

"It's supposed to be a very strong place. Less than twenty years ago the Greeks held it, and they must have a record of its defences.

I shall ask Taticius. I suppose Count Raymond went forward with his own men? He didn't lead a mixed force, with knights from other followings?"

"Well, no. That would be an odd way to behave, wouldn't it? My knights follow me and Raymond's knights follow him. But beforehand he explained his plans in full council. It wasn't a private foray, like Baldwin's raid into Cilicia or your Tancred's. I am sure if you had been there you would have approved, but you happened to be away."

"Yes, I happened to be away, so Raymond happened to try to snatch Antioch. Curious how these things fall out, isn't it? Luckily I can count on one thing: if the Turks hold a place Raymond can't take it unless I help him. Thank you for telling me. And Baldwin has gone off eastward? The pilgrimage is diminishing. But you and I and the other Normans can take Antioch without help from any Frenchman. I shall talk it over with Taticius. Do you think you can get your men on the march tomorrow morning?"

Taticius produced a map of Antioch. It looked huge, but he explained that houses did not fill all the space within the walls. He had never been there when it was in Christian hands, but before he left the city he had talked with an elderly engineer who had once helped to repair the towers.

"Here's the Orontes," he explained, pointing at the map. "Not a very big river; but it flows all the year round, which is more than some rivers do in these parts. The main traffic of the town is by barge to the river mouth, so most of the houses are here, on the south bank. Here's a whacking great bridge, leading to a little castle on the north bank. There's no bridge lower down. About a day's march upstream there's a bridge in open country, with no town beside it. It's called the Iron Bridge, though it isn't made of iron. No one can explain these local names. It has some kind of permanent fortification, though I don't know how strong. So much for the Orontes: two bridges, no easy fords. An awkward obstacle to an army coming from the north."

"But with Christian ships at Tarsus we can build a bridge of boats," Bohemond interjected. "The Orontes won't stop us."

"No indeed. But then you come to the walls of Antioch. They

were built by the mighty Emperor Justinian. Sixty feet high, dotted with towers, no way down into the town except stairs inside the towers. A very long circuit, because Mount Silpius dominates the whole place. On the summit is the castle, to the north a gentle slope, precipices on the other three sides. The walls climb up to enclose the whole north side of the mountain. They must be about eight miles long altogether, too much for any garrison to hold in force. But the defenders can see everything the besiegers are doing. and anyway you can't get near the south wall because of the precipices. You won't get in by surprise."

"Will your men help us to build siege-engines?"

"That won't help you. The river is a moat to the northern wall, and Mount Silpius guards the other sides. You can't get near enough to batter effectively."

"Then we must starve them out."

"It's a very big place, with grazing for cattle on the mountain. The Turks have been gathering provisions. You might starve first."

"In fact you don't think we can take it. But the Turks took it from the Emperor."

"The Turks didn't take it from the Emperor. After Manzikert the local commander declared himself independent. After he was dead his son took fright and sold it to the Turks. Antioch has never been taken by force."

"No Franks have tried to take it, so far. My father took Bari and I have taken Durazzo, both strong fortresses built by Greeks. If the Turks man the wall we can close with them and use our swords. But thank you for your advice."

"I try to help you. Of course I hope you will liberate Antioch." Taticius spoke with a pleading smile. "There's one other thing, my dear Count. Could you ask your followers not to be so rough with my men? They are scouts, you know—not our best warriors. They complain that whenever they leave their tents pilgrims threaten to cut their throats. I know that some of your common foot are angry with the Emperor, but they ought not to take it out of men who have guided them across Anatolia."

"I'll do my best. But if men would love one another at my command there would be no wars. I hope no one has threatened you personally?"

"No. I am not often threatened by common foot." With a smile Taticius touched the hilt of his sabre. "I have got into the habit of guarding this precious nose of mine." He did not look like a man whom it would be profitable to threaten.

With mixed feelings Bohemond prepared for the next advance.

CHAPTER X

Before Antioch

————————————————————★————————————————————

On 20th October 1097 the pilgrims descended into the plain of Antioch, the verge of the Holy Land they were vowed to liberate. The plain was fruitful, and a good harvest was stored in the numerous villages. From the look of the fields and vineyards they could see this was a new land; they had traversed Anatolia from end to end and at last come to Syria.

A few Turkish scouts hovered in the distance, but rejoicing Christian peasants lined the road. Interpreters reported that the whole country had risen; the Turks were shut up in a few strong towns. The army of the pilgrimage straggled over several miles of road, as eager knights pressed forward and less enthusiastic footmen loitered with friendly village girls.

Bohemond rode in the van, with Taticius and the papal legate. It was a good country for an ambush, cut with steep ravines and hidden valleys; but the friendly peasants could be relied on to give warning. So long as every man was armed there was no need for further precaution.

"There's the Orontes," said Taticius, grinning. "That's the Iron Bridge straight ahead, with those two towers guarding it."

Bishop Adhemar understood no Greek, but he followed the pointing finger. "A great cloud of dust. It may be the Turkish army. Come on, Count Bohemond. We can see more from the top of this mound."

"No army," he said a moment later. "Something even better. A herd of sheep and cattle on the far side of the river. Supplies for Antioch, I suppose. We must have them. In this land of bread you never taste decent beef. Why are you waiting? There may be Turks in the towers, but the bridge was built so that men might cross the river."

His horse got off to a good start. As he galloped he pulled his shield in front of him and couched his lance.

Bohemond hesitated. This was absurdly rash, even if the pilgrims were in need of fresh beef. There were Turks in the towers, and an unknown number of Turks driving the cattle; if the men holding the towers knew their job they would have dug some obstacle to halt charging knights within convenient range of their arrows. But Bishop Adhemar took in a situation very quickly. At Dorylaeum he had attacked the infidels in the rear when even such a good knight as Godfrey thought only of charging to the rescue of his fellow-pilgrims. By now the Bishop was several lengths ahead; it would be wrong for a Hauteville to ride second in a charge. He chanced a short cut down a steeper slope until he was beside the legate.

He was aware of hoofs behind him. Another horseman drew level, and then correctly dropped back. It was the squire who carried his banner on the march. A squire, without knightly mail, should not be so far up in front; and in addition the whole mesnie of Apulia would be galloping behind their lord with banner displayed. Without warning the legate had started a battle.

Here was the bridge, a fine solid structure with ample room for three horses abreast. There was a tower full of Turks at each end, but they had only just begun to bar the road with posts and planking. Even now the workmen were scuttling to shelter below the river bank. The Bishop, setting his horse squarely at a post fixed in the earth, bowled it over. Two arrows thudding against Bohemond's back brought a shudder of fear. But his mail stopped them. Once more he drew level with Adhemar. A moment later they were the first Christian knights across the Orontes since the Emperor Heraclius had been driven from the Holy Land more than four hundred years ago.

On the southern bank of the river the fight became just another galloping skirmish, like any summer cattle raid in Europe. As more pilgrims pounded over the bridge the mounted Turks fled. No one even shot at the later arrivals. The infidels in the towers slipped out on foot and dodged upstream sheltered by the river bank;

everyone was too eager to get to the front to harm them. Hardly any Turks were killed, though the booty was most rewarding.

Obviously they had snapped up a belated convoy on its way to Antioch. Besides sheep and cattle there were mules and donkeys laden with sacks of grain, even a herd of spare horses as remounts for the garrison.

No time was wasted in dividing the spoil, since the Count of Blois would look after it. Bishop Adhemar called to Bohemond.

"There's another six hours of daylight. Why don't you bustle along to Antioch and make them close the gates? You may catch another convoy, and at least you will bother them. There's no danger. The infidels are not in the mood for battle. The rest of the army will arrive tomorrow, I promise you. I'm afraid we may have missed a chance by stopping to take over these bullocks. If we had ridden hard after the Turks we might have got inside Antioch with them. I reproach myself for having squandered time. I have been told that in warfare, time may be more precious than blood."

"Had you seen before you charged that it was safe to cross the bridge?" asked Bohemond.

"As safe as such things can ever be," answered the Bishop. "It might have been an ambush, but I didn't think Turks would use such a rich convoy as mere bait. I knew that the Turks I could see would be no danger to us. I'm sorry if I was slow."

"You couldn't have been quicker. I must apologize for my unworthy suspicions. I supposed you were charging recklessly. You also saw the way to the Turkish rear at Dorylaeum. Now if only the Pope had appointed *you* commander of the whole pilgrimage I would follow you gladly."

"But he didn't. He expected the Emperor to take command, with my Count Raymond as his deputy. I have no skill in military affairs. If you thought I was charging recklessly you were brave to follow so close. But we mustn't waste time. Please move on to Antioch."

To be in the very van of the army of liberation was exhilarating. Taticius and his guides had vanished, but it was impossible to mistake the broad paved road. Soon they could see Mount Silpius. Christian peasants ran out of their cottages to cheer; some had murdered Turkish stragglers, and displayed their heads proudly.

The road led straight to the great east gate of Antioch, between the mountain and the river. When Bohemond got a close look at the walls he pulled up in dismay. Sixty feet of sheer masonry, studded with towers twenty feet higher. The gate was closed, and there were sentinels on all the towers. No hope of rushing in before the Christian army was expected. All the same, the siege had begun twelve hours before the infidels looked for it; the gallop from the Iron Bridge had not been entirely a wasted effort.

The legate had promised that the main army would arrive next day, and Bishop Adhemar could be relied on. But until the Apulians were reinforced they would be in some danger. They had no cross-bows, no foot of any kind; and they must be greatly outnumbered by the infidel garrison. At least there were some light horse who had ridden behind the knights; these lesser men could look after the warhorses. Bohemond laid out a bivouac, guarded on the north by the river. For most of the night he sat on the bare ground, though when he felt very sleepy he stood up and strolled about. He dared not sleep, for he had no subordinate with him who could be trusted to relieve the sentries punctually. But there was plenty of bread for supper, given freely by Christian peasants.

It was a very long night, and a gloomy one. After his hurried look at the walls Bohemond could not imagine how to capture Antioch. While that mighty curtain stood undamaged they could not storm it; the rising ground made it impossible to bring siege engines close enough to batter it. Still, if Taticius was right the walls made a very long circuit. They might find a weak spot somewhere. Perhaps after the whole army had come up some other leader might have a bright idea.

By sunrise there was still no threat of an infidel sortie, and Bohemond slept until noon. Tancred woke him, with news that the army would be in position by nightfall. He was no longer in command of an advanced detachment. Freedom from responsibility made him feel less tired.

Tancred shared with him a lump of salt pork; for supper the army would feast on as much fresh beef as the greediest pilgrim could hold. This was war as it should be. Tancred suggested that to celebrate their arrival they should ride round the town.

"I'm sorry I wasn't with you yesterday," he explained. "I'm

sure you know that when I see your banner displayed I follow it;
I don't claim to lead a mesnie of my own. I have just come back
from a look at the Syrian Gates into Cilicia, and a talk with
Guynemer the pirate."

"And how did you leave your fief? Are your vassals obedient?"

"There's no fief for me in Cilicia. The quarrel with Baldwin
has botched everything, and anyway I suspect the Armenians are
too strong to submit to Frankish rule. Some of my men hold
Mamistra, but they will come on when they have gathered all the
plunder. The Syrian Gates are such a dangerous obstacle that it
would be difficult to rule Cilicia from Syria. But Guynemer gave
me some encouraging news."

"Let the Armenians keep their land. They dislike the Greeks as
much as we do. They will give us ample warning of a stab in the
back. That may come at any moment, you know, and it worries
me more than any move from the infidels. What did the pirates tell
you, and are you now at peace with all your fellow-pilgrims?"

"You mean Baldwin? I haven't met him, since he has gone off to
the east. But when we meet I shall keep the peace. I have thought
it over, and that formal reconciliation must bind me. Guynemer
is a ruffian, of course; a man of low birth with appalling manners.
But he fights well, so I'm told, and for the present he is an earnest
pilgrim. His sailors are taking over all the harbours between
Tarsus and the mouth of the Orontes, and they have picked up a
rumour that a Genoese fleet is on the way. Before winter we shall
have our safe communication with Italy, one that Alexius cannot
interrupt."

"That's very good news. Confound Alexius. He's brave and he
never gives up. Without him to lead them the Greeks would be no
bother to anyone. Perhaps he will be poisoned: that often happens
to Greek Emperors. I am genuinely afraid of Alexius, especially
when I don't know what he is doing. I don't think I have ever been
afraid of anyone else in the world."

"Cheer up, uncle. Alexius in the city is a very terrible foe, but
when he comes within reach of a Frankish lance he runs away.
You have proved it in the past. Now let's look at these walls."

They rode round the south of the town. At first the wall was
close on their right, but soon the steep cliffs of Mount Silpius

drove them farther away. Narrow tracks led up these cliffs to the castle on the summit, but these were dangerously exposed to Turkish arrows. No main road entered the town from the south, again because of the mountain. After a long scrambling ride they came to the south-west gate and a good road to the coast, on the left bank of the Orontes. The south-west gate still stood open, but no Turks came out to attack the two tallest knights in the whole army of the pilgrimage.

They looked north-east, where the wall ran nearly straight by the left bank of the river. "We can't go any farther," said Bohemond. "The infidels would catch us between wall and river bank. The east gate and my bivouac must be about four miles in that direction. We have seen the whole circuit of Antioch, and there is no easy way in."

"In fact the pilgrimage is stuck, unless we can frighten the Turks into going away. It seems to me about time to call on God for a miracle."

"Leave that to the clergy. It's none of our business. Something may turn up. A great deal of war is waiting for something to turn up. Now we must go back the way we came."

When they got back at sunset the whole army had arrived and the tents were being pitched. The Apulians kept their proud position outside the main gate of Antioch; peasants told them that it was named after St. Paul. They were on the left of the line, but also the closest to the enemy.

On their immediate right Count Raymond made camp opposite a small entry named the Dog's Gate. Beyond him Duke Godfrey occupied a bend in the river, from which he could block the imposing Duke's Gate. There was no room in the front line for the rest of the pilgrims, who were camped along the road to the Iron Bridge. This disposition was nowhere near an investment of Antioch. The pilgrims faced little more than a mile of the wall; the great Bridge Gate, leading over the river to the main road to the port at its mouth, and St. George's Gate, leading south-west to the Syrian coast, were both open to infidel traffic.

The next day was spent settling in. The Turks made no move, except occasionally to shoot an arrow at some pilgrim who wandered too close to the wall. Evidently they trusted entirely to the defences built long ago by the mighty Justinian; it seemed only too likely that their trust was well placed.

But at the council meeting, next morning, the lesser Counts who carried no responsibility for managing the campaign were feeling very cheerful. The autumn weather was delightful, the camps were not crowded, and food was abundant. For the first time since they had embarked on this pilgrimage they were living as pleasantly as if they had been making war on the borders of their own fiefs.

The Count of Blois made them feel less cheerful.

"Gentlemen, please persuade your men to live more frugally. I was shocked at the amount taken yesterday from our central store. I know we have great mounds of wheat and barley, and a large herd of cattle. But there are no more cattle in the country, no more grain until next year's harvest. The peasants were so delighted to see a Christian army again in these parts that they gave us all they had; or perhaps we bought some of it and took some of it by force. Anyway we have it all. I don't know how long this siege will last—nobody knows. But it may very well drag on until Christmas, and by then we shall all be hungry."

"Then let's end the siege at once," said Count Raymond briskly. "The Turks must meet us at close quarters, and that's what we have all been waiting for. We can't blockade such a long wall, and battering or mining will be a waste of time. Let's make scaling-ladders for the next three days, and then go straight up and use our swords. That is my proposal. Has anyone a better plan?"

Bohemond had been thinking on more or less the same lines; but as soon as he heard Raymond's plan he knew it must be wrong. Raymond had no feeling for military possibilities, or for what the lesser knights were thinking. So far they had not met a discouraging defeat; if they were now repulsed from the wall many pilgrims would go straight home. Besides, if Raymond proposed such a plan it must be to benefit the Greeks; he had become almost a Greek himself, so eager was he to serve the Emperor.

Bohemond rose to speak. "I have faced many walls built by Greeks, at Durazzo and Corfu and elsewhere. They are always hard to capture, until they have been thoroughly battered. I say this escalade has no chance of success. Battery will be no use either, because we can't get our engines close to the walls. We must extend our lines until the infidels are shut in. In the end they will starve. That may take a long time, but then I am used to long sieges. You have all heard how my father took Bari."

"Norman land-pirate," exclaimed Raymond. "The Greek Emperor will lend us long-range siege-engines. If the escalade fails we must seek his help. Let me remind you that the Pope, who asked my advice before he preached this pilgrimage, told me that we must stay friendly with the Greeks. At that time, of course, he supposed that you gentlemen would choose me as your leader."

"If the Pope had appointed you leader those who came on this pilgrimage would have given you willing obedience," answered Bohemond. "I for one would have stayed at home. Pope Urban does not know the full wickedness of the Greeks, who shot an arrow into his legate. Pope Urban is my personal friend also. Indeed he is my secular lord, the only lord to whom I owe fealty. Count Raymond serves lords of greater temporal power. He holds Toulouse from the King of France and Provence from the German Emperor. It is unfortunate that both these great lords should lie under the ban of the Church. I am sure that if either of them had happened to be in communion with Rome he would gladly have joined this pilgrimage. I am more fortunate. My temporal lord is also my spiritual lord. At the beginning of Pope Urban's reign he remarked to me that the Normans of Apulia were the only secular rulers who recognized his authority. My father, by his own might, restored Rome to its true Bishop when the German Emperor held it for his anti-pope. Gentlemen, I have spoken at some length about past history, which has nothing to do with the campaign before us; because I want to kill once and for all the ridiculous rumour that Count Raymond enjoys some special degree of papal favour."

Of course Count Raymond jumped up to reply; a speech of such bitter personal animosity was unprecedented in the council of leaders. But Duke Godfrey intervened.

"We are not now discussing the supreme command, or what were our relations with the Pope before we came on this pilgrimage. As most of you know, I served the Emperor Henry until I heard what had been decided at Clermont. I am still the Emperor's faithful vassal, which in no way hinders me from fighting in de-

fence of Christendom. This is a council of war to fix on an immediate plan of campaign. What shall we do, now that we have
reached Antioch? Shall we try an escalade? That must be considered carefully. If it works, the Turks will be finished. No more
trouble from them. They will not dare to hold Jerusalem against
us. But supposing we are driven back? From this camp there can
be no retreat. We hold the Iron Bridge, upstream. But the Turks
hold the bridge here. If we begin to withdraw they can cross it, and
we shall find them waiting for us on the right bank of the Orontes,
between us and Romania. I don't think we ought to start any
large-scale fighting until we control the whole north bank of the
Orontes. Let's first block the Bridge Gate, and build a temporary
bridge of our own. Then we can get in touch with the Christian
pirates who are said to be holding the port of St. Simeon at the
river mouth. When our communications with Europe are secure
we can get on with the siege. Finally, though we may have differed
about the powers of Pope and Emperor when we were at home,
we came here to liberate the Holy Sepulchre. Until that has been
done we are a band of brothers."

Others got up to report that their men had been shaken by the
terrible crossing of the mountains, and that it would be better to
postpone the assault. Most of them had already chosen sides in the
quarrel between Bohemond and Raymond, and were unlikely to
be swayed by a single speech. But Bohemond's party was slightly
more numerous, and the more often Raymond spoke the less he
was liked. He was a prudent lord and a skilful diplomatist; but he
did not look or sound like a mighty warrior.

By the end of the council the plan for an escalade, without
previous battery, had been shelved indefinitely. Bohemond still
wondered whether he had been right to oppose it. If they could
take the place in a sudden rush they might never have to fight
Turks again. But it was true that if they were beaten they would
have no way of retreat. Reluctantly, he uncovered the real reason
why he had opposed it. No one had said anything about what
would happen to Antioch afterwards.

Antioch was his. In private Alexius had agreed that he should
have it. He had not actually turned down the suggestion that
Bohemond should be Grand Domestic, commander of all the

Greek forces in the east. He had not accepted it either; it had been left on one side for further discussion. But Alexius had been willing to entrust Antioch to Bohemond.

Afterwards Alexius had broken his side of the feudal compact, by refusing to march with the pilgrimage. So all the oaths sworn to him were void, and Bohemond need not hold Antioch as a vassal of the Greek Emperor. But that did not weaken the force of the gift: Bohemond was by right the Christian lord of a Christian Antioch. Perhaps the argument should not be examined too closely. If Alexius had the right to dispose of Antioch then his offer to Bohemond had been withdrawn; if the place was not his to give, then no particular pilgrim had more right to it than any other. But to think on these lines was mere legal pettifogging. Bohemond would be rightful lord of Antioch, because Antioch had been at the centre of his thoughts ever since he left Constantinople. He must take care that Raymond did not steal it from him.

The Apulians continued to hold the left of the Christian line, opposite St. Paul's Gate. On the right Duke Godfrey extended the line, prudently. All the boats between Antioch and the Iron Bridge were made into a pontoon bridge to the north bank. This bridge was almost opposite the Duke's Gate, which was thus closed to traffic. The main camp, with the stores and the non-combatants, was moved to the north bank of the river. When this camp had been suitably garrisoned the great Bridge Gate of Antioch was nearly blocked. A journey down river to St. Simeon was about equally hazardous to Christian and infidel.

The pilgrims could not hope to invest Antioch; even their numbers were not enough for the task. But by extending their line they might block the gates on east, north and west, which would stop supplies to the infidel garrison. Only a trickle of messengers and reinforcements, without waggons or pack-animals, could get in by the rough tracks from the south which climbed Mount Silpius.

To economize manpower they built counter-forts opposite each gate. The tower which covered St. Paul's Gate and the road to the east was named Malregard; it was held by Apulian cross-bows, fed from Bohemond's private stores. Since Count Raymond, on his right, was so often sick with fever, Duke Godfrey took over the blockade of the Bridge Gate; here the winding river ran close to the walls; siege-engines were set up as well as another tower.

That left open only one big gate, St. George's, on the left bank of the river at the head of the main road to Syria. But it was very close to the Christian cross-bows on the right bank, and the infidels used it with reluctance. Soon there would be hunger in Antioch.

Bohemond found, to his astonishment, that it was fairly easy to discover what was happening in the town. Every day Christian peasants visited his camp with small luxuries for sale, a handful of radishes or perhaps the virtue of a daughter. Probably some of them were spies; but that could not be prevented and in any case it did no harm. The Christian army was very numerous, very well armed, and for the present adequately fed. Unwarlike spies reporting to the Turks would not make it sound less frightening than it was.

Then Tancred came to him with a strange story. "Some of the locals in our camp are not peasants; they are burgesses of Antioch. Among themselves they speak Arabic, supposing that no Frank can understand it. They cross the ridge of Mount Silpius, and wander down the slope until they come into camp from the south. What is really amazing is *why* they come. They visit us to compare prices. They have food hidden and don't care which side buys it. If the Turks offer famine prices they will get it; as soon as we begin to starve it will come to us."

"Do you mean they don't care who rules them?"

"They don't. Disgusting, isn't it? If you question these men you can find out what is happening in Antioch."

"Then catch one and bring him here. I should like to know more about the domestic affairs of the Turks. Taticius is quite out of his depth on this side of the mountains."

When the man was brought in he explained, of course. that he had left his wealthy home to throw in his lot with his Christian deliverers. He did not intend to return to Antioch. Bohemond pointed out that, according to his own story, he had left his wife and children in the town. Unattached grass-widowers were not trustworthy recruits. If he would bring his family and his money the pilgrims would welcome him. Meanwhile he might go freely back to Antioch, and report all he had seen, if in return he would tell all he knew of what was happening in the town.

When the interview was ended Bohemond turned cheerfully to Tancred. "I begin to see why the Turks claim to be sprung from the same stock as the Franks. Their political arrangements are very like ours. I wish I could pronounce the name of the present lord of Antioch; but Cassian is the nearest I can get to it. Cassian is a vassal, there is no doubt of that. But three different Turkish emirs claim his fealty; at one time or another he has given his oath to all three, and made war on all three. So while three Turkish armies are gathering to relieve him he is not quite sure that he wants to be relieved. If he can beat us off by his own power he will be independent, but whoever relieves him will certainly be his lord. Have I got it right?"

"I think so," answered Tancred. "I can't manage these Turkish names either. You need another set of teeth half-way down your throat to do it properly. But I can manage the names of the places. His suzerains are the lords of Aleppo and Damascus, fairly close; and the lord of Mosul who lives further off but is more powerful. Yet Cassian has ruled Antioch for the last ten years. He must be clever at managing his superiors. I hope he is not equally clever in war."

"He may be clever, but he's not enterprising. We have been here for more than a fortnight, and he has done nothing. If he sticks behind his wall we must get him in the end."

CHAPTER XI

Christmas in the Field

────────────────────────★────────────────────────

By mid-November the siege had settled into a routine. The walls of Antioch were so strong that only a few sentries were needed to guard against sudden escalade. The Turks never sallied out, and seldom shot arrows.

In fact the besiegers saw more of the Christian burgesses than of the infidels. These burgesses were not too badly oppressed by Turkish rule. They reported that until recently the cathedral had remained open and the Patriarch had functioned freely; though since the siege began the cathedral had been used as a stable and the Patriarch had vanished into a dungeon. One day a cage was hung half-way down the wall by the Bridge Gate, the only stretch of wall which could be battered by the engines of the besiegers. Almost immediately it became known that the Patriarch was in this cage. The engines could not be used. A dirty trick, the pilgrims agreed; but few of them had expected the engines to harm the wall anyway.

Bohemond and Tancred had both thought of buying a way in, as soon as they found they could talk with the inhabitants. It was an idea that would occur spontaneously to any Norman of Apulia. A large proportion of the garrison were renegades from Christianity, warriors who would rather bear arms for the Devil than not bear arms at all. Such men might be bribed to change sides again. The difficulty was to get in touch with them.

"It's our best chance, all the same," said Bohemond to his nephew. "In fact it's our only chance. Those walls are too strong for us. It may take a long time, but in the end we shall find our traitor. Such a numerous garrison must have at least one rogue in

170

it." In spite of the mounting cost of food they kept a bag of gold handy for when he should appear.

Bohemond was worried because in the ever-shifting opinions of the ordinary pilgrims, his prestige was sinking as Raymond's rose. He had been the first leader to reach Antioch, but from the beginning of the siege his men had been busy before St. Paul's Gate. Now Godfrey was sick; which meant that Raymond was in charge of all the new and exciting developments towards the west. The south French built the bridge of boats and the camp north of the river; they were feeling their way to clear the coast road.

Though the Turks of Antioch did nothing, other Turkish bands were becoming a nuisance. There were rumours of an army of relief mustering in the south, though it was unlikely that the lord of Antioch would be glad to see them. Another band, of uncertain allegiance, held the town of Harenc to the eastward, beyond the great bend in the river. These were enterprising men, who made a habit of intercepting parties of Armenian merchants coming down from the mountains to the Iron Bridge. Bohemond, anxious to perform some exploit that would keep him in the news, decided to deal with them.

It ought to be easy, if everyone did as he was told. Unfortunately the Armenians would not. Bohemond wanted to use one of their convoys as bait, while he himself lay in wait for the raiders from Harenc. But when he explained his plan the Armenians said it was too dangerous. There was nothing for it but to risk good Frankish Apulians. A party of sick, looking more debilitated than they felt, marched slowly across the Iron Bridge from the south, as though to recuperate in the mountains.

Even Apulians would not obey orders to the letter; though they should have known, after more than a year oversea, that a plan devised by Bohemond would work out safely. As soon as the infidels appeared some of them drew their swords and stood firm, instead of running away with cries of terror. Bohemond had to gallop out of his counter-ambush to rescue them, when he had hoped that the Turks would ride by him at close range.

But everything came right in the end. Bohemond had not asked these invalids to stand and fight, because a lord cannot sacrifice his own followers even to gain a military advantage; but when they fought of their own free will they absorbed all the attention of the infidel. It was always easy for mailed knights to kill Turks, if they could catch them. Bohemond's knights killed all the Turks before they had time to kill more than two Apulians.

After the knights had searched the money-belts of the dead and rounded up spare horses they prepared to ride back to camp. But Bohemond believed in pressing his luck, once luck had shown itself in his favour. "I wonder how many Turks are left in Harenc?" he said. "Here are a great many dead, perhaps the whole band. The simplest way to find out whether Harenc is empty is to go and see." He led his knights eastward.

Harenc was unwalled, though a little castle stood in the middle of it. Bohemond found a Greek inhabitant who admitted that he could speak Turkish.

"You are going into the castle to give a message to the infidels," he said. "Perhaps they will kill you as soon as you enter; but I shall certainly kill you if you do not, so you had better try it. Tell the Turks to send out someone who speaks Arabic to negotiate a peaceful surrender. I have men in my following who know Arabic."

After an interval the Greek emerged from the castle, though he prudently scuttled away to hide in the town. He was followed by a Turk, mounted but unarmed, who rode steadily towards the Christian banner.

"Ralph, you will interpret," said Bohemond to a knight from Sicily. "They mean to yield. I never heard of a garrison that began to parley and didn't surrender at the end of it. Offer them the usual terms. We may as well keep the rules of war. They may take their arms and anything else they can carry, so long as they leave the castle empty and undamaged."

After a brief conversation in Arabic Ralph asked for further instructions.

"They will go if they may take everything that moves. He means their women and children, their cattle and spare horses."

"Obstinate, aren't they? I have something to persuade them, but we won't mention it just yet. Spare horses, no; one horse for each warrior. Cattle, of course not; we lack beef more than they do. Women and children; that's a poser. As pilgrims we ought to keep away from Turkish concubines but some of their women will be captive Christians. Tell him this: Women and children are to come out singly, on foot. Each will be questioned by a respectable Christian woman of Harenc. Those who wish may go with their husbands. Those who choose to stay in a Christian land may do so. See what he says to that."

Some knights looked disappointed. They were pilgrims fighting in a holy cause, but a Turkish concubine or two would help to pass the long winter evenings. However, there was no point in saying that to Count Bohemond, who was notoriously indifferent to female society.

In a few minutes the interpreter was back again.

"Your terms are refused, my lord. The man says that Turks don't care about castles, they would just as soon live in tents. But their animals and women are their wealth. They will fight to keep them. He added that they need hold the castle only for a few days. An army is gathering in Damascus for the relief of Antioch, and soon we must retire. That may be a lie; but he said it as though he believed it."

"That's no evidence either way. There's very likely an army of relief, but no one would choose an envoy who couldn't lie convincingly. What matters is that our terms are refused. You all heard that, gentlemen? I have kept the rules of war as though we were fighting a civilized foe, and now by the same rules of war they are at our mercy. Some mercy they shall have, though not very much. Tell the envoy that within an hour I shall set fire to the four corners of Harenc. Whichever way the wind is blowing they will be roasted alive. That's their own fault, for putting their castle in the middle of a town and letting someone build wooden sheds right up to the walls. In Apulia we have more sense. If they don't want to be roasted they may come out unarmed. Their women and children will not be killed, though I suppose someone will enslave them as soon as we go away. All I promise the warriors is that when they are killed it will be swiftly, without torture. They have just an hour to come out, mind. Then the town burns."

Less than a score of warriors came out of the castle; though there were hundreds of women and children, the families of those infidels who had been killed in the ambush. At once Bohemond set off for Antioch with his prisoners and cattle. He did not care to watch the Christians of Harenc tie up their new slaves before driving them over the mountains. Every great man among the Greeks and Armenians kept a numerous household of slaves, so slavery could not be unchristian; but it was a peculiar institution for which there was no room among the more honourable customs of the West.

On the day after Bohemond arrived back in camp they told him that the Patriarch was once more hanging on the wall in his cage. So Bohemond brought his prisoners down to the Bridge Gate, where the besieging lines were closest to the town, and there had their heads struck off one by one, to vex the garrison. The best thing to do with an infidel Turk was to kill him, and such a swift death was merciful.

That same evening he had great fires made in his camp; visiting Greeks and Armenians were told that these were to roast the bodies of the slain. Everyone knew that the pilgrims, though not yet starving, were very short of meat. When the Turks of Antioch heard of it they would wonder. As a general rule Christians were not cannibals, but the giant Bohemond might do anything. . . .

About the same time came news that a fleet from Genoa had occupied the port of St. Simeon at the mouth of the Orontes. This was a much safer communication with Italy than a fleet of wandering pirates from beyond the Straits of Gibraltar. The road to St. Simeon was still exposed to infidels' raids, but it was used increasingly.

The fast of Advent was well observed in the pilgrim camp, where the price of food was soaring. A small ration of grain was given out daily to each warrior, enough to keep him from dying of hunger; but if he wished to eat better than his horse he must buy everything else from his own purse. Peasants brought in a few vegetables for sale, and there were dead baggage animals. A very strict law forbade the killing of a warhorse for food, and any normal knight would rather starve to death than fight on foot; but warhorses were sometimes stolen from their rightful owners to be killed and eaten.

The council of leaders hanged a few Greek and Armenian horse-thieves. No pilgrim was caught stealing a horse; it was not the kind of offence for which any hungry Frank would denounce a comrade. The leaders themselves were not yet very hungry, but the prospect of starvation before the next harvest affected them in various ways.

Because the ration of grain was given out only to able-bodied warriors family life collapsed. The many women who had accompanied the pilgrimage would do anything to get food for their children. This appalled the papal legate, who pointed out that if they offended God by promiscuous adultery they could never hope to liberate Antioch. He organized processions of intercession, and proclaimed fasts even more rigorous than necessity compelled. Bohemond, who had seen severe famines in Italy, was less worried than some other leaders. He reminded his knights that according to the old story the Normans besieging Bari had eaten their shoes and their saddles, but not their horses. A long siege was always a hungry business.

The Count of Blois, in charge of the central store, was nearly mad with worry. To everyone he met he suggested that it was time to wind up the pilgrimage, take passage on the ships at St. Simeon, and go home. But he did not make the suggestion formally in the council of leaders, perhaps because it was obvious that only great men would be able to pay the shipmasters. He was after all a knight; he could not stand up among his equals and propose that they should leave the poorer pilgrims to be massacred by the infidel while they saved their own skins.

Taticius was also frightened; though his was a different fear. He called on his old friend Bohemond to ask for a guard of Apulian knights. "I'm ashamed of myself," he said with the ghost of a smile. "A general of the Empire should be able to look after himself in any throng of barbarians. I suppose you know that in the city they call you barbarians? Christian barbarians, of course; but they are known to be more dangerous than the most barbarous heathen. I'm not afraid that I shall die of hunger. I've got a bit of money put by where even you, my friend, can't find it; and my imperial commission still carries weight among the Armenians. But a good many pilgrims blame the Emperor for their misfortunes. They can't reach the Emperor, so they take it out on me, his representative. All my horses have been stolen except the one Arab mare I keep by my bed. Turkish ponies are stouter, but only Arabs are properly house-trained. Whenever I leave my tent some-one waves a knife under my golden nose. My unfortunate guides are too frightened ever to go out. I can't use them for a bodyguard. But your men obey you, within reasonable limits. If you would detail two or three of them to guard me while I sleep I should get more rest."

"There are knights who will obey me, though not perhaps a great many. They blame the Emperor, you know, and in my opinion justly. One difficulty is that being a bodyguard isn't work worthy of a knight, unless he guards his own lord. I shall have to proclaim that you are my guest, under my protection. To guard the guest of his lord won't hurt anyone's dignity."

"I'm afraid it would hurt mine. The Emperor would be furious when he heard of it. I can't openly seek the protection of an in-dividual Frankish lord. That's why I came to you in private. I was hoping to hire some knights and pay them a regular wage."

"That's out of the question, though I'm sorry to say it. Any Frank who chose to enlist with the Emperor just now would be kicked to death by his fellows. I can't help you. Don't take offence at this, but I feel I ought to say it: Why don't you go back home? The Emperor sent you to show us the way, and to explain Turkish tactics. You have done both. But we shan't be moving for some time, and anyway you don't know the country ahead of us. It seems to me that you have accomplished your mission."

"I still have one duty to perform. It's my job to install an im-perial governor of Antioch. A governor satisfactory to the Franks, of course, but still an imperial governor. This is the limit of the Empire, and I shan't come with you any farther. But while the siege continues I must stay. I'm sorry you can't let me have a guard, but I quite understand. I shall hire some Armenian cut-throats, and move my tent to the edge of the camp so that only one side need be watched. Don't worry. I'll manage. I've seen worse in my day."

When old Golden Nose had gone Bohemond thought hard. So the Emperor still hoped to grab Antioch, though he had not lifted a finger to liberate it. But he had promised it to Bohemond. How could Taticius think of offering it to anyone else? The trouble was that most of the leaders liked Taticius, a gallant warrior who had always done his best to help them. If he were still here when the place fell he might be an awkward nuisance. There ought to be some way of removing the old boy, of course without hurting him.

During the rest of Advent, Apulian grooms and cross-bows shouted threats at Taticius whenever he left his tent. If Bohemond passed by he would rebuke them sternly, but as soon as his back was turned they began again.

The pilgrims celebrated the liturgy of Christmas 1097 with great ceremony. The legate sang all three Masses in full pontificals at the magnificent portable altar of the Count of Provence, assisted by all the other pilgrim-Bishops. It was the most solemn and splendid religious function that most lay pilgrims had ever seen.

The feasting afterwards was on a lesser scale. Though great lords distributed gold and silver among their followers no one had very much to eat. But the Count of Blois saw to it that everyone had a portion of meat, though it might be only camel or mule. If only it had been possible to foresee what they would have to eat at Epiphany it would have been a fairly cheerful occasion.

One thing was still in their favour, it was agreed at the council of leaders which met on St. Stephen's Day. The garrison of Antioch was cowed. Since the siege began there had been no sortie, and the enemy never harmed them except by pouncing on lonely stragglers. But something would have to be done to gather fresh supplies.

The suggestion came from Count Robert of Flanders. He was a lord of great power, leader of a strong and disciplined force; but such a disinterested, dedicated pilgrim, quietly behaved and lacking in ambition, that he seldom spoke in council. It seemed strange that he should take the initiative, though as usual what he proposed would not benefit himself.

"I expect that by now you all know something about the curious course of the Orontes?" he began. "It rises far to the south of us, turns sharp west just above the Iron Bridge, and continues southwest to the sea. If we follow it upstream we shall reach the heart of the infidel lands, the only direction in which our foragers have not yet explored. The Turks are so quiet in Antioch that I think we may safely divide our forces. I shall lead all my men up the river, as far as we can go in unravaged country. I shall return when I have collected a good herd of cattle and loaded my waggons with grain. But for such a deep raid I don't think my Flemings will be enough. Will any other lord join me with his mesnie? And do you all agree that it is safe to divide the army of the pilgrimage?"

It was most flattering that the other leaders, except Raymond, looked spontaneously to Bohemond for his opinion. They were all expert warriors, but he was the expert among experts. It was a challenge he could not refuse.

"I shall be honoured to ride under the leadership of Count Robert of Flanders," he said quickly. "Whether the garrison of Antioch will stay quiet I am not so sure. From the castle they will see us go. It's a chance no warrior can ignore. They may very well try a sortie. But you should be able to hold the camp. Even if they don't see us the visitors who sell us food will tell the Turks. So the sooner we start the better. Tomorrow, at sunrise?"

There was a general murmur of agreement, and not a whisper of dissent. The great Bohemond of Apulia recommended an important tactical move, and not even the jealous Raymond dared to speak against it. That was most satisfying.

On the last day of December the foragers were deep in unknown country. At the great bend of the Orontes they had turned south, but the broad valley had proved disappointing; it was a natural road for warring armies and quarrelsome Turkish factions had harried it bare. The pilgrims ventured farther east, to the open country bordering the desert. They had passed the night in the little town of Albara, a town inhabited only by infidels in which there was not a single Christian church. The natives fled at their approach, leaving enough stored grain to make a good supper, but not enough to carry back to the hungry camp before Antioch. The foragers were completely lost, except that sunrise had shown them the east. Now Count Robert was debating with Bohemond in which direction they should continue their march.

"Damascus and Jerusalem must lie south," said Robert. "Plenty of infidels round there. The mountains to the west must also be full of them. We came here to plunder, not to fight. I suggest we go on to the east, where the country seems empty."

"It's very open," Bohemond objected. "I don't care to fight Turks in open country, where they can keep out of reach while they shoot arrows. I would feel safer among the mountains. If you push those Turks up against some obstacle you can charge them. They may pop out suddenly from an ambush, but in the long run mountains are safer."

"Well, you know best," said Robert doubtfully. "I suppose we must turn west and fight before we forage. We came out in strength because we didn't want to fight. The idea was that such a strong force could forage without opposition. But perhaps we have come too far to get back without a fight. My men will go ahead, if you agree. Then you in the rear can see what happens, and do as you think best if something unpleasant turns up."

Count Robert was a charming colleague, but Bohemond found it difficult to cope with such open diffidence. He was used to giving orders, or perhaps to obeying them ; it was hard to strike the right note with a great lord who was so willing to be persuaded and yet might not be commanded. Obviously, if the Flemings agreed to march west Count Robert must be allowed to lay down the order of march. The Flemings would have first pick of any plunder found, but in these small things Bohemond must fall in with the wishes of Count Robert.

The Flemings were nearly as well trained and obedient as Apulians. Within an hour they were marching west, though they had been expecting to continue east. They had gone about two miles, and Bohemond was getting ready to follow them, when the Turks came in sight.

The ground was wet, so no dust-cloud hid the horsemen. Bohemond could see all that went on. He knew that this was a crucial test. It would be easy to rescue the Flemings but he was expected to do more. He was the expert who annihilated Turkish armies. If Count Robert acknowledged his superior skill he would support him against Raymond in the council of leaders.

As he watched he muttered aloud, to help clear his own thoughts.

"Those Turks haven't come out to defend their own herds. They are too many, and they attack too eagerly. They are shooting now, at very close range, but they are getting ready to charge with the sabre. That's not how men fight who are defending their homes against great odds. Ah, I see it. An infidel army coming up from the south to relieve Antioch. They heard of plunderers in these parts and turned aside to wipe us out. Tut tut, all those light horse and they don't bother to scout before they charge. They think the Flemings are all they have to deal with. They still haven't spotted my Apulians, among these houses."

His knights were getting into line, shield on neck and lance in hand. They waited for him to lead the charge, but they would not wait much longer. He *must* time it right. If he charged too soon the Turks would get away; if he delayed too long the Flemings would be massacred before their rescuers could arrive. He rode down the line to steady his knights, his eyes still fixed on the fight. Two miles of muddy plain to cross, say ten minutes at the outside. The Turkish drums were beating a sustained roll like thunder; the mass of galloping horses contracted towards its centre. With his banner-bearer half a length behind him Bohemond set off towards the battle.

The loose line of Apulian knights enclosed the scrimmage on three sides. As they arrived the Turks had charged in with the sabre, against a compact mass of Flemings. Flemish cross-bows, grooms and baggage mules were all mixed up with their knights in a dense knot which no Turkish pony could penetrate. The out-numbered Flemings were fighting stubbornly for their lives. A good many Turks were down, for their flimsy mail and light weapons put them at a disadvantage in close combat; but in a few minutes the Christians might break. No one on either side had eyes for anything beyond the reach of his arm.

Bohemond's lance took his first Turk in the small of the back, which seemed an unknightly way to join a battle. Then he had drawn his sword to struggle against wiry desperate men who slid to the ground and tried to dodge under his horse's belly as the best chance of escape. Since the throng was too dense for his horse to move he dropped the reins and fought with both hands, sweeping his heavy shield to the left as he waved his great sword on the right. A pony gripped his thigh, but could not get its teeth through the mail; his horse bit the pony in the neck until it let go; the rim of a little Turkish shield, banged into his kneecap, brought acute pain but did not break the skin.

Suddenly it was over. Count Robert, bloody and sweaty, waved in welcome; and there were no more Turks. "A nice little battle," said Robert. "You came in just at the right moment. Some of my men are dead, but that was what they risked when they left Flanders. We have killed many more Turks. Look, that's all that's left of them, the little band riding off westwards."

"Others got away on foot. Your cross-bows and grooms can hunt them down. Mine are still two miles away in Albara. Are any of your knights fit to gallop? These people must have been coming to the relief of Antioch, which means that they have a convoy with them. If we follow the fugitives we may find it."

A convoy had been there, but they never caught it. Turks used pack-animals instead of waggons, and travelled fast. The pilgrims were not quite empty-handed; they picked up some lame cattle and foundered pack-ponies, as well as the personal wealth of the Turks they had killed. It was not what they had hoped to find, but it was better than nothing. Robert and Bohemond agreed that after such a stiff fight, with so many armed Turks to the south-ward, the foragers ought to return to the main army.

Before they reached the Iron Bridge they turned west, to sweep the southern approaches to Antioch. They might catch another infidel convoy, and anyway their journey must inconvenience the garrison. They were surprised to meet pilgrims and camp-followers straggling over the mountains to the south-west. These told vague stories of a terrible attack on the camp; though the stragglers were not fugitives from defeat, but hungry men and women looking for something to eat. When they saw victorious knights they were glad to come back under their protection. Bohemond abused them for cowardice. Ever since they left Nicaea he had feared that the pilgrimage might disperse into little groups of hungry foragers. Most of the lesser pilgrims were not following the lords who ruled them at home, and with no leader except that slow and clumsy council of war it was hard to keep an army together.

Time was no longer on the Christian side. Most pilgrims had

made their vows in 1095, and now it was the beginning of 1098; after such a long campaign enthusiasm must slacken. All things considered, they had done amazingly well; Alexius had expected that they would be slaughtered in Anatolia. But they could not take Antioch unless they bought a way in, and so far no traitor had appeared. A serious defeat, even a continuation of the hungry winter, might scatter the army. He would be lenient with people who left their posts to look for food without intending to withdraw from the Holy War; but he must persuade the council of leaders to make an example of the first man who tried to go home to Europe without leave.

Robert and Bohemond were cheered as they rode into camp; for it was still considered a notable exploit to ride round the walls of Antioch. But everyone was plainly disappointed at the scanty plunder they brought with them. Bohemond was eager to hear about the great battle which had been fought in his absence. While he washed in a tub of cold water (fuel was too scarce for a hot bath) Tancred told him the news.

"The pilgrims are really in a bad way. Armenians sell us food, but at such a price that only the rich can buy. The Count of Blois has stopped the issue of free corn, because he has none left. In St. Simeon there is food, though not enough for the army. Genoese sailors send what help they can. So, curiously enough, do the Greeks of Cyprus. The Patriarch of Jerusalem fled there. Of course he counts on the pilgrims to get him back into the Holy Sepulchre. The Patriarch is Greek, but he knows the Emperor won't help him. With odds and ends from here and there we can keep going; at least we Apulians can keep going. The veterans insist on telling me about grandfather Robert and his siege of Bari until I could scream with tedium. Hunger is a hardship, but it never yet stopped an army that meant business."

"I wish I could offer you supper, but you know how it is. Will you take a cup of wine? I have a little."

"No, thanks. You are very kind, but it doesn't sit well on an empty stomach. I manage all right. For dinner I had a bit of camel, and tomorrow there will be a cabbage and some oats. I am half a Hauteville, which means that when there's fighting to be done at least half of me can go without food. No, what's far more worrying than this little bother about supplies is that the Turks of Antioch have got back their courage."

"Ah yes, the battle. Were you in it? Did you see it all?"

"Everyone was in it. They attacked right along the line. I didn't see it all, because most of it happened in the middle of the night. That was what made it such a muddle. Let's see, when was it? Oh yes, the second night after you left us. This is how it went."

Tancred sat on the ground. Most of the Bohemond's chairs had been burned for firewood, and a hungry man found it tiring to stand.

"Since we arrived the Turks had sat quiet behind their wall, apart from catching an occasional straggler. Suddenly, about midnight, they beat their drums. Men carrying torches soaked in oil came out in front of the wall. The glare dazzled us so that we could not see their archers on the battlements; but they could see us. I am afraid that after such a lull we were all a bit slack. We had sentries out, of course, but the rest of us had taken off our mail and were sleeping in blankets. Our sentries fell back out of range. I told our cross-bows to shoot at the torchbearers, and they began to explain why this couldn't be done. You know how obstructive they can be. It was too wet for their bow-strings, or too dry, or perhaps too foggy. No weather is just right for cross-bows, and no knight knows enough about their horrid little machines to contradict them.

"You can say the Turks drove us from their wall," he went on, "until the knights were armed and ready. Then of course we drove *them* back. In our following no one of any importance was killed, though we lost a few sentries. The worst of it was a sleepless night, and a certain amount of thieving during the confusion. I lost a bit of bacon I had been dreaming about for days. I was saving it until I felt really hungry. But what depressed me more than anything was the courage of the Turks. A month ago they were afraid of us, now they are not.

"Duke Godfrey missed all this. He has fever, so he sleeps in a cottage some way back. His men fought well enough without him. You can rely on them. They are nearly as good as Normans.

"The real Turkish attack came over their bridge and our bridge of boats. The rest of it was just a demonstration to stop us reinforcing Count Raymond. On the two bridges there was real hand-to-hand fighting. In the beginning the Turks nearly got among our tents. Count Raymond behaved very well, though I don't enjoy saying it any more than you enjoy hearing it. As soon as he was armed and mounted he charged the Turks. They stood their ground and fought back as they have never done before. Of course the legate rode behind Raymond. I wish he wouldn't. It gives a wrong impression, for all that Raymond is temporal lord of Le Puy. No Bishop is the vassal of the lord who happens to protect his cathedral city. Anyway, the legate fought like a paladin, and lost some good knights from his mesnie. His banner-bearer was killed on the bridge. That was when the Turks were beginning to give way. It ended with Raymond chasing them over the bridge, and very nearly carrying the Bridge Gate by assault. For a moment there was no one to stop him, so I'm told. But all this happened in pitch dark, except for those flaring Turkish torches. Something galloped out of the dark. It may have been the Devil with horns and tail, it may have been a riderless horse—accounts vary. Anyway, Raymond's men flinched, and the Turks got their gate shut. So here we are, just as far from Antioch as when you left us, and a good deal more frightened."

Tancred rose to go.

"By the way," he added, "there was a slight earthquake next night, and strange lights shone in the sky. Earthquakes happen constantly, and I am told by pilgrims from the north that they have similar lights in their country. Neither can affect the Holy War. But those of our men who were already frightened felt all the more frightened. That's what happens when things begin to go wrong. Now you know all the news. No, I really won't eat or drink anything."

"It's time for a miracle—or a traitor," Bohemond called after him as he left the pavilion.

CHAPTER XII

The Hungry Winter

————————————★————————————

All through January the famine increased. Great lords did what they could for their sworn followers, and for lesser folk who came from their own fiefs; but a great mass of poor pilgrims followed no lord. These had been expected to look after themselves. So far they had managed on the free supplies of the Greek Emperor, by foraging, or by earning wages from those who had money. Now they died of hunger. There was nothing to be done about it.

Numbers of horses died also, from lack of fodder in the crowded muddy camp; for anyone who was caught killing a horse for food was hanged immediately. In a military sense the loss of horses was a greater weakness than the loss of unwarlike camp-followers. The charge of Frankish knights was the new weapon in which those leaders who did not expect a miracle trusted to conquer the infidel east. Without a horse a knight could defend a wall; but he could not attack and could scarcely march.

Anyone who had food ate it alone, in secrecy. There was an end of visiting from one great pavilion to another. Bohemond and Tancred, in fact all the Apulian knights, were proud of being able to keep alive on very little; it was a military tradition of their fathers. They guarded their horses, did not steal from other pilgrims, rested as much as they could—and watched for the first sign of collapse among Franks accustomed to an easier life.

Taticius was in fact the first to weaken. He sought out Bohemond to explain why he must leave. "The Emperor sent me to guide you," he said. "I can't do that any more, because I don't know the country ahead. I was also to report to the Emperor on your progress, and that again is impossible. The Armenians will not allow imperial couriers to ride through their land. My money is finished. My men have deserted, I suspect to join the infidels. I must return to seek fresh instructions. The Emperor is with his army somewhere in Anatolia, so I shan't have to go all the way back to the city. Will you explain all this to your colleagues on the council, so they don't accuse me of running away?"

"My dear fellow, no Frank would accuse you of cowardice. We have seen you fight. You are not under the orders of the council of leaders. You need no man's permission to withdraw. All the same the lesser pilgrims won't like it. They may try to keep you here by force, as a hostage for the Emperor. You must give out some soothing reason for your journey. Why not say you are going to arrange another convey of supplies? By the way, why doesn't the Emperor send supplies? God knows we need them."

"I can't say why any more than you can. It's a long time since a messenger got through from imperial headquarters. I can make guess, of course. One reason is that you are just too far off. By road it's a very long way from the city to Antioch, with Armenian mountaineers barring the route. It would be easier by sea, but again there are difficulties. Our sailors could reach St. Simeon, but they may be afraid to venture into harbour. It has always been the port of Antioch, within the Empire from time immemorial. They may be waiting for you to install a Greek governor. At present Italians hold it, and they haven't even asked for a copy of our import regulations. I fear that in the laxity of war they may not be enforcing them. Would you like me to take over the port? I am sure I could get Greek shipping moving at once."

"That's obviously the right thing to do, my lord Taticius. But unfortunately I don't see how I can do it at present. The Italians, Genoese I believe, are not my men and would not recognize my authority. Of course I can't use force against them, since we may not fight fellow-pilgrims. But they will help you on your way, if you are seeking supplies from the Emperor."

"I suppose they will recognize the authority of the full council of leaders? Shall I come before the next meeting of the council, with my interpreter of course? I can promise your army plentiful seaborne supplies as soon as I am in possession of St. Simeon."

"That's the honest straightforward course, which comes

naturally to you since you are an honest straightforward man. If you speak to the council I shall speak in your support, you may be sure. All the same, I advise against it. The Genoese are Italian, and pretty civilized. But also in St. Simeon there are those pirates from the far north, Guynemer's men, tough savages. They have got it into their heads that they fought their way through the Straits of Gibraltar, and restored the whole coast of Cilicia to Christendom, without help from the Emperor or the Greek army. Pirates, as you must know, are inclined to keep what they have taken. I fear the council of leaders may not be able to help you. And of course there is always the slight risk that they might fetter you as a hostage. That would be a shocking way to treat a loyal ally, and I should vote against it. But it is my duty to warn you of the danger."

There was something in the very act of speaking Greek which made it easy to convey a threat under a veil of courtesy. Bohemond and Taticius understood one another. Alexius would feed the pilgrims if they gave him St. Simeon at once and Antioch when it fell into their hands. Bohemond did not consider this a fair bargain.

After many protestations of undying goodwill Taticius took his leave. As he walked back to his tent on the edge of the camp a burly Armenian guarded his back; even brave old Golden Nose was worried by constant threats of assassination.

Next to the knights, the most valuable warriors in the pilgrim army were the cross-bows. Their weapons were a novelty in the east, so that Armenian lords were eager to hire them. In general they were poor men, unable to buy food at current prices; their lords tried to look after them, but they were strongly tempted to desert.

The council of leaders decided that mounted knights should patrol the road northward to the mountains, to check the desertion of such skilled soldiers. A mounted patrol was hard on the starving horses; but Tancred, bored by the siege, volunteered for the task. A very little extra forage was collected as a reward for his public spirit.

It was tacitly agreed that he should not arrest non-combatants and unskilled foot of negligible military worth. There was a constant trickle of such men to the delusive safety of Armenia. This safety was delusive because the Armenians did not want them. Any food they had to spare was sold at high prices in the Christian camp; deserters who did not starve in the mountains were sped on their way back to Europe. None of them got farther than Anatolia, where wandering Turks killed the weak and captured the able-bodied for the slave-market. That left the pilgrims with fewer mouths to feed, and suited all parties.

But as darkness fell on the evening after Bohemond had spoken with Taticius, Tancred hurried back into camp, too speedily for the welfare of his hungry horse. He hurried straight to his uncle's pavilion, though it was supper-time and in that dearth the wrong hour for a social call.

Bohemond sat before a cup of wine diluted with water, chewing on the strap of an old spur. It was a dodge he had heard his father recommend. It did not seem a useful dodge. The leather exercised his teeth; but his stomach still ached with emptiness, and he knew that if he swallowed the strap it would ache worse than before. What he wanted was something exciting to take his mind off his longing for food.

That was provided by Tancred's news: "You remember, uncle, that I have been ordered to hang captured deserters in public, as a deterrent. But this afternoon I caught a couple of fish rather too heavy for my net. I suppose I ought to bring them before the council for judgement, but that will cause scandal. The scoundrels I caught sneaking off to the bread and beef of Armenia are Peter the Hermit, that holy man, and the lord William of Melun. I have them here, safely bound. What shall I do with them? Hang them, or take them before the council, or just let them go quietly?"

"If you take my advice you won't bring them before the council. People will take sides, and it may end in an open breach. If they are safely bound chuck them down in the entry of this tent while we talk it over. William of Melun, eh? Isn't he supposed to be a mighty warrior? And the famous Peter? This needs thinking out. I wish I could offer you some refreshment. God's teeth, but I will. Not food, of course, but I have a little jug of wine. I was saving it for an emergency, and this is an emergency. We can't think straight without something inside us. Here's a cup, and here's the wine, hanging on the peg behind my mail. Now then. Peter and the lord of Melun, you say? I see your difficulty. If men like that can set a bad example unpunished, then everyone will run away. On the other hand, I don't think I am great enough to judge them, and certainly you aren't. H'm."

As the wine glowed inside them, they sat, looking judicial.

"Let's take Peter first," said Bohemond. "It's a tricky case."

"Surely William matters more," Tancred exclaimed. "A good knight, wealthy and well born. It's the worst thing that has happened since the pilgrimage began. As for Peter, he's neither a priest nor a monk. I doubt if he would rank as a clerk. Just a stray holy man, very dirty, with no kin behind him. Does anyone care whether he lives or dies?"

"You don't and I don't, of course," Bohemond answered soothingly, "but we are knights. This Peter once raised a great army. The Turks killed his men, naturally, while he hid in the imperial palace. All the same, once he had an army. He rides a donkey, too. Beware of men who ride donkeys and raise armies. If we hang him we shall spread alarm and despondency among the lower orders. I won't meddle with him, I won't even talk to him. I'm scared of Peter, because I am always scared of the unknown. I can cope with rational men, who defend their own property, try to steal the property of others, take a bribe, serve their lords. I can't cope with an enthusiast.

"You deal with Peter," he went on after a pause. "Tell him off. Warn him that you have your eye on him. Say that if you catch him running away again you will skin him alive and then report him missing, believed killed. Explain it so that he understands. Then take him back to his tent and say no more about it."

"We can't hush it up," Tancred objected. "I was not alone when I caught him. A score of our knights saw it. The story will be all over the camp."

"Better and better," his uncle chuckled. "The story is known, but it isn't official. Peter may have run away, but very few noticed and here he is back again. He will have to behave himself, but no one can openly call him a deserter. No other Count will blame us for keeping it quiet. No alarm, no despondency, no more trouble from Peter. Now what shall we do with William of Melun?"

"Nothing, tonight," Tancred answered with a yawn. "My stomach is so empty that a single cup of wine has left me muzzy. Sleep on it, and then do as you wish. I leave his fate in your hands. Thank you for the drink, and good night."

"Right. Tonight I shall think about it, and so will William. That will be part of his punishment, perhaps the worst part. Drop Peter by his tent as you go home. I hope your horse is none the worse?"

Next morning Bohemond woke early. To doze again in his blankets as long as possible would be wise, but the gnawing of his stomach would not let him rest. Instead he worked up a fine glow of moral indignation about the wickedness of William of Melun.

For a knight to desert his lord in the field was the worst crime he could commit. Wait, had William deserted his lord? He had come in the company of the Count of Vermandois, but Count Hugh was not his natural lord. It was unlikely that he drew wages, though he might have been paid during the ride across Romania. But he had perjured himself. The pilgrims had sworn to liberate Jerusalem unless they died in the attempt. The vow would bind the survivors until they had actually heard Mass within the Holy Sepulchre. Odd, by the way, how the Count of Vermandois had faded from the public eye. He rarely attended the council of leaders; perhaps he was sick. But he had not run away. A fool, but a brave fool. The Duke of Normandy was such another fool, though he talked so much that one could never ignore him. Bohemond's thoughts were wandering. He was on the edge of another doze.

He jumped up and shaved with care. In these days it was important to keep up appearances. Then he sent a servant to fetch William, who still lay bound, like a heap of rubbish, in the entry of the pavilion.

William was too wretched, and too frightened, to attempt any defence. He could only beg for mercy. Bohemond recalled that the scoundrel had once before deserted from an expedition against the infidel, one of the many raids on the Moors of Spain. He was not afraid of fighting; in fact he was a famous knight. He must be one of those unlucky men who cannot bear cold and hunger. It was easy to upbraid him as a disgrace to knighthood, and to the whole race of the Franks.

But he could not be punished. The lord of Apulia, indeed the whole council of leaders, had no right to punish a knight who owed allegiance only to the King of France. Bohemond began to feel anxious about what would happen after his copious flow of abuse had dried up. Once more Tancred came to the rescue.

Tancred introduced a deputation of eminent Frenchmen, who came to beg that their compatriot should be spared any greater punishment than open disgrace. The point, as Bohemond saw at once, was that these great men were asking the grandson of the petty lord of Hauteville to grant them a favour. He allowed himself to be persuaded. William of Melun promised that never again would he desert his comrades in the field. He was then graciously allowed to go free. As Bohemond, and indeed every other sensible man, had foreseen, a few days later he deserted again, this time with success. He was perjured and dishonoured; but he was a knight of the Franks, one of the few genuinely free men in the world. If he craved life on those terms no one had power to punish him.

About midday the leaders met in formal council. Duke Godfrey presided, and Bohemond took a lowly seat; but the north French, the most independent section of the council, remembered that earlier in the same day they had been asking him to do them a favour.

The first business was the reception of an embassy of infidels. This was most exciting, as proving that the infidels were divided; but the proposals of the ambassadors could have little bearing on the immediate progress of the campaign.

Everyone who had bothered to inquire knew that the religious head of the infidels was a kind of hereditary Pope called the Caliph. He lived beyond the furthest bounds of Christendom, within a town named Baghdad. The Turks and Arabs were his servants, though he had little temporal power. They were not always obedient servants, any more than the German Emperor always obeyed the Pope in every particular; but they would not deny that in theory they owed him obedience.

Now it appeared that there was a rival Caliph, in Egypt, far to the south. His envoys stated that he did not consider Turks to be the right kind of infidel. He would always be at war with the Turks, and with the false Caliph they supported; though the clerks among the pilgrims had discovered after cautious inquiry that he was not a Christian and did not intend to become one. All the same, he would like to help anyone who fought Turks, and he had sent this embassy to discuss an alliance.

That led to a long though wandering discussion. It would be splendid if a great army were to attack the Turks from the south while the pilgrims marched on Jerusalem from the north. Afterwards, though no one was so tactless as to say so, the pilgrims might go on and conquer this other breed of infidel.

Bohemond did not believe that such an alliance could ever come into effect. The distance between Antioch and Egypt was so great that military operations could not be concerted. The prospect fascinated some pilgrims; but they were the kind of men, there are altogether too many of them in the world, who thought that a war could be won without the hazards of actual fighting. Presently Bohemond grew bored with the endless and circular discussion. By putting a few direct questions to the interpreter he got an admission that the Egyptians claimed Jerusalem and would not return it to Christian rule; though of course Latin pilgrims would be welcome at Christian shrines. That could be dealt with later, thought the more warlike Counts. Bohemond next discovered that the Egyptians already had a treaty with the Greeks.

That produced an awkward silence. The pilgrims were all very hungry, and only Alexius could send them food; it would be rash to defy him while perhaps a convoy was on the road. But Greeks were not trusted, and neither were their allies. After a pause Duke Godfrey delivered a polite but empty speech. Envoys from such a great ruler were very welcome; but difficulties of religion must be discussed in private by the learned clerks who guided laymen in such matters. For the present the envoys might remain in the pilgrim camp, though they must feed themselves from their own stores; the lack of hospitality must be excused by the rigours of active service. Would they like to inspect the pile of Turkish heads preserved by Count Bohemond as a memento of his capture of Harenc? That would prove that Franks also made war on Turks.

The interpreter for the embassy spoke gracefully in reply, and the envoys withdrew. A few days later they went quietly home by sea, as had been expected.

It was unfortunate for Taticius that he was the next to speak. The Counts were all thinking of how Alexius had left them in the lurch, and they did not care to be reminded that they were still nominally his allies. What he said was in substance what he had already privately told Bohemond. As soon as he reached the Emperor he would arrange to send provisions. He had thought of one more bait. With the provisions the Emperor would also send horses.

He knew that his audience was unfriendly, and he spoke as tactfully as he could. But from sheer habit he referred to the imperial fortress of Antioch, and his too-faithful interpreter repeated the phrase. Every Frank was reminded that, according to the Greek version of their oaths, Antioch, as soon as it had been won by Frankish blood, must be restored to the Empire.

In reply Duke Godfrey hardly bothered to be polite. He said that Taticius might go as soon as he wished, with the goodwill of the whole pilgrimage. Since he proposed to take ship from St. Simeon the council of leaders would give him a safe-conduct, addressed to the Genoese and to Guynemer the pirate. Perhaps the sailors would respect the safe-conduct, perhaps they would not. But nothing more could be done, for neither fleet had formed part of the original pilgrimage.

Taticius, that brave warrior, put a good face on it. He said he would leave next day, by a Greek ship which would take him to the imperial army in Anatolia. He would come back as soon as possible, with everything the pilgrims lacked; and as proof that his absence was only temporary he would leave in the camp his tent, his servants, and all his gear. Then he said good-bye. Of course no one expected him to come back, and he did not.

Bohemond considered this a good time to clarify his own position, while everyone remembered the perfidy of the Greeks. He got up to make a personal statement.

"My lords, it seems that we must still capture Antioch, and then hand it over to the Greeks. As you know, Antioch was promised to me, as a fief, before we left the city. So I myself have been cheated twice, as you were all cheated once when the Greeks would not march with us. In these conditions it just isn't worth while to go on with the war. Perhaps by a mighty effort we could take Antioch. But then we shall be too exhausted to continue to Jerusalem. The Holy City will never be liberated, and Alexius will be the only gainer. I for one will not persevere any longer. I shall go back to Italy and ask the Pope, a personal friend of mine, to release me from my vow. I advise the rest of you to do the same. But if some of you feel bound by the vows you made in France, at a time when we all thought the Greeks would help us, at least you ought to abandon this hopeless siege. Antioch is too strong to be taken. I suggest that the whole army withdraw to the mountains of Armenia, where you will find food and fresh horses. I say 'you' because I shall not come with you. It is possible that Alexius will join you in the mountains, and I do not wish to meet him. I doubt if my life would be safe. So this may be the last council I shall attend. I hope you will agree that while I was on the pilgrimage I did my duty as a good knight."

Consternation kept the other leaders silent. It was hard to imagine the Holy War without Bohemond. He never lost heart, he always knew what to do, under hardship he set a shining example, he got on with the local Christians, at Dorylaeum he had saved the whole army. Count Raymond alone was delighted. He rose to clinch the matter.

"We shall all be very sorry to part with Count Bohemond, but if those are his views he is right to leave us. I myself never heard the Emperor promise Antioch to Count Bohemond as his private fief, though since we left the city I have heard Count Bohemond often refer to that promise. I don't suggest for a moment that he isn't telling the truth as he sees it; but recollections of private conversations sometimes differ. As I see it Antioch ought to go to Alexius. You all promised to restore his old frontiers. As it happens I did not, but I promised to do him no harm while I was within his dominions, and I am now within his dominions. There it is. Antioch must be given to the Greeks, even if it means losing that splendid Apulian contingent."

"This will never do," said the Count of Flanders as soon as Raymond had finished. "You all know that I don't want eastern fortresses. All I want is for the pilgrimage to succeed. If we are going to free Jerusalem we must compromise our private quarrels. I now beg Count Bohemond to compromise. Let him stay with the pilgrimage until midsummer, or until Antioch falls if that happens earlier. At this time of year it won't be easy to get home anyway. As to what happens to Antioch once it is ours, here is what I suggest. If the Emperor comes with his army and helps to take it, let him keep it. If he doesn't, and Count Bohemond wins the place by his own efforts, let *him* keep it. If the Emperor doesn't come and Antioch falls to the whole pilgrim army we can decide who gets it. But fall it must if we keep our vows; for God is on our side."

"That's a good compromise," Raymond said quickly. "If Bohemond gets us into Antioch it shall be his, and otherwise not. Will you all remember that?"

"I also accept it," Bohemond answered. "I suppose if Antioch falls to Count Raymond it goes direct to the Greek Emperor, whom he has chosen for lord?"

"Private quarrels are in abeyance until the pilgrimage is finished," said Duke Godfrey sternly. "No more of those remarks from either of you. You are both trying to make the other draw his sword first, so that you can fight him with a clear conscience. Now, Count Bohemond, will you stay with the pilgrimage and fulfil your vow?"

"I suppose so, if you really want me."

The answer was a most satisfying roar of agreement from all except the south French.

The council was about to break up when a knight pushed his way into the semi-circle. He was covered with mud and sweat, and clamoured to be heard. Duke Godfrey vouched for him. "This is a knight of Boulogne who follows my brother Eustace. He has been watching the eastern road. Tell us your news, Sir Odo."

"A huge Turkish army in Harenc, my lords. Thousands of them, all horsemen. I suppose they will reach here some time to-morrow evening."

"Then we must retreat," Godfrey said sadly. "There are more Turks in Antioch than there are pilgrims outside it, unless you count the non-combatant foot. If we march against Harenc they will come out and pillage our camp. If we stay we shall be attacked in the rear. We must pull back to the mountains, and beg help from the Emperor. There's no time to waste. It means leaving all our tents and baggage. Count Bohemond, can you get all your men north of the river by sunset? If we march through the night we can take up a strong position at dawn, and perhaps fight a defensive battle. Very likely they won't pursue. Once Antioch has been relieved they may go home without fighting." He sighed. He knew that such a hurried retreat would be very hard to stop. This looked like the end of the pilgrimage.

"Wait a moment. Listen to me," Bohemond shouted. "We can't retreat and then fight. Many of our knights are dismounted. They can't march on foot in their mail, and we have no baggage animals to carry it. Their mail will remain in camp, and those knights are out of the war. There must be a better plan. Let me see, Harenc to Antioch. The Turks must cross the river, I suppose by the Iron Bridge. But a few miles east of the Iron Bridge is a narrow pass, between a lake and the river. We could fight them there, if we can hold the camp behind us. I've got it, my lords. Listen to my plan. The dismounted knights, with the foot, hold our camp for a day or two. All those knights who still have horses ride east. I can't promise success, but it may come off. If it does it will be a very pretty battle, something for our grandsons to boast about."

In his mind he could picture the whole double action. As though from a great height he saw the lower Orontes, from Antioch up to the lake. Dismounted knights, with their mail and their great swords, could hold the palisaded camp against any Turkish charge; between the lake and the river the infidels must advance in column to fight at close quarters, instead of shooting arrows. How many fit horses had they in the pilgrimage? Not enough, but only the best knights had them. The Frankish charge must go exactly right; there would be no hope of a second. But if it went right the numbers of the infidel would not matter; nothing could withstand it.

As he blinked he saw another picture: thousands of pilgrims toiling on foot up the steep mountain road. They would have no bedding, no tents, no mail. Turkish arrows would pick off the horses of the mounted rearguard. When the order came to halt everyone would press on a little further, so as to leave plenty of other Christians between himself and the enemy. Many of them would run until their strength gave out. About midnight the Turks would ride in with their sabres. Hardly enough pilgrims would survive to carry the appalling news to the Armenians.

Count Raymond, naturally, disagreed. "I've got the flux. I can't charge though perhaps I could sit a horse. If we retire in good order we can join the Greeks. Or we may be able to hold the camp."

"We have to hold the camp anyway," said the Count of Flanders. "It's full of sick, helpless sick, suffering from something worse than a touch of the flux. If we retreat we must leave them to the infidels. Some of them are my own vassals, and I'll be killed before I desert them. But if we just wait to defend the camp the combined Turkish armies will break in within a week. Bohemond's plan is our only hope, and a slender one at that. But if all the mounted knights get themselves killed in this pass the men in the camp will be no worse off than before, and we shall have earned martyrdom. Even if you can't ride, Raymond, I suppose you have a horse? Lend it to some other good knight, and while we are away you shall command the camp. I shall ride with Bohemond."

"So shall I," said Duke Godfrey.

All the great Counts had horses, and they approved of a plan which gave them such a noble and prominent part. It was agreed that all mounted knights should muster within the hour.

As they drew up in column on the north bank of the river Bohemond did his best to number them. He made the total about seven hundred men; which in Italy would have been an army but here in Syria seemed a pitiful little force to represent the fighting strength of the great pilgrimage. What was even more daunting, to Bohemond, was that they were all great men, many of them better born and more powerful than himself. Except for Count Raymond all the leaders were present; there were few below the rank of baron. Yet because he had devised the plan they all looked to him for orders.

Dusk was gathering as they set off eastwards; but catcalls and hoots of triumph showed that the garrison of Antioch had observed their withdrawal. Next morning would certainly bring an attack on the camp. It was an added difficulty of this terrible siege that infidel sentries on Mount Silpius could see all they did.

Tancred rode beside his uncle. Amid the jangling of bridles and the clanking of scabbards they could talk without being overheard. "Here are all the leaders of the pilgrimage," said Bohemond abruptly. "Which is the greatest man among them?"

"Duke Godfrey, I suppose, unless it's the Duke of Normandy," Tancred answered. "They are both good knights, and they both lead splendid mesnies. But then there's the Count of Flanders, and the Count of Blois who married the daughter of the mighty King of England. You see? I can't make up my mind. It's impossible to choose."

"They have splendid mesnies, but they have left them in camp. No one here has as many as fifty knights behind his banner. Forget their followers. Who is the greatest man in himself?"

"Duke Godfrey again, I imagine. Everyone admires him. It's still very hard to choose. Of course Count Hugh, brother to the King of France, is the knight of highest birth. Is that what you mean?"

"I think that's the answer I have been looking for. Count Hugh, brother to a King. Even a great lord would not feel slighted if he were asked to take orders from Count Hugh."

"It wouldn't be a slight. It might be the mortal sin of suicide," said Tancred with a laugh. "He's the man Alexius held hostage all winter, and Hugh never noticed it because his meals came regularly. He's brave enough, but he's got no sense. I'd have to be riding a much faster horse than this before I would follow his orders in battle."

"Nevertheless, I shall ask him to take command of this very small force of very noble knights. I expect you to back me up."

Tancred thought for a moment. Then he looked up smiling.

"You like a gamble, don't you, Uncle? The Hauteville half of me agrees, while I hear my father whispering caution. Still, it may come off, and if it does we may beat the Turks. This is a crazy scheme anyway. You may count on me to make it even crazier."

They reached the chosen position an hour before dawn, the most gloomy hour of the night when tired and hungry men feel most tired and hungry. The knights halted when Bohemond gave the word, and then stood about like a herd of cattle as their horses snatched at the dead winter grass.

"Gentlemen," called Bohemond in a low but carrying voice, "it is time to array our line. I suggest that the Count of Vermandois, son and brother of Kings, allot us our places and later give us the word to charge."

"Don't forget I am a king's son too," the Duke of Normandy objected. "Oh, I see what you mean. My father wasn't a king when I was born."

"But I don't know the ground, or the time, or whence the enemy will appear," Count Hugh said at once. "Besides, I have never commanded in a great battle. I shall be proud to charge with such gallant knights, but someone else must give the word."

"And that someone else must be Count Bohemond," said Duke Godfrey. "He has chosen the spot where we should fight. He saw exactly what we must do while my messenger was still speaking. I also will be proud to charge with such gallant knights, under Count Bohemond as my leader."

Tancred exhaled a gusty sigh of relief.

"Very well, gentlemen, if you insist," said Bohemond in a winning tone. "I shall array the line as I think best, and from a sense of my own unworthiness I myself will lead the rear-battle."

He was in a daze of glory as he, Bohemond of Hauteville, ordered famous Dukes and Counts to the places where they would fight and, very probably, die. But it was so clear in his head that never once did he hesitate. He draw up five long lines, each in a single rank. Widely spaced they completely filled the ground between the river and the lake. He himself led the sixth line, about a hundred men. They were all Normans of Normandy or Apulia, and they formed up close together in two dense ranks. Then everyone stood at his horse's head and said a few prayers in lieu of breakfast.

The sun was barely up when the Turks appeared. They rode in a narrow column, just as he had hoped. Before they could open out and string their bows he ordered his first line to charge.

He had planned a succession of shocks, as more likely to break the Turks than one great charge. It also concealed his small numbers. But it did not seem to be working. One after another the first five lines charged. The Turks, clubbed in a solid mass, pushed them slowly back. Then Bohemond turned to Robert fitzGerard, who bore his banner and rode beside him.

"This is it, Robert. We must scatter those Turks, or die on the field. If we retreat to the camp they will follow, and probably break through the palisade at our heels. I suppose it's my fault. No leader should put his men in a position where they must conquer or die. Or perhaps it's the fault of the pilgrimage. A mad idea from the start, but we all joined it of our own free will. We swore to die for the Holy Sepulchre, and now is the time for it. Come on, gentlemen, our last charge, and the fiercest we have ever delivered."

Robert lowered the banner until it pointed forward like a lance. The final reserve moved forward, well closed up.

By the time they reached the enemy they were in a wedge, with Bohemond a length in front. He picked a gap in the failing Christian line and crashed into the Turks without checking his pace. His hungry horse just managed it; another furlong would bring it to a faltering trot. But if this charge should succeed there would be spare horses in plenty. It succeeded.

Turks in their flimsy leather cuirasses were slashing with light sabres, their ponies at a stand or barely edging forward. Before the heavy mailed Normans they went down in heaps. More Turks were pressing forward in the rear, but between the river and the lake they had no room to get into action. To begin with they turned about to find more room to fight, but once they were on the move they could not stop. Soon the whole throng of mounted men was galloping upstream towards the Iron Bridge.

At the narrow entry to the bridge the infidels were checked. The pilgrims made a great slaughter; many knights mounted well-fed Turkish ponies whose owners had been killed. Those Turks who got over the bridge continued without stopping to their base at Harenc, and the knights still pursued.

At the edge of unwalled Harenc, Bohemond reined in, and ordered fitzGerard to display his banner upright. The Christians were quite ready to end their exhausting pursuit. Bohemond organized a search through the town, and was amazed at what he found. There were hundreds of mules and camels, a great troop of

spare horses, flour, oxen, sheep and goats. He asked the Count of
Flanders to take back the spoil to the camp. It was not the kind of
work knights did cheerfully, but Count Robert was a level-headed
and willing pilgrim who saw it must be done. Bohemond hurried
back to Antioch with as many knights as could still get a gallop
out of their horses.

He reached the camp before sunset on the same day. He found,
as he had expected, that the Turks of Antioch were attacking the
palisade; but the infidels withdrew into the town when they saw
knights riding to the rescue. It was hard to conceive that one day
had brought such great changes. Now the besiegers had food and
fresh horses in plenty. It was Shrove Tuesday, 9th February 1098,
and a very auspicious beginning to Lent. All the pilgrims agreed
that their good fortune was due to the skilled leadership of Count
Bohemond of Hauteville, and that was best of all.

CHAPTER XIII

The Road to St. Simeon

──────────────────★──────────────────

The supplies taken at Harenc did not last long. The Count of Blois was a scrupulous guardian, who divided fairly everything he had; but he lacked the force of character to say No and stick to it. Any blusterer, even a non-combatant who could curse fluently, would leave the central store with a decent ration. By the end of the month the store was empty. The Count of Blois had seen this coming, complaining of it to everyone he met. When it had come he could do nothing but wring his hands and lament.

Once more the hungry army depended on supplies bought from Armenians and Syrians, who admitted quite frankly that they also sold to the Turks in Antioch. It was all a matter of price, they explained, spreading their hands wide; they were peaceful merchants who made a living by selling grain. Surely the pilgrims, who were under God's special protection, would conquer the infidel anyway; it would be impious to doubt it. In the meantime poor unwarlike men must support their families by selling to the infidel what would otherwise be taken by force.

Tancred, of course, led the faction which proposed that these traitors to Christendom should be hanged before they left camp. The more responsible leaders forbade it; better to share food with the infidel than to have no food at all. Bohemond in particular was glad to see plenty of strangers in camp; though the siege had continued all winter he still hoped that a traitor would appear from Antioch.

The only other source of supplies was irregular convoys from St. Simeon, the port at the mouth of the Orontes. The Greeks of Cyprus sent a certain amount of free aid, collected by the exiled

202

Patriarch of Jerusalem; the Genoese and the pirates sold what they could spare from the plunder of Cilicia. Even some of this reached the Turks, though no one was so base as to sell it to them. The coast road was exposed to raids from Antioch; small parties of sailors were sometimes captured by the infidels.

The whole pilgrimage was fretful and discouraged. Few died of starvation, but everyone was hungry; they did not seem to be any nearer the capture of Antioch and there was no reason why the siege should not endure for generations. The Normans of Apulia did not make things any better by boasting of the four-year siege of Bari; learned clerks who mentioned the ten-year siege of Troy were rudely advised to find some more inspiring example from the past.

At the beginning of March came news of more ships in St. Simeon. The news was unexpected, though not especially important, as Bohemond explained to Tancred while they were inspecting the Apulian horse-lines.

"They said this was an English fleet," he said, "but it is not another armed passage through the Straits of Gibraltar. I have been talking to Greeks from the port. The ships are Greek, though the men are English enough. It seems that a lot of Englishmen take service with Alexius, since they don't want to fight for the son of Duke William who conquered them. This fleet sailed from the city. How do we take that? Are they Latin pilgrims, come to help in the siege? Or are they some of the Emperor's soldiers, come to bag Antioch as soon as we win it from the Turks?"

"The English are faithful to the Pope," Tancred answered. "In Italy everyone knows that. Exceptionally faithful, in fact. No heresy or schism in England. So they must be pilgrims, even if the Emperor pays them."

By next morning the pilgrims had learned more about the new arrivals. They were indeed English Varangians from the city, and their ships were Greek; but a number of Frankish late-comers had joined them instead of making the dangerous crossing of Anatolia, and their leader was an English nobleman of high rank. After a routine meeting of the council the Duke of Normandy told his friends all about it.

"He's the chap who would be King of the English today if my

father hadn't conquered the country. Edgar, the only survivor of the ancient royal line. No connection with Harold the usurper, of course. He's quite respectable. His sister is married to the King of the Scots, he fights on horseback and speaks French and has all the other manners of a gentleman. I have invited him to join my following. We share a common hatred of my brother William, who has done us both out of the same crown. Unless one of us gets it we have no reason to quarrel. Some of my knights hold land in England. They will be glad to see Edgar. This pilgrimage is really bringing all Christendom together."

Bohemond noted that Duke Robert did not expect to gain England. The Duke was quite happy on this pilgrimage, except for the temporary lack of food. He was the only great leader who was never tempted to hurry home to look after his fiefs. When he was at home he did not look after them.

Everyone was tepidly pleased to learn of the reinforcements; but Tancred alone thought their arrival ought to affect the campaign. He still burned to take the offensive, while most pilgrims were content to hang on before Antioch. He pointed out to the other leaders that one gate was still open to Turkish conveys. The west gate south of the river, known as St. George's, had long been considered out of reach of the besiegers. The great Bridge Gate, where the Turks clustered most thickly, barred the way to it from camp north of the river; Christians could reach it only by the long and rough ride round the south of Mount Silpius. Tancred now volunteered to hold a castle opposite this gate. He made conditions. Since his followers were now penniless they must be paid by the whole army; and carpenters from the English fleet must help him to build the castle. Perhaps among the new pilgrims would be cross-bows and other foot willing to join the garrison.

"It sounds reasonable," said Bohemond. "On a campaign like this to do almost anything is better than to do nothing. If anyone can hold this castle right behind the Turkish lines my nephew Tancred is the man. By the way, St. George's Gate. In Romania all sorts of things are dedicated to St. George. Who was he?"

"A very great saint," Bishop Adhemar said at once. "One of the most famous martyrs of the days before Constantine. He has a church in Rome down by the Tiber, a fine church lined with coloured marble."

"He was a soldier," Count Raymond said severely. "A soldier in the pagan Roman army who defied the persecutor Diocletian. You see his image everywhere, armed and mounted, so I suppose he was a knight. I thought everyone knew of him. Perhaps Normans who invade the lands of fellow-Christians are not so well instructed."

Bohemond answered in anger. "In my town of Bari we have the complete body of the famous St. Nicholas, brought from Romania to save it from the infidel Turks. My old friend Pope Urban consecrated the shrine for me. I don't know the names of all the saints venerated by schismatics. Perhaps that's because I am the immediate vassal of the Pope."

"Doesn't your younger brother the Duke of Apulia stand between you and the Pope?" muttered a south Frenchman.

"No one holds the fealty of the mighty Bohemond," Tancred shouted. "He came on this pilgrimage without leave from any lord, certainly without consulting his younger brother. I follow him, and will gladly prove on the body of any French knight that he is more free than a Marquis of the German Emperor."

"Until this pilgrimage has been accomplished you may not prove anything on the body of a fellow-pilgrim," said Duke Godfrey in a tone of reproof. "Do you wish to say more to this council?"

"I am sorry, noble Duke. Now that your brother Count Baldwin no longer attacks my men I shall not wage war on any pilgrim. My immediate plan is to get in touch with the English at St. Simeon, but I have not enough knights to escort a convoy. Will any other lord join me with his following?" It was a legitimate score off the brothers from Boulogne, though a rash remark in full council. But Tancred never allowed prudence to control his tongue.

"I shall ride to the port this very day," said Bohemond at once. "I suggest that my nephew Tancred stay here and plan his castle on the ground. My knights can escort the convoy from the ships."

"I also shall ride to the port," said Count Raymond. "Two mesnies are stronger than one, and this convoy is important. The sooner Tancred builds his castle the sooner we can restore Antioch to its rightful lord the Emperor."

Even in public council no one concealed the enmity between the south French and the Normans of Italy. Raymond was determined that the Apulians should not ride off where he could not see what they were doing.

That afternoon two strong mesnies set off on the fourteen-mile ride to St. Simeon. The Turks of Antioch saw them go, but there was no way to stop that.

After one night in the port they began the return journey. St. Simeon was not a place where Bohemond cared to linger. The little settlement at the river mouth was unwalled, and the ships anchored in the stream or moored to the shore were not in his military eye a useful fleet. Pisans and Genoese and Frisians had fought hard to get there, and the English Varangians were famous warriors; but now that they were in harbour they did not obey their commanders, and men who were pirates by trade kept their hands in by stealing from one another. There were men in complete mail who claimed to have been knights at home; but they had brought no horses and must take their place among the lowly foot.

Every sailor from the Mediterranean could use a cross-bow, and so could some of the Franks who had taken passage on the Greek ships. Luckily the English and Frisians preferred to fight on foot with axes, and Edgar the Englishman proposed to sail with them to the sack of various infidel or Greek ports. That was all for the best. Englishmen in a French army would be tempted to fight the battle of Hastings over again, instead of forming part of a united front against the infidel.

Bohemond and Raymond, working independently, each collected a force of Frankish cross-bows and carpenters, to help Tancred build his new fort. There was a certain amount of food; and some useful timber and tackle for making siege-engines. Altogether there were two useful convoys. Normans and south French were by now too hostile to work together, but each watched the doings of the other and the two convoys set out at the same time. Where the road narrowed Count Raymond went ahead, whereupon Bohemond and his knights fell back to guard the rear.

Like all the valleys of northern Syria this was ideal country for an ambush. Count Raymond was experienced in wars against the infidel; but he was himself too old and sick for hard riding, and he did not always make his knights carry out his orders. Bohemond did not trust his scouting. But to send out Norman scouts after Raymond had declared the way safe would be an insult that might end in bloodshed. Bohemond kept his knights in good order and waited for the Turkish attack. He was not at all surprised when it came.

Unfortunately no one else was ready for it. The cross-bows and skilled workmen marching on foot beside the waggons trusted in the south French knights riding ahead. The advance guard expected an attack from the front, the Apulians in the rear were looking over their shoulders, for they knew that Turks liked to attack from behind. A cloud of mounted bowmen suddenly popped out of a deep ravine to charge the straggling column in the middle.

In a moment the Turks were so mixed up with the Christian foot that Bohemond dared not charge. Besides, he still waited for another Turkish attack from the rear. There seemed to be more Turks ahead, since the south French knights were dressing their line to charge forward.

Bohemond turned to his banner-bearer. "The artful devils, they have caught us. This broken country is a curse, you never see all your enemies at once. You and I are safe enough. Light horse cannot harm mailed knights. But I don't see how we are to save the waggons. Halt. Send scouts to the rear. Open ranks to let fugitives through. Wait until the Turks have the waggons and begin to move them back to Antioch. Then we can pelt after them and perhaps take back their plunder."

The centre of the column quickly dissolved in rout. Those foot who had not been cut down in the first onset took refuge behind rocks on the steep hillside. They were at the mercy of the mounted infidels, but luckily the Turks did not pursue. They were too busy rounding up the waggons and controlling the oxen who drew them.

With a great gabbling and shouting the Turks got the waggons under way. They were in a desperate hurry, apprehensive of what seemed to them too easy a victory. Bohemond shut his eyes, to see behind their closed lids his imaginary map of the valley.

"Gentlemen, this battle isn't lost," he called to his excited followers. "The infidels must cross the river with their waggons. That's it. The Bridge Gate. If they drive the oxen at that speed there will be a lovely jam there. Follow me carefully, and make sure that none of you charge before you see my banner lowered. We'll hustle the Turks without actually charging them. Shout the warcry. Make all the noises you can. But don't actually get among them before we reach the bridge."

Oxen can make good speed if their waggons are lightly loaded and the men riding beside them are nervous and flustered. The Turks ought to have dropped a rearguard to delay pursuit, but perhaps there were not enough of them. Bohemond noted that with apprehension. Another infidel army must be attacking the camp. If that should have fallen by the time they reached it they must fight their way back to St. Simeon and then sail away to Europe; they might be among the few survivors of the disastrous pilgrimage.

But so far the second stage of this muddled battle was going well enough. When a waggon lost a wheel the Turks abandoned it, proof that they dared not stand to defend the plunder they had seized. The Apulian knights kept just out of arrow range; but they rode closed up, shield on neck, ready to charge. A mile ahead they came on the knights of Count Raymond, prudently drawn up on a hillock just north of the road. Without a word they fell in beside the Apulians. Raymond might be unwilling to speak to his rival, but he was not too proud to conform to his movements in the field.

Bohemond could not recall perfectly every mile of an unfamiliar road, but the castle of Antioch, perched on Mount Silpius, was a handy landmark. As they approached it Bohemond heard, above the clatter of hoofs and the warcries, a distant roar of battle. On the spur of the moment he changed his entire plan of action. He gave up the slow pursuit of the convoy and led his knights at full gallop in a northerly half-circle. He had guessed right. They came over a rise to see a strong Turkish force closely engaged with the palisades of the pilgrim camp.

The Turks saw them at the same time, but because of the ridge could not estimate their numbers. Men who fight by ambuscade will be nervous of being ambushed in their turn. At once the Turks disengaged and began to retire over the bridge into Antioch. Bohemond charged towards the bridge-head, Count Raymond beside him.

It was all working out. Bohemond felt a glow of godlike omniscience as for the second time in one afternoon his enemies did exactly what he had expected them to do. He had guessed that they would attack the camp while they ambushed the convoy, and that the attackers would retreat rather than face Christian reinforcements. Now he must drive them over the great bridge before the first waggon could reach it. He squeezed his horse.

The Turks fought badly. Everything was going wrong for them; all they wanted was safety behind the walls of Antioch. Some ass must have feared that the besiegers would enter with the fugitives, for the gate was closed and barred before more than the head of the column had entered. The rearmost Turks lost heart. Some tried to make their ponies swim the river, and were drowned; others pulled cloaks over their eyes, so that they would not flinch when a Christian sword cut them down. No one sought quarter, and none was granted.

Suddenly Bohemond saw mailed knights all round him. Duke Godfrey leaned out of the saddle to embrace him; he had led the pursuit as soon as the Turks began to withdraw from the camp. He called out to inquire after the convoy, and Bohemond pointed to the road behind him.

There stood as many of the waggons as had survived the hurried journey. Their oxen grazed peacefully, as oxen will graze peacefully in the midst of any disaster. No man was near them, either Christian or Turk.

"I was in too much of a hurry to drive oxen myself," said Bohemond, "so I got the Turks to do it for me. I knew they would drop them somewhere handy. Look, there are the last of the infidels, down by the river. Let's go after them and kill those who hesitate before drowning."

At the end of the day the pilgrims estimated that fifteen hundred Turks had fallen, and among them they found the bodies of nine eminent leaders. By supper time all the Christians were safe behind the palisades of their camp.

For the moment there was enough to eat, and knights went

visiting among the pavilions. Tancred came to talk over the day's fighting with his uncle.

"There was a time when things looked very bad here in the camp," he said. "Duke Godfrey did more than anyone else to organize our defence. I was out with some engineers on the site where I plan to build my castle, and I had to ride right round Mount Silpius to get back. So you won't hear much of the part played by the Apulians. Of course all sorts of rumours were flying about. Some of your light horse, grooms and such, fled from the convoy as soon as the fighting started. To excuse themselves they told us that you and Count Raymond had been killed, with all your knights. It might have been true, for all I knew. It may happen tomorrow, as it may happen to any of us. If it does, your remaining followers will probably seek my advice. What shall I tell them?"

"What will you do yourself?"

"Go on until I am killed, or until I have liberated the Holy Sepulchre. That's what I vowed before I left Italy. But I have no right to order your followers to get themselves killed. Do you order it?"

"I do not. That's an order I shall never give. Every knight, every warrior, is the guardian of his own honour. He must decide for himself whether to fight or whether to run away. It is wrong to compel a man to be killed for you, though sometimes in a bloody war it can't be helped. If that happens it's because the leader has made a mistake, but it may be too late to alter it. I always try to remember that my troops may be beaten, and that they ought to have some way of escape."

"But we are bound by oath."

"My dear Tancred, tell your confessor that you are bound by oath to commit suicide, and see what he answers. Take this case you mentioned. If Count Raymond and I had been killed with all our knights the remaining leaders would have decided for retreat; and that would release you from your oath. If I happen to get killed and the pilgrimage still continues, of course my followers will march with it. If the leaders decide on retreat my men retreat with the rest, and I hope you do also. That's all the advice I can give you on a case that hasn't happened yet."

"Just one other point bothers me, uncle Bohemond. Don't take offence. I must ask you. A good many pilgrims have suggested that if we win Antioch you will stay in it, instead of continuing to Jerusalem. I suppose there's no truth in that?"

"Unless we win Antioch before next winter we shall all go home. We can't stick it out here for three years, as our fathers stuck it out before Bari. I suppose you agree that's reasonable? Now if I take Antioch, I myself and not the pilgrimage as a whole, I shall have to consider carefully the exact terms of my vow. I swore to fight the infidel until Jerusalem has been liberated, and to hear Mass in the Holy Sepulchre before I go home. If I am lord of Antioch I shall be fighting the infidel every day, and I shall also aid the pilgrimage. St. Simeon is our only way home, now that we cannot trust Alexius. We can't go on to Jerusalem leaving a hostile Antioch behind us; and it will be as hostile in Greek hands as in Turkish. Some Frank must hold it. Why not I, who want it? One day before I go home, if ever I go home, I shall hear Mass in the Holy Sepulchre. My vow will be fulfilled to the letter."

"Well, every knight is the guardian of his own honour, as you have just said. I see that when Antioch falls, if it falls, we must part."

"I shan't try to keep you; though you are my best knight, if indeed you are a knight of mine. I also think we should part. There won't be room in Antioch for two knights of the Hauteville stock."

"So that is cleared up," said Tancred with a shrug. "If you can't hold Antioch no Frank can; and some Frank must hold it. I shall do what I can to win it for you. Tomorrow I begin building my castle before St. George's Gate."

Later that evening the Turks, who also felt a strong attachment to holy places, crept quietly over the great bridge to bury their dead in an ancient infidel cemetery just north of the river. The pilgrims saw what they were doing, but did not come out to fight. In the morning Christian foot, protected by cross-bows, dug up the infidel dead. They piled their heads where the garrison of Antioch could see, for Armenians had told them that the mutilation of dead infidels caused their comrades great distress; the deluded fanatics believed that at the Resurrection they would rise in the condition in which they had been buried, instead of returning to Hell. The knights would not permit the pilgrim foot to inflict other, more amusing mutilations on the corpses, for one day their own bodies might fall into the hands of the enemy.

The foot gained an unlooked-for bonus. The Turks, still barbarian at heart for all their pretence of being cultured infidels, had buried their leaders with all their personal wealth. The pilgrims had not only a little food from St. Simeon; they had money to buy more from Armenian merchants.

Within a few days two castles were built. Raymond's castle, by the infidel burial ground, commanded the northern end of the great bridge and kept the road to St. Simeon firmly in Christian hands. Tancred's castle, a perilous post, blocked St. George's Gate. No more convoys could get into Antioch, though single messengers might still climb over Mount Silpius.

By the end of April everyone felt more hopeful of victory. The weather was warmer, a great comfort to an army which had burned all the firewood within foraging distance. It was rumoured that the garrison of Antioch was beginning to feel hungry. Tancred had snapped up the last caravan from the north, a long column of waggons and pack-animals collected by Armenian merchants. The Armenians lost all their possessions and barely escaped with their lives. Henceforth they must sell their wares to the pilgrims, for the Turkish market was closed to them. Many more native Christians were to be seen in the camp.

But news from the outside world was disturbing, so disturbing that the council of leaders met in special session to discuss it. The great Caliph of Baghdad, religious leader of all the infidels, had begun to gather an army of relief. It was under the command of Curbaram, the Caliph's favourite general and the ruler of all Persia. He had enlisted horsemen from all the infidel world, as far as Khorasan and the borders of India. He would arrive by mid-summer, as soon as he had conquered the castles held by Count Baldwin on the eastern bank of the Euphrates.

It was hard to find out what happened so far to the east, but by April news had seeped through that Baldwin was lord of the strong town of Edessa. He had married the daughter of its Armenian lord; soon after the people of Edessa rebelled against their ruler, murdered him, and installed Baldwin as his heir. There was a strong smell of treachery about the whole business, but no one had denounced Baldwin formally for treason to the lord who was said to have adopted him as a son.

Tancred, like most Apulians, took it for granted that Baldwin was capable of any villainy; but everyone agreed that he was a good knight who would defend the fortress which had so curiously come into his hands. That gave the besiegers of Antioch a little time in which to make up their minds; but only one decision was possible. When the council met Duke Godfrey announced it bluntly.

"Gentlemen, we are only just strong enough to fight the Turks at present in Antioch. To divide our forces is out of the question. It is doubtful whether we can defend ourselves against the great army of Curbaram. Certainly we can't fight the two Turkish armies combined. So we must go back, at least as far as the mountains. That may be regarded as settled. The only question still open for our decision is whether we halt among the mountains until more pilgrims join us from Europe; or whether we wind up the whole enterprise and ask the Pope to dispense us from our vows. The Emperor supposed we would never liberate the Holy Sepulchre, and I am beginning to agree with him. What are your views?"

Amid a murmur of regretful agreement Bohemond got up to speak. "Let's wait a week or so. Baldwin is no friend of mine or of my kin, but he can defend a castle. There is no immediate danger. But I want a firm answer to a question I have asked before: if I get us all into Antioch will you recognize me as lord of the town?"

"Why the devil should we?" asked Count Raymond. "Who besieged Antioch, Bohemond or the whole army of the pilgrimage? When we starved, when we fought the Turks, my men did not serve Bohemond. I have given him no oath. On the contrary he has sworn to serve the Emperor. The Emperor is the key to the whole campaign. Without him we can do no more. But we have all heard that he is somewhere in Anatolia with his mighty army, completing the conquest of those Turks who fled before us. If we take Antioch, let the Pope's legate give it to whichever lord he thinks most suitable to rule it. I shan't attempt to decide for him. It's a matter for the Church. But before we take it we must seek help from the Emperor. I agree that there is no hurry. There is time to send a messenger to imperial headquarters. Once we know Alexius is marching to help us we can retreat just enough to join him."

"Suppose he doesn't come?" asked Bohemond.

"Then we must make other plans. But surely he will come. In any case we have another week or ten days. That is my suggestion, gentlemen. Send a message to the Emperor and wait for the answer. Since opinion is divided we ought to put it to the vote."

"Who is entitled to vote on such a great matter?" asked Bohemond. "Every Count in the pilgrimage, or just those Counts here today? How many of us rank as Counts? That has never been decided. In a civilized country every man knows whether he has been born with a vote in the assembly or not, but in this pilgrimage we have never made up our minds. At this stage we can't take a vote. Before evening we would be fighting one another. Gentlemen, with the welfare of the pilgrimage at heart I withdraw my proposal. I shall fight with the army so long as we stay here. Let us send a messenger to Alexius. If he joins us I myself will go back to Italy, since he is my foe and may very well murder me. But you and he together will liberate Antioch. I hope he pays you your due wages. I am not his mercenary soldier, so I shall not fight under his orders. Good day."

Without looking back he walked to his pavilion.

After the leaders had decided to send yet another messenger to the Emperor they adjourned in some dismay.

Bohemond squatted on his folded blankets, for by now his pavilion was completely bare of furniture. That walk-out had been a fine gesture; and necessary, for if he had stayed longer he might have drawn his sword on the Count of Toulouse. But the future looked bleak.

If the other pilgrims sought the Emperor he must go back to Apulia. It was quite likely that he had no home, for some other Hauteville would have taken his fiefs. Why wouldn't his comrades let him have Antioch? No one else wanted it as he did, no one else had been promised it by Alexius, no other Frank was so fitted to rule it. He spoke Greek, he understood orientals, he could plan a battle better than any other Count. But Raymond was his enemy, and that was just enough to prevent the council making any decision. Why had he come on this absurd pilgrimage? If he had stayed at home he would have conquered most of Italy by now. To kill Turks was a good thing, they were unpleasant people who needed killing; but it was not his personal duty. If it was a question of freeing Christians from infidel oppression Spain was a better place to do it. The Spaniards were decent western Franks, obedient to the Pope and willing to fight for their freedom. Greeks were schismatics who would never fight in any cause; Armenians would fight, but only each for his own hand. They did not deserve help from the west. He had been wasting his time, and there were not very many years of active campaigning before him; he was in his forty-fifth year, and he had no son to come after him.

Perhaps a comfortable monastery, with a decent winter climate, would be the best solution. It was lucky that he had never been tempted by women. He owed a duty to his followers. He must lead them home in safety. As soon as he was back in a sensible Frankish land he would hang up his sword before St. Michael on Monte Gargano and enter religion. He could read fluently, so they would make him a full choir-monk, perhaps a priest; he would not care to be a mere lay brother, at the beck and call of every literate monk. Probably he had not much of a vocation, but his will was strong enough to keep him to the rules. He would miss riding, and all the fussing over horses in the evening which was the favourite pastime of every good knight. But old age would put him out of the saddle one day, even if he remained a layman.

He was beginning to plan his journey home. When the Emperor had joined the pilgrimage he would lead his men towards the west, by one of the great roads made by the men of old. Before they reached the city they would swerve southward and sack some flourishing Greek port. With money they could buy a passage home on Italian ships. Then they would disperse.

It was the end of a dream. When he first heard of the pilgrimage he had hoped to found a strong fief in the east. Perhaps he could still make himself King of Italy; but first he would have to kill all his half-brothers, and the price was too high. He had it in him, he knew, to be a great commander. He saw what the enemy were about to do, he could see a whole battlefield, a whole countryside, something in his mind told him that exact moment to charge. Well, all that was over. It was possible that never again would he kill a man.

He squatted with his eyes on the ground, imagining the painted page of an office-book before them. In the cloister there would be hot sun and the sound of bees, but the great church was always cool and still within. His mother would be surprised to find him a monk, though she would approve. He still saw her from time to time, a very old lady; but he did not often think of her since she had left him so long ago, a child who still needed her. Life had been unfair to him. They had taken away his mother, and now they were going to take away Antioch. Self-pity is a very pleasant sensation, so long as you see it clearly for what it is.

A spearman stood in the entry to the pavilion, keeping a careful eye on a nondescript Armenian. "This man insists on seeing your lordship alone," he said anxiously. "I have searched him for weapons, and he has promised me a gold piece if I bring him here. My lord, I need the money. Will you speak with him?"

"Make him pay in advance and then go away. I may as well gossip with local merchants as sit here thinking about Italy. My part in the war is nearly over and I have plenty of time to waste."

CHAPTER XIV

The Towers of Antioch

---★---

The man who came in was a middle-aged Armenian; Bohemond had seen enough of the varied races of Syria to know that he was not a Greek or a local peasant. But he was not the kind of Armenian who usually came to the camp. There were two very different types of Armenian: the soft plump traders who looked, if that were possible, even more dishonest and shifty than they were; and the tall hawk-nosed mountaineers, who walked with long strides and looked undressed without a sabre and a beltful of knives. This man was a warrior.

He bowed with both hands at his breast, like a humble merchant; but he did it clumsily, as though he were unused to the gesture. After looking carefully round the pavilion to make sure they were really alone he spoke in Greek, in a very low voice.

"I know you are the lord Bohemond, for you are the tallest of the Franks. We may be able to do business together, just you and I with no third parties. It must be done swiftly. What price do you offer for secret entry into three towers on the western wall of Mount Silpius?"

Bohemond sat up with a jerk. At the last possible moment, when he was planning the life he would lead in Italy after the failure of the pilgrimage, God had sent him the traitor he had been seeking for eight months. It seemed too good to be true. He must find out more about this man.

"I can't offer a great fortune. The siege has dragged on so long that the pilgrims have no money left. But if money was what you wanted you would have spoken sooner. The man who lets me into Antioch will be under the protection of all Christendom, with sufficient land and gold to live without ploughing his own fields. I promise only what I can perform. If that is enough we can begin to talk business. In the first place, who are you and how do you command three towers? You are not a Turk."

"Your offer is enough. I want to die of old age, I don't seek riches. The executioner comes closer every minute, and what is one more treason after all my past sins? I may even dodge Hell after I am dead, and that's something I had given up hoping for. So here, very briefly, is all about me.

"I am an Armenian, a baptized Christian. I shall not tell you my name, since I have brought disgrace on my kin. When I served the Greek Emperor I was known as Pyrrhus, the Turks now call me Firouz. It's ten years since I fell into the hands of Yaghi-Siyan, emir of Antioch. I had fought well, and I was offered life if I would deny Christ. I did so. We can't all be martyrs. Now that I see a chance of dying a Christian I want to change sides again. That is enough."

"It's not nearly enough," snapped Bohemond. "Since October the pilgrims have lain before Antioch and now it is late in May. Why did you fight for your masters all through the winter, and why have you now decided to change sides? What's all this about the approaching executioner?"

He must hear a convincing explanation of what might be a trap. But he liked his first impression of this double traitor; the man had said honestly that fear had made him a renegade, when he might have tried to find excuses for his wickedness. Besides, it could have been pride as much as fear. Warriors of noble birth found it unbearable to live as taxpaying serfs even when the infidels granted mercy.

"Yaghi-Siyan won't be emir of Antioch much longer. His men will yield unless relief comes soon, but any Turkish lord who drives the pilgrims from Antioch will keep the fortress for himself. My emir likes me and trusts me; for that matter I like him. He's a stout warrior and an honest man. Kerbogha, or any other Turkish lord, will probably take away my sword and sell me as a slave. I might be castrated and put to look after the women. That justifies any treachery, doesn't it? Anyway, my present lord is beginning to suspect me. I am afraid."

"He suspects you? And you command three towers? You must tell me a great deal more."

"He doesn't suspect my fidelity. You see, I am *his* man, whom he relies on to protect him from discontented Turks. Turks might set up another emir, but they wouldn't follow an Armenian. That part of it is safe enough. But there are other troubles. One is about money. Turks like money, but they can get it only by the sword. They won't work for it, and they don't know how to buy and sell. Every Armenian can do that, even an Armenian warrior. When food grew scarce I sold bread to the Christians of Antioch. I would take nothing but gold, and I did quite well by it. Presently the emir found out. He took my gold, gold I had earned by my skill as a trader. I explained that I had been acting as his agent all along and that it was all his anyway. But he suspected that if he had not found out about it I might have kept some for myself. Any emir feels himself cheated if all the gold in his country does not belong to him. He thinks I may still be cheating him. One day he may torture me, just to make sure. The other trouble is about my wife. The emir is her lover. There is nothing I can do about it, and in a way it keeps me safe. As a mistress she amuses the emir, because a woman reared as a Christian is not so submissive as the women of the infidels. But I suspect that Anna has begun to think of joining the emir's household, to better herself. The infidels are very hot against adultery. She could only enter that household as a widow. The suspicion puts me off my food, which she cooks. I don't see a very long career for me as the trusted captain of the emir Yaghi-Siyan. But today I am his trusted captain, trusted to command three towers."

"It seems to me that you gained very little by denying Christ," said Bohemond. "I see why you are in a hurry. The deal must go through before the army of relief arrives, and Curbaram is now before Edessa. Well, it's agreed. Now when we get in there will be a bloody sack. Are there any members of your family whom you want to keep safe? Presumably you will let your wife take her chance."

"I have a brother in one of the other towers; he joined the Turks when I did. I would like to save him but I dare not tell him anything. He must take his chance with my wife. The only one who *must* be saved is my ten-year-old son. He will be in the tower with me when you enter, and you must swear that he will be first out of the town, before the fighting begins."

"That I'll swear. Meanwhile you have named your hostage. He will be first out of the town, as you say. But he will be in the Christian camp before the first pilgrim enters Antioch. If we find a trap waiting for us he will be burned alive."

Pyrrhus reflected, and then shrugged assent. "Of course you must have a hostage. Clever of you to find out so quickly which member of my household is really dear to me. Since no treachery is intended my son will come to no harm. The difficulty will be getting him into your camp. He can slip down from the wall unobserved; but he lives in my tower and my men will soon notice his absence. I can't send him to you before the day of the assault."

"That will be soon enough. He will be in my hands before I trust myself to you. That is the only condition, but we must not waste time. It will take a day or two to arrange this. I must get the whole army under arms, without telling the men why. I am not in supreme command, you know; we have no supreme commander. Can you come here again to see me?"

"I can get here fairly easily, when I can be absent from my post. In Antioch I pass as a Turk and wear Turkish dress, so the other Armenians won't recognize me. It must all be done within the week. Do you know that Kerbogha has decided to raise the siege of Edessa and march here? When he arrives you will have to retreat. Now forgive me, my lord, but I should like to have some idea of the reward that awaits me."

"Here is a key. Open that box. It is full of gold bezants, given to me last year by the Emperor Alexius in person. You may count them and test them, and for that matter take the key home with you. I hung on to that gold all winter, even when I might have bought food with it. I expected that one day I would need it at short notice. Besides the gold, when I am lord of Antioch I shall give you three or four villages."

"I shan't open the box. The word of the giant Bohemond is good even among the infidels. I don't want land. All I want is a few more years of life, until my son is old enough to carry a sword and defend himself. Only you can give it to me. There is one more promise I must have from you. Swear on your sword that you will not tell another living soul before you climb the wall."

"Until an hour before I climb the wall. I won't climb it alone, and my followers must be told where they are going."

"An hour, no longer. You wouldn't have made that condition unless you intended to keep your word. Will you give me your hand on the bargain? I shall be here again tomorrow or the next day. Then we shall fix the time of the assault, before Kerbogha can arrive. It will be a tight fit."

Bohemond put out his hand without hesitation. Pyrrhus was a double traitor and a double renegade. But he seemed to be the kind of warrior who would keep a solemn promise. In Apulia he had met Normans who were even greater scoundrels.

Soon after Pyrrhus had slipped away Tancred came in to discuss the stormy council of that morning. Bohemond found it hard to keep his promise not to let anyone into the secret. Tancred was in despair, continually talking about the need to find a traitor just when one had in fact appeared. They agreed that the outlook was hopeless. When Curbaram approached the pilgrims must evacuate the left bank of the Orontes; as soon as the two Turkish armies united they must retire to the mountains of Armenia. It was possible that they would advance in the spring, with Greek help; but the Apulians and many other pilgrims would continue back to Europe.

Every morning the leaders met in council, to hear the latest reports of Curbaram's advance. With a handful of knights and many allied Armenians, Count Baldwin was holding the strong fortress of Edessa. Perhaps Curbaram had sat down to besiege it; or he might have passed by and continued his march on Antioch. Christian peasants continually reported the arrival of more Turks. But they were peasants, inexperienced in war. Were these Turks foragers, gathering supplies for a siege? Or were they the vanguard of the army of relief? The peasants were agreed that Edessa was still in Christian hands, but they could not be more definite.

Bohemond, putting himself in Curbaram's place, guessed that a veteran Turkish commander would leave Edessa to fall by its own weight after the pilgrims had been driven from Syria. That would be the wiser plan. But the Turks were boasters who hated to admit a check. Curbaram might be so angry with the weak garrison of Edessa that he would stay to kill every Christian in the place. Everything hung on Curbaram's movements. The pilgrims must retire before him, but there was just a chance that they might win Antioch before he could arrive.

Since Bohemond had sworn not to speak of the intended treason of Pyrrhus the advice he gave the council was even more gloomy than his private thoughts. Tancred loyally backed him up, though he was a little puzzled by the faint heart of his famous uncle. After a few days the council was unanimous on one point: that very soon the whole army of the pilgrimage would suffer a terrible defeat. Nevertheless the Counts were divided into two factions: those who would die where they stood, and those who wished to retreat into Armenia.

The climax came on the morning of the 2nd of June. At day-break the Count of Blois rode out with a company of north Frenchmen, fully armed and shield on neck. They said quite openly that they would not face another Syrian winter, neither would they cross again the awful mountains of Armenia. They were on their way to the Cilician port of Alexandretta, whence they would take ship for France. If other pilgrims barred their way they would fight rather than be turned back. They added that those pilgrims who still lingered before Antioch were in danger of the mortal sin of suicide.

Tancred, watching the road with his little patrol of knights, sent to ask his uncle for instructions. Bohemond jumped on the nearest horse and rode out all unarmed to see what was going on.

"It would be rather fun to charge them," he said to Tancred. "I bet I could bowl over the Count of Blois as I am, in my gown, just by bumping my horse into his. Some of his knights are better stuff, but they can load their dishonour on his shoulders. A vassal cannot be blamed for following his lord. So we must let them go, rather than start a civil war. Report to the council of leaders, if ever the leaders meet again. But this looks like the end of the pil-grimage. I shan't be the next to go, but we ought to get our Apulians packed and ready."

In silence Tancred leaned over his horse's shoulder and with the point of his lance scratched a line in the dusty earth.

"Confound you, my boy," said Bohemond. "A grown man who takes a dare is a fool. But I have no lord below the Pope, and I can be a fool if I choose. Very well. I also stay south of that line. You and I will kill a lot of infidels. Perhaps we may kill them all before they kill us. As far as I can see that's our only hope of survival."

"We never had any other hope, since we left Apulia," Tancred answered.

As they rode back to camp Duke Godfrey hailed them. "Blois has gone," he called, "and a lot of north French with him. What happens next? Do we follow?"

"My nephew has decided to stay," answered Bohemond. "I shall stay to keep an eye on him. I owe that much to my sister. If you stay also, so will the others."

Godfrey shrugged. "This pilgrimage was never safe. I'm sorry it will end here, when I had hoped to liberate the Holy Sepulchre. I wonder if we can get the women away before the end?"

"It can't be done," Bohemond explained. "They would be enslaved by Greeks, or Armenians, or by casual pirates. So if Turks don't capture them they can buy them. Perhaps your knights might escort them through Armenia."

"No, I stay and my knights with me. It's too late to escape, anyway. Within three days Curbaram will be here, and he would overtake our retreat. What on earth made the Count of Blois flee so disgracefully? A man of his birth, married to the sister of the King of England—I can't understand it."

"His abacus scared him, of course," said Bohemond cheerfully. "If you just feel hungry you hope for a good dinner tomorrow. But if you have figures to prove that there will never be enough food you look for a way out. I wonder what his wife will say when he gets home? A pity we shall never hear an account of that meeting."

"You may think like that, you must not talk like that," said Godfrey sharply. "We may win, though it needs a miracle. Anyway we don't want to discourage the foot. We are all looking forward to a jolly battle."

They separated, each going to see if there was any breakfast in his pavilion.

As Bohemond dismounted, a spearman came forward. "I hope I did right, my lord. There's a young boy in your bedchamber, a local of some kind, Christian or infidel. I searched him, and he's unarmed. He can't speak any proper language but he keeps on asking for the lord Bohemond. They are the only Frankish words he knows. He's too young to be a spy but he might be a messenger, so I let him wait for you."

In the inner apartment Bohemond found a boy about ten years of age. He wore silk, though he was thin and grubby; but then so was everyone else on both sides by this stage of the war. He spoke in careful though clumsy Greek.

"My father Pyrrhus sends me as a hostage. He says you must come tonight or not at all. Until dawn he will wait for you in the Tower of the Three Sisters. You must put a ladder to the window, and enter the tower itself so that you cannot be seen from the wall. If you are not there by dawn my father will climb down a rope and flee to the mountains. He thinks that tomorrow he will be arrested, or at least dismissed from his post. There is no time to be lost."

"I see. Where are you supposed to be at this minute?"

"That's another reason for haste. The soldiers think I am with my mother, my mother thinks I am in the tower. Often the emir visits my mother, and if he comes tonight he may send for me. You cannot delay. And my father said to remind you that you have sworn on your honour as a warrior that no other Frank will know the secret until an hour before it happens."

"I shan't tell anyone. You are as safe as any Frank, which isn't saying much. But this needs thinking out. I can't tell the pilgrims, I must persuade them to follow me blindly."

Bohemond sat with his head in his hands. He might not give orders, and he had twelve hours or less to arrange the assault. Perhaps it was too late anyway. While they were fighting on the walls Curbaram might crash into them, and they would all be martyred.

Such a man as he could reasonably expect to die in battle, one day. It was natural to postpone the event as long as possible. He did not look forward with pleasure to martyrdom, as did Tancred. He did not greatly care about the liberation of the Holy Sepulchre. He did not even hate Turks, so long as they did not come near

Apulia. He had volunteered for this pilgrimage because there were too many other Hautevilles in Italy. Even when Tancred had persuaded him to heroism he had been secretly hoping that after the final lost battle a knight of his strength and skill might be able to cut his way through to St. Simeon. Now, within a few hours, he must risk all on one throw of the dice.

The risk must be taken. By tomorrow he would be in Antioch, the magnet that had lured him half across the world. He might be dead there, but it was a good place to die in. If he was still alive he would be lord of the great fortress. All he had to do now was to plan the means.

Today there would be no meeting of the council of leaders. Everything was still too disorganized after the flight of the Count of Blois. So he must unofficially persuade the whole army to follow him. That might not be too difficult. Everyone knew there was a crisis, everyone would be ready for a sudden move. He spoke Greek, and if he pretended to private information he would be believed. Most people took his advice on the battlefield; at Dorylaeum he had saved the whole pilgrimage; when they were starving he had taken convoys from the infidel. He must issue his commands at the last minute, so that Count Raymond had no time to object. Who would proclaim his orders?

It ought to be someone fairly well known, but not a knight who might query Bohemond's authority. At the entry of his pavilion he happened to see a foot-sergeant. That man would do. He had a loud voice and he was well known. At the siege of Nicaea, more than a year ago, he had ventured so close to the wall that a Turk had emptied a bucket of filth on him; that narrow escape was the greatest adventure which had ever befallen him, and he spoke of it constantly. As a result his comrades knew him as Dirty Crown.

"Hey, Dirty Crown, come here. I have a job for you. This afternoon I want you to take that Turkish pony, and that Turkish drum. You must go through the whole camp, beating the drum and crying my message. Curbaram is near. Our only chance is to destroy him before he reaches Antioch, as we destroyed the last army of relief in the battle by the lake. Proclaim that at sunset every man must be armed and ready to march out. We shall march east to surprise Cubaram's camp in the dark. I shall lead you. And by the way, Dirty Crown, if anyone asks you whether this has been decided by the whole council of leaders you may as well tell the truth. It hasn't. It's no more than what I think best. But there's no need to say that until they ask you."

Dirty Crown laid an enormous finger beside an enormous nose. "I understand, my lord. Every pilgrim will know what's expected of him, and if anyone queries your authority I may not be able to hear him."

That afternoon most pilgrims ate the last of their stores. They would fight better after a meal, and there was no future to provide for. At sunset they mustered in arms. No one lagged behind, no one asked by what authority Bohemond led them.

In gathering darkness they marched east. Count Raymond took the rear and followed where the column led; Godfrey sought out Bohemond to ask where they were going. "I'm sorry, my lord, I can't tell you," said Bohemond apologetically. "It's a secret I have sworn to keep. When the time comes I may give you an hour's warning, no more. I assure you that we have a chance of victory."

"Treachery, is it? Then I shan't ask more. By God we need a traitor. Pardon me, Count Bohemond, but I never supposed you were leading us to perish with honour but without hope. Now if Tancred had suggested it I would be more cautious."

"So far it's all going according to plan. The sentries on the castle have seen us march out against Curbaram. Can they see us now, do you think? Perhaps it's time to turn south and get round to the west of the town."

All night they stumbled over rough slopes and loose stones; it was hard on the horses, but they would not be needed in the fighting. An hour before dawn Bohemond told Tancred the whole plan, and asked him to pass it on without noise or cheering.

Dawn was pink in the eastern sky when the van reached the Tower of the Three Sisters. A party of trusted foot had carried a ladder all the way, under Bohemond's eye. Now he told them to rear it against the tower, from which a dim lamp glowed. The first man began to climb.

After the long stumbling journey Bohemond did not feel like climbing ladders. He moved aside, staring towards the south. Far off in that darkness lay the Holy Sepulchre; in a few minutes they would know whether it was to be liberated. For a moment he wanted to see the campaign as a whole. He did not fear that Pyrrhus had laid a trap; but Pyrrhus might have been discovered, the Turks might even now be stealing up in the open. This was a dangerous time, a good time to meditate on the Four Last Things.

An Apulian sergeant plucked at his shoulder. "My lord, you must climb into the tower. This man Pyrrhus is very much afraid. He says, as far as we can gather, that there are not enough Franks, and that the mighty Bohemond must lead them. Come up at once, my lord."

With a weary sigh he set himself to climb the ladder. In the little tower room Pyrrhus beat his breast in a frenzy, as he groaned: "So few Franks." But there were already enough knights on the wall to capture any strong place.

As Bohemond stepped off the ladder it broke, too late to wreck the enterprise. Men set off down the stairway inside the tower, to open a postern from within. Bohemond led the rest uphill along the wall towards the castle.

The door into the next tower stood open, for Pyrrhus had commanded it. The circuit was so long that on a quiet night the garrison did not hold every tower. But soon they came to a barred door, made of thick oak planks. A sergeant had a hatchet, but Bohemond did not want to make a noise. They waited outside it.

At that moment the alarm was given in the town below. Drums beat, trumpets sounded, Turks set up their gobbling warcry as they rushed into the street. All the way down to the Bridge Gate pilgrims outside the wall shouted *Deus Vult*. Bohemond snatched the hatchet to beat on the door.

That tower was soon overrun; but there were four hundred towers on the walls of Antioch, each barred off from the rampart walk. As Bohemond led his men uphill resistance became continually stiffer. In the streets below the pilgrims were getting the better of the fighting; the Bridge Gate had been thrown open so that knights might ride in, and some of the native Christians were helping them. Turks who could not make head against their enemies took refuge on the ramparts. There they might retreat to the strong castle on Mount Silpius, or at the worst escape into open country. As the pilgrims took over more of the town more Turks appeared on the wall.

Bohemond plodded on. His legs were weary, but this was *his* town that the infidels were trying to keep from him. Unless he held the whole wall Count Raymond might steal part of his town from him. Here was another tower—Turks shooting arrows—the door barred. With bent head he shuffled towards it, swinging the hatchet instead of his sword. His shield kept out the arrows, and as the door came down the Turks fled uphill.

At the next tower they waited for him, which seemed unusual. He knew that he must look very frightening, a head taller than most men, covered in steel, waving a bloody hatchet. Turks ought to run away when a knight of Apulia walked up to them.

It was quieter than it had been. He looked round. Good Heavens, there wasn't another pilgrim in sight. He was trying to capture Antioch single-handed. Was he the last Christian left alive?

As he dodged back into the shelter of the tower behind him he understood. On his left, now a little behind him, one of the wealthiest towns in the world was being sacked; even the knights of Apulia, those warriors, could not resist such a temptation. All his men had faded away from the bloody and unrewarding battle on the ramparts to help pillage the great warehouses by the river.

He could not go any farther by himself. But he had climbed well above the town, to within a quarter of a mile of the castle. He would not abandon any of the wall he had won. The doors of this tower were stove in, of course; but if he stood in an angle of the masonry he would be sheltered from arrows. Stand here, put the hatchet on this ledge, draw sword. A Turk could get in only by this door. Here he was, the brave man, scouting ahead of his comrades. Bohemond's sword made a bloody mess of the infidel head. Don't move the corpse. It lay just in the right place, a warning to other infidels that this tower was in Christian hands.

Bohemond settled down to wait. The light was growing; in a few minutes the sun would rise. He heard steps behind him, and shrank against the wall. If the infidels should attack him from behind he would be in a tight place. But he had been in tight places before; you wore hot and uncomfortable mail so that you could get out of a tight place. He felt sure that he would not be killed on the wall of his own predestined fortress. He looked quickly behind him. An Apulian cross-bow shuffled gingerly along the rampart.

"This is as far as we've got," Bohemond called. "Don't come any farther until I give the word. But if we want to keep Antioch we must win the whole wall. You'd better go down among the houses and fetch up some of my men. What's it like down there?"

"I can't describe it, my lord, and you can't imagine it. Pilgrims and native Christians are killing the last of the Turks. All those great houses, full of women and children, it's nasty. There was wine. It's mostly in the gutters now. Oxen too, though so far no one has found a pig. Gold and silver and silk and velvet, and wine and beef and bread. I had a good feed and filled my wallet with silver. It's a funny thing, but I have never enjoyed rape, especially with a crowd looking on. So when I had all I could carry I came up again on the wall."

"Silly fools, that's all the food in these parts. If they waste what they can't eat they will be hungry the day after tomorrow. Besides, it's mine by rights, and I never said they could take it. You are a good man to come back to the fight so soon. I shan't forget you. Now take this ring to prove you speak in my name, and get as many knights and cross-bows up here as you can. For the last twelve hours we have been marching or fighting, but we must win that castle before sunset or see Antioch a permanent battle-field. Bring that ring back, by the way. It's valuable."

Bohemond felt very sleepy and very thirsty; he was hungry also, but he had been hungry for so long that he had grown used to the sensation. He stood up to make sure he stayed awake, and waited for reinforcements.

Presently a score of cross-bows and a dozen knights arrived, led by his banner-bearer. Most of them were drunk, and all were exhausted; but then the Turks must feel pretty frightened. Bohemond waved his sword as he trotted along in front, and the others raised a wavering warcry.

This upper wall ran over a rocky slope, far from any house. It was almost as steep as a stair, pointing to the castle on Mount Silpius. All the way along were towers, each within a short bow-shot of the next; but that was chiefly because the mighty men of old, who fortified Antioch, had wished to complete the pattern of defence. There were no Turks in the towers, and no litter of occupation; throughout the siege they must have stood empty. But Turks withdrawing to the castle must have come this way. Bohemond followed slowly, giving time for his men to get their wind.

He had a clear view over the barren slopes of the mountain. On the left he could see two or three steep tracks, dotted with wounded Turks who could climb no higher. Those who had escaped from the town unhurt would be already within the castle; the pilgrims, more specifically the pilgrims of Apulia, must hold that castle before they could say that the fortifications of Antioch were within their control. Ahead and to the right he could see a track winding down the southern slope of the mountain; on it were a few Turkish horsemen, though the going was really too steep for horses. He hoped they would get down safely, and thus encourage the rest of the garrison to escape into open country. There was no need to kill more Turks; what mattered was secure possession of the castle.

They were nearly there. For a hundred yards or so the wall ran level through the ground did not. The ancients had carried the battlements over a narrow gulley, the headwaters of a torrent now dry which in winter must flow south. The gully was spanned by an arch; the wall ran above the arch, which was closed by a metal grille. There must also be a hidden postern, for he could see the beginning of the southward track. This was the last tower before the castle; he paused to inspect the obstacle ahead.

It was a nasty place to carry in a single rush, without battery or scaling-ladders. But now was the time to try, while the infidels were shaken and disorganized. He saw a stout oak gate in a twenty-foot wall, peppered with arrow-slits. Somewhere there must be a bigger gate for horses, since there were stables in the castle; probably it was round a corner. Anyway, he could not look for it now. If he was to get another charge out of his weary followers he must not let them stop to tell him how tired they felt.

His hatchet would make no impression on that door. He must scale the wall, and it would be better to plan his route before the arrows began to fly. If only he were feeling fresh he could jump and get a knee on that boss, catch that arrow-slit with his right hand, and then with another jump balance his belly on the parapet;

one of his men would give a shove from behind and he would be standing on the gatehouse. Against an active foe it would be suicide; but probably the Turks would flinch from the wall, and cross-bows would cover him at the critical moment.

The first jump would be the trouble. His shield had never felt so heavy, and he had been wearing mail for more than twelve hours. As he sheltered behind the tower he called to his banner-bearer. "Sir Robert, undo my leggings and tie the skirts of my mail round my waist. We must climb over that gateway before Antioch is truly ours. Come on, gentlemen. This is the last charge in this long siege."

The other knights stripped off their mail leggings, and tucked up the skirts of their mail shirts. They were true Normans of Apulia, who would follow their lord into any danger; but their lord must go first.

The whole party dashed out together from the shelter of the tower. As always, Bohemond was the most conspicuous, taller by a head and obviously in command. He saw several Turkish arrows coming straight at his face, too many for him to dodge. He raised his shield high; and as they thudded into it another Turkish arrow transfixed his left thigh.

Since his leg would no longer bear him he sat down with a bump. He felt no pain until a cross-bow seized him under the arms to pull him to shelter. As the arrow-head scraped along the stone rampart-walk he felt a great deal of pain. His knights protected him with their shields and no other arrow hit him. Safe within the tower he examined the damage.

"The vein isn't torn. No need yet for a priest. Sir Robert, you know what to do. Push the arrow-head through and then cut it off. Pull the shaft out backwards. There, it's not bleeding too badly. I'm afraid we must leave the Turks their castle. We've done enough for today and all the other pilgrims will be drunk. Fly my banner from this tower and put a guard on it. The infidels won't be feeling like a counter-attack but this wall is ours and we don't want other pilgrims to steal it. Let's see if I can stand. No, indeed. You must carry me on my shield. Don't take me back to my pavilion. Antioch is ours and we may as well use it. Listen, take me to the house of the Turkish emir. Drive out anyone else who tries to lodge there. I won this town with my own sword and now it belongs to me. Ask Duke Godfrey. . . ."

He fainted from pain and shock.

It was nightfall when Bohemond came to his senses. He was lying on a comfortable bed in a cool room walled with white marble. Water tinkled nearby, and a servant stood beside him with a bowl of snow-cooled fruit. For a few moments he lay luxuriating, though his leg throbbed. This was his own house in his good town of Antioch. He had accomplished all he had wished for when he set out on this long pilgrimage.

"Count Tancred wished to speak with you, my lord, as soon as you are awake," said the servant. "Duke Godfrey also wishes to see you when you are recovered. Are you strong enough to talk?"

"With Count Tancred, yes. He can tell me the news. Send a knight, not a servant, to ask the Duke to wait until tomorrow. I am strong enough to hear what happened, but not yet strong enough to make decisions."

Tancred hurried in. He was very clean, dressed in a brown silk gown with his hair and beard carefully combed. It was so long since Bohemond had seen his nephew unarmed that he must look twice to recognize him.

"Ah, Uncle, you are awake. I've looked at that leg, and it won't keep you in bed for long. Within three days you can stand on it, and after a week you will be riding. I suppose you want to know what is happening in Antioch? Some good news, some less good. I shall tell you the good news first, to encourage a sick man."

"Before you begin, what has happened to Pyrrhus? He is on my conscience. He is a renegade and a double traitor; but I owe him a debt and I like to pay my debts."

"He went off before midday, with his son and the box of gold you meant him to have. I offered him land also, because I knew that was what you intended. But he wasn't having any. He wants to disappear, and I think he is sensible. He was glad to learn that his wife had been killed in the sack but sorry when I told him his brother was dead also. Apparently he wanted to save his brother, though he was too frightened to warn him beforehand. He will settle down under a new name in some part of Armenia where no one need know he has served the Turks. You will never see Pyrrhus again, or if you do see him don't recognize him. It's all for the best. You could never trust a man with that record, anyway."

"No more Pyrrhus. I'm glad to hear it. I don't like traitors, though they should always be paid promptly. He was wise to disappear. Any pilgrim would guess he had money, and kill him for it. What's the good news?"

"An Armenian peasant outside, waiting to show you the head of the emir of Antioch. A goatherd who lives in a hovel on the southern slope of Mount Silpius. The emir panicked and tried to gallop down the track. His horse fell with him and he went into this cottage to recover. The goatherd recognized him and cut off his head with his own sword. The man won't go away until you have seen the head, though I have already paid him his reward: the weight of the emir's head in silver, because after all he murdered his own guest. If he had killed him under the open sky I would have given him gold instead of silver. He hasn't done badly anyway. Someone bought the emir's sword for sixty gold pieces. The point is that he wants to show the head to you, the mighty Bohemond. All the native Christians take it for granted that you alone captured Antioch, and that you command the whole army of the pilgrimage."

"I did capture it alone, or with only Pyrrhus to help me. The point is, do I hold it now? Is this the emir's palace?"

"Well, no, it isn't. When you were wounded you didn't know the situation in the lower town, so I took it upon myself to change your plans. Count Raymond is in the emir's palace. His men hold part of the wall facing the river, and Duke Godfrey holds another stretch to the eastward. The Turks are still in the castle. I have collected all the Apulians, and persuaded some of Duke Robert's Normans to come in with us. We lie right across the upper town, facing the castle. The Turks won't stay there long. When they leave we can walk in, or at least no one else can walk in without your permission. We aren't strong enough to hold everything, and since we must choose I thought it better to keep the castle and Mount Silpius, even if Raymond holds the Bridge Gate. Oh, and there's one more thing. The Genoese in St. Simeon have sent an envoy. He wants a big defensible warehouse, under the Genoese banner, held by a Genoese garrison. I said you would be happy to grant it, provided the Genoese recognise you as lord of Antioch. It's a sound deal that will benefit both parties. You can still go back on it—nothing has been sworn. But you ought to ratify it."

"You have done splendidly. Soon I shall have Antioch."

Bohemond slept.

CHAPTER XV

Curbaram

─────────────── ★ ───────────────

By the time Duke Godfrey called in the morning Bohemond was feeling much better. The thoughtful and efficient Tancred had found among the captives a skilled bath-attendant; his massage had started Bohemond's wound bleeding again, but the leg was no longer stiff. Within a week he would be able to sit a horse. He was clean, he wore a cool silk gown, there was a good meal of beef and wine inside him. He wanted to rest for one more day on this comfortable bed, but he was quite ready to discuss high politics.

"It's nice to find someone in bed and alone," said Godfrey cheerfully. "The confessors will be busy for the next day or two. But we are warriors as well as pilgrims, and one must make allowances. I might have known that you and Tancred would be living decently. It was an ugly sack, you know. Most of the burgesses are Christian, which makes it worse."

"I am keeping my virginity for the King of France's daughter. That saves me a lot of trouble when people offer me female captives. How are things going? When will the men be ready to fight? What news of Count Raymond? Is my banner still on the tower next the castle? Where is Curbaram?"

"What a lot of questions. All the wine has been drunk, and the men are ready to fight this minute. They may not know where to find the right banner, but they are full of courage. Antioch is a great prize, and we shall none of us forget that you found the way in. I *think* we can hold it. But there is a meeting of the leaders tomorrow, and you look as though you will be fit to attend. We can go into that then. I really came to see you about this feud with

Count Raymond. You will be reasonable, won't you? He's in the emir's palace, and Tancred says you want it. Let him be. At his age he likes comfort. His men hold the wall by the river, so it's convenient for him. Your men hold all the upper walls and the street facing the castle, the only part where there is any fighting at present. When you are up we can arrange about reliefs for them. Get well soon, and don't quarrel with Raymond."

He bustled away on other urgent business. Duke Godfrey was the only perfectly honest and disinterested pilgrim leader who also did more than his share of the work. Robert of Flanders and Robert of Normandy, equally disinterested, thought only of fighting; Raymond, an efficient quarter-master, was covetous. Godfrey and the legate, and a few knights of the middle rank, made up the nucleus of honest hard-working men without whom any army will dissolve into a band of brigands. They ought to canonize Godfrey, or at least make him Lord of the Holy Sepulchre, thought Bohemond lazily as he turned over again to sleep.

On the morning of the 5th of June, Bohemond attended the council of leaders. He limped, leaning on a stick; but tomorrow he could wear mail. As they took their places, with Duke Godfrey as usual in the chair, everyone exchanged rumours about Curbaram. He had been seen—he had turned back—he was only a mile off. No one knew, but no one thought of anything else.

Then came a distraction. Two Greek priests ushered in the Patriarch of Antioch, wearing full pontificals including the crown-like Greek mitre. He was a gaunt old man who moved with difficulty; his face had been a good deal battered by the Turks. Since he spoke no language but Greek he could not take part in the discussion, but he was obviously entitled to sit among them.

An interpreter came over to Bohemond. "The Patriarch John sends you his special blessing. If the town fell the Turks were going to impale him on a stake. You got in so quickly they had no time to sit him on it before they fled. He owes you his life. As soon as the cathedral has been reconsecrated your priests may use it according to your western rite."

"I believe they would have done that anyway," Bohemond

answered. "We Franks hold this place. But give my thanks to that holy confessor the Patriarch. As ruler of Antioch I shall respect his privileges."

It was good to know that the clergy recognized his lordship. But so did all the other Syrians. Many of them supposed he was formally the leader of the whole Frankish army. His trouble would be to persuade his fellow-pilgrims to recognize that accomplished fact.

Duke Godfrey rose to give the latest intelligence of the enemy. "Curbaram will be here before sunset tonight. We must move all our baggage within the walls. Tomorrow we shall defend the place we attacked all winter. We owe it to Count Bohemond that we have a good wall to shelter us. If everyone does his duty we may still reach Jerusalem."

Of course Raymond could not let that pass. "We are here because a traitor let us in. He happened to seek his bribe from Count Bohemond, either by chance or because he recognized Count Bohemond as a man accustomed to dealing in treason. We have been saved by Count Baldwin's stout defence of Edessa. If Curbaram had reached here three weeks ago we would now be dead."

Godfrey looked to Bohemond, who made no answer. What Raymond said was true in its way, and he was too tired for argument. If Baldwin held Edessa and was content with it, that was one rival out of the game.

Godfrey continued: "Gentlemen, we must see to the manning of our wall. Knights and cross-bows in the towers, I suppose, while the common foot bring in the baggage. There is a banner on nearly every tower, so we know who claims to defend it. South French and my men along the river, the Normans of France and Italy on the slopes of the mountain. Others fit in wherever they are wanted. Get that done by midday; it's important. We ought to find food inside the town, though there doesn't seem to be any forage for our horses. There's no other business, and no time to waste. We meet again the day after tomorrow."

As they dispersed Tancred came up to Bohemond. "Did you hear Godfrey? 'We may reach Jerusalem?' I suppose from time to time we have all thought of failure, but never before have I heard anyone speak of it in open council. You and I came oversea to die, either tomorrow or forty years hence. But I hope someone gets home to tell of our deeds."

"The Count of Blois can tell of Dorylaeum, if he's not too ashamed to open his mouth. He fought well until he felt hungry. But we must get the pilgrimage to move on, whether Jerusalem is liberated or not. How can I rule my fief of Antioch if all the great lords of the Franks are stuck in it? You and I must deal with Curbaram. That calls for skill as well as courage. But I'll see the tail of his horse before winter, unless a Turkish arrow finds me first. Here I am in Antioch. If I win one more battle I shall get my rivals out of it. Think about Curbaram."

By evening Curbaram had arrived. A huge Turkish army was encamped on the plain north of the river, where the pilgrims had been encamped since October. Next day Curbaram put a garrison of his own men in the castle, as could be plainly seen by pilgrims on the wall. They made probing attacks here and there, to find out whether all the defences were manned; but their main assault came downhill from the castle. After desperate fighting it was repelled by the Normans of Normandy and the Flemings, fighting on foot behind an improvised barricade. When plans were to be discussed everyone ignored the Duke of Normandy, scatter-brained and improvident. But in the forefront of a hot battle he was a hero. His men regarded him with affectionate contempt, knowing that he would be in no position to reward loyal service if ever he got back to Normandy; but no knight would give ground while such a paladin led him.

Altogether that was a very nasty day, though Bohemond stayed at home to nurse his wounded leg. Various Normans of Normandy or Apulia won great honour in the defence of individual towers; a rash sally from the lower town brought heavy casualties when the pilgrims retired in haste and jammed the unfamiliar gate; for an hour the Turks established themselves on a stretch of rampart and had to be expelled by a bloody counter-attack. That night the servants could find nothing to cook for supper.

In the dark a party of north-French knights escaped over the wall with ropes and fled on foot to St. Simeon. It was said that they sailed away on the last Frankish ships in the port, which was immediately occupied by infidels. But no one in Antioch really knew what was happening beyond the walls of the town.

Inside Antioch all the pilgrims were trying to buy food. Because Antioch had been sacked amid great confusion the leaders had been unable to collect a central store of provisions. Before the place fell the burgesses had been hungry, and most of their reserves had been wasted in the orgy of plunder. No rations could be issued, even if anyone was willing to take on the vacant job of the fugitive Count of Blois. There was an open market, in which fragments of horseflesh, even of horsehide, were sold at fantastic prices; for hundreds of horses were dying of starvation. Bohemond heard rumours of cannibalism; he did not believe them, but he recognized a symptom of grievous famine. An army where men whispered of cannibals was very far gone. In the streets miserable figures, both pilgrims and burgesses, squatted to wait for death.

Ten days later the mood had changed. Everyone who was not already dead of hunger talked about the miraculous relics which must save the pilgrimage. Hitherto no one had remembered that Antioch was on the fringe of the Holy Land. St. Peter had ruled the Universal Church from Antioch before he moved to Rome. It was sacred ground. Apostles, even Our Lord Himself, had been appearing in dreams to the most dissolute pilgrims.

"It's a strange story," Tancred told his uncle. "Among the south French is a poor pilgrim named Peter Bartholomew. He is tonsured but he can't read, so he's not exactly a clerk. His comrades say he is a notorious adulterer, but that doesn't mean he tells lies. He told the legate, and also Count Raymond his lord, that St. Andrew the Apostle had appeared to him, to say that the lance with which St. Longinus pierced Our Lord on the Cross was hidden under the floor of the cathedral. They dug for it and they found it. Raymond has it now."

"Of course he has," Bohemond answered. "Wrapped round the lance was a charter, sealed by St. Andrew, appointing Raymond supreme commander of the pilgrimage, I suppose? Raymond never stops trying, I'll say that for him. Do you believe this is a genuine relic? Does anybody?"

"The poor pilgrims believe in it, even those who know Peter Bartholomew. The legate asked some awkward questions, so I'm told, but he did not denounce it. Raymond pays great honour to the lance, and of course his knights follow him."

"And you? What do you believe?"

"How can anyone believe—or disbelieve. St. Longinus pierced the side of Our Lord. That's certain. He may have given the lance to St. Peter, and St. Peter may have brought it to Antioch. But why bury it under the floor of the cathedral? And where does St. Andrew come in? On the other hand, when the south French dug they found their lance."

"An iron lancepoint, I suppose, not a complete weapon? Then this Peter could have brought it with him and dropped it into the hole. We can't be sure of anything. I won't go out of my way to venerate it, but I won't scoff at it either. It's neither here nor there. But the change in the spirits of the pilgrims is a fact. We must allow for it in our calculations. It's the right time to fight our battle. Come up the mountain with me and we'll look at the Turkish lines."

As they walked on the ramparts they saw fires burning down by the river. Tancred exclaimed in alarm, but Bohemond told him that the houses had been deliberately set alight. "Half the pilgrims were skulking in those comfortable mansions when they should have been fighting Turks. The easiest way to get them out was to burn the houses over their heads. They aren't afraid, just lazy. When they have nowhere to sleep they will fight well enough. Tut tut, I see the emir's palace burning. I took great care to point it out to my men. I explained that it must be spared, since Count Raymond lodges there. It would be wrong to discommode the great Count of Toulouse. Now the fire has spread to it. A pity, but in war accidents happen."

Tancred laughed.

Presently they reached the farthest tower in Christian hands, where a knight guarded the banner of Apulia. Below them burgesses worked to build a wall of mortared masonry, under the direction of Duke Robert's Normans. Farther below lay the town and then the great Bridge Gate. Beyond it they could see the river and the old camp site, now held by Turks.

"A good day to plan a battle, bright sun and no mist. We can see everything," said Bohemond.

"How do we fight without horses?" inquired Tancred lazily. "Tomorrow the last of them will be dead of hunger."

"Then we fight on foot, naturally. For some of the knights it will be a new experience, but they came oversea to seek new experiences. If you are on foot how do you persuade a horseman to fight you, when he can ride away? That's the problem. Soon we must fight, or die of hunger."

They stared at the plain beyond the river, dusty with scurrying Turks, smudged by the sprawling tents of the nomads.

"That plain must be pretty foul," remarked Tancred. "October to June—the latrines of a huge host—offal—dead horses—dead Christians for that matter. The Turks will die of sickness if they sit there through a hot August."

"Antioch is no better. We shall have sickness here by July. There's no time to lose, even if we can find something to eat."

"I've got it," said Bohemond a moment later. "We can make them stand and fight. That must be Curbaram's own pavilion over there, with all those flags. There are the tents of his nobles round it. Those nomads keep all their wealth in their tents. Old Golden Nose said so, and it was proved at Dorylaeum. They won't strike those tents in a hurry, especially if Curbaram himself is fighting. His women must be in his pavilion, and you know how they like to keep their women private. Say two miles from the Bridge Gate. We march out on foot against their camp. They stand to defend it. We knock them off their horses. There's our battle."

"There are a great many Turks. They will ride round behind and charge us in the rear," Tancred objected.

"Not if we fill the whole plain as far as the mountains. If necessary we'll fight in a hollow square. March on that pavilion and they must meet us. At close quarters they haven't a hope, no matter how many they are. If our line breaks we are killed, but it's our best plan."

"Are you sure that is Curbaram's pavilion?"

"Of course not. But we can send envoys to find out. Never mind what message they bear. A simple defiance if we can't think of anything better. We'll send holy men, not warriors. Than if the Turks don't observe the laws of war our army will not be weakened."

"It may come off, if everyone does as he is told. Let's think it out. Uncle, you are Curbaram. I am Bohemond leading out the pilgrim host on foot. What's your next move?"

From their airy height they discussed the projected battle, moving squadrons and clumps of spears as though they were angels leaning out of Heaven. It could succeed. If everyone did what he was told it must succeed. That was the flaw in it—the pilgrims must march and wheel and halt like the trained professional soldiers of the old Greek army. But the pilgrims were not in the habit of obeying orders, and there was no reason why they should obey orders coming from Bohemond.

At last the two Hautevilles came down into a town engrossed, not by the pressing Turkish threat, but by the manifestation of what was already known as the Holy Lance. Peter Bartholomew had moved into Count Raymond's lodging, where he was living in pomp and luxury. The legate had finally come down in favour of the new relic, though he was careful not to vouch for it. In their next battle it would be the chief banner of the whole army. Meanwhile there would be three days of fasting, with special processions and appropriate Masses, in gratitude for its miraculous arrival.

Count Raymond bore it in these processions, and at night it was lodged in his portable chapel. That was one up to Count Raymond. On the other hand he was suffering from a flux, and might not be able to fight if the battle came soon. Bohemond went to lay his plans before Duke Godfrey.

No one else had a plan of any kind, except to die gallantly when the end came. That helped. The idea of sallying out from the shelter of their strong walls to give battle in the open was so crazy that it appealed to the streak of craziness that had brought each pilgrim from Europe in the first place. The common foot had complete faith in Bohemond as a commander, and would have followed him over a precipice; the lesser knights felt the same, so that only the leaders needed persuading.

At a special council summoned to discuss the plan the two Roberts, of Normandy and Flanders, supported it; both were brave honest men who wanted to end the crisis, and did not much care whether they died tomorrow. After the leaders had been wrangling for some hours Count Raymond withdrew, to take to his bed with a high fever. By the end of the meeting the other leaders had agreed to march out, and had further agreed that on the day of battle the whole army should obey Count Bohemond. As a climax to the meeting they went in public procession to the cathedral, where they took oath that they would fight until the Holy Sepulchre was free or until they were dead. Count Raymond was carried in a litter to swear; Tancred swore further that he personally would go on so long as forty knights would ride with him. Strictly speaking the oath was superfluous. They had all sworn as much before they left Europe. But they all felt the better for taking it.

The Count of Vermandois had suggested an excellent embassy to Curbaram. Let their principal envoy be Peter the Hermit. He was known among the infidels as a great leader of the Franks, so Curbaram would hear him; if the Turks did not respect the sanctity of an envoy Peter would get no more than he deserved for his attempted desertion. An Apulian knight would go with him to put his message into Arabic. This Herluin would behave very humbly, keeping in the background; he would probably get back, even if some misfortune befell Peter. He was an experienced veteran, who could tell at a glance whether that great pavilion was really the headquarters of the infidels.

On Sunday the 27th of June 1098 the embassy set out, and after a few hours returned safely. Curbaram had received them in person, listened courteously to their offer of safe-conduct if he would retire immediately, and answered with a courteous refusal. Sir Herluin was sure that the pavilion was the permanent dwelling of the famous emir, housing his women and his treasure. If the pilgrims attacked the Turks must stand to defend it.

After the leaders had heard Herluin's report they decided to fight next morning. Count Raymond was too ill to be present, so for once there was no disagreement. The great moment came when Duke Godfrey turned to Bohemond and asked him to order the Christian line of battle.

"You are really seeking my advice? Well, I have been thinking about what we should do, so here is my plan. Remember that it is advice only. I am Bohemond son of Duke Robert, no more. It is not for me to give orders to valiant Dukes and Counts."

That went down well. They pressed him to continue, and Tancred smiled encouragement.

"To begin with, there is the matter of Count Raymond. You all know that we seldom agree, and you may suppose that I want to leave him out of the battle, since by mischance he is too weak to ride. On the contrary I ask him to defend Antioch while the able-bodied pilgrims are north of the river. The Turks in the castle are sure to attack downhill as soon as they see us cross the bridge. That's why they are there. My lord legate, will you ask Count Raymond to hold our new wall against them? He can lie behind it in a litter, in his mail, and stand only when there is fighting to be done. There are about two hundred other knights who are too sick to ride or march, and a great number of clerks and other noncombatants. All these will help Count Raymond to defend his wall. If Antioch is taken while we are fighting in the plain we shall be finished. Count Raymond has a most responsible task. It's really too much to ask of a sick man; but for more than a year we have all been running the most fantastic risks. So I beg him to display his knightly valour in this duty. I am confident that he will accept."

All the leaders were surprised and pleased. This was how rivals in the same army should compete with one another. By birth Count Bohemond might be only a Hauteville, but he displayed the sentiments of a paladin.

"The rest of us will march out in many small companies, every man under the banner of his chosen lord. *Every* man, you understand. Knights, sergeants, cross-bows, archers, spearmen, grooms, all in line and closed up. Any knight who still has a horse may ride it, to carry the weight of his mail until we meet the foe, but we all keep in line and advance at the pace of the foot. If I have judged our numbers correctly our line should stretch from the river to the mountains, so the infidels can meet us only in front. Agreed?"

There was a babble of questions. Who would go first? What would happen if the Turks attacked them as they crossed the bridge?

"We want the Turks to close. If they charge us as we cross the bridge they can't at the same time shoot arrows from a distance. In that case we push them back until our left wing rests on the mountains before we turn right-handed to attack their camp.

That's quite simple. As to our order of march, let's stick to precedence because everyone knows it. The Count of Vermandois
leads the van. But remember that he is also entitled to take the
right of the line; so as soon as he is across the river he halts, turns
right, and waits for those coming behind him to take post on his
left. Duke Godfrey leads the largest mesnie, so he commands the
main body. Count Tancred and I, with the Normans of Apulia,
march in the rear and take post on the left. The legate will I suppose carry the Holy Lance, the chief banner of the whole army. So
he must be somewhere in the centre. The rest of you sort yourselves
out, as formally as if you were walking in procession to a wedding.
But remember—every Count in the middle of his own mesnie,
knights at the head of their own men, no division between horse
and foot. That's what matters. We can take our time about arranging the column, in the main street behind the closed Bridge Gate.
Muster tomorrow, immediately after the dawn Mass. Eat what
you can tonight. Tomorrow night we shall feast, either in Heaven
or in a peaceful Antioch."

The meeting broke up in a buzz of congratulations. But as
Bohemond walked back to his quarters Tancred seized him by the
arm.

"Uncle, you have given us the lowest place and the hardest
fighting. I don't complain of that, the Normans of Apulia can do
it. But what happens if Count Raymond seizes Antioch while we
are fighting, and won't allow us back?"

"He can't seize Antioch without the castle, and he's too sick to
capture it. I believe. Does it matter if he tries to keep us out? By
this time tomorrow, what will I be?"

"Dead, I suppose, with the rest of us," said Tancred without
hesitation.

"Very likely. But we have faced one mad risk after another
since we left the city, and here we are. I think God must be really
helping us, though we don't deserve it. But if we beat the Turks
tomorrow I shall be the leader of the whole pilgrimage. The south
French will have fought under my command. If Count Raymond
tries to keep me out of Antioch his vassals won't obey him. I shall
be the most famous knight and the most worshipful in all Christendom."

"If we win, you will be. It's a new kind of battle, and we *might* win. I for one don't expect it. But a lot of Turks will be killed, and our vow will be fulfilled. I suppose you and I have ancestors buried on every battlefield in Europe, Vikings and such. We shall be buried in Syria, a long way from Normandy. That is the right end for Normans. I am content."

"It will be a good end. Make sure you kill plenty of Turks first. See you in the morning after Mass."

The 28th of June 1098 dawned fine, with a promise of great heat later. After Mass the pilgrims assembled in the main street of Antioch, a broad avenue leading to the Bridge Gate. Bohemond still had a horse, though it was very weak; to spare the miserable beast he rode a donkey as he arrayed the column. The crowd stretched from the gate right up the slope to the temporary wall where Count Raymond lay on his litter, and Bohemond must continually move up and down the slope to get the men in order.

There could be no argument about the precedence of Count Hugh, brother to the King of France; and any unattached north Frenchmen were proud to march under his banner. So it all began easily enough, once the knights had grasped that they must really mingle with the common foot. Bohemond had feared a quarrel about the right to second place; luckily those disinterested pilgrims, the Count of Flanders and the Duke of Normandy, had reached a private agreement. Some might say that a Duke should go before a Count; but there was only one Count of Flanders whereas the King of England disputed Normandy with his brother. So the Flemings came second and the Normans third. Normans were the best knights in the world, but north Frenchmen and Flemings were nearly as good. The right wing would be formidable.

Duke Godfrey led the main body, divided into three corps. Luckily two excellent subordinate commanders were available, the Counts of Toul and of St. Pol; they were neighbours of the Duke of Lorraine and were themselves of lesser rank so that they could obey his orders without loss of dignity. Duke Godfrey understood exactly what Bohemond planned to do, and had promised not to advance until the line was fully formed. He could control his men.

The third battle was the most tricky to array. The south French, of course, were willing to follow Bishop Adhemar since Count Raymond was too sick to lead them. But the small contingent from Brittany did not like to march behind the small contingent from Aquitaine, though neither was led by a very great lord. The Gascons complained that they had been insulted, as happened to them far too often. Since they could not have the right of the line they insisted on taking the extreme left. The only way to get them on the field was to transfer them to Tancred's rearguard, where they would march behind the Apulians. Bishop Adhemar could be trusted to keep the main line in order. He was in fact an extremely skilful commander, as he had shown at Dorylaeum; but he thought it his duty as a Bishop to obey the orders of any lay nobleman on the field. So long as he kept possession of the Holy Lance none of his men would charge before he gave the signal.

After two hours of hot and exasperated shouting Bohemond had his army in array. Every pilgrim understood that he must march across the bridge and keep going until he took post on the left of those in front. Then he must stand still until the whole line was in order, and advance only when he got the command. Never before had any of them gone into battle like that. As a rule Christian armies marched in the order in which they would fight. But never before had knights marched out on foot from the shelter of strong walls to attack ten times their number of horsemen. Never before had anyone fought in such a desperate attack. Bohemond was the only pilgrim who knew his own mind, the only pilgrim who had a plan. They trusted him.

At last Bohemond climbed on a tower beside the bridge, and commanded that the gate should be opened. As he saw Hugh of Vermandois ride out, a magnificent figure in princely mail on a very thin horse, he looked across the river. Splendid. On the far bank were only a few Turkish skirmishers; the main body of the infidels were still in camp. He could get his army over the river without fighting.

He waited only long enough to make sure that Count Hugh was following instructions. When the north French were in line and Godfrey ready to march he came down and joined his own mesnie, the hindmost detachment in the column. There was a nerve-racking wait before he got through the gate, but he could hear no sound of battle. The Turks must be waiting to receive the attack of the pilgrims. This was going to be easier than he had feared.

At last he rode through the gate, into sunshine and a brisk west wind which seemed another world from stinking Antioch. On his right were the backs of the van, in their proper place. When he had led his men to the far left, so that the Christian line stretched from river to mountain, the charge could begin. All was going well.

Then a mass of Turks charged him head on, riding in close to use their sabres. These were not skirmishing bowmen, they were desperate heroes; and there were a great many of them. The column of Apulians and Gascons widened into a solid clump; but they still advanced, very slowly.

It was hard to see what was happening in the dust-cloud, among the hoofs of excited ponies. But the foot stood shoulder to shoulder, and the few mounted knights did not charge. This could be Dorylaeum over again, without the arrows which had made that battle so dangerous. Turks could not break into the solid clump of western swords. On both sides men fell, but it did not occur to Bohemond that he might be in personal danger. His great size and his mail had brought him out of many such fights in the past.

His men kept together, but the numbers of the enemy began to push them back. This would never do. He understood what was happening. These Turks were trying to take the Christian line in the rear; he must drive them off, or Bishop Adhemar would be surrounded. Tancred was a length ahead, standing his ground while the others retired; a Turk was behind him. Bohemond pushed forward to guard his nephew's back.

If the Turkish commander had any sense he would leave enough men to keep the Apulians busy and still go on to take the pilgrims in the rear. But no Turkish savage would think so clearly in the heat of battle. All the same, the Christians were in great danger. If the Apulians were driven to retreat the pilgrims would be fighting back to back, unable to charge in any direction. At all costs he must hold his ground.

It was not the kind of fighting his men understood. They could charge, or they could die bravely if hope was gone. But they had never before been told to hold firm in the open, in line. They must learn it now. He shouted to his Apulians that the Gascons were holding, and then edged along until he could tell the Gascons to stand their ground like Apulians. For a short time that would keep them steady.

Then Christians came up from behind; not fugitives but reinforcements. The Count of Toul shouted that all was going well in the attack on the Turkish camp, and that Duke Godfrey had sent him to help.

That was very good news in itself; and even better as showing that Duke Godfrey understood the plan of battle and had the main body under control. The Turks began to yield ground. Presently they broke off close action and began shooting arrows. Someone among them set fire to the dry grass, either as a signal to Curbaram or to cover his retreat. Arrows still came out of the foul black smoke, but the danger of defeat was past.

Rainald of Toul was shouting something. Now that he was not using his sword Bohemond could hear. "The Saints have left Heaven to fight for us. We all saw them, St. George and St. Demetrius and St. Mercury, riding white horses and bearing white banners. They charged down from the mountain and Curbaram fled before them. We have taken his pavilion and all his camp."

"Then those men in front of us will retreat, though certainly we haven't beaten them," said Bohemond. "I should like to have seen St. George. It's a pity I was fighting with my back to him. Did you get a close look at his mail? Have the armourers of Heaven any dodge that we haven't yet thought of on earth?"

"They all saw him," said Tancred severely. "I suppose we were not worthy of such a vision, and I'm not surprised. It is not an occasion for jokes. This whole battle has been a miracle. Men on foot charged ten times their number of horsemen, and drove them from the field. Look, it's not long after midday. I never expected to see another sunset, and I'm still alive. I wonder whether there is anything left in the Turkish camp, and whether this poor starved nag can carry me there. Have I permission to leave your banner?"

"It's too late. There will be nothing left, and you might get into a fight with the south French. No, we shall bind up our wounds, strip the infidel dead and collect our own for burial; and then return, slowly, to my good town of Antioch. As for a miracle, this battle went exactly according to plan, the plan you and I devised together. Any miracle was performed by *us*."

Bohemond was too excited and gratified to display the modesty appropriate to a hero.

They slouched back, leading their foundered horses over a plain dotted with corpses. There was not a living infidel in sight, as the Count of Toul remarked in wonder. "Except up there," answered Bohemond with a jerk of the head. "That's an infidel banner on the castle. But the commandant must have seen the whole battle. Unless he is a very steadfast hero he will now be looking for a safe way out of there."

They entered a town that was already drunk with joy and relief. Christian burgesses, and stragglers from the pilgrim foot, were bringing in the first plunder of the Turkish camp. For the first time for eight months no armed foes threatened Antioch.

As the Apulians entered the Bridge Gate a clerk hailed Bohemond. "My lord, will you please go and see Count Raymond at once? He is too weak to come down here, and so he sends his apologies for not waiting on the conqueror of Curbaram. He is now arranging the surrender of the castle, and he needs your help."

"Come, that's very čivil of him," Bohemond grinned with delight. "I'm not so spry as I was thirty years ago, but I shall be pleased to wait on the mighty Count of Provence. Run and tell him that I am on my way." He must go on foot, for his horse could do no more.

Count Raymond sat in his litter, for he was still too weak to stand in full mail. Around him were a group of unarmed Turks. He saluted the conquering hero with a wave of his hand, and then lay back in a faint. He was really very sick, and he had done his duty to the full.

The infidels recognized Bohemond at once. They knew that in the pilgrim army there were two champions taller than ordinary men, and that the elder was Bohemond. One of them spoke in Greek.

"My lord, we wish to yield, if you will grant us the usual terms of honourable capitulation: free passage with horse and arms and what else we can carry. We sent down to ask for your banner, but this lord gave us his instead. That would not do at all, and our commander sent it back. We will surrender only to the mighty Bohemond, the conqueror of our lord Kerbogha, the great leader of the Christian host who can guarantee us protection. If you will now send up your banner you will be welcome in your castle when you wish to enter it."

"Since the walls of the castle are intact those terms are fair. Take my banner. I shall enter my castle before nightfall. Would you like an escort of my men, to see you safe into Turkish territory?"

"Some of us would be glad of an escort, my lord. Others have been impressed by your miraculous victory. Your god must be the stronger and we intend to worship him. When your priests have admitted us into your religion we should like to take service in your horde, for we know no trade save war."

"That's a very sensible idea. I came east to kill infidels, but converting them will do just as well. Those who intend to become Christians may remain in the castle, and I shall send priests to instruct them. Now be off with you."

He turned to a servant who stood by Count Raymond's litter.

"Tell your lord, when he recovers from his faint, that for the moment the war is over. He will find me in the castle of my good town of Antioch. Of course he may remain in my town until he has thrown off his fever. I don't press him to leave at once. But these matters can wait until we are both at leisure. Give him my congratulations on his gallant conduct today. While I won the battle he sat his litter like a true knight."

CHAPTER XVI

The Lordship of Antioch

--------------------------------- ★ ---------------------------------

On the night after the great battle no one slept very much. Bohemond and Tancred inspected the castle, and tried to make up their minds about these Turks who wanted to change their religion. It was the kind of problem that Bohemond had faced often before, when foreign mercenaries sought to enlist under his banner. Were these men just well-armed bullies, who made an easy living by looking fierce and who would run away from any tight place? Were they genuinely willing to fight as Christians, or had they chosen the easiest way of dodging captivity? What was the standard of fidelity among their people? Were they expected to die fighting to save their lord, like a Frankish knight? Or did they at once overthrow a beaten commander, like Greeks, and try again under another leader?

Of course they were looking their worst, like any other member of a garrison driven to surrender. It was an added difficulty that few of them spoke Greek, or Arabic which Tancred could understand.

In the end Tancred made up his mind for him. On a weekday, after a stiff battle, Bohemond was inclined to forget religious differences. Tancred reminded him that an infidel who had submitted to baptism would be killed at once by any other infidel who caught him; in the Holy War these recruits could not change sides again. The Turks were allotted to various Apulian mesnies, exhorted to learn Frankish as soon as they could, and baptized by a compliant priest before their religious instruction had begun. Henceforth the way back was closed to them.

It sounded as though the town below the castle was fairly peaceful. As yet there was no organization to enforce order, and no law.

But all the infidels had been killed in the first sack, and the Christians who remained were glad to be liberated. Most pilgrims were too tired for further pillage, all the wine had been drunk, and public opinion disapproved of the rape of Christian women. Perhaps property was changing hands with little formality, but it did not sound as though much blood was being shed.

The Apulians in the castle were proud of themselves, but a little discontented. In the great battle they had fought harder than anyone else, and suffered the heaviest casualties. They did not care to guard the castle while other pilgrims enjoyed themselves in the lawless town. Bohemond sympathized, but it had to be done.

Soon after midnight Duke Godfrey arrived, after climbing on foot from the river bank. He wore a gown instead of mail, and his face and hands were clean; but the shadows round his eyes showed that he had not rested since the battle. He answered the sentry's challenge in a hoarse croak; but he was too tired to stop walking and wait for permission to enter. As soon as he was through the door he sat on a handy chest and closed his eyes.

"Phew, what a long day, and still there's more to do. The leaders meet tomorrow morning, I suppose I ought to say today. There are important questions to be decided, and no one has had any sleep. You'll be there, I know, Count Bohemond. Then I hope we can all rest for a few months, to recover from this campaign."

"I'll be there. I can keep going until midday. That will be about my limit. A night of planning, a day of battle, another night to sort out the men and the plunder. By afternoon we shall all be flat on our backs. I suppose there is something you want to discuss with me privately before the meeting. May Tancred hear it?"

"Of course. It concerns all the knights of Apulia. But without your consent there is no chance of its going through. It's about this castle. Count Raymond says you ought not to be holding it with only your own men. He says that all Antioch, including the castle, belongs to the Greek Emperor. According to the oath we swore at Nicaea the pilgrims as a whole ought to hold it in trust for him."

"That's something we can discuss in the morning. Or, better still, discuss it after a few days, when we are not so sleepy."

"That's what I said, of course. My dear Bohemond, I know you got us into Antioch, I know the Turks yielded the castle to you, after refusing to yield it to Raymond. You have a better right to it than anyone else, and in council I shall support that right. But Raymond served us well, you know, by holding the town when he was too weak to stand. His fever is trying to the temper. He threatens that before dawn he will send his men against the castle, unless you will allow them to come in peacefully. Anything is better than open war among the pilgrims. Please allow some south Frenchmen to come in. Your men need not leave."

"If a south Frenchman shoots a single arrow at this castle I shall call on Count Raymond," said Tancred. "Give me a minute to put on my mail. I suppose he is still in what's left of the emir's palace? If he is too weak to stand I shall cut off his head as he lies on his litter. He can't take other men's castles and then plead sickness to dodge the consequences."

"I command here," said Bohemond quickly. "Before you leave, young Tancred, you must swear peace with Count Raymond. Otherwise I shall put you in chains. Godfrey is right. Any injustice is better than civil war among the pilgrims. Besides, if these south French come inside the castle they may not stay with us for very long."

"I'll swear peace rather than wreck the pilgrimage," Tancred answered. "But can you get an oath from every Apulian, and will they all do as they have sworn? If the south French come here there will be swords drawn in this hall before sunrise."

"That's true, you know, Godfrey. My men don't like the south French, and certainly I won't withdraw them from the castle."

"I thought of an answer to that, if you will agree. Robert of Flanders says I may use his knights as I think fit until this has been settled. He doesn't care where they are stationed. He still plans to go home as soon as Jerusalem is free, and that won't be long now. My knights will go where I tell them. What about this? For every Apulian in the castle we bring in a south Frenchman. Raymond must admit that is fair. Then for every south Frenchman we bring in a Fleming, and for every Apulian a Lorrainer. They will keep the peace between the factions. No great lords will come with them, so you, Bohemond, remain in command."

"A crowded garrison, but it will be rather fun to watch

them. By all means let's do that. Even Tancred can't object."

As dawn was breaking the supplementary garrisons arrived. Soon every foot of floor was occupied by a sleeping pilgrim. If they had been close kinsmen, reared in the same nursery, such crowding would soon have brought quarrels.

The congregation for the dawn Mass in the cathedral was tired and bleary eyed. It was a solemn Mass of thanksgiving for victory, offered by the legate in person with several other pilgrim Bishops on the altar; so it went on rather longer than an ordinary weekday Mass. The Patriarch sat politely in the choir, surrounded by Greek clergy, until all was finished; and then began a much more elaborate liturgy in his own rite. The pilgrims slipped away to breakfast.

By mid-morning the leaders were gathered once more in the cathedral, which seemed to be the best place for a council. The Patriarch sat on his throne and the legate gave him precedence. Antioch had taken no part in the quarrel between Rome and Constantinople; the Patriarch, seated in his own cathedral, was acknowledged by every Christian to be the legitimate successor of St. Peter. But he could not preside over the council since he spoke no Frankish.

Count Raymond was there, so weak that he was supported until he sat down in a choir-stall. His chaplains brought in the Holy Lance and placed it with ceremony on the High Altar. Even Bohemond and Tancred bowed as it was borne by, for after it had led them to their miraculous victory no one could doubt that it was a true relic. Then, after a gesture of politeness to the silent Patriarch, Duke Godfrey declared the meeting open.

It was a stormy meeting. Tancred lost his temper early and went on speaking after Duke Godfrey had commanded him to sit down; so that everyone began to shout at once. There was no foe within miles, no need to be ready to fight; the sketchy discipline which had bound the pilgrims together was beginning to evaporate. There were two different subjects to be decided: who would be lord of Antioch and when the army should resume its advance. But everyone discussed both at once, without listening to other speakers.

From the babble of voices Bohemond could distinguish two main opinions. No other leader wanted Antioch for himself, and most of them were willing for Bohemond to keep what he had won. But the south French would fight rather than leave Bohemond in possession; and some churchmen close to the legate, who kept silent, still held that they were bound to oath to give it back to the Greeks. If heads were counted the majority would be in his favour; but the minority were so strongly against him that they would fight rather than yield.

At last Godfrey rose from his seat. He did not attempt to close the meeting, for he could not be heard above the noise. Instead he went up to a few great men, indicating that they should follow him into the Lady Chapel behind the High Altar.

They stood there, rocking on their feet from weariness, blinking away the spots before their eyes, trying to shut out from their aching heads the clamour in the choir. They could just hear Godfrey speak.

"This must stop, before bloodshed defiles the cathedral. It's my fault. We met too soon. I should have given you all another day of rest. But those Greek clergy are watching. Gentlemen, what will they think of us? Will you agree on this compromise? Let the army disperse until All Saints, the 1st of November. You may go off to plunder the infidel, or you may rest here. But for God's sake separate, before your men start fighting one another. As to the lordship of Antioch, that is really two questions. Ought we to give it to Alexius? If not, who gets it? I suggest that we give Alexius one more chance. Send him a messenger, someone of high rank. Tell him that Antioch is now Christian. Give him until All Saints, the day we are to muster. If he is here then, with his whole army, we shall return Antioch to him. If not, we shall decide at leisure who shall be its lord. During the summer the present mixed garrison shall hold it. If you agree, gentlemen, persuade your men to disperse."

"My objection is formal only," said Bohemond. "We should not offer to *return* Antioch to Alexius, for he has never held it. If you propose to give it to him, provided he comes in good time, I am willing to seal the letter. Of course my seal will be placed below that of Count Raymond, as is fitting to my rank. By the way, who will be the messenger?"

"I agree with my whole heart," said Count Raymond. "I shall seal the letter as soon as it is written. I recognize with gratitude the public spirit of Count Bohemond, who has put the welfare of the pilgrimage before his personal interest. Permit me to embrace you, my lord. I should like to carry this message of reconciliation, but I fear that for many weeks I shall be unfit for hard riding."

"I will carry the letter," the Count of Vermandois put in eagerly. "I suppose the legate will dispense me from my pilgrim's oath? I swore never to turn back until I had heard Mass in the Holy Sepulchre, and I can't visit the Emperor without turning back."

"Of course you are dispensed, in such a worthy cause," Bishop Adhemar said. "Bless you all, my comrades. With a special blessing for Count Bohemond, who has made such a great renunciation for the Glory of God. Now let us disperse, and forget all our quarrels. When we meet again, on the auspicious feast of All Saints, we shall go forward like a band of brothers and quickly liberate the Holy Sepulchre. I would add only one thing. So long as we are in Antioch you must pay all due honour to the steadfast Confessor John the Oxite. He is the lawful Patriarch, the rightful successor of St. Peter. He is no schismatic, for he is in no way subject to the erroneous Patriarch of Constantinople. Respect all priests of the Greek rite. If they could understand our language I would ask you to confess to them."

When the lesser pilgrims saw their lords come out of the Lady Chapel in complete agreement they dispersed willingly. It was a sudden and surprising change of temper; so curious indeed that Tancred tackled his uncle about it as they plodded together up to the castle.

"Why on earth did you cave in like that, just when you had Antioch so nearly in your grasp? Those pilgrims who intended to go home afterwards don't care who holds the place—the Flemings and Duke Robert's men and so on. Duke Godfrey has come round to your side since you won the great battle for him. Some of the clergy are worried about our oath to the Greeks, but they could easily be shown that Alexius has broken his side of the bargain. Only Count Raymond is against you, and if it came to open war not all his men would follow him. If they do support their lord the

Apulians could kill them all in an afternoon. South Frenchmen—
no better than monkeys."

"Are you so sure that I caved in? I made a noble gesture which
must win public opinion to my side, but I didn't really give away
very much. I could hardly keep my face straight when the Count of
Vermandois wriggled so neatly out of his vow. Do you think that
after he has found Alexius he will come back? I don't, though I
may be uncharitable. He will travel on to France, and speak highly
of the great Bohemond once he gets there. No one can call him
forsworn, that's the beauty of it. Of course Count Raymond thinks
he has got the better of me—but I know the Greeks better than he
does. Consider the passage of time, as advised by the wise men of
old. If Count Hugh does not mean to come back he must pack his
baggage. He's not the most energetic of travellers, and the mountains of Armenia are a troublesome obstacle. Once he is over them
he must find Alexius. That letter won't be delivered until late in
July. Say three months for Alexius to get here, and he won't dare
come without his army. You know how Greeks prepare for such
an expedition. Orders must go out from the city to gather provisions and money. The mercenaries won't start until they can see
the waggons. They will fight for their pay, they won't starve for it.
I think Alexius will still be absent when All Saints' Day comes."

"I see. A very pretty plan. And there is something more that you
forget to mention. Alexius is now fighting the Turks, but he must
have arranged to go home for the winter. He can't leave the city
for a whole year, or he will find another Emperor waiting for him
when he gets back. Perhaps he will start some of his soldiers on
the long march to Syria; but he himself will have to visit the city
first, and such a careful man will take his guards with him. From
the city to Antioch in three months at the most, and with a great
army? It can't be done. You have behaved generously. Alexius
will be in the wrong, and yet Antioch must be yours. I wish I were
clever enough to negotiate like that."

"You are quite as clever. It's just that you are younger and
haven't seen so much of the wickedness of the world. By winter I
shall have Antioch."

In the castle a servant announced that envoys fom the Genoese
fleet at St. Simeon were anxious to talk with the mighty lord

Bohemond. But he asked them to wait for a full day, while he slept. Genoa was an important republic, and it would be prudent to keep on good terms with her sailors; but a wise man would not negotiate with Genoese envoys while he was too sleepy to have all his wits about him.

Negotiations with Genoa took time. The treaty was not sealed until the 14th of July. In it Bohemond lord of Antioch granted the Genoese a market, a church, and a block of houses to live in; this factory would be governed by the laws of Genoa, and ruled by a consul appointed from Genoa. In return the Genoese should have recognized him as lord of Antioch, but they would not openly take sides in such a disputed question. All they would promise was to support him against any pilgrim who tried to take the town from him—with the exception of Count Raymond, the only pilgrim who might do it. In a war between Raymond and Bohemond they would stand neutral.

This was not recognition of Bohemond's lordship; in fact it was the very opposite. But it indicated that Genoa would be content to accept his rule if he could enforce it. The council of leaders would not meet before November; if by that time he was supreme in the town the leaders would recognize accomplished facts.

Meanwhile Antioch stank, and went hungry. Everywhere in the plain and in the town itself were lightly buried corpses; and this year there would be no harvest, for the peasants had not dared to cultivate their fields after the fighting had started last autumn. No one was surprised when plague broke out.

Bohemond lodged in the crowded castle, with his followers nearby in the upper town. Count Raymond lay sick in the emir's palace, by the Bridge Gate which his sentries controlled. The hall of the castle was divided among the four contingents of its garrison by coloured lines drawn on the floor, and food was cooked in four separate kitchens. Apulians never went downhill, south French never went uphill; so that in general peace prevailed.

All the same, Antioch was no place to lodge in for pleasure. The great lords who were not concerned in the dispute rode off elsewhere. The Duke of Normandy went down to the coast, where Edgar and his English fleet helped him to plunder various seaports. But the two unlikely allies were not bent on setting up a permanent fief, and presently Greek mercenaries from Cyprus opposed them. It was known that Duke Robert would continue to Jerusalem with the main pilgrimage, so intending settlers and Italian merchants did not seek his protection. As usual, the Duke of Normandy might be disregarded when there was no fighting to be done.

Duke Godfrey took most of his men to Edessa to help his brother. He also would be going on in the autumn, so he could not distribute land among his vassals. But he had been for so long the most respected of the great leaders that his absence from Antioch seemed to forebode anarchy.

A straight fight between Apulians and south French, with no third parties intervening, would be a level contest; Bohemond was not sure he would win it. But suddenly Fate turned against Count Raymond.

He himself had lain sick for a very long time, and was not expected to be strong enough to take the field before autumn. During his absence the legate had become the acknowledged leader of the south French. In the latter half of July he also fell sick, and most of the leaderless south French went off in a body to plunder up the valley of the Orontes. Their self-appointed commander was a knight named Raymond Pilet, who took much booty and several strong towns. But Count Raymond was left with a very small mesnie.

About the same time the Count of Flanders and Duke Godfrey sent for their men who were in garrison in the castle. The detachments were glad to leave stinking Antioch and ride in the cool air of the Armenian mountains. The south French, fearing to be isolated among the Apulians, left at the same time without orders. Most of them went off to join Pilet, though a few stayed with their sick lord. Bohemond had the castle to himself. In return the south French closed the Bridge Gate, hoping to blockade the upper town. But Tancred still controlled St. George's Gate and could communicate with St. Simeon.

On the 1st of August the legate died. He was buried by the Patriarch in the cathedral. Bohemond ventured down from his castle, with a strong escort, to attend the funeral, though there were many south French among the crowd. The Requiem was sung in Latin and the eulogy was spoken in French, in spite of the fact that the Patriarch knew not one word of either tongue. It was a very good eulogy, which had the whole congregation in tears. Bohemond was so moved that at the end, when they were closing the grave under the floor of the cathedral, he spoke out.

"Mark the place well, and don't mortar the gravestone," he said. "Bishop Adhemar was the noblest pilgrim in the whole army, and he had vowed to visit the Holy Sepulchre. I swear in my turn, before all these witnesses, that I shall myself see his body buried in that holy spot."

It was a very proper vow to make, greeted on all sides with murmurs of sympathy. But as Bohemond left the cathedral Tancred took him aside.

"Have you changed your plans? I thought you were going to remain in Antioch while the rest of us marched on to Jerusalem? I hope you won't ask me to stay and hold Antioch for you. I want to be the first man on the wall of the Holy City. I won't stay behind to fight Greeks when I might be fighting infidels."

"I was carried away by my admiration for Bishop Adhemar. A holy man and a leader who always brought his knights to the charge at exactly the right time in exactly the right place. Do you remember him at Dorylaeum? If we had all backed him up when we first crossed the Iron Bridge we might have won Antioch in a rush, without all the miseries of the siege. You don't expect to find those two qualities in the same man. I spoke without thinking. When I entered the cathedral I didn't intend to say anything."

After a pause he continued. "Of course I shall fulfil this vow. I usually keep my solemn promises. But I haven't changed my plans, and I see a way out. There was no time-limit to my vow. Remember that I am under another vow, to finish the pilgrimage by hearing Mass in the Holy Sepulchre. I can fulfil them both at the same time—one day. One day when I am secure in Antioch. Quite soon I shall be secure in Antioch. The death of the legate is a loss to us all, but it is a much heavier loss to Raymond. The legate was so scrupulous in deference to his lay lord that it looked to some ignorant pilgrims as though the Count of Toulouse had the support of the Church. That won't be true any longer. Some clerks, I know, don't like the way Raymond clings to the Holy Lance as though the relic had been revealed to the south French only, instead of to the whole pilgrimage. Besides, he is much too friendly with the Greek Bishops."

"Well, so are you, Uncle. That's another thing. Aren't they all schismatics, who ought to be thrown out of their Sees? There are holy clerks in the pilgrimage who have marched and fought all the way from Europe. They deserve a reward for their valour."

"They will be rewarded, after the government of these parts has been settled. You must learn how to be a pilgrim, my boy. It isn't enough to charge gallantly against the infidel; not enough for you to grab a fief worthy of a Hauteville amid this band of pious and ravening wolves. Patriarch John has never fallen into schism, and he has suffered as a Confessor for the Faith. All Christians should support him, as I do. But no one comes out of a Turkish dungeon as strong as he went in. In a year or so the Patriarchate of Antioch will be vacant, and the secular lord will select a suitable candidate, Latin or Greek. If a successor were needed this minute the choice would be made by the council of leaders. You understand?"

"Yes indeed. I am only half a Hauteville and I don't see these things as quickly as you do. A pilgrim's life is more complicated than it seemed when I landed at Durazzo."

"The life of a successful pilgrim. Any good knight can win martyrdom, but you want to lay a sound foundation for the future. That gets easier every day. Count Raymond is out of luck."

Count Raymond was indeed out of luck. On the 3rd of August, two days after the legate's funeral, Peter Bartholomew announced that he had been granted another vision. It was a most embarrassing announcement.

The disreputable discoverer of the Holy Lance had been living softly in the household of Count Raymond, while his lord gained great esteem as guardian of the precious relic. But Peter had never forgiven the legate for his tepid reception of the great discovery. Now he said that St. Andrew had again appeared to him in sleep. St. Andrew announced that Bishop Adhemar had very nearly been condemned to Hell for his disbelief in the Holy Lance, and had barely been saved by the combined prayers of all the pilgrims. He also laid down a programme for the future. The whole army of the pilgrimage must set out for Jerusalem by November at latest—all prelates of the Greek rite must be expelled, whether they were schismatic or heretical or in full communion with the Pope—their benefices must be given to worthy Latins—Bohemond should be recognized as lord of Antioch as soon as he had installed a Latin Patriarch.

When Bohemond heard of this he rode in state to call on the Patriarch John, and in the evening gave a feast in his honour. No Greek could doubt that he was a faithful son of the Universal Church, admitting the right of any prelate in communion with Rome to conduct his liturgy in his accustomed language. Meanwhile poor Count Raymond was in an awkward dilemma. Most pilgrims believed that Peter Bartholomew must be a rogue, and his Lance a bogus relic, since he cast doubt on the sanctity of the holy and gallant Bishop Adhemar; but Raymond was so fully committed to reverence for the Lance that he could not give it up without looking very foolish.

Bohemond saw that time was working for him, and Antioch was by now a most unpleasant town to stay in. He rode north to Cilicia, where he received the homage of several isolated Latin garrisons. If Alexius should march on Antioch this barrier of fortified towns would cushion the shock. Any Franks who felt themselves in danger were glad to seek protection from the mighty Bohemond, whatever the legal rights of the position; he was acknowledged to be the best knight in the whole pilgrimage.

By September the plague had abated in Antioch, and the leaders returned. Godfrey called them to a meeting in the cathedral of St. Peter, where they all sealed a letter to the Pope. They had just learned that Alexius had returned to the city with all his men, and could not appear in Syria before next summer at the earliest. Obviously he took no further interest in the pilgrimage; he had used the Franks to crush the Turks of Anatolia, and now the sooner they were destroyed by the infidel the better he would be pleased.

The letter to Pope Urban asked for another legate in place of the late Bishop of Le Puy; all the pilgrims were unanimous on that point, since none of them knew the rights and duties of the native clergy. Raymond suggested that the Pope should be invited to come out in person, to take command of the whole expedition. Bohemond seconded the suggestion, which duly found a place in the letter. It was unlikely that the Bishop of Rome would have time to manage Antioch as well, since the care of those two great Sees at once had been too much for St. Peter. But each of the rivals for the lordship of Antioch was certain that his close personal friend, Urban, would back his claim. Either of them would have submitted if the Pope in person had decided against him.

Godfrey and Raymond went off together to plunder the infidel lands to the east. Bohemond remained in hungry and battered Antioch, where he was lord of all the walls and towers except a little patch on either side of the Bridge Gate. No one could convince the natives that he was not the official commander of the whole pilgrimage. They had seen him lead the army in battle against Curbaram. He was the most gallant and most terrible of all these foreign knights. It was widely believed that he and Tancred together dined every day on two thousand oxen and four thousand swine. When pilgrims tried to explain that they were governed by a council of equal nobles the Syrians admired all the more the cunning of these deceitful foreigners.

On the 5th of November the council of leaders met again in the cathedral of St. Peter. Ostensibly they were gathered to plan the advance on Jerusalem; but for the first time the question of the lordship of Antioch was openly discussed. Bohemond would not plead in person to claim property for himself, fearing for his dignity; but he had briefed a group of friends to speak on his behalf. They made two points: that Alexius had withdrawn from the Holy War, and that Bohemond was competent to defend this vital fortress. Raymond answered that the Emperor might now be on his way to Antioch, and that every pilgrim was still bound by the oaths sworn in the city. The other leaders favoured Bohemond, or at least did not oppose him; but none of them would speak openly to advocate the breaking of a sworn oath. The discussion continued for several days, and decided nothing. Some of the lesser knights were so bored with their long delay in Antioch that they threatened to pull down its walls unless the leaders soon marched on Jerusalem.

At the end of the month Raymond and the Count of Flanders laid siege to the infidel town of Marra. After a few days of hesitation Bohemond followed with all his men, save for those holding the castle of Antioch. Marra was a very strong fortress, and the pilgrims had no siege engines. On the 11th of December they broke in by escalade. In a long day of confused and bitter fighting some assaults were thrown back and others gained a lodgement on the walls. At sunset Bohemond sent one of his baptized Turks to offer quarter to all infidels who would assemble in a certain mansion beside the main gate. Next morning the pilgrims burst in, and the south French took particular pains to kill all those infidels who had trusted in Bohemond's offer of protection.

Duke Godfrey and the clergy just managed to prevent open war between the Apulians and the south French; but Marra during that melancholy Christmas seemed to be Antioch over again. Raymond held most of the town but Bohemond hung on to a few towers on the wall; his men built barricades and allowed no foreigners to enter. Just to make things worse, there was very little to eat.

Peter Bartholomew did what he could to help his lord. He related more visions, in which the pilgrims were commanded to march at once on Jerusalem. The Apulians replied by denouncing the Holy Lance as a blatant forgery. On St. Stephen's Day a mob of common foot and lesser knights clamoured that if Raymond would advance without delay they would obey him as commander-in-chief of the whole pilgrimage.

Bohemond at once withdrew to Antioch, though Tancred and some other knights pointed out that they must help to free Jerusalem even if it meant serving Raymond. Raymond himself hovered undecided. At last he had been offered supreme command of the pilgrimage, the goal he had sought since he left Toulouse; but if he accepted he must say good-bye to Antioch. He accepted in words; and then moved to Rugia, half-way between Marra and Antioch, ostensibly to prepare for the great march.

The pilgrimage was breaking up. Most of the lesser men were starving at Marra, the Apulians were in Antioch, the other great lords were said to be conferring with Raymond at Rugia. But on the morrow of Epiphany important guests arrived in Antioch, Duke Godfrey, Duke Robert, the Count of Flanders and Count Tancred. They were escorted only by a few of Tancred's Apulians, which showed that they came in peace.

Antioch was beginning to revive, largely because of its new trade with Genoa. The south French still blocked the Bridge Gate, but there was a road fit for horses from St. George's Gate to the castle. The leaders could ride all the way, and Bohemond had time to turn out a guard of honour to welcome them.

Soon they were seated in the great hall, in careful order of precedence. Pages set wine before them, and a squire carved with lavish flourishes the last joint of pickled pork in the store room, for all Syria was hungry. Bohemond, standing to receive his guests, waited for Duke Godfrey to speak first; but Tancred could not keep silent, though he was the least of the company.

"Uncle," he burst out. "Count Raymond has offered me a bribe. Worse, he offered it publicly, in the presence of these gentlemen. He is now in Marra. Come with me, and bring all your men, so that we can burn the town over his head."

"Please don't, Count Bohemond," said Godfrey. "He didn't mean it as a bribe, and he made the same offer to all of us. Count Raymond has his own views of the conduct proper to a good knight. But we must live with him if we are to liberate the Holy Sepulchre. It's odd—he is well born—the Pope likes him—Bishop Adhemar was his faithful vassal—yet sometimes it seems to me that Count Raymond lacks the instincts of a gentleman."

"You heard that, my dear Tancred?" said the Duke of Normandy with a chuckle. "Isn't that all the revenge you want? Better than if you were to ride Raymond with a saddle and bridle after the German fashion? Godfrey says Raymond lacks the instincts of a gentleman, and he has said it before witnesses. A melancholy occasion it was, too. The only time in my life when someone has offered me a large sum of money and I have been compelled to refuse it. I can still hear the chink of those lovely silver pieces."

"Will someone please tell me exactly what happened?" begged Bohemond.

"Count Raymond invited us to confer with him in Rugia," Godfrey explained. "The common pilgrims have offered to recognize him as leader if he will march at once on Jerusalem; and he thought, most wisely, that his position would be stronger if we also would obey him. He suggested that we might serve him as vassals in return for a money-fief. Not a bribe at all, Count Tancred. We have money-fiefs in the German Empire, and respectable noblemen take them. All the same, we turned down the offer. For one thing, we came out here as pilgrims, not as mercenary soldiers. For another, I'm not sure that to accept the military direction of Count Raymond might not incur some of the guilt of suicide. But if he marches I must march too, to care for the common pilgrims and save them from the infidel."

"How much did he think you were worth?" asked Bohemond. "Forgive my vulgar curiosity, but that's the first question everyone will ask."

"Ten thousand silver solidi for me," said the Duke of Normandy sadly. "I could have used every penny of it, and the amount will always be engraved on my memory. If he had made it gold pieces I might have sold my honour. But perhaps if he has all that money he will leave some of it to me in his will," he added in a more cheerful tone. "Ten thousand to Duke Godfrey, six thousand to the Count of Flanders. He thought Count Tancred would come cheaper, so he offered him only five thousand."

"I see. He was hiring your knights at so much a head," Bohemond summed up. "Tancred, you ought to feel flattered. Apulians are valued higher than Normans of Normandy. You haven't half as many knights as Duke Robert. The money came from Alexius, of course. But Greeks are not often so crude. A real Greek would have wrapped up the bribe more gracefully. That means that Alexius has no agent among the pilgrims, except the maladroit Raymond. A cheering thought. All the same, you intend to march with him, if he gets the army moving? I suppose you are right, but I shall stay to hold Antioch."

On the 13th of January 1099 Raymond marched from Marra. His faithful followers burned the town behind him, lest he be tempted to turn back. The garrison of the Bridge Gate of Antioch followed him; and so, after an interval, did the other leaders of the pilgrimage. Only Bohemond remained, sole lord of Antioch.

CHAPTER VII

Accomplishment

——————————————★——————————————

The 24th of December 1099 was the first Christmas Eve for more than 450 years on which free, armed Christians might celebrate the Nativity in Bethlehem. The great marble basilica built by the great Constantine was packed to overflowing. Many of the congregation had been there all day, to make sure of getting in; but places had been kept for the distinguished lords come down from the north, Bohemond of Antioch and Baldwin of Edessa, and tall Tancred had pushed his way in to kneel beside his uncle.

The Midnight Mass of Christmas, after the Latin rite which was now the only use in Bethlehem, was to be offered by Daimbert, Archbishop of Pisa, the newly arrived papal legate with the pilgrimage. The new legate was evidently as tough as his predecessor; for he proposed, after offering the Midnight and Dawn Masses in the Church of the Nativity, to ride to Jerusalem and sing the Morning Mass of Christmas within the Holy Sepulchre. Of course he had been fasting throughout the Vigil of Christmas, and he must continue the fast until dinner on Christmas Day.

When the clergy entered Bohemond had been kneeling on the marble pavement for some hours. This was the very place, the very time, of the Incarnation; the manger in which God had become Man was only a few feet away. To be free to kneel here at this hour the best knights in Christendom had left their homes; for three years they had marched and fought, until the greater part of them were dead; but the survivors had accomplished all they set out to do. Tears streamed down Bohemond's cheeks as he tried to thank God for the Incarnation. Then he began to pray for the souls of dead comrades. But they were martyrs who had gone straight to Heaven. They would not need his prayers.

He was accustomed to long hours in church, to kneeling on bare stone pavements. But it was difficult, tonight of all nights, to keep secular thoughts out of his head. Our Lady had lain on this spot of earth in the agony of childbirth, while St. Joseph cleared up the droppings of the ass and the ox. But it had been a tricky moment when Tancred pushed in to kneel on his right, within arm's length of Count Baldwin kneeling on his left. Luckily the two had smiled at one another; this was not a place for enmity.

The bell tinkled for the Consecration. God was present again in body as He had been for the first time more than a thousand years ago. Peals thundered from the tower in token of rejoicing. That brought a comforting memory. Only a few months ago Tancred had hung those loud bells. The infidels who had ruled here so long did not tolerate bells in Christian churches.

Here was the Pax coming round. They had brought it to him gratifyingly early, probably the first among the laity. But politics could not be ignored even on this sacred occasion. He motioned to the subdeacon to present the little olive-wood carving first to Baldwin and then to Tancred. As he himself kissed it in third place he knew with joy that those two had once again exchanged the Kiss of Peace. In a few minutes they would receive Communion side by side. In Cilicia Baldwin had compassed the deaths of many Apulians, and the injury was still unavenged; but after such a reconciliation in such a place the blood-feud could never be revived.

As he received Communion the love of God entirely filled his mind. But he was not a mystic, and he could not keep his soul at full stretch for very long. As often happens, the Devil began to tempt him while he was making his thanksgiving. Was he worthy to receive the Body of God? Was he truly in a state of grace? Was he genuinely a pilgrim?

Such thoughts must be faced, and dismissed. No Christian was worthy of anything, but in receiving Communion he was obeying the Will of God. If there was such a thing as a Church, he was in a state of grace; he had been absolved by a priest who had received the power of absolution in unbroken descent from the Apostles.

Was he also a pilgrim, entitled to the Great Pardon promised by Pope Urban? Two answers were possible.

Like many other Normans Bohemond saw the Laws of God and the less important regulations of civil society as a set of rules, to be obeyed or dodged or very occasionally defied. He had fulfilled to the letter all the obligations of the pilgrimage. He had left home to fight his way clean across the civilized world; his life had been continually in danger; he had killed countless infidels; soon he would worship in a liberated Holy Sepulchre; with the possible exception of Duke Godfrey he had done more than any other knight to liberate it. By midday he would be free of his vow and entitled to the pardon.

But had he ever been a true pilgrim? The nagging doubt remained. All his life he had fought to win a great fief, either from the Greek Emperor or from the infidels. Now he had Antioch, and he was content. Duke Godfrey had certainly fought for the love of God, though he had been rewarded with a great lordship. The Duke of Normandy and the Count of Flanders had served an even purer motive, for they had not asked or received any temporal recompense at all for the blood and treasure they had squandered. It could be said that he had fought solely for his own advantage.

Well, that was not positively wrong. No one suggested that his mighty father had done wrong when he drove the Greeks from Apulia to rule it himself. The Normans of Italy were the most faithful defenders of the Church, which needed secular defenders in this fallen world. Before he left Italy, Pope Urban had been his close friend and companion, at Bari and Monte Cassino and in many other places. It was sad that Pope Urban had not lived to know of the liberation of the Holy Sepulchre, though in fact he had been ruling the Universal Church when it was liberated. His successor, Pope Paschal, would think well of the renowned Bohemond of Antioch.

In battle he had done his duty, though perhaps no more. Poems were sung about his prowess, but other knights might be more reckless; he was usually the tallest and strongest man on the field, so it was only natural that he should charge in front. But without his mind to tell them what to do, and the natural authority which made his equals follow his advice, all the pilgrims would have died in Anatolia. He thought back to the rolling plain of Dorylaeum, two and a half years ago. At that time nobody knew by experience how to fight Turks in the open field, no knight who saw a mounted foe could think of anything except to charge and knock him off his horse. Bohemond had seen what must be done; unless indeed he had been directly inspired by the Holy Ghost. What was it they sang of the hero Charles Martel, who had turned back the Moors at Poitiers long ago? "The men of the north stood like a frozen wall." At Dorylaeum the Normans had done it again, because Bohemond said so. Behind his closed eyes as he knelt in prayer he saw what so easily might have happened: the futile charge into a cloud of horse-bowmen, the plain dotted with the scattered corpses of dismounted knights. As for the great battle against Curbaram, eighteen months ago, there had never been such complicated manœuvring since the days of Julius Caesar; in the end men on foot had driven an army of horsemen from the field and plundered their camp; and though St. George and other warrior saints had given their help the supreme commander, by request of all his peers, had been Bohemond.

If he had marched from the city with the object of liberating Antioch, rather than the Holy Sepulchre, that was in itself a praiseworthy object. His motives might not have been so pure as Duke Godfrey's, or Tancred's; but they were good enough to earn him the pardon. He was in a state of grace, he was a virtuous pilgrim. It was time to turn his thoughts from politics to worship; the Dawn Mass of Christmas was nearly finished.

The congregation surged out of the church. Great lords gobbled bread soaked in wine as they stood waiting for their horses. Archbishop Daimbert was too exalted by the greatest experience of an eventful life to notice his hunger, though some of his clerks looked rather sorry for themselves. Soon they were all riding to Jerusalem.

They rode two by two, well closed up behind a screen of scouts; for there was still no road in all the Holy Land that was safe from infidel raids. Bohemond motioned for Tancred to ride beside him. He had not spoken freely to his nephew since they had parted in the previous spring.

"A fine church, isn't it?" said Tancred, looking back. "I liberated it, or rather the infidels fled before I could catch them.

But I was the first knight to pray there with a sword at my side. The natives gave me a great welcome. They had all remained true to the Faith under infidel rule, and of course for centuries they had been forbidden to carry arms."

"I didn't know you had liberated Bethlehem. Were you alone, or did others help you? I have heard another tale, that you tried to liberate Jerusalem all by yourself. What's the truth of that?"

"My mesnie were with me at Bethlehem. As a matter of fact Count Baldwin of Le Bourg was there too. He's a kinsman of the Boulogne brothers, but a good knight all the same. Anyway, I have forgiven Baldwin of Edessa, as you must have noticed just now. I did as a matter of fact try to be the first knight on the walls of Jerusalem, but well-meaning friends interfered and the assault was called off. When we did break in the first knight on the wall was a Fleming, Litold of Tournai from Duke Godfrey's mesnie, a very good knight. I hope we shall see him at the Holy Sepulchre. His children will have something to remember."

"Yes, but tell me about your unsuccessful try."

Bohemond liked to hear Tancred talk. The combination of unabashed boasting and scrupulous fairness to rivals was an example to all good knights.

"It's a long story. I wasn't the first to reach the Holy City, because I was driving a herd of bullocks I had captured from the infidel at Bethlehem. When I got there I saw the pilgrims making camp as though we had all the time in the world. But I knew an infidel army was on the march from Egypt and that we ought to hurry, and I was greatly encouraged when I ran across a Christian hermit who had been hiding on the Mount of Olives. You'll never guess what he was doing. He had come out to look for Hautevilles. He was a Greek, but he could speak some Frankish. He said that he had been born near Durazzo, and that years ago when his home was burned by the mighty Guiscard he had come to live as a hermit beside the Holy Sepulchre. He knew that pilgrims from the west were here to free Jerusalem, but he didn't think they would succeed unless the Hautevilles were among them; for the Hautevilles were the only warriors who had made the Greek Emperor flee before them. So I reminded him that in the same year that you chased Alexius your father was chasing the German Emperor; and

I added that I was at least half a Hauteville, on my mother's side. So he exhorted me to go straight on and conquer. When I reached the camp they were making scaling-ladders, but only one was finished. I carried it to the wall and set it up. That wasn't really dangerous, you know. The infidels in Jerusalem were Egyptians, and anyone who wears mail can walk right through Egyptians. They don't fight like Turks. But some of my faithful comrades wouldn't see it. They were too busy saving my life to hold the ladder steady for me. Instead they tried to take the ladder away from me. I had slung my shield on my back, the best place for it during an escalade; so I hooked my left arm in the rungs and no one could separate me from that ladder. I was still standing on the ground, looking up to dodge any stones from the wall. So Richard of the Principate made a jump for the sword in my right hand, and snatched it away while I wasn't looking. Imagine it—disarmed as though I were a little boy too small to play with grown-up weapons. I was going to swing the ladder at him and squash his helmet down to his waist when I remembered that I had sworn not to wage war on a fellow-pilgrim. So I gave way to public opinion and postponed the assault."

"I see. A pity, when you might have won such glory. But you might have been killed, and I'm sure Richard meant well. Did you get any good plunder when the town fell later?"

"Oh yes, all that was in Solomon's Temple. The infidels had fitted it up for the worship of Mahound, and there was a lot of good stuff in it. But again my fellow-pilgrims did me down, if you can call the south French fellow-pilgrims. The infidels in the Temple surrendered to me, so I put my banner on the roof to show that they were under my protection. But there was still a lot of fighting in the streets, so I joined in. When I came back next morning the south French had killed all my captives, just to spite me. What made it worse was that the infidels who surrendered to Count Raymond got away. Of course I went to look for them. But they were in the Tower of David just by the Jaffa Gate, so they could get out to Ascalon without passing through our men; whereas my temple lay in the middle of the city. Count Raymond tried to hang on to that tower, by the way; but I'm glad to say we have turned him out. Now he's up north somewhere near Tripoli."

"You still have your temple, I hope."

"I gave it to Duke Godfrey, when we chose him Advocate of the Holy Sepulchre. He needs somewhere of his own, now that the Patriarch is grabbing all he can. Besides, there are too many houses round it. I don't like neighbours so close. But of course I kept the plunder, and now I have liberated Galilee. Nice open country that, and my only neighbours are infidels. I can go my own way there."

"Does Count Raymond still keep the Holy Lance?"

"I suppose so. At least he hasn't publicly thrown it away. An odd relic, that. I wish I could make up my mind about it. Peter Bartholomew really believed in it, you know. He passed through the fire of his own free will. I saw him."

"But it didn't save him. Or did it? He took a fortnight to die. It might have been an ordinary sickness."

"Perhaps he told the same story so often that he came to believe it. That can happen. I shan't make a pilgrimage to bow to the Holy Lance, but if I meet it on the road I shall dismount, just to be on the safe side."

"Anyway, Count Raymond has lost an asset."

The clergy began to sing an appropriate hymn, and conversation died away.

That Christmas Day went on a long time. Bohemond was too tired after his vigil to take in much of the appearance of Jerusalem; and within the Holy Sepulchre he seemed to fall into a dream.

It was a huge basilica, of a pattern he had seen often in Italy. Like the basilicas of Italy it had been patched and sacked until little remained of the original design. Heathen Persians had plundered it, and then the infidels; the mad Caliph of Egypt who thought he was God had ordered its complete destruction, though he had been murdered by his own infidel subjects before his orders could be carried out. Only the ground-plan remained of the work of the mighty men of old. Now that it was once more in Christian hands it could be made into a seemly Frankish church.

But that little marble hut over there was the tomb in which the Body of God had been laid. He was only a few yards off, under the same roof. He was carrying his sword, and he called no man master. The Mass followed the Latin rite. It was for this they had all left home.

His thoughts ranged back over the last three years. He saw once again the bullying Patzinaks, and Tancred charging against them all unarmed; Thracian peasants lamenting beside their sacked cottages; murdered Franks and Greeks outside the city; the deluded followers of Peter the Hermit lying rotting at Civetot; the gallant knights and stout sergeants killed under the walls of Nicaea; the women and children and clerks cut down when the Turks broke into the camp at Dorylaeum; the terrible crossing of the mountains; the starvation, plague and misery before Antioch. Of all the myriads of pilgrims who had left the Latin west not one-tenth had lived to see the Holy Sepulchre. Yet here they were, the survivors of that multitude. The shrine was open to all Christians. It had been worth doing. He would start again tomorrow and do it all over again if, which God forbid, it should become necessary.

When the Mass ended he lay flat on his face, his arms stretched in the shape of the Cross, to continue his prayers. Presently he joined the crowd of other newcomers who inched their way forward on their bellies to kiss the outer wall of the tomb.

Presently a clerk announced in a loud voice that the legate and the Patriarch called on all laymen to leave the basilica, where the Canons of the Holy Sepulchre wished to meet in private. Bohemond remembered that he was to dine with Duke Godfrey in Solomon's Temple, the only building allowed by the clergy to their Advocate. If Tancred had not graciously yielded it Godfrey would have had to lodge in his pavilion.

In the temple was a fine marble hall, which the infidels had used for the teaching of their false religion. Duke Godfrey kept considerable state, more than one would expect from the Advocate of a clerical fief; Bohemond was gratified to be seated at his right. There were a number of other guests, but some of them were strange to him. Already many of the great lords who had led the long campaign were on their way home.

Everyone was very hungry, and a poet made a great noise shouting out a song he had composed in honour of the hero-pilgrims. This was a new development. Godfrey explained that even gentlemen of good birth who had fought in the pilgrimage were composing songs about it. Everyone in France was eager to hear of these great deeds. Poetry had become smart, as in the old days when Bishop Turpin sang of Roland. Bohemond heard his own name often enough to know that the poet had his facts right, but otherwise the new fashion did not appeal to him. He was glad that under the noise of poetry and hearty eating he could talk privately with Duke Godfrey.

His first question was natural, though blunt. "Who rules here, you or the Patriarch?"

"The Holy City must belong to the Church. The head of the Church, of course under the supreme authority of the Pope, is the Patriarch. But every knight within these walls takes his orders from me."

"Then since I am a knight I shall take orders from you, so long as I am here. Is the Patriarch a decent sort of man? I never heard of him."

"Arnulf? Well, there's no harm in him; though if I had been a Bishop I might have chosen someone else. They say he's a scholar, and certainly he preaches well. The real point is that he was a favourite clerk of Duke Robert's, who fought very gallantly and got nothing for his pains. The Normans worked it, I believe, to block the election of some south French follower of Count Raymond. A pity there wasn't a more outstanding candidate, but all through this pilgrimage we had to work with the material to hand."

"Does he tell you what to do?"

"I'll say this in his favour—he doesn't. His position is shaky, you know. The election was hurried, and some say his consecration was irregular. The legate is inquiring into that this afternoon. Besides, Duke Robert has left for home, and he was Arnulf's chief supporter. I rule in these parts just as much as if I were King. But it seems more decent to call myself Advocate. Certainly I regard Pope Paschal as my superior."

"The legate holds court this afternoon? A glutton for work, that holy man. Since midnight he has sung three Masses. I know, because I heard them all. On top of the fast of Christmas Eve, too. But he's a good man in his way, with the right ideas about Greeks. None of those schemes of reunion with Constantinople that fascinated poor dear Adhemar. Daimbert came to land first at St. Simeon, and rode with me from Antioch. He brought out the whole war-fleet of Pisa as escort, and on the way he fought a con- siderable battle against the ships of Alexius."

"Did he indeed? Who won?" Godfrey liked to hear news of battle.

"It was more or less a draw. Greek Fire gives Alexius an unfair advantage, and will do so until I find a traitor to sell us the secret. The Greeks captured one of the biggest Pisan ships; then luckily the weather grew worse. The coast of Cyprus was dangerously close, and of course in a storm Pisans sail better than Greeks. The legate got away in fair order. But I don't think he will bother us by upholding the rights of Alexius in these parts. Alexius who makes war on a legate of the Pope."

"Down here we forget Alexius. I suppose he is rather a menace to you in the north?"

"Why not say that I menace him? Years ago, long before this pilgrimage, I saw the tail of his horse. I may see it again before I die. But the road from the city to Antioch is barred just now, the road we followed the year before last. That's why this excellent Pisan fleet is so important. It's my only link with Italy."

"The legate is our link with Rome. While the Pope supports us Frankish knights will get here by one road or another. That's why I give such honour to the Patriarch. The Pope must do more than wish us well, he must send out reinforcements."

At that moment a steward called for silence. A Canon of the Holy Sepulchre stood in the door, with thurifers and clerks. He bore in his hand a roll of paper, from which he wished to read aloud. Bohemond wondered idly what would happen to a clerk who came in and told him to be silent in his own hall; but here in Jerusalem the clergy seemed to be in control. It was only good manners to copy the submission of his host.

The Canon announced that the legate desired the presence of these great lords within the Holy Sepulchre an hour before sunset, to hear the papal judgement on a cause of grave importance. He added that certain Bishops elect would be consecrated, for which as many witnesses as possible should be present.

"Good Heavens, does this legate ever eat?" exclaimed Bohemond as the Canon withdrew. "He was fasting all yesterday, and he can't have had much dinner today. It must be a very important judgement, at least to Archbishop Daimbert. Do you mind, Godfrey, if I rest until we go there?"

Attached to the Holy Sepulchre was a chapter house for secular business, since it would be indecorous to discuss such affairs before the actual tomb. There all the great lords in Jerusalem assembled. Godfrey as Advocate had the place of honour, but Bohemond, Tancred, and Baldwin of Edessa sat in a row just below him. Opposite them the Canons sat side by side on a dais, on either side of the Patriarchal throne, which was empty. Knights, clerks, and a few pioneer traders from the Italian towns crowded the rest of the building. The proceedings began with an inspection of Daimbert's legatine commission. It was carried round by a Canon escorted by armed sergeants so that all present might verify the papal seal.

It seemed strange that neither the Patriarch nor the legate was present; but the ecclesiastical manner of conducting business often baffles the layman.

Then the same spokesman read out a long legal judgement, whose import left the audience gasping. After due inquiry the legate had discovered defects in the election of Arnulf as Patriarch, and indeed in his consecration. It was not certain that he was validly a Bishop, or even a priest; before election he had been merely a sub-deacon. That left the Patriarchal throne vacant. But in these troubled times a Patriarch was necessary, so the Canons had immediately proceeded to a valid election. Their choice had fallen on Daimbert, Archbishop of Pisa and papal legate. An hour ago he had been solemnly enthroned, since for an Archbishop no consecration was needed.

"I spotted that Daimbert was hurrying through something he thought important. I never guessed how important it would be, to him. But what a man for getting things done. If he had been our legate when we lay before Antioch he would have got us inside the walls in a week, not after eight months," muttered Bohemond.

At this stage the Patriarch Daimbert entered, in his full pontifical robes. He mounted the throne and addressed the congregation.

"My first duty as your Patriarch is to provide for the defence of
our conquests from the infidel. Remember that I am also the
legate of the Pope, your suzerain. As Advocate and defender of
the Holy Sepulchre and the Holy City I appoint Duke Godfrey.
My lord, will you come forward and do homage?"

"Your Beatitude, there is no need to repeat the form. I have already done homage to Pope Paschal through the person of the
Patriarch Arnulf, who was at that time his representative."

"Very true, and we are pressed for time, at the close of the long
ceremonies of Christmas. Duke Godfrey, your homage is on record, and the Pope has it. We may proceed to the next business."

Everyone in the hall was at a high pitch of excitement. This was
how political business of great moment should be conducted: in
public, and with splendid mouth-filling phrases. It was already
evident that Daimbert had tried to put Godfrey in a position of
inferiority, and that Godfrey had politely rebuffed him. There
could be no doubt who would bear rule in Jerusalem tomorrow.
After such a furtive and hurried election Daimbert was in no position to make trouble.

"There are other lands to be defended," the Patriarch continued. "Lands outside the immediate control of the Holy Sepulchre. As papal legate, but not as Patriarch of Jerusalem, I demand
the homage of Prince Bohemond for his Principality of Antioch."

In a bound, more speedily than dignity permitted, Bohemond
was on his knees, his hands clasped between Daimbert's. Prince.
That was a title unknown in France, rare even in Italy. A Prince
had no secular lord at all, not even the German Emperor who
claimed to be the secular suzerain of all Christendom. A Prince
was immediately dependent on the Pope, with no intermediary.
Bohemond had expected to hold of Jerusalem, in some form or
another; though while he lived Antioch would not be a sub-
servient fief. He saw that Fate had helped him at the last minute.
Because Godfrey had refused to renew his homage Daimbert had
deprived him of control over Antioch. No one could give orders
to the Prince of Antioch, except the Pope who lived a very long
way off.

All the same, he must not make Godfrey his enemy. They were
the last great lords of the original pilgrimage still in the land over-

sea; when the infidel returned to the attack they would have to stand together. After he had given his homage to Daimbert he turned about and stood before Godfrey. Very slowly he began to bend his knee.

Luckily you could always depend on Godfrey's courtesy. He was genuinely without ambition, except to liberate the Holy Sepulchre; which was perhaps why he had risen to the top. Before Bohemond could kneel he had risen to his feet. They exchanged the embrace of equals, both standing, right cheek to right cheek, then left to left. "Prince," called Godfrey loudly so that all might hear, "when we fought Cubaram together I was proud to carry out your orders. Never shall Antioch kneel before Jerusalem."

Even in that holy place there was a hum of applause. The two best knights among all the Franks would fight the infidels as comrades, without jealousy.

After that it was rather an anti-climax when Baldwin was invested with his County of Edessa, as a fief subordinate to Jerusalem. But then Edessa, though a mighty fortress, was far away beyond the Euphrates with the infidel on three sides; it needed a protector nearer than Rome. Anyway, an Advocate busy with the defence of Jerusalem would have no leisure to interfere with Baldwin, in the distant north-east. Everyone was satisfied.

Then it was time to leave the chapter house, for the consecration of the new Latin Bishops within the Holy Sepulchre itself.

On the Eve of Epiphany 1100 Prince Bohemond and Count Baldwin set out from Jerusalem to assume the government of their lands. They planned to travel by an inland route, along the continuous valley formed by the upper Jordan, the upper Litany, and the upper Orontes, so as to widen the bounds of Christendom. Every castle on their way was in infidel hands, until they should reach the plain of Antioch.

As they left the city Bohemond recognized Tancred, sitting his horse athwart the road so that they must halt or ride him down. As they came up he called gaily: "Prince and uncle, I do not bar your way. You have my permission to ride through my land of Galilee. But first I should like to exchange the embrace of equals. By grant of the Patriarch I also am a Prince. Prince of Galilee—

Prince of Antioch. My great-grandfather and namesake ought to be proud of his seed. We have come a long way from the manor of Hauteville."

Ceremoniously they leaned from their saddles, the two tallest knights in the world and the fairest. As their heads came together Bohemond muttered: "Lord of Hauteville—Count of Bari—Prince of Antioch. But Emperor of New Rome is an even grander style, and I am not yet forty-six years old."

He turned back for a last look at the banner blazoned with a Cross which floated over the gate of the Holy City.